BILLION DOLLAR VOW

SHARON WOODS

For the ones who find someone like Oliver Lincoln who makes it easy to trust again. You're not your past. You're proof that healing is possible and love can be safe.

CONTENT INFORMATION

THIS BOOK CONTAINS EXPLICIT sex scenes and strong language. It also includes mentions of infertility, breast cancer, fostering and adoption, and parental neglect.

PROLOGUE

KARLEY

THE AIR IS THICK with the scent of freshly baked hors d'oeuvres and leather in the crowded living room of my brother Declan's condo.

I say a quick hello before he's deep in conversation with a couple. He suggested I attend his party tonight to spend some time together. After growing up with not much contact since I was eight, we've been trying to make up for that since we reunited when I was twenty-one, one year ago.

I grab a glass of champagne and walk around. Pausing to the side, I don't initially see anyone I recognize until I spot Oliver, my brother's best friend, across the room. My stomach drops. He has three girls practically draped over him, giggling at whatever words fall from his lips.

He looks the part of a player... Messy dark hair like he's just rolled out of bed, a smirk that could melt steel, and that lazy way he leans against the kitchen island, like he doesn't have to try.

Like everything just comes to him.

And maybe it does.

I glance at the girls around me. They're beautiful, with glossy hair, manicured nails, designer jeans that show off their curves. I tug at the hem of my black tank, acutely aware of my paint-streaked jeans and Chucks. Even the thrifted sweater tied around my waist feels like it doesn't belong.

Oliver's eyes roam the room until his blue gaze lands on me. A wolfish grin spreads on his face, and it causes my stomach to flutter.

I shift my gaze to take in the house, and when I bring my eyes back to Oliver, he's still looking at me. He leaves the group and heads my way. I let out a shaky exhale as nerves dance in my stomach. Needing to wet my mouth, I take a sip of my drink.

"Hey, Karley." He winks as he stands in front of me, wearing black pants and a white shirt and tie.

"Hi, Oliver. How are you?"

His presence is all-consuming, and when he gives you his full attention, it feels like it's just you and him in the room.

He's holding a glass of amber liquid, and gives me a slow, sexy smile. "I'm good. It's nice to see you again. How are you?"

I shift my weight, one arm crossing lightly over my stomach, as if I can settle the flutter there. I don't want to seem flustered, but I feel heat creep up my neck anyway.

"Truthfully? I want to go home. There are a lot of people in here."

"It's okay, I've got you." He reaches out to rub my arm, the touch soft as the air crackles between us.

"Thanks, but I know you're busy." I notice the girls looking over, waiting for him to return. "I'll leave in a few hours. I just wanted to see Declan."

"You'll see him, but talking to him?" Oliver shifts, dropping his arm, trying to locate Declan, but the crowd is in the way. "I don't think either of us will get to spend much time with him. So you can't bail on me."

I smile, enjoying this conversation. Usually, we aren't talking alone when Declan's here, so this feels different.

"Okay, deal."

"Who are all these people?" I ask, regarding the unfamiliar faces.

Oliver leans in closer, his voice dropping to a whisper. "Mostly business associates, clients, ass kissers. Your brother knows how to network."

"Always has," I reply, sipping my drink. "Even as young kids, he was the social butterfly."

"And you, I bet, were the quiet artist in the corner," Oliver says, his blue eyes softening.

My heart skips. "I was."

"I love that you know exactly who you are. That's rare." He steps closer. "Most people in these circles are just pretending."

"And what about you? Are you pretending?" I ask boldly, eyebrows raised.

"Right now?" he says huskily. "Not even a little."

Leaning even closer, his hand gently grips my waist. "Can I tell you something I've been thinking about for a while?"

His lips are right there. So damn close.

I don't answer because when my mouth opens, I lose my words, and all I can muster is, "Mmmhmm."

For one glorious second, I swear he's about to meet me halfway. But then— "Whoa." He jerks back, his hand dropping from my waist like I just burned him.

The rejection slams into me like a gut punch.

"I-I," he stammers, his eyes darting around the room. "I don't think that's a good idea."

"No, no, I'm sorry. I don't know what happened." I cover my mouth to hide the way my wobbly voice betrays me.

His expression eases, but that only makes it worse. There's pity in his eyes now, and I'd rather he hated me than look at me like that. Like I'm fragile.

He shakes his head, sighing. "Look, I get it. But I'm the last thing you need."

The words hit harder than they should.

No one wants someone who's broken.

I shake my head, blinking hard against the sting at the back of my eyes. "I was just—" I swallow, stepping back. "Never mind. I'm heading out."

"Wait—" He starts to say something, but I don't let him finish.

I walk off, discarding my drink, forcing my steps to stay balanced, even though the ground feels a little too wobbly beneath me. I have to focus on one foot, then the other, ignoring the burning in my chest, and the humiliating fact that I just made a complete fool of myself. Because, of course it had to be my brother's best friend. The one guy I was never supposed to want... let alone try to kiss.

CHAPTER 1

KARLEY

6 MONTHS LATER

I exhale loudly as the crowd on the Manhattan sidewalk flows, and the woman in front of me abruptly stops. My usual fast pace means I crash right into her. "Sorry," I mutter breathlessly, trying to muster a smile, but the sun blazes in my eyes as I adjust the strap on my bag that slipped off my shoulder when we collided. At twenty-two, you'd think I'd have mastered the art of navigating busy streets by now.

She apologizes and steps aside. I'm running late again. God, I wish I had my shit together like those women who glide through life effortlessly. You know the type... Always fifteen minutes early, never digging through their purse at the checkout or scrambling to find their keys. Their bills are probably paid a week in advance. They've got clean cars, perfect nails, and color-coded calendars that they actually use.

Meanwhile, I'm standing here in a coffee-stained sweater, juggling an oversized tote that's basically my portable junk drawer, with a phone full of unpaid reminders. My life isn't just a little messy, it's a full-blown disaster zone. Like one of those "before" pictures on an organizing show. Except, for me, there's no neat "after" waiting at the end.

I move past her, eager to continue my walk to The Lincoln School of Art. I've been here for a few months now, pouring myself into painting, pushing my skills further with every brushstroke. It started when I was a kid. I've always loved drawing, not just with crayons or colored pencils, but on anything I could find. Worksheets, napkins, the backs of old receipts—if there was a blank space, I'd fill it. My brother still teases me about the time I drew on the back of his homework. *"You turned my math into flowers,"* he said, like it wasn't an improvement.

But painting? That was different. I remember the first time I held a proper artist brush. It was hard in my grip, solid and real, yet somehow, it felt like holding possibility itself. Like I could take all the broken, unfair things in the world and turn them into something beautiful.

I was fourteen, and my adopted mother, Amber, handed me a palette full of bright, shiny colors. She said, *"Here's your chance to make something that feels alive."* I didn't know what she meant, but as soon as the brush hit the

paper, I felt it. The way the colors moved and blended...
It was like magic.

From that moment, painting became my thing. My escape. My joy. While other kids were braiding each other's
hair or playing dress-up, I spent hours in the art room, trying to figure out how to mix the perfect shade of green. My
adopted parents even let me paint on a wall in my room.
I still remember the freedom that simple act gave me, like
someone finally saw the real me beneath all the labels and
case files. My fingers trembled holding that first brush,
afraid they'd change their minds, but they just smiled and
closed the door behind them.

Even when life felt like it was falling apart, painting
made everything make sense. It was the one time when the
chaos in my head settled into something beautiful. And
now, walking to The Lincoln School of Art every morning,
it feels like I'm exactly where I'm supposed to be.

I jog up the steps of the concrete building, take the elevator, and hurry down the hall, past offices and classrooms.
My heart's racing as I push open the glass door to class.
Inside, students are unpacking supplies... and some are
already set up. I nod a quick hello and slip to my usual spot
in the back corner. Tucked beneath the fluorescent light,
the empty desk awaits. It's hidden, and that's exactly how
I like it.

Dropping my bag to the table, I open it to pull out my
brushes, including my hake, laying them out, and then

place my bag near my feet. My body sinks into the plastic chair as I scan the room. There are a total of fifteen students in this class. The school is owned by Eliza Lincoln, my brother's best friend's mother. I don't see her often, but I look up to her. She's also a painter, but better known for her art galleries, which she started on her own. She established the art school for people who couldn't afford formal classes, like me. She supports the school with the best teachers and supplies, including high-quality paper that's perfect for those of us... like me, who love watercolors.

"Good morning, class." Mrs. Bennett enters, wearing her classic blue distressed overalls and a white cardigan covered in sunflowers, brightening the room.

We all respond in unison. "Good morning."

She settles at the front of the class, her messy brown hair in a bun, soon to be filled with art brushes, no doubt. We will have to wait and see to figure out how many.

I peer over at Evelyn, my friend's empty chair. As usual, she's running late, probably because she slept in after studying all night.

"Has she started?" Evelyn asks not even a minute later, dragging out her chair with a screech that echoes through the room. There's something reassuring about her presence. No matter how late she is, Evelyn always shows up.

She drops her bag onto the floor with a thump, unconcerned about the eyes on her. She's the opposite of me. I try to avoid attention, but even if she were quiet, she'd draw it anyway, with her striking green eyes, faint freckles, and shiny red hair.

"No, she just walked in," I whisper.

"I slept in because I stayed up late studying and watching a new show."

"What was it called?" I ask, thinking I'll try to watch it if I'm home alone tonight. I've finished binge watching *Dream Home Makeover*. I've been obsessively taking notes of every built-in shelf and kitchen island, saving them for the house I want.

She scrunches her nose as she snaps her fingers. "Damn it. I forgot. It'll come to me."

I giggle as she unpacks before settling in her chair.

"Alright, class," Mrs. Bennett starts, and the room falls silent. "Today, we'll focus on line work. For the first half of the class, you'll watch me, and then you'll try it yourselves. I'll walk around and offer help. Any questions?"

We spend the next thirty minutes watching her sketch the Empire State Building, explaining her techniques as she goes. As expected, by the time she's finished, she's got at least eight pencils tucked into her messy bun.

Now it's our turn. We're free to draw whatever we like, as long as it's based on lines. I don't hesitate. I already know what I want to draw. Before I know it, I'm lost in my drawing of a peony, only snapping out of it when Evelyn taps my shoulder.

"Hey, what's up?" I ask.

"Time for a break."

I glance at the clock, surprised to see that an hour has already slipped by. As much as I want to skip our break, I know I need it to keep me going today. I lower my pencil and stretch my arms over my head. Grabbing my purse, which is filled with an old phone and crumpled sketchbooks, paint-stained receipts, and dried color tubes that mean everything to me, I follow her out of the classroom, where I finally notice what she's wearing.

She usually wears dress pants to class and changes tops before heading to her afternoon or night shift at The Charles Hotel, working as a concierge.

"Why are you in jeans? I thought you had a shift at the hotel right after class."

"Brittany begged me to swap shifts."

"So, when are you working?"

I know she needs the hours. I can't help but worry about what it means for her money.

She crosses her arms. "Saturday afternoon."

We step into the break room, soft conversations humming around us. A small table is covered with free snacks, all provided by Mrs. Lincoln, who insists on taking care of her students. I appreciate it and usually grab a handful. In the corner, a simple vending machine stands. A few students lounge on green sofas, the concrete walls and exposed pipes, adding to the industrial feel of the room.

"Bummer, we can't hang out on Saturday then," I say, walking over to a small counter, where a friendly staff member is arranging more free snacks on trays. I help myself to a red apple, some cheese, and crackers from her neatly organized selection.

Evelyn grabs cookies. "Hopefully, your brother goes out so you don't have to deal with him."

By *him*, she really means him and his girlfriend, Amarni. I live with him while I save for my own place. It's also close to the school. I'm happy he found someone, and it helps to keep his focus off me.

"God, I hope so. They're all over each other like a rash, and I'm over it." I sigh.

We make our way to the coffee and tea station.

"If you were in love, you'd be the same."

Evelyn makes her coffee with cream and sugar, while I make tea. "Not happening anytime soon. I've got more important things to focus on." I'll never be in love like that.

We take our things to one of the wooden tables and chairs and begin eating. As we settle in, I can't help but feel a little disappointed that we can't hang out on Saturday. It's not like I was planning anything special, but I had hoped for a chance to maybe talk more. When she asks how I am, she actually means it. She doesn't push, doesn't pry; she just listens. And when she talks, it's never empty. It's thoughtful, fun, and real.

I don't trust people easily, but with her, it's different. She gets me in a way no one else does. She doesn't try to fix me or tell me what I should do. She's just... there. And that's more than I've ever been able to say about most people.

"Are you still thinking about that property?" she asks.

I pause, slowly chewing the crisp, sweet apple, a little surprised. She hasn't asked about it in a while, and I kind of thought she'd forgotten. But I feel fine with her bringing it up now. "Of course."

She shakes her head. "I know you love'd it, but man, it's so expensive."

I take another bite of my apple, letting her words sink in. She's not wrong. "I'll worry about that after I see it."

I could hate the house. I've only seen pictures online and know how airbrushed and staged they usually are. Plus, it's hard to let myself think it's real sometimes. I can barely afford lunch, but that's the point. Every penny I save now is one less reason I can't buy the house later. I keep telling myself it's worth it... cutting corners, living with my brother, selling my paintings, skipping fancy meals I actually want. But it's hard to ignore the gap between where I am and where I want to be. It feels like a dream, but if I keep working and saving, I'll get there.

I'm making sacrifices now, because this house is more than just a place to live. It's the future I want. And somehow, even though it feels like a stretch, it's the one thing that keeps me going.

"What did you decide to draw today?" I ask to change the subject.

She gives me a knowing look. "The hospital."

I smile. "Manifesting."

"Exactly. When I finish both of my studies, I'll be the best doctor that hospital's ever seen. They won't say no when I apply."

She's studying to be a doctor, but she's also an artist. Although she has scholarships to cover her college tuition, she still finds time to hone her craft by taking classes with me. We're like-minded in that when we set our minds to something, we do what we can to achieve it, knowing we've been through worse obstacles.

"No one can say no to you anyway." I giggle.

"True," she says. "What did you draw?"

"A giant peony. Surprised?" I smile around my cup of tea as I sip it, waiting for her reaction.

She smirks. "Not at all, but I'm excited to see it."

"Are you staying after lunch to paint the hospital?"

"Yeah, I've got time before I head home to study," she says, shifting in her chair.

"Good. I want to paint too." Smiling, I tuck a loose strand of hair behind my ear.

She glances at her phone. "Don't you have work?"

"Not until five."

"Okay, let's hope it doesn't take that long to paint."

"It won't." I glance at my watch. If we leave now, we should have plenty of time. "We better head back."

She nods, grabbing our garbage to throw it away as we exit the room.

Inside the art room, the familiar smell of paint fills the air. The space feels like a second home, with walls lined with student work, sketches, unfinished canvases and a few bold splashes of color. The light from the windows reflects off the wooden easels and scattered art supplies.

While waiting for the next lesson, I set my purse down to finish my line work. When it's time to set up my paints and easel, Mrs. Bennett comes over to check on us, giving me a soft smile. "What color flower are you painting today?"

I return her smile, a little spark of excitement bubbling up. "Pink."

"I can't wait to see it," she says, moving on to Evelyn's work.

I'm known for my nature paintings, something that started when I was young. When things were tough at home, I'd escape to the garden. Flowers were my hideout. My foster parents had a garden too, and when they found out I loved flowers, they expanded it. The garden grew with me. Even now, I make a point to visit their garden whenever I go to see them. And when I buy my own place, I want a large garden.

I get so lost in painting the soft pink and white peony that when Evelyn walks over and gasps, it makes me sit back to admire my finished work.

My head feels heavy and my knuckles ache, but gosh, it's worth it.

"That's incredible," Mrs Bennett says, coming over.

"I'm really happy with it," I say, feeling a mix of shyness and satisfaction at her compliment.

Looking at the finished painting, I can see what I pictured in my head. There's one spot where the shadows could be deeper, but I'm not fixating on it. Not after Mrs. Bennett's validation.

She moves on to the next table.

"Will you sell it?" Evelyn asks.

I shrug. "I'm not sure." I'm torn between keeping it as a milestone in my artistic journey, while the practical side of me knows sales will fund my future house and garden. I usually sell my paintings at the shop here for extra money. They sell for a crazy amount, due to the Lincoln name.

I walk over to check out Evelyn's painting, and it looks just like New York City General Hospital, brought to life with her vibrant colors.

I lean in for a closer look. "I love how yours turned out."

Her eyes light up, and she beams, practically bouncing on her heels. "Thanks, I'll hang it in my bedroom."

I snicker, but it dies on my tongue at the sound of heavy shoes walking through the classroom. Designer shoes are not what you'd usually hear around here. Naturally, it draws my attention, my gaze focusing on the man walking toward Mrs. Bennett. I'd recognize that build mixed with swagger, no matter how many months have passed. A cold wash of dread spreads through my chest.

Him.

My fingers tighten around the edge of the desk until my knuckles whiten, but I force my expression to remain neutral. I lower my eyes to the canvas, pretending to concentrate on a detail in the bottom corner while positioning my body so my hair falls forward, partially covering my face. The last thing I need is for him to recognize me.

"Well, hello, Oliver," Evelyn mumbles.

"No, Evelyn, we don't like cocky pricks." *No matter how hot they are.* I don't hold back. He's my brother's best friend, but that doesn't mean I have to like him, even though he's probably here looking for his mother, as she teaches classes.

She turns on me so fast, leaning across the table to argue. "Are you kidding? Look at him."

"I am, unfortunately. You'd think with his money, he could afford a suit that fits." As I glance around the room, I can see every student here has their eyes set on him. The women straighten their posture, and the men want to shake his hand. I return my gaze to his pinstripe suit that sticks to him like glue.

"I bet you like him. You just pretend not to." Evelyn snorts.

I stare at her, momentarily speechless, before muttering, "Trust me, that couldn't be further from the truth." The fact is, I did until he turned me down.

His shoes click, and he winks at me, as he comes to my side in front of Evelyn's work. "Nice," he says to Evelyn. She tucks her hair behind her ear, as if she's loving his compliment.

I shift my weight slightly away from him, creating distance without being obvious about it.

He turns his attention to me, his eyes lingering a moment too long. My chest tightens as the familiar scent of his cologne brings back memories I've tried hard to bury. I breathe through my mouth instead of my nose, pretending he doesn't affect me at all.

"I'll make sure to tell my seamstress that her alterations need work."

My mouth parts as a gasp slips. Fuck. He heard what I said. But I don't let him see my embarrassment. Instead, I bite back. "It can't be comfortable wearing a shirt that looks like it's going to pop a button."

He smirks, cocking his head slightly. "Are you checking me out, Karley Maddox?"

"You fucking wish." I roll my eyes. What is it about him that has me seeing red? Plus, I hate it when he uses my full name. It reminds me of the times with my parents.

"Then how would you know I'm going to pop a button? My eyes are up here." He points to his face, where his blue eyes are gleaming with delight. It adds to my temperature rising.

"Valid point," Evelyn mumbles. My eyes dart to hers. I widen them to convey a silent *are you serious?*

She pinches her lips together, but the edges slip up.

"Even your friend agrees." Oliver's light tone pulls my gaze back to him. His eyebrow lifts in a silent challenge.

I'll never admit to checking him out. "She's a fan of yours. I'm not."

He tips his head back and chuckles. Inside, I cringe at the attention he brings to the table. Several heads turn in our direction, curious eyes darting between us, whispers starting to spread. Mrs. Bennett pauses mid-sentence at the front of the room, her eyebrows raised. I can feel Evelyn's wide-eyed stare boring into the side of my face, along with at least half a dozen students who've stopped what they were doing to watch this unexpected interaction.

"There's still time to win you over."

"I've known you for a while now; it's not going to happen."

His phone rings and he pulls it out. Hope blooms in my chest that maybe he'll leave now. "I'm coming," he says to whoever is on the line. He straightens his posture, and the smug grin is replaced by a tightness around his eyes. "Sorry, I'm going to have to end this conversation."

"What a shame," I say in a sarcastic tone.

He shakes his head as he slips his phone into his pocket.

"Goodbye, ladies," he says, moving his gaze from Evelyn's to mine before walking away.

After he's out of earshot, Evelyn grabs my forearm. "God damn, he's hot. And he better not tell his seamstress anything. The image of his ass in those pants is branded on my brain forever."

I roll my eyes and step away to return to my seat. "You need to get laid."

"I do. Let's go out to a bar."

If she wasn't working, we could've gone out on Saturday, even though I don't usually go out because of a few factors. One is work, two, I'm exhausted, and three, money. I don't have money to waste when I'm saving for a house.

"Next time we both don't work, let's go to the one with the mechanical bull?"

Her face brightens, and her eyes shimmer. "You want to ride one?"

"Yeah, it looks like fun, and the guys would be less pretentious at one of those bars."

The thought of talking to another guy like Oliver at a fancy bar makes my stomach churn. They hold their power above everyone, which is why I'm determined to stay focused on my house.

"Let me know when you're free, and let's do it."

I try to refocus, but the image of him walking in makes everything shift.

My pulse quickens, tension creeping into my shoulders. It's not just that he was here... It's *him*. I've tried to bury my shame, but seeing him again makes something inside me snap. I try to calm my racing heart, but my body still reacts like I'm back in that moment. The time I tried to kiss him, and he rejected me. That feeling, that sting, comes rushing back in a flash. It's been buried under a lot of other things—work, school, life—but it doesn't take much for it to surface again.

I take a photo of my painting to send it to Amber, and for a moment, I just look at it, *really* look at it. It makes me feel something I haven't felt in a while: proud. As I pack up my things, Mrs. Bennett offers to hold on to my painting until I decide whether to sell it.

After saying goodbye to Evelyn, who takes the subway home, I walk to work. I have plenty of time to get there. I work at Tills' Sip N' Paint, a small business where I teach painting classes to anyone who wants to drink wine and try art. I love it. It's messy and loud, but it's also creative and fun in a way that makes the hours fly by. The streets are still buzzing with energy, as always, in Manhattan. I pull out my phone and call Amber, my adopted mother, as I weave through the crowd. I like checking in with her on my walk; she always wants to know how class went, what I painted, if I'm eating enough.

"Hi, sweetie," she answers with a cheerful greeting.

"Hey, Amber," I say, already feeling a little lighter just hearing her.

"How was class today?"

"Good," I reply, smiling at the thought. It wasn't perfect, but it was fun. The only thing shaking me up was Oliver's surprise drop-in.

"What did you focus on today?" she asks. I love that she's always invested in what interests me and hearing my progress.

If it weren't for Amber, I probably wouldn't have found the courage to go back to school. Her loving support and meeting Evelyn, who instantly pulled me into friendship with her bubbly personality, was exactly what I needed. I have a habit of being critical of my art, but Amber's encouragement and Evelyn's enthusiasm give me the boost I need to keep going.

I tell her about my day, when she cuts in with a question I should've seen coming because I forgot to hit send. "Did you take a photo?"

"I sure did. Hang on a sec." I pause my walk, stepping to the side as I scroll through my phone to find the best picture. Sending it off, I wait for her response.

"Oh my, it's beautiful," she says after a moment.

"It's one of my favorite pieces," I admit, feeling proud as I think back to the soft pink petals I carefully painted.

"Why's that?"

It reminds me of this one time when I was thirteen. It was after a really hard night missing my family. I'd been crying, and then I saw a bloom just like it outside my window, soft and beautiful, similar to this one. I started drawing, and somehow, that feeling of hope took over because Amber and Wren adopted me soon after. The piece brings me back to that moment. "I don't know... It's just so pretty. I'm not sure I can sell it."

"Then don't. If you're not ready, there's no rush."

"We'll see..." I trail off, resuming my walk. The streets are a little less crowded now as I near the quieter neighborhood where my job is. "How's Wren doing?"

"Take a wild guess."

I giggle. I can easily picture him, my adopted father. "Let me guess. He's in his chair, snoring, with the sports channel blaring."

"And don't forget Rufus on his lap," Amber adds with a laugh.

I snigger. Rufus, their white Scottish terrier, is Wren's constant companion. They're inseparable.

"Call me after work, okay? I want to hear how it went," she adds.

"I will," I promise, even though she asks me the same thing every time I have a shift. I know she worries about me walking home and catching the subway, but it's never felt unsafe to me. Not really. It's loud, crowded, and chaotic, but it's nothing compared to what I grew up with. The shouting, the uncertainty, the constant feeling of being on edge with my parents and other foster homes. They treated me worse than any subway ride ever could. So, the bumping of bodies, the strange looks from strangers, it doesn't faze me.

As I near the end of the block, the familiar sight of the small brick building comes into view. I hang up the call just as I reach the front door, ready to start my shift, eager to see who'll be in my class tonight.

CHAPTER 2

KARLEY

INSIDE, THE SCENT OF paint instantly hits me as I unlock the door. I head to the small desk in the corner where the art supplies are neatly organized. Turning on the radio, music fills the room as I begin setting up for the party of six. Something catches my eye in the light: a white note folded by the paint jars.

Karley

I brought new paints. They're in the cupboard. There's only one party tonight, so feel free to stay back and paint if you want.

Tills

I smile at her generosity. I've been working at Tills' for a few years now. Tills is my brother's girlfriend's mom, and this place has become a second home to me. My brother mentioned my love of art, and he was the one who encouraged me to ditch my part-time office assistant job to work here. I couldn't say no; it's a dream come true. It hardly feels like work. Till trusts me completely and lets me use supplies whenever I have spare time, no questions asked.

Hosting the parties is fun too. Occasionally, I get a few stuck-up guests; the kind who roll their eyes when they can't figure out the brushstrokes or sigh dramatically when the paint doesn't do what they want. They're the ones who treat this like a joke, dismissing the process with every complaint. But I've learned to let it roll off me because it's just a part of the job. Most of the time, though, it's pure joy watching them create. Those moments make the annoying ones worth it.

I start setting up wine glasses beside each easel and arrange platters of fruit, sandwiches, and pastries that Tills has ordered from a nearby deli. Grabbing canvases, I prop them up on the easels and get the idea book ready for the birthday girl to choose from.

With a few minutes to spare, I switch the radio to the work playlist. Chatter outside the door draws my attention. I glance at the clock, seeing it's five. Right on time. Moving closer, I open it and greet them with a smile. Most of the women look to be in their late twenties, wearing flowy dresses and laughing a bit too loudly already. But I can tell the vibe's going to be fun.

"Hello, welcome to Tills' Sip N' Paint! I'm your host, Karley. Who's Natasha?" I ask, scanning the group.

A woman with long blonde hair and a black pant suit steps forward, her hand raised, wearing a badge that says thirty-two. "That's me."

"Happy birthday!" I greet her warmly.

"Thank you!" she says, her smile wide and bright.

"Come on in. Introduce yourself as you pass by so I can catch everyone's name," I say, stepping aside.

Natasha steps in first, followed by Jennifer, Gracie, Ava, Abigail, and Sara. I close the door behind them, watching as they squeal over the setup.

"This is adorable," one of them gushes, eyeing the easels and food spread.

While they settle in, nibbling on the food, I head to the fridge, grab the wine, and pour each a glass. "Alright, sorry to interrupt, but Natasha, I need you to pick which painting everyone will work on tonight." Part of me hopes she chooses a challenging piece to make the class more interesting.

She jumps out of her chair and walks over to me. Flipping through the idea book, she points to a giraffe with flowers on its head. "This one."

"Good choice." I smile. The design is cute and girly, perfect for the group. I pin it up on the wall so everyone can see. "Feel free to put your own twist on it. Change the flowers, the background, the colors. Make it your own. But first, let's get a group photo."

They gather at the front of the room, huddled close together, arms around each other, their happiness palpable. I snap a picture before they put on their smocks and take their seats. Once settled, I give them step-by-step instructions, making sure they understand the basic techniques. When I finish, I announce, "Now go have fun." They chatter and dive straight into their painting, brushes dipping into colorful palettes. I walk around, snapping candid photos of their progress to send Natasha later, offering advice, topping off drinks, and making sure they have everything they need.

Over the next hour, the room grows louder and messier as paint splashes everywhere. The chatter picks up, a mixture of laughter, jokes, and the occasional clinking of wine glasses. Once they've put the final touches on their paintings, I call them together.

"Alright, everyone, let's see your masterpieces. Natasha, you go first."

Laughing, she steps forward, holding her painting up for everyone to see. Her giraffe has a big head and a bright pink background. It's adorable. We make our way around the room, complimenting each person's work, but when we get to the woman whose name I've been trying (and failing) to remember, she stares at her canvas like it's betrayed her. "Okay, I have to warn you... it's really bad," she blurts out, then laughs too loudly, like she's trying to cover up how uncomfortable she is.

I take a look at the painting, it's not what I expected, so I give her a reassuring smile, wanting to let her know that it's okay. I've seen plenty of paintings that weren't perfect, but that's part of the fun.

Natasha requests another group photo, so they all line up, holding their paintings with smiles. Just as I'm about to take it, the same woman who wasn't feeling confident in her painting suddenly rips her canvas in half, letting the torn artwork fall to the floor.

The sound makes my blood run cold, and suddenly, I'm back in my childhood home. My mother's cruel laughter echoes in my ears, mocking my drawings, while my father rips them up right in front of me. *"No one wants to see that,"* he'd say. *"You're useless."* My mother always agreed. But my brother would comfort me once they left, telling me I did a good job, that I'm talented, and to not give up.

I take a deep breath, shaking off the memory, wanting the birthday girl to have a good night. I'm cleaning it up as the woman who'd been frustrated helps gather the scraps of her artwork. The others exchange some glances. One even offers a soft, "Hey, it's okay. You can always start again."

She nods silently, still holding the torn pieces of the canvas.

The party's atmosphere has turned awkward, and before I can speak to turn it around, Abigail clears her throat and changes the subject. "I've been looking to buy art for my husband," she says. "It's our wedding anniversary soon."

My ears perk up at the mention of art. "Do you have a place in mind, or do you need a recommendation?" I ask.

"He loves a piece from Lincoln's Gallery. I have an appointment with a consultant named Oliver."

My stomach tightens at the mention of his name. I force a smile. "It's one of the best galleries in New York," I say sweetly, though bile rises in my throat.

Abigail's face relaxes. "Good. It's very expensive."

"You're in good hands with Oliver," I assure her. "Now, let me call your ride."

As they take selfies and get ready to leave, I organize the ride service and help them into the car. Once they're gone, I begin cleaning up, but my muscles are tense from the torn canvas and at hearing Oliver's rich and entitled name. I need to relax before going home to my brother... *his best friend*.

I grab a blank canvas and decide to paint the giraffe myself, drawn to its flowers. At first, my strokes are shaky, but after a few minutes, I lose myself in the painting. My body sinks into the chair, and my movements become smoother. I let the music fill the space, pushing away any thoughts from my mind, savoring the peace that washes over me.

CHAPTER 3

OLIVER

"Do you have any leads?" I grip the phone tighter.

"No, sir," Sam, my private investigator, replies.

I drag a hand over my face and lean forward, burying my head in my arms on the desk. My temples throb. My jaw clenches. "Why is it taking so long?"

"They've got some good security on them," he mutters, like that's supposed to be an acceptable excuse.

I flop back in my chair, the leather creaking under me, my pulse thumping in the base of my neck. "Try harder," I snap, hanging up before he can respond.

I march over to the bar cart, shoulders tight, and pour two fingers of whiskey into a glass. The scent hits before the burn does, but it's a welcome distraction. I'm raising the glass to my lips when my mobile phone buzzes in my pocket.

What the fuck is it now?

I answer without checking. "Yes?" I bark.

"Woah. What's crawled up your ass?" Harvey, my brother, grumbles.

I close my eyes and exhale through my nose, willing myself to stay calm. It's not his fault I can't find the damn mystery artist. "Nothing," I mutter.

He snorts. "Doesn't sound like nothing."

"Just tell me what you want." I take a slow sip of my drink, letting the whiskey warms its way down my throat.

"Did you still want a lift tonight?"

I freeze.

Shit.

Harvey chuckles, smug as ever. "You forgot, didn't you?"

I grit my teeth. "Yes. But it's fine. I'll meet you there. I'll head straight from the office."

"You sure?" he asks, but I'm already mentally rearranging my evening.

"I'm sure. I have to get to this meeting, but I'll see you later." I hang up before he can start in on me again and toss back the rest of the drink.

Later, I'm having a drink with my brothers, and the tension is thick enough to slice.

We're at Top Secret Bar, one of those quiet, luxurious places tucked into a corner of Midtown, a spot only the right people know about. The booths are a deep brown leather, stitched with precision, and the lighting's just enough to see the drink in your glass but not so much that anyone could read your expression too clearly.

The four of us take up the corner booth... Me, Evan, Jeremy, and Harvey. Each of us in suits, ties loosened to say we're off the clock, but not off duty. Gold-rimmed glasses rest on the polished table, not quite ready for another round.

Jeremy nurses a bourbon, always trying to prove he's got more taste than the rest of us. He's the brother who's about to get married. Harvey, the youngest Lincoln, is sipping something amber and overpriced, legs stretched out like he owns the room. Evan, the oldest and grumpiest brother, hasn't touched his drink yet. And I've already gone through two fingers of whiskey, the burn not doing nearly enough.

Evan breaks the silence first, tone clipped like he's running a board meeting. "So, for Jeremy's bachelor party, don't forget, the plane leaves at 9 a.m. sharp. There's a private dinner when we land. The chef's doing a multi-course tasting menu. Then a cigar and whiskey pairing on the terrace."

Jeremy raises an eyebrow, and Harvey leans back, unimpressed.

"Do we get matching robes too?" Harvey mutters into his glass.

I swirl the ice in mine, not bothering to look up. "Why is Evan in charge?"

Jeremy stiffens slightly, then leans forward. "He's the oldest."

I glance up and lock eyes with Evan. He's already glaring at me, posture military straight, like he's waiting for someone to challenge him.

"We all should've had a say in your bachelor party," I argue.

"It's my choice," Jeremy replies coolly. "When it's your turn, you can choose who you want."

"Well, it sure as hell won't be you."

Harvey chuckles under his breath, like this is better than whatever show he's been bingeing. Jeremy hides a smirk behind his glass.

"Petty children," Evan mumbles, shaking his head, finally picking up his glass.

"You wouldn't be saying that if you weren't involved," I fire back.

His lips thin into that flat line he always gives when he's done arguing. Discussion closed.

I lean back into the booth, dragging a finger down the side of my glass. "I went past Mom and Dad's today. Mom was putting the students' work in the basement."

Jeremy blinks. "What? Why?"

"They needed more classrooms," I say. "She lost the display space."

"Shit," Harvey says. "She loved that gallery wall."

"She didn't say anything?" Jeremy asks.

"She never does. But I could tell. She kept holding this one canvas like she couldn't decide if she was proud of it or heartbroken."

A silence settles in again, this time heavier. I glance at the drink in front of me, then back up at my brothers.

"She deserves more than a basement," I say quietly.

The Warne Gallery flashes in my mind again. Its high ceilings, white walls, the way the light spills in during the afternoons. Mom used to take me when I was a kid. I still remember the way her eyes lit up when she talked about it. Not like she was simply describing a building, but something bigger. She had plans. And damn it, I want to make them a reality.

Chapter 4

Karley

Later that night, I step into the house I share with my brother, dragging my feet as I head toward the kitchen. Everything about it screams Declan—glass, chrome, and cold, gray tones that look like they were pulled straight from a catalog. I let my bag slide from my shoulder, hitting the floor with a dull thud. The sound barely registers as I freeze in the doorway, my face tightening at the sight in front of me. Declan and Armani making out on the sofa, completely oblivious to my presence. A flush rises to my cheeks as I stand there, torn between slipping away and making my presence known. Clearing my throat, I say, "Hey."

They pull apart and turn to face me. Armani's face is beet red. "Hey."

"How was work?" Declan asks, seeming completely unfazed as he straightens his shirt.

I shrug. "Alright." Moving to the cupboard, I grab the pasta and a can of tomatoes. As I pull out a pot, my brother makes his way over to the kitchen and settles onto a stool at the counter. Armani hovers near the doorway, tucking her hair behind her ear as she glances at her phone.

"How was your day?" I ask, steering the conversation away from me.

"Busy. I got home five minutes before you," he says, eyeing the bag of pasta.

"Want me to make you some dinner?" I offer, immediately regretting the words as they leave my mouth. Why do I always do this? Cook for him, clean up after him, when he's capable of doing it himself.

"If you don't mind."

"Not at all." I pour double the amount, making sure there's enough for him and Armani.

"I noticed you haven't started packing," he says.

Which is code for: he's been snooping. One thing I hate about living with him is the lack of privacy. I desperately need my own space. *Just a few more weeks of this*, I remind myself.

"I don't have much stuff. It won't take long to pack."

I can feel his eyes burning a hole in my head, and I already know the question before he asks, because he wants me to change my mind. "Have you decided if you'll come to Florida with me?"

"You make it sound like you're going alone. Armani's going to be there. You don't need me," I say, filling the pot with water and turning on the burner. He makes no effort to get up and help, and I feel the pulse in my temple start to pound. Part of me wants to escape apartment living, move somewhere warm with beaches. But Florida means living under my brother's roof again, watching him and Armani build their perfect life, while I hang around like a third wheel. Here, at least, I have independence.

"I don't understand why you'd want to stay here," he says.

Crossing my arms over my chest, I lean against the counter. "I like it here. Amber and Wren are here."

"But don't you want a fresh start?" His eyebrows lift slightly. He waves his hand, as if Amber and Wren are friends, not the lifeline parents they've been for me.

I uncross my arms and grab a pan, then reach for the tomatoes, garlic, onion, and a basil leaf. My childhood home is in another state, and New York is filled with great memories. "No. Why would I need a fresh start?"

"You've been here and unhappy for years."

I laugh, but it turns into a sigh. "I'm not unhappy, and you know that. What's really going on?"

He scratches his temple before clasping his hands on the counter, his eyes firmly on me. The smell of sauce fills the air, making my stomach growl again. "I can't watch over you from Florida," he admits.

A familiar mix of irritation and affection washes over me. Part of me is touched by his concern, but the bigger part hates being treated like a helpless child in need of supervision.

So that's it. "I don't need you to. I'm twenty-two."

"I know..."

"I'm not irresponsible, either. If anything, I stay home more than you do."

"I know. I just don't want anything to happen to you."

"I have friends here. I'll be fine. Quit worrying about me." A small part of me does worry what it'll be like without him close. But I need to stand on my own, prove to myself that I can build a life that's entirely mine.

He snorts, and I turn to stir the sauce, adding the pasta to the boiling water. I know where this is coming from... He's still haunted by not being able to help protect me when we were kids. We were separated and fostered by different families. He's always felt responsible. It's written all over his face. I reach out to squeeze his arm. "If I hate it here, I'll be on the first flight out."

"I'll always make room for you," he says softly.

I smile. "I know, and I love you for that."

Do I think this is the end of the conversation? Not at all. He'll keep trying until he leaves for Florida. He wants to erase the past, and while I understand that, those experiences made me who I am. I wouldn't change that. My hardships gave me strength and independence. Those scars are part of me.

He wipes a hand down his face. "I still don't like the idea of you struggling on your own."

My muscles tighten. I hate that he sees me as weak just because I don't have a fancy job like him. But he encouraged me to work at Tills', and I wouldn't want to be anywhere else. I'm not cut out for corporate life. "I'm not going to struggle. I also couldn't find the art school like I have here."

"Don't take this the wrong way," he starts, and I raise an eyebrow, already disliking where this is going. "But do you want to follow art all your life?"

"Why does it matter to you?" I snap, stirring the sauce even though it doesn't need it. Art is a part of me, my therapy. I could never give it up. I thought he knew and supported that.

"You're so smart," he says, and my nostrils flare as I try to take slow, calming breaths.

"Smart people work in many fields, not just corporate jobs," I bite back, knuckles whitening around the wooden spoon.

He sighs. "I know, but I didn't think you'd stay at Tills' this long."

"Let's drop this topic right now." My voice trembles with a mix of hurt and anger that threatens to spill over.

He tugs at his tie. "Fuck. I'm sorry. I'm messing this up."

I move to check on the pasta, steam rising around my face. "I don't think you are. You've mentioned my job more than once. I wish you'd support me."

"I'm letting you stay here," he says, and I freeze mid-motion.

"Letting me?" My voice turns to ice. "I pay bills and cook you dinner."

Armani slides up beside him, placing a gentle hand on his back. "Drop it. She's right. Let her live her life. She's happy."

I exhale shakily, grateful for her support. I've never had the urge to slap my brother before, but I'm dangerously close tonight. Armani must've sensed the extra tension in the room. "I'm moving, but I'm staying in New York."

"I'm sorry. I just feel responsible," he mutters as his eyes drop to the countertop.

"And I keep telling you not to. Now, sit and wait for your dinner."

"I'm going to miss this," he says with a smirk.

"Hey, I can cook. You just never give me the chance," Armani teases, and they stare at each other with hearts in their eyes and a flicker of heat. I turn away, rolling my eyes despite the small pang in my chest.

Once the pasta is done, I assemble my bowl and head to my room. They get too touchy for me to hang around. "Help yourselves. There's plenty for seconds," I call out, though I'm not sure they heard me.

As I sit on my unmade bed, peace finally settles in my chest. My room is small, but it's mine, walls filled with art, colorful pillows and blankets thrown across my sheets and comforter. Art supplies cover every surface. I take a deep breath and dig my fork into the steaming pasta. The first bite melts in my mouth. I close my eyes, shoulders relaxing for the first time today. After this, I'll just hide here for the rest of the night, sketching or watching something till I fall asleep.

I'm starting to feel like I can breathe again.

Until the doorbell rings.

Who could that be? I'm not expecting anyone, and Armani's already here. I hope they stop making out to answer it.

"Hey, you're just in time. Karley made pasta," I hear my brother say loudly.

"Sweet, I haven't eaten yet," a deep, familiar voice replies. Oliver. He's been stopping by more frequently since my brother's announcement of his move.

I have to force myself to stay put, resisting the urge to march out there and tell him not to touch anything I've cooked. But that would be childish, and it would mean facing him, which I'd rather avoid. I've had enough of people for tonight.

"Where is she?" he asks, and my heart skips a beat.

Why does my body have to react this way? I need to remember he's a heartbreaker. His charm is designed to pull people in.

"She's in her room. I think I upset her," my brother replies.

"Think?" Armani adds sarcastically. I may not be a fan of their public displays of affection, but I like her. She's always been supportive, like the sister I never had. "You definitely upset her."

"What did I do?" he asks.

"You're trying to dictate her life," she replies.

"It's my responsibility," he counters.

Even as my blood boils, I understand why he feels this way. But his job is to be my brother, not my parent. "We're moving, and I can't watch over her," he adds.

It kills him to feel like he's losing control, like he did when we were kids. But things are different now. We're adults. We make our own choices.

"I can help look after her," Oliver jokes, and it makes my temperature rise. I don't need anyone's help. I'm a grown woman. Why do they treat my past like it's still holding me down? I survived those years, Declan didn't.

I don't want Oliver's help. I'd rather he just forget about me. Sure, I'm his best friend's little sister, but once my brother leaves, there won't be any reason for Oliver to keep crossing my path. *Unless he drops in at the school again...*

"That would be amazing," I hear my brother say.

No, it wouldn't. My hands clench around the bowl. The last thing I need is for Oliver to be involved in my life in any way. Not after what happened last time. I can't let him think I'd ever want that... Not again.

"This is some good fucking pasta," Oliver comments, and I can't help but feel a small flicker of pride.

My brother chuckles. "Slow down, or you'll fucking choke."

I smile to myself. I do love cooking, and I'll miss it when they leave next month. I can't believe it's happening so soon, but maybe the distance will be good for them. It'll give my brother space to focus on his relationship without worrying about me.

"I have a big mouth," Oliver jokes.

"Speaking of, how's that girl you were seeing?" my brother asks, and I straighten up, even though I shouldn't care who Oliver is hooking up with. Still, I stay quiet and listen.

"Fun," Oliver says casually. I roll my eyes, wanting to not care, but I can't stop the wave of jealousy that's rising in my chest.

"But?" Declan pushes.

"She wants more." Oliver exhales heavily.

"When are you going to settle down?" my brother asks.

"Soon," Oliver replies, his voice light, almost dismissive.

My brother laughs. "You always say that, but trust me, this is the happiest I've ever been."

"Good answer," Armani says.

"I'm focused on my career right now," Oliver replies. "It's just not a priority at the moment."

At least he's honest. I'll give him that. I shake off any warm thoughts about him because I believe in artists, and he only believes in money...

"Maybe you need to find the right girl," Armani says.

"Maybe... but I doubt it," Oliver says.

They all laugh. Nothing will get Oliver to settle down. He's been around for a while with no one permanent. Just like me. The thought knots my stomach. I'm not *like* him. I'm not someone who can just move on without a care, without wondering if I'll ever find someone who stays.

"How's the search for the blue lotus artist going?" Declan asks.

I freeze for a second, holding my breath.

"No luck so far," Oliver replies. Then, an outburst— "What? That's a penalty? You've got to be kidding me!"

Their conversation veers into sports talk, and I quietly return to my pasta, chewing through the unease. The talk about the latest football game adds to my already tired state. With a full belly, drowsy, I put the bowl on the nightstand and lie back on my comfy mattress, letting their voices wash over me until I drift off into a restless sleep.

I wake in a cold sweat, haunted by the memory of that one time I tried to kiss Oliver, and he turned me down.

CHAPTER 5

OLIVER

"WHAT'S GOING ON TODAY?" Declan asks, loud enough to be heard over the EDM music blaring through the gym speakers. He's standing behind me, spotting and waiting his turn. I slowly press the dumbbell up and down beside my chest, focusing on my form. We're both squeezing in our workout before work. I've got an hour to burn before heading to my office. I'm actually looking forward to work today, likely because I'm sourcing new art for our collection.

"I'm going to visit Dan Warne to discuss the Warne Gallery he's selling."

"Do you need another gallery to handle? Surely, you're busy enough?" he asks, as I finish my eighth rep. I sit up on the bench, grab my towel, and wipe the sweat off my forehead.

"This one's different. It's on West 24th street."

I stand and step aside. He takes my spot, lifting heavier weights. "What's so special about it?"

"My mom has always loved it, but he never put it on the market. Until now." I can't keep the excitement from my voice. This is the opportunity I've been waiting for... one I won't let slip away.

"So you're buying it for your mom?" he asks, straining as he pushes through his eighth rep.

"Not exactly. She's happy teaching. She's not interested in running galleries again."

He drops the weights, puts his hands on his hips, and paces as he catches his breath, before I continue.

"I want to showcase her students' work there. They mean a lot to her, and after helping me get a head start with my galleries, this feels like the best way to thank her." I can't help but smile as I share my plans, certain Declan will appreciate the mix of strategy and heart.

We switch positions, moving from chest presses to dumbbell flys, and I grab a lighter set of weights.

"So will it run like a normal gallery?" he asks.

"Yes, everything will be for sale, and I plan to hold auctions," I say, lying back on the bench and press.

"She'll love it."

"That's what I'm counting on," I reply, completing my eighth rep before dropping the weights to the black-padded flooring. Her approval means everything; it's not just about business this time. If she doesn't love it, I'll have missed my chance to finally repay her for all those years of sacrifice. The gallery needs to be perfect. We switch again, and I ask, "What about you? Busy day?"

"Transfer meeting this morning. After that, just the usual grind." He grunts, pushing through his first rep.

Declan's in corporate finance, where he handles managing companies, buying and selling them, overseeing mergers, the whole lot.

Even though we were on different paths, we clicked after meeting our sophomore year of college. While I spent late nights working on business projects, he was grinding through internships at investment firms, already planning his future. He's always thinking three steps ahead of everyone else, whether it's in business, poker, or life, while I go with my gut. Over time, we settled into an easy friendship, him trying to convince me to save money, and me reminding him that not everything needs a spreadsheet. He plays it safe; I take risks. It shouldn't work, but somehow, it does. Maybe it's because, no matter how busy he was, he always made time for me. When I struggled with my business degree and felt like I was falling behind, he showed up with takeout and refused to let me spiral. He knew my dreams were to own art galleries, and he didn't let me forget them. When my grams got sick, he sat with me at home, no questions asked. And when I nearly backed out of my first real art show, convinced I wasn't good enough, he gave me a speech about how I was going to take over the art world one day.

"Is the transfer meeting with the New York team or the Florida team?"

"Florida," he says, putting the weights away. "I'm trying to prepare, so I've been signing in to their important meetings to stay in the loop."

"I'm going to miss you, man. I'll have to find a new gym partner."

"I'm irreplaceable," he says, giving me a playful shove. I stumble but catch my footing, laughing.

"You fucking wish," I tease, my grin falling when I realize how much I'll miss seeing him every day. He's been one of the few people in my life. Adjusting to him living far away is going to take some time.

I pull into the nearby parking garage of Warne Gallery. After I park and push my door open, the low growl of an approaching engine catches my attention. My head snaps up, muscles tensing instinctively. A sleek red Lamborghini pulls into the spot beside me, the driver taking his sweet time shutting it off before stepping out like he owns the entire city.

Liam fucking Carter. Of course he stopped by to chat to Mr. Warne at the same time as me. Asshat.

That irritatingly self-satisfied smirk is plastered on his face like he was born with it.

"Oliver," he says smoothly, adjusting his cufflinks. "I'm surprised you made it out of bed this morning. I thought you'd be lying in a pool of your own tears after a restless night of dreaming about your failures."

I shut my car door and match his smirk. "It was hard to get out of bed, considering I was entertaining your ex-girlfriend. She kept going on and on about how she was glad to be finally dating someone successful."

Liam lets out a low chuckle, shaking his head. "You almost had me there. But we both know you don't have the time, or the money, to keep up with a woman like her."

"That's rich, coming from a guy who throws money at problems because he doesn't have the brains to solve them."

"Money wins in the end, Oliver. You'll figure that out eventually."

I step toward the gallery entrance, and he falls into stride beside me. This is how it always is. Business, life... hell, even women. If I want something, Liam Carter wants it too. It drives me fucking insane.

He gives me a sideways glance. "So, what is it this time? Looking to add a little class to your sad excuse of an office?"

I let out a dry laugh. "Please. Unlike you, I actually appreciate art beyond its price tag."

"Oh, is that so? I just assumed you were here to beg the gallery for a payment plan."

"Bold of you to assume I need one when you're the one who thinks buying this place will finally make you interesting."

Liam grins, pushing open the gallery door. "Guess we'll see who walks out of here as the new owner."

My heart hammers against my ribs. This isn't just another business acquisition... It's personal.

He pauses just inside, his grin sharpening. "Speaking of interesting," he says, glancing over his shoulder. "Heard you've been on the hunt for that hidden artist everyone's whispering about. Any luck?"

I keep my expression neutral, masking my surprise. "Didn't realize you had an interest in them."

"You know me, always curious about what keeps you up at night," he replies smoothly.

I force another smirk, refusing to give him the satisfaction of a real reaction. "Sleep's never been an issue. Maybe you should try worrying less about me and more about your own overrated collection."

My jaw clenches. The fact that Liam is sniffing around the same anonymous artist only confirms what I already suspected. Whoever created those pieces is the real deal. Now, I'm not just determined to acquire the gallery for my mother; I need to find this artist before Liam does. His interest has just turned my curiosity into an obsession. Two battles on my hands, and I refuse to lose either one.

Right now, I want to talk to Mr. Warne about the gallery, and seeing Liam here makes my stomach uneasy. If Liam buys it, he'll only ruin it like he's done with the others by turning them into overpriced, soulless showrooms. He guts their originality, strips them of real artistry, and replaces it with whatever flashy, high-ticket pieces will sell the fastest. No loyalty to artists, no real appreciation for the craft, just another playground for the wealthy to throw money around.

That's not what I want for this place. This gallery has history; real character. The artists here deserve a space that respects their work, somewhere that fosters creativity instead of choking it with neon lights and overpriced champagne bars. If Liam gets his hands on it, all of that disappears.

Not happening. I won't let it.

The sun beams down on me, heating up my suit as I walk toward the building, leaving him behind. I have a meeting to get to, and I won't be late.

The tall brown brick gallery has a special charm, a mix of sophistication with neutral tones and gold accents, art on display with warm accent lighting, and the scent of fresh wood polish. It's perfect. This place matters to me, and I know exactly what I'd do to make it even better. Incorporating my mom's students' art. I can already picture her face when she walks through these doors... That slight widening of her eyes she gets when she's truly surprised, followed by that soft smile that crinkles the corners of her expression. She'd slowly walk the space, maybe even tear up a little, but try to hide it.

I stride straight to Mr. Warne's office. I've been here countless times over the past few years, practically begging him to sell the gallery to me. This time, Trudy, his assistant, told me he was selling.

When I reach his assistant, she smiles, but she won't be smiling for long. Once I buy this place, she's out. Cora, my assistant, will be taking her position.

"Hi, Trudy. I'm here to see Mr. Warne," I say, leaning on her desk. "Can you do me a favor and delay Liam joining me?"

"I shouldn't..." She hesitates, glancing around.

I flash her my devilish grin and edge a little closer to her. "I just need a few moments alone with Mr. Warne."

She sighs lightly. "Alright, but you owe me."

"What do you want?" I ask, popping my eyebrow.

"Dinner," she says with a hopeful smile.

"Sure," I say with a wink.

"Go ahead, I'll stall him," she agrees, touching my hand briefly before I pull back and head to the door.

I knock, and then turn the silver metal handle, the sound of Trudy greeting Liam hitting my ears as I step inside the office and close the door behind me. Mr. Warne's dark head looks up from his paperwork, his gray eyes piercing through his black-framed glasses.

The man is well into his sixties, but he has a presence that demands attention despite his quiet demeanor. I've known him for years, though our relationship has always been more professional than personal. He's a tough negotiator, a man who values legacy over quick money, which is exactly why I need to convince him that I'm the right buyer.

"Good morning, Mr. Warne," I say, approaching his large wooden desk.

"Good morning. Have a seat," he says, gesturing to the navy fabric chair across from him.

I sit, smoothing my tie as he studies me. "I appreciate you taking the time to meet with me."

"What can I do for you?" There's a flicker of surprise in his eyes.

"I wanted to talk about the Warne Gallery and the possibility of me buying it."

Warne nods, lacing his fingers. "I'm curious to hear your vision for this place."

I lean forward slightly. "I want to preserve what you've built... Keep the integrity of the gallery intact, continue showcasing artists whose work deserves to be seen, not just those with the biggest bank accounts."

His expression gives nothing away, but I can tell he's listening. "And financially? Running a gallery isn't cheap."

"I have a solid plan," I say. "Strategic partnerships, curated events that bring in serious collectors while keeping the focus on the art. I'm not looking to turn this into a social club with a few paintings as decoration."

Warne exhales, tapping a finger on his desk. "It's rare to find someone who actually cares about the art. Most people just see dollar signs."

A subtle wave of relief washes through me. His words validate what I've been trying to prove. The fact that he sees my genuine passion gives me an edge I hadn't counted on. I straighten slightly; maybe this negotiation won't be as cutthroat as I'd prepared for.

A knock at the door pulls his focus away from me.

I close my eyes, exhaling sharply. Trudy couldn't keep him distracted a little longer?

Fuck me.

"Hi, Mr. Warne. I hope I haven't missed anything. I'm right on time," Liam says, taking a seat next to me. Mr. Warne checks his watch. "Looks like you both are, which is great because I need to make this quick. I have to meet my wife." He puts his glasses down on the desk. "I know you're both interested in buying this gallery, and I've narrowed it down to you two."

My shoulders tense as reality hits... I'm not the only contender here.

Mr. Warne leans back in his chair, pointing at us. "But there's one thing neither of you has."

My eyebrows pinch involuntary as I sit up straighter. I try to figure out what he could be talking about, but I come up empty.

"What can I do, Mr. Warne?" Liam asks.

I remain quiet, waiting for more information. Whatever he needs, I'll make it happen.

"You're both excellent in business; your galleries are performing well. Thanks for sharing your figures. It made it easier to cut out the competition. But there's more to it than that. You know how much I adore this gallery. There's so much love here. I need to trust that whoever buys it won't ruin it for greed."

"That won't happen with me," I say, my voice firm.

"Same here," Liam adds, giving me that trademark smirk. "Oliver here curates for museums and old money while I bring fresh blood into the market. My clients may like their champagne, but they also dropped thirty million on artists last year."

I resist rolling my eyes. Yes, Liam's sales numbers are impressive... You don't become a finalist otherwise. But there's more to this business than turning quick profits. One of my galleries has helped build three major museum wings and launched exhibitions that changed how we view twentieth-century art. That's the kind of legacy Mr. Warne wants to protect.

"As much as you both say that, I need more than words," Mr. Warne continues.

My knee bounces rapidly under the table. I force it still with a firm hand before Liam notices. What the fuck could he want that will get me over the line?

"What do you need?" I ask.

"Both of you are single, right?" Mr. Warne looks between us.

"Yes," Liam confirms.

I nod slowly, my mind racing back to my recent conversation with Declan about settling down. I'd laughed it off then, but now, with Warne's gaze drilling into me, I wonder if my personal life is becoming a professional liability.

"I'm engaged," I blurt out.

Liam twists to face me with an eyebrow raised. "To who?"

Fuck, I can't think. My mind blanks completely as panic floods my system. An ex? No, too messy. A friend? They'd need convincing. Make someone up? But what if Warne wants details, or worse, wants to meet them? Who could I say that would work, that won't fall in love with me? Luckily for me, Mr. Warne interrupts.

"That's not relevant, Liam. I need you both to be serious."

"And how does being in a relationship show that?" Liam asks in a biting tone.

Is he upset at me one-upping him or at Mr. Warne for making this a requirement?

"Being in love softens your heart, makes you see things differently. It's a feeling, like art, and it's something I'm looking for," Mr. Warne explains, his gaze shifting to me.

I force a smile, pretending I understand. His eyes crinkle, and the corners of his mouth lift. "My father and I made a promise. When he sold me this gallery, we agreed that its next owner would understand the importance of family. That's why he insisted on the contract."

My heart sinks as the pieces click into place. A contract? Now Warne's strange questions make perfect sense. I'm being judged not just on my work, but on my personal life too.

Liam shuffles in his chair beside me. "So, I need a girlfriend to buy the gallery?"

"You need a wife." Mr. Warne's voice carries the weight of decades. *A fucking wife?*

"My father believed that someone with a family would protect the gallery's legacy, not just its profit margins. He wanted its future owner to understand what it means to build something that lasts beyond yourself."

I have no interest in marriage and kids right now, but I need this gallery for me and my mom. I want the most respected gallery in the world to have the name Lincoln.

How on earth will I convince someone to marry me?

"Maybe we could double date, and I could meet your fiancée, Oliver?" Liam sneers.

My chest tightens, and I tug at my collar, suddenly feeling like I can't breathe.

"That sounds great. Let me know when and where, and we'll be there," I say.

"Let's plan for next week," Mr. Warne suggests.

My stomach plummets. A week? Mentally, I try to find someone to convince in just seven days.

"Can we move it a few weeks?"

"Why?" Liam narrows his eyes.

I keep my expression neutral. "I have my brother Jeremy's bachelor party."

"That's right. Good man, Jeremy," Mr. Warne mumbles.

Jeremy bought an art piece at a recent charity auction Mr. Warne hosted.

I think I've gotten myself some time. But I wasn't lying about my brother's party, though. It's happening, and I'm a groomsman. Between that and now needing to figure out this relationship dilemma, I've got my hands full.

Mr. Warne pushes his chair back and rises. "I need to head out, but my assistant will coordinate with yours to set it up. Now, if you'll see yourselves out."

I stand, a strange mix of relief and dread swirling in my gut. Relief that this unexpected interrogation is over, but dread at the ticking clock I now face. I force my expression to remain confident as I offer my hand. Mr. Warne shakes it firmly.

"Liar. You're not dating anyone," Liam hisses as we walk out.

I ignore my thumping heart to sneer under my breath. "I am, Liam. Don't be a sore loser when I buy the gallery. Maybe you'll do better next time."

"This is... fucked," Liam hisses under his breath as we reach the doors to leave.

I couldn't have said it better myself, but I don't have time to argue. I need a plan, and fast.

"Mom?" I call out, peeking into her office. It's cluttered with paintbrushes, canvases, papers, and easels, but there's no sign of her. I know she's here somewhere, because I called on my way over. *"Just stopping by to check on you,"* I'd said casually, not mentioning anything about Warne or the gallery.

I head toward the classrooms, glancing through the window of the first one. But it's a different teacher. I move to the next door and step inside. The walls are filled with students' artwork, some framed, some curling at the edges, splattered with spray paint. Stacks of canvases lean against the back wall, some wrapped in protective plastic, others exposed, displaying bold strokes of color and intricate details. I pause to study a particular cityscape piece. This is exactly the kind of talent I want to showcase when I take over Warne's gallery. These artists deserve more than a classroom or basement; they need walls that will have audiences who will truly see them. The faint smell of turpentine and clay fills the space, mixing with the underlying musk of old wood and paper.

"Mom, are you here?" I call out into the classroom.

Her brown head pops up from behind the desk. "Hey, you're here."

I walk over, noticing the smudge of blue paint across her forehead, and kiss her cheek, getting her usual warm smile that makes me feel like I've done something right just by showing up.

"Looks like you're in the middle of something," I say, gesturing to the scattered supplies and half-organized chaos around us.

"I'm setting up for the next class."

"Want some help?"

"Yeah, can you clip the paper on each easel?" she says, pointing to them.

"Sure."

I follow her to a drawer, where she pulls out some paper, my mind spinning with everything left unsaid between us. How do I even begin this conversation? *"Hey, Mom, I need to find a fake fiancée to secure a multi-million-dollar gallery that I want to surprise you with."* Stupid. I run my fingers over the soft material as I take it from her. I love how she always uses the best supplies for her students. This is why

I want to make sure she gets the gallery. The students here deserve a chance to showcase their work, and Mom should be recognized for all the free classes she offers. She gives back so much, and I want to give back to her too.

"How many students today?" I ask.

"Twelve."

I go around clipping twelve sheets of paper while she arranges the brushes and palettes on tables. I think about possible approaches. *Just be direct. No, just ease into it. Maybe start with a hypothetical?* The routine task keeps my hands busy while my mind races.

"What brings you by today? Are you still stressed about finding the artist?" she asks, glancing with a raised eyebrow.

"Can't a son visit his mother?" I say, a grin tugging at the corner of my mouth. My stomach tightens with guilt at the deflection. For the first time, my mind hasn't been on the mystery artist who paints their signature with a blue lotus instead of their name. It's driving me mad. But today my mind is on The Warne Gallery.

She straightens, giving me a knowing look. "Oliver, I wasn't born yesterday. What's bothering you?"

I wish I could tell her, but I want the gallery to be a surprise. I'll tell her as soon as I finalize the purchase, but for now, I need to keep my concerns off my face.

"Girl trouble," I utter. I mean, it's not a lie, but I can't tell her what kind of girl trouble, because she would demand the full truth.

She pauses sorting the paint. Her eyes meet mine, and her face is lit up. "Who's the lucky lady?"

I shake my head, hating that I need to lie to her. I feel like young Oliver, lying about not taking her paint brushes from her home studio. But I don't need a girlfriend; I need a fucking wife. I'm so fucked.

"No names, I don't need you looking her up."

She tries to bite back a smile. "I would never."

"You're a terrible liar. You've looked up Nova, Chelsea... You even stalked Summer's socials." My brothers' fiancées and friend.

"It wasn't stalking, just researching," she says, heading to the drawer for more paint bottles. Following her lead, I grab and place them around the room, mimicking her movements. The irony isn't lost on me... Here I am, about to make up a whole fake fiancée, while lecturing my mother about boundaries.

"Call it what you want, but she's staying anonymous for now." *As anonymous as someone who doesn't exist can be.*

She returns to putting the paints on the table. "Fine, so what's the problem with this no named woman?"

I laugh inwardly at her clear disapproval before I focus on why I came to her in the first place. "I'm just wondering... when's the right time to make things official? Like, when's too soon?"

Her face brightens. "There's no such thing as too soon."

"Of course you'd say that."

"I'm serious. If you were under twenty-one, I'd be saying something different, but you're mature. You have your own place, a good job, and a good head on your shoulders." She walks over, pausing in front of me and putting her hand on my cheek. "Follow your heart. Let it lead you."

"Thanks, Mom."

She glances at the clock on the wall, and I take it as my cue to leave.

"I'll let you get back to it," I say, leaning down to kiss her cheek.

She holds my face in her hands, keeping me close. "Make sure we meet her soon."

I roll my eyes and sigh, guilt twisting in my chest. How many more lies will I need to tell before this is over? "Yes, Mom. Have a great class. Talk to you tomorrow."

She turns back to her desk, and I head out, only to collide into someone. My hands instinctively reach out to steady the person, and I'm hit with the sweet scent of floral and caramel. I stare into a stunningly familiar set of blue eyes.

Karley.

Chapter 6

Karley

I stand toe-to-toe with Oliver, his piercing blue eyes locked on mine, a crooked grin spreading across his lips. Why does he have to keep showing up here? I know that his mom owns the school, but seriously? He's popping up everywhere this week like it's his full-time job.

My gaze drops quickly over his outfit. He's wearing a tailored navy suit that hugs his frame perfectly, paired with a white shirt and a matching navy tie. I force myself to look up, avoiding his lips, the same lips that have starred in countless of my dreams, and most humiliating nightmares. His eyebrow is slightly arched, as if he knows exactly what I was doing.

Where has he been, all dressed up? A meeting. An art auction. A date? The thought twists the fluttering in my stomach into tight, uncomfortable knots.

"Hi, Karley," he says, voice smooth, with the tiniest smirk playing on his lips.

"Oliver."

"Are you going to tell me your thoughts on today's suit?"

It's the same as the other one... Tight and dangerous.

I cross my arms. "You wearing overly tight clothes is none of my business."

"It's not tight; it's tailor-made."

"You should consider telling your assistant to look for a new tailor," I mumble, ready to take a step around him to go home.

His hand reaches out in front of me, stopping me from moving. "How was class?" he asks.

My annoyance eases when I notice his eyes soften at the corners.

Today, I got to paint a bird of paradise, something I've never tried before, and I'm pleased with how it turned out. I used acrylic paint instead of watercolors, playing with textures and layering. Tomorrow, I get to finish a new large bouquet of peonies, a watercolor piece I've been working on.

I step back, putting distance between us. "It was good. Did you see your mom?" I ask, hoping to steer the conversation away from whatever annoying game he's trying to play.

"What if I came to see you?" He leans in slightly, that smug grin still sitting on his face.

I ignore how my heart stutters and roll my eyes at him. "Funny."

"I'm not joking." His expression is suddenly serious, eyes holding mine without a trace of humor.

I shake my head. "Oliver, I'm going home. I don't have time for this," I say, moving around him, but I catch a whiff of his scent, which is fresh, clean, with a hint of something warm like wood. The scent lingers, making my skin prickle. The fact that he smells so good only adds to my irritation. Not just because he won't quit, but because being near him still does something to me. No matter how hard I try to shut it down, that pull... that old, inconvenient spark... refuses to die.

His hand juts out, gently grabbing my arm. A shiver ripples down my spine as he spins me back to face him.

"I'm sorry. It was nice seeing you. I'm heading off too. Do you want me to drive you home?" he offers.

"No, I'll order a ride, thanks." I walk away, pushing down a flicker of surprise at his offer. Oliver drops his hand from my arm, but he matches my pace. I also need to meet a real estate agent at a house I'm planning to buy. My brother doesn't know I've been looking at properties outside of Manhattan, which means Oliver definitely can't come along.

"Right," he says, but there's a flash of something that passes his eyes. Disappointment? Embarrassment? His cheeks darken slightly, and for a moment, I almost feel bad.

We step into the elevator, where a few people are already inside. I make sure to stand on the opposite side so someone has to stand between us. The electricity crackles even with people in here. I can almost feel his gaze on me, but I keep my eyes straight ahead, watching for the ground button to light up. The last thing I need is to get lost in his blue eyes, or worse, get lost in a soft look of his, the one that always messes with my head.

It's a short ride, and as soon as the elevator doors open, I rush out, throwing a casual wave over my shoulder, brushing off any tension between us. "Goodbye, Oliver." I don't even bother turning around. I can already feel his eyes on me. I need to focus on me and the house.

"Bye, Karley. I'll see you soon," he calls out after me. I can hear the grin in his voice, but I don't let it distract me. Instead, I clench my jaw and quicken my pace, fighting the unwelcome warmth that threatens to spread through my body.

I get into the rideshare and let out a long breath, checking the address the realtor sent before giving the driver directions. As I sit staring out the window, I try to push thoughts of Oliver out of my head, but his words ring in my ear. Despite my irritation, anticipation builds inside me at the idea of seeing him again, which only frustrates me more. When we finally pull up, I get out, thank the driver, and walk up the driveway, pausing to take in the house.

It's a classic brownstone, with a red brick façade, black wrought-iron railings, and tall windows with elegant creamy white trim. There are freshly cut hedges lining the front, and a smaller unit tucked away at the back, almost hidden behind a few neatly trimmed green trees. The whole place feels like a mix of old charm and cozy warmth, not modern, which is exactly what I'm looking for.

The air smells fresh, with a faint hint of floral. The porch light casts a warm, welcoming glow, making my heart swell. This place feels like hope. It's not just a property for me. Growing up in foster care, both Declan and I weren't able to meet up. So I want to create that space. A safe, welcoming place for foster kids to reunite even if it's just for an hour.

"Karley?" the realtor calls out, snapping me away from my faraway thoughts.

He looks to be in his fifties, with gray hair and a short frame, wearing black suit pants with a blue shirt open at the collar, no tie. He approaches with a friendly smile.

"Hi, Hugh."

"Are you ready?" he asks, pointing toward the door.

My lips part into a wide grin, and I have to swallow my excitement. "Yes."

We walk along the concrete path up to the front door, painted a rich, deep navy with only a few faint marks. I take a deep breath as he unlocks it and pushes it open, revealing a long hallway. It has light wooden floors and soft lighting illuminating the walls, which are painted a creamy white. I take a left into the living room; it's a large open area with big windows that let plenty of natural light seep through the curtains. It's full of potential as I picture the family conversations, laughter, and connections that could happen here.

We make our way to another room on the opposite side of the hallway. The potential of this house is flashing in my mind, lighting me up from within.

Continuing down the hall, we pass a living room, a small den, and finally the open kitchen and dining room. There's plenty of counter space, cabinets, and a big dining table. I can already see it, families sharing meals, playing board games, or just being together and having conversations.

The backyard is huge, with a swing set, a large, luscious grass area, a shed for more storage, and even a trampoline. It's a perfect setup for kids to run around and play. I'd love to add a couple of little tables for families to enjoy a meal or simply get the chance to talk. Every part of this house feels right, and when I spot a blue lotus, my eyes fill with tears. It's a sign. This place is meant to be mine.

But then we walk to the cabin out the back. This is where I would live.

I step inside, and the tiny home is better than I imagined. It's modern with white walls, wood accents, and navy details. Everything blends so perfectly. There's a double bed on one side, with storage overhead, a compact kitchen in the middle, and a small dining area that could double as an art workspace. The other end has a small sofa, facing a TV mounted on the wall. It's small, but it's perfect for just me. I won't be here all the time anyway. I'll be working, studying, or helping run the main house.

Standing in this tiny home, a warm rush floods my veins. This is my dream. I have to make it happen. If I lose this house, it could be months or even years before I find something else this perfect.

"What are you thinking?" he asks.

I turn to him, my cheeks aching from smiling so much. "Honestly, it's perfect."

"The owners heard your story, and they were moved by it. They want to sell it to you. And truthfully, I want that too. But if you don't commit soon, we'll have to consider other offers."

"I'll buy it," I rush out, panic rising at the thought of losing this opportunity.

"When?" he presses. "I need to give the owners a deadline."

"Thirty days, maximum," I say. I only have fifty-five thousand saved. It's not enough. I need another fifty thousand for the down payment, and I have no clue how I'll get the rest within a few weeks.

He nods. "That'll work."

As we walk out, my smile drops, the wheels spinning in my head, trying to figure out some options to get fast cash.

But I take one last look at the house, soaking in every detail. I'll figure out the money somehow. For now, I just want to hold on to this feeling, this tiny bubble of hope, and not let it pop.

"I'll keep in touch," Hugh says as we part ways.

"Thanks for showing me around. I'll talk to you soon."

Leaving Hugh behind, I walk slowly to the sidewalk where I call a ride. A light warm breeze sweeps through, and I can't wipe the smile off my face. I have to find a way to make this place mine. I haven't smiled this much since the day I found out I was going to be adopted.

The ride home in the rideshare is a blur, my thoughts alternating between ideas to raise money and visions of foster siblings laughing together in that living room. I imagine hanging string lights in the backyard, maybe even hosting holiday gatherings. I need this house to work out.

Once I get back to the city, I'm heading to an empty house. My brother won't be back until late, so I have the place to myself. The quiet is a glimpse of what's coming.

Inside, I turn on the TV for background noise, deciding to have breakfast for dinner. As I put bread in the toaster, the doorbell rings, cutting through the quiet.

Who is that? And, more importantly, what do they want? I check through the peephole. My breath catches. Oliver. Still in that infuriating come-fuck-me navy suit.

I hesitate, then open the door just enough to speak through the gap. "He's not home," I say flatly, and before he can respond, I try to shut the door in his face. But his hand shoots out, catching it before it closes.

"That's okay. I'm not here to see Declan. I'm here to see you."

Chapter 7

Oliver

I catch the door before it slams in my face, my heart pounding harder than I'd like to admit.

She opens her mouth, then closes it, before slamming the door behind me.

"Is there a problem?"

"No. Just go sit down," she says, as the toaster pops.

"What's for dinner?" I tease, noticing she's changed from jeans into baggy light gray sweats, hair in a messy ponytail. The casual look suits her; she seems softer somehow. She glances up at me, eyes lingering a beat too long, like she's reading my thoughts.

"I'm making myself some toast. You can make your own or order something."

I bite back a smile at her bluntness. I should probably feel bad about invading her space, but there's something about the way her eyes flicker to mine that makes me think maybe, just maybe, she doesn't mind as much as she pretends to.

She moves to the counter in front of me and grabs the peanut butter.

"No jelly?" I ask.

"No. I prefer it without. Now, go sit down and stop watching me," she says, waving her hand dismissively. I lean against the counter, unable to tear my eyes away despite her command. I spot paint smudges on her hand as she spreads the smooth peanut butter over the toast and takes a big bite, her eyes fluttering shut for a moment before opening again. I wonder if she even knows she does that. The little moment makes my chest tighten in a way I wasn't prepared for. Maybe I should've thought this through more before showing up. Being alone with her feels more dangerous than I anticipated.

There's always been something about Karley. This easy way of pulling people in without even trying. I remember when Declan asked me to help make her feel welcome, back when they had just reconnected. It wasn't supposed to be anything more than that. Just a favor. But the banter started quickly, and before I realized it, talking to her became my favorite part.

I chortle at her adorable reaction. "I think I'll make some toast."

"Help yourself," she says, her tone lighter now. Maybe she was just hungry.

I'll keep that in mind. *Karley gets snappy when she's hungry.*

I wander around the kitchen, grabbing a plate and some jelly from the fridge. I feel her eyes on me as I move, and when I glance up, our gazes lock for a brief moment before she looks away, continuing to eat. She makes it clear she's not going to start a conversation.

"What are we watching?" I ask, glancing across the room at the TV screen.

A sigh escapes her. "I'm watching something that will hopefully make you leave."

"Is it reality TV? Because I hate to break it to you, but I secretly love that shit." I wink.

"It's a drama rom-com called *Nobody Wants This*."

I reach for the cupboard door, and her eyes widen slightly as I lean in. "Sounds amazing. I can't wait to watch it after I eat."

I smile to myself as I grab a plate.

"God, you're annoying. I don't know why my brother likes being your friend."

I move to grab a knife when my toast pops, and I spread on the peanut butter and jelly. On impulse, I hold it up to her lips. "Try it with jelly."

She pushes my arm away. "I know what peanut butter and jelly tastes like."

"But I make it the best."

She arches her eyebrow. "It's peanut butter and jelly. It's not difficult."

I wink again, trying to rile her up more, hoping a little fun might soften her. "You'd be surprised."

She huffs, her cheeks flushing, and I expect her to snap at me. "Fine. Give me your amazing toast."

She closes her eyes, parting her lips before she takes a bite, then opens her eyes, her bright blue gaze assessing me critically.

After she swallows, she replies, "As I thought... No difference."

I hiss, pretending to be offended. "Harsh critic. Maybe you should be on *MasterChef*?"

"I have no desire to do that." She spins around, putting her plate in the dishwasher, and moves to walk past me.

"Wait up," I call. My heart races. This isn't going how I planned. I seem to be upsetting her when my goal was just to hang out with her until Declan gets home.

She pauses, her eyebrows knitting. "What?"

I step forward and swipe my thumb gently across the corner of her full bottom lip, ignoring the slight hitch in her breath. She pulls back and wipes her mouth roughly herself. "I got it," she says, turning and heading into the living room. I finish my toast, watching her walk away.

My mind drifts to that night at the party; her hopeful expression just before she leaned in, the hurt in her eyes when I pulled back. I'd been trying to do the right thing; she's Declan's little sister.

"Oliver!"

"Sorry. I'm coming."

I leave my plate and move into the living room. I keep getting distracted by the little things she does, like the way she wrinkles her nose when she's annoyed at me, or how her eyes brighten when she's about to deliver a smart remark. I need to focus.

I move into the living room where she's curled up on one sofa, while the other is empty.

I choose to sit next to her, knowing it will annoy her. Our thighs touching.

"No need for personal space," she mutters under her breath, but a small grin tugs at my lips as I lean back.

We sit in comfortable silence until I notice she's huddling.

"Do you want a blanket?" I ask.

"Sure, that'd be nice." I get up to grab one from the closet. "Maybe take off your shoes. You're making me uncomfortable in that suit."

I look at her, noticing a slight pink flush on her nose. "Why didn't you say something earlier?" I ask, slipping off my shoes, loosening my tie, and pulling it off. I untuck my shirt and undo a few buttons before heading back. Her eyes drop for a moment, but she quickly darts them back to the screen.

"Is that better?" I ask, lifting an eyebrow.

She nods, her throat bobbing slightly. "Hurry up, I want to watch the whole episode before I shower and head to bed."

We watch one twenty-six-minute episode in a silence that gradually shifts from awkward to relaxing. I steal glances at her when she laughs at certain scenes, noticing how different she is when her guard is down.

She turns it off and sits up. "That's it for me tonight. I don't know when Declan will be back, but don't watch the show without me."

The casual comment catches me off guard; it's the first hint she might be okay with hanging out with me again. "Same goes for you."

She frowns. "This is my house."

I shake my head with new confidence. "I can come back every night until we've watched the whole season. I'm invested now."

The truth is, I like the show, the easy silence between us, and just unwinding after a long day. I haven't done this in so long, and I suddenly feel like I could do this every day.

She spins around, calling over her shoulder. "So strange, but whatever. Goodnight."

"Night."

I watch her walk away until I can't see her anymore. I can hear her turn on the shower, and my mind drifts to her... specifically, her body covered in water and her hands rubbing soap.... Fuck. Oliver, no. I shake my head, realizing I'm tired. I shouldn't be thinking about her like that. I need to be figuring out how to find a wife in a few weeks.

My head rests where hers was. Her scent lingers on the sofa, a mix of her perfume and soap. It's an unusual blend of floral meets caramel.

The house is quiet, except for the faint noise of the TV, left on whatever channel she flicked it to before she left. As I lie here, I wonder if she's already finished showering and tucked up in bed. I can't tell because her door is closed.

I pull out my phone and scroll through my social media. It's the same shit... family photos, my mom sharing random recipe posts, or worse, Grams uploading baby photos of us. I exit the app and switch to Instagram. This is more interesting, with a lot of art, specifically paintings that align with me. But even here, I can't escape posts from snotty wealthy people flaunting their shopping sprees, which I'm sure are a result of maxed-out credit cards. But a post from Liam, five minutes ago, makes me sit up straight.

I run my hand through my hair as I take in the image of a candlelit dinner at Le Bernardin, one of New York's finest restaurants, where you rub shoulders with the elite. It's the kind of place with a year-long waitlist unless you're an A-list celebrity. The caption reads, *Date night.*

He said he was single today. He must be gearing up to find a partner to show off. That bastard is trying to one-up me. But I'm one step ahead because I've already told Mr.

Warne that I'm engaged, so the transition to 'wife' is more believable. I've started making a mental list... a small wedding ceremony, purchase quality wedding bands, and a suit. And the most important... *a wife!*

In the business of buying art galleries, it's all about charm and deception to get what you want. Usually, I have charm in abundance, but lately, it seems I'm losing my touch.

I close Liam's picture and search for the artist I've been trying to find. Still nothing. I get that they're introverted, but I just want one meeting to discuss a collaboration. No one else has these paintings, so it would be exclusive to me and this up-and-coming artist. They don't even have to show; I'll be the face for them. But I can't host an auction or a viewing without their collaboration. I first saw their painting at the school, but my mom has no clue where it came from; she's never seen anyone paint the flower where a signature should be. I've looked online at every possible option, and I even hired a private investigator.

I've talked to my brothers about this, but they don't get why I'm so determined to find this artist. At first, I thought it was a woman, but they pointed out it could be anyone. And fuck, I have no leads. I've even gone to underground galleries to get a clue-in on who the artist is.

I send an email to Cora, my assistant, to see if she's heard anything.

At my mom's school, they have a website and shop where artists list their work for sale. I've managed to buy a few pieces, all of which are watercolors and flowers, but recently, there's been nothing new. Mom even told the shop assistant, Ray, to set them aside for me and call when a new one arrives, but it's been weeks since the last piece. Right now, I have two paintings. One in my office and one at home. Each time, I get frustrated by how undervalued they are. Another reason I need to contact the artist. These paintings could sell for hundreds of thousands, even millions, yet I've bought them for just fifteen thousand each. A fucking steal.

I go to exit Instagram, but there are more stories from Liam. I can't help myself... I click on them. This time, it's a picture of his date. She's pretty, but not my type.

A noise from down the hall interrupts my thoughts, followed by a faint "fuck" from Karley's room. I sit up straighter, listening. Did she fall? Is she hurt?

"Karley?" I call out, already half-rising from the sofa. "Everything okay in there?"

There's a pause, and I'm about to head down the hallway to check on her when her voice comes back. "I'm fine. Just knocked something over."

I settle back down, relief washing over me at the same time it hits me.

She's the perfect wife...
Beautiful? Check.

Loves Art? Check.

Funny? Check.

Easy to get along with? If you're not me... Check.

Charming? Check.

Knows me well? Check.

But there's still one major problem: she hates me.

Do I have any other choice? I need this gallery. She loves my mom, so maybe she won't do it for me, but she might for her, at least until I can buy the gallery. But what would she get out of it? Maybe money? I know the classes she attends are free, and her part-time job is minimum wage. I bet the tips from drunk women aren't worth much.

The door clicks open, and Declan walks in, looking exhausted, with dark circles under his eyes and his tie loosened around his neck. His presence brings me back to reality, reminding me that I still have to ask the most important person.

"Sorry, I'm late."

"It's alright." I get up from the sofa and clean the kitchen to keep busy, which is still messy from the toast. I smile. I haven't had toast for dinner in years, not since I was a teenager. And fuck, it was good.

"Did you eat? Or did Karley leave this mess?" he asks, dropping his keys on the side table. "Actually, don't answer that. I already know it was her."

Declan is like me; he likes things neat and tidy, but it slipped this time because I was watching TV with Karley...

"Both."

His eyes narrow, giving me that brotherly warning I've heard a thousand times. *"Don't touch my sister."*

But I need to ask him the craziest fucking thing. Maybe I should get him a drink before I bring it up. This would help both me and Karley. He can trust me not to touch her. I've pushed her away once before. Her sad, broken eyes still haunt me, if I let myself think about it, but we could never work. She needed to build her own life, and she deserved that chance.

Besides, her brother, my best friend, had forbidden it. He was still hurting from being separated from her, the guilt, so not touching her was the least I could do for him, no matter how tempting she was. And still fucking is. Now she's older, with more confidence, sass, and curves. Tonight alone, the room felt hotter, and I doubt she even noticed how hard it was for me, literally.

"Where's Karley?" Declan asks.

"In bed. She went a while ago."

He nods and heads to the fridge, pulling out a bottle of water and handing it to me. I take it, immediately drinking some to soothe my dry throat. I don't know why I'm sweating... When he hears my dilemma, he'll agree. At least, I hope so.

We settle on the sofas. He takes the one I was on, so I move to the other. I place my water on the coffee table and clasp my hands, keeping my gaze fixed on him. "I need to ask you something."

He looks at me, still in his suit, and I understand why Karley said I looked uncomfortable earlier. He does now, too.

"What is it?"

"I had my meeting with Mr. Warne today—"

He nods. "That's right. The Warne Gallery. How was it?"

"Yeah, the one I want for my mom." I feel like I need to mention my mom. Declan knows how much the gallery and students matter to her, and it might soften what I'm about to ask.

His expression stays neutral as he tosses his jacket over the back of the chair. I take a deep breath to steady my anxiety of knowing what I'm about to ask.

He rolls his eyes. "What did Warne say?"

"It's down to me and Liam."

"He's a douchebag. Surely, he wouldn't give it to him. You're a much better fit."

I hesitate, rubbing the back of my neck. "He... he will if Liam gets married first."

His eyebrows pull together as he shuffles to the edge of the sofa. "What?"

"He thinks we're both immature. He's told me before that he thinks I pretend to like art." The words sting, making me feel like a fraud even though I've dedicated my entire career to this.

"No way. That's bullshit."

"It's true."

"It's your life. You haven't had one because you dedicate all your time to the galleries."

I nod, but Declan's staring at his hands, missing my gesture completely. "He needs one of us to settle down, some family agreement. Once that happens, then he'll choose."

My hands are trembling slightly, and I cross my arms to hide it.

"You could date anyone. That'd be easy."

"Liam was out tonight on a date."

His hand flaps around in the air. "Well, call someone."

"When was the last time I was with anyone more than once?" I ask, raising an eyebrow. If he reacts badly to this, it could ruin everything: our friendship, the gallery, my mother's dream, my entire career plan.

He scratches his brow. "I don't know... a year?"

"Two."

And even before that, it wasn't much. I've never had a reason to. I want the kind of love my brothers and parents have, so I'd rather wait and focus on making money.

"Fuck, that's a long time."

I laugh, but it quickly fades. "You could say that. But that's not enough for Mr. Warne."

"What do you mean?"

"He wants Liam or me to be married. He wants to hand over the gallery to a happily married man because he wants to make sure it will follow the family tradition."

Declan bursts out laughing, then laughs harder until tears form in his eyes. "You're kidding."

I force myself to maintain eye contact, even as his laughter cuts deep. I clench my jaw, counting to ten before responding.

"I wish. I told him I was engaged." The words leave a bitter taste in my mouth. Saying it out loud makes the lie feel even more pathetic.

"You did?" He laughs again. "Fuck, you're digging yourself into a hole."

"And that's why I need to ask you something." My heart pounds so hard, I can feel it in my fingertips. I've run through every possible scenario, exes, friends, dating apps, professional matchmakers, but none of them would work fast enough. I need someone who could convincingly play the part of a fiancée without raising suspicions. And there's only one person who fits.

"You can't have my missus. That's just fucking weird."

I scrunch up my face. "I wasn't asking for her."

His laughter fades, and his expression shifts to confusion. There's a moment of silence between us as his eyes narrow slightly. "Then who?"

I take a deep breath. The words feel like crossing a line I can never step back from. "Your sister."

Fuck, that came out so wrong, and I quickly say, "I mean, as a fake thing."

"No." His face falls flat.

I hold up my hands, leaning forward on the sofa, watching Declan's face carefully for any sign he's about to explode. Right now, I'm not opposed to begging him on my knees, if that's what it takes.

"Hear me out first. I need this gallery for my mom. She's wanted it all her life, and Warne would never sell it. But now he's willing, and she has no idea. She's retired from galleries, and he won't sell it to her. He wants someone young who can run it for years."

I pause as Declan's face tightens around his eyes, his jaw clenching and unclenching. He hasn't thrown me out yet, which is already better than I expected.

"Your sister knows art, and I could help her."

"How?" His voice is dangerously calm.

"I could give her money to buy a condo."

"I can give her money."

"I can give her more, and you know she won't take your help." The words come out before I can soften them, and I immediately regret my bluntness.

He's tried before, but she's stubborn and refuses to take anything from him.

He crosses his arms, and I can see the flash of hurt in his eyes before he masks it. "She won't take yours either."

"I think I can convince her." Doubt creeps in even as I speak. Will Karley really agree to this crazy plan? The same woman who tried to slam a door in my face just hours ago? But I'm desperate enough to try. "It would only be until I buy the gallery."

"And how exactly are you planning to convince her?" His voice rises.

"She has a soft spot for my mom, and if she knows it's to help her, I think she'll agree."

He rises, paces the room, and shakes his head. "I don't know."

"I promise I won't hurt her. This could benefit her too."

"How?"

"I'll help her find her footing in the art world. Introduce her to the right people and help her build connections for when she's done with school."

He rubs his hand over his face before he stops walking and meets my gaze with his conflicted expression. "Alright, if she agrees, I'll go along with it. But there's one condition... you don't fucking touch her."

"I won't." A wave of conflicting emotions hits me. Relief comes first. Declan's blessing is more than I dared to hope for. But it's quickly followed by dread as the reality of what comes next settles in. Tomorrow, I have to convince a stubborn, sharp-tongued Karley, who can barely stand being in the same room as me, to pretend to be my fiancée.

CHAPTER 8

KARLEY

I'M AT TILLS' IN the middle of a class when my phone rings. The women are painting on canvases with wine glasses in hand, their laughter filling the studio. I take a glance at the screen, half expecting it to be a telemarketer, but no, it's Oliver.

What could he possibly want?

I hit decline and put the phone on my desk to refocus on helping one of the women who's struggling to blend her colors. My hands move easily, showing her how to create a smooth mix, but my mind is still on Oliver. If it were urgent, there'd be a message, a voicemail, or text. Knowing him, it's probably something trivial, like needing to confirm my brother's birthdate for some paperwork.

The class wraps up, and as I'm cleaning brushes and putting away easels, my phone rings again. I miss the call because it's across the room, but when I check, it's Oliver. Again. I sigh, deciding I'll call him back once I'm done cleaning up. It's been a long day, and all I want to do is go home, collapse on the sofa to watch some TV, and then fall asleep.

I'm wiping down the table when there's a knock on the door. I freeze, my heart suddenly pounding.

It's late; no one should be here.

I tiptoe over to the peephole, peering out into the dark, and see Oliver standing there under the outside light, dressed casually in a cream sweater and dark pants. He's not in his usual suit, which throws me off. This relaxed version of him is harder to resist.

I open the door a crack. "It must be something important if you've called me twice and now showed up at my work."

"It is," he says simply.

My stomach drops. Whatever annoyance I felt dissolves into concern. I pull the door open wider. "Come in. It's cold out there, and I'd like to go home before midnight."

It's an exaggeration. I could finish up here in fifteen minutes, but I want him to hurry up, tell me what he wants, and leave. As he steps inside, the familiar scent of his cologne hits me. I tell myself to ignore it, to push down the warmth creeping up my chest, but it's impossible not to inhale just a bit deeper.

He doesn't ask where to sit. He strides toward one of the empty chairs and looks around the studio. He's never been here before. There's a slight frown on his face, and I suddenly feel self-conscious, as if he's judging this small, messy space I call work. I imagine him comparing it to his sterile office, with modern art, glass walls, and everything in its place. Deep down, a flicker of resentment rises in me at the fact he had two loving parents who supported him, who gave him a head start in life, while I bounced between foster homes after my parents' addiction took priority over raising children. No safety net, no inheritance, no connections... just survival with nothing but my stubbornness keeping me going. Until I was adopted by Amber and Wren.

I start putting away the easels, feeling his eyes on me the whole time, which only makes my body tense.

"I need to ask you a favor," he says, breaking the silence.

I pause, glance over my shoulder, then turn to face him fully, one eyebrow lifting. "You need *my* help?" I ask, surprised. He's usually the one who has everything under control.

"Yes." He runs a hand through his hair, something I've rarely seen him do. "That's why I've been trying to reach you."

"Well, I'm sorry, I was working."

He runs his hand down the back of his head. "I know. I'm sorry. It's just... a little urgent."

I continue picking up the easels, deliberately avoiding his gaze. Why am I still tidying up when he clearly has something important to say? It's to keep a distance between us and to keep control in my space. When I reach the one closest to him, his hand closes over mine, stopping me. A jolt of electricity rushes through me. I try to ignore it, looking down at his hand, then back up, keeping a blank face. "What do you need, Oliver?"

Standing over him, I notice how different he seems, almost vulnerable, without the usual power he exudes. And I hate how a small part of me still finds it endearing, being in the same room with him, even after everything.

"I need you to marry me."

"What the fuck, Oliver?" I spit out, the words escaping before I can stop them. My mind floods with questions. Is this some kind of sick joke? A bet with my brother? A prank?

"I'm serious."

I yank my hand back, my mind struggling to process his words. This is fucking crazy. I actually start laughing because there's no way he means it. "No."

Marriage isn't even on my mind right now. Maybe in the future, but certainly not now.

"I'll pay you," he pleads.

The suggestion hits me like a slap. Heat floods my face as anger rises in my throat.

"I'm not a whore, Oliver," I snap, crossing my arms over my chest, hating that he confirms that the powerful always take advantage of the weak.

He grimaces. "Shit. No, Karley. Clearly, I'm not explaining this well. I didn't mean it like that."

I shake my head vehemently, trying to process what's happening. Part of me wants to laugh, but the other part is insulted that he thought I'd agree. "I don't want to get married."

"What do you want?" he whispers with uncertainty in his eyes. Oliver Lincoln unsure of himself is unsettling.

I point to the wooden door. "For you to leave. Like I said, it's been a long day."

He stands and waves his hands around the room. "I'm offering to pay you enough so you don't have to work here anymore."

My chest tightens as his words confirm his dislike of my work. "I like this job, and I have no intention of quitting."

His blue eyes flare, clearly taken aback, as if he never considered that someone could actually enjoy this kind of work. But there's a freedom in teaching, in watching people create, that I can't give up, not for any amount of money. And more importantly, not for him.

"Your brother said it would be okay," he adds.

I go completely still as a sharp ringing fills my ears, replaying his words over and over. He has to be fucking kidding. "My brother said it was fine for you to marry me?" The betrayal cuts deep. I can almost picture it: Declan and Oliver discussing my future.

"Yes."

I close my eyes and rub my temples, feeling a headache coming on. What exactly had Declan told him? That I was desperate enough for money? Or maybe it's connected to Declan's upcoming move; this is his way to take care of me while he's gone.

I drop my hands and look at him. "Declan isn't my father, Oliver. He doesn't get to decide for me."

"I understand that, but he's my best friend."

"Yes, I'm well aware."

I turn to the table to continue cleaning, needing something to distract me. Part of me wants to throw him out, but another part wonders what kind of money he's talking about. I spray down the table and start wiping it.

"It's not a real marriage. It would be for a short time," he says, watching me. He shifts, rubbing the back of his neck. "Can you please stop cleaning and just listen?"

A fake marriage? Is that supposed to make his proposition less insulting? More tempting? I'm not sure which is worse.

"No." My hands need to stay busy while I process what he's asking. "I'm not marrying you, Oliver. Please leave."

For a moment, there's nothing but silence, then I hear his voice, softer, almost pleading. "Come on, Karley."

I swear there's a break in his voice, and it makes me hesitate. I close my eyes, drop the cloth, and then slowly sit down in the chair next to him, facing him directly.

"You need to explain why. You can't just show up at my workplace and demand I marry you."

"Do you know the Warne Gallery on West 24th Street?" He leans forward slightly, his voice low, like he's sharing a secret.

Of course, I know it. Everyone in the art world knows it. I nod. "Yes."

His eyes are intense. I feel my heart flutter under his gaze.

"The owner, Dan Warne, is finally selling it."

I wait, sensing there's more. "I want to buy it, but the owner won't sell it to me. Or to Liam."

Liam. The guy's a jerk. I saw him once at one of Oliver's gallery parties, trying to flirt with Jemima just to rile up his brother Harvey.

"Why won't he sell it to you?"

"He will only hand it over to a married couple. He wants to make sure it's in a good family's hands."

"And that's where I come in?" His plan leaves me somewhere between insulted and suspicious.

"Yes."

This is ludicrous. A fake marriage, legal documents, lying to Warne. All the complications that would follow. "I want to help you, Oliver, but you'll have to just buy another gallery. I'm not doing this." I sigh and stand up, but as I move to walk away, he catches my wrist. A shiver runs down my spine, starting at the point where his fingers touch my skin and radiating through my entire body. I wish he'd stop touching me because it's messing with my head.

"It's not just for me. Let me explain."

The sad look in his eyes makes me reluctantly sit back down, and he lets go of my wrist. Immediately I miss his touch.

"It's for my mom," he says, and my heart softens.

His mom is like a second mother to me. "Your mom's retired. She doesn't need a gallery. I thought she was busy with her school?"

"It's to display her students' work," he says quietly. He's nervous admitting that? But why...because I'm one of those students?

My heart skips a beat. *My work.*

The thought of having my art displayed in a world famous gallery is too good to be true, a dream I never let myself consider. But shame fills me. How could I let Eliza down by saying no? Not just me, but all the other students, people like me who never thought they'd have a chance. People she's believed in. But I've always stayed in the shadows, and this would put me on display. Which means I can't do this.

"I can't help you, Oliver. Find someone else."

"There isn't anyone else," he says firmly. "No one who knows me, who understands art, and who could make it believable."

"But it wouldn't be real." The words come out softer than I intended. Why does that matter? Shouldn't I be relieved it would be temporary?

"We'll annul the marriage as soon as I secure the gallery," he insists. "I'll do anything. Name your price."

I stare at him, searching his face for any sign of a playful smirk, a flicker of humor, really anything that might tell me he's joking. But the familiar spark is gone, replaced by a heavy, desperate look that I hardly recognize. His shoulders slump, his eyes dark and distant, as if he's carrying the weight of something he can't put into words.

"You're serious?"

"Yes." He reaches out, trying to touch my hand, but I slip off the stool, putting some distance between us. I need space to think.

The idea of helping his mom is sweet, and I can't deny that. Eliza gave so many students like me a chance when the art world wanted nothing to do with us. A gallery dedicated to showcase our work could change lives. Even if I chose to keep my own art hidden, could I really stand in the way of others getting their big break?

"What does your mom think about all this?"

"She doesn't know," Oliver says, his voice dropping to nearly a whisper, eyes softening with what looks like genuine affection. "I want it to be a surprise. She's always dreamed of having this gallery, but Mr. Warne never seemed interested in selling before."

I cross my arms, hesitating. Something about the timing feels off. "I heard his wife had a health scare." It's a rumor that's been circulating in the art community for weeks now.

His eyebrows knit together, a flash of surprise crossing his face.

"I overheard Mrs. Bennett talking about it at school," I explain.

He nods slowly, processing the information.

"So, what do you think? Will you marry me, Karley?" His expression is a mix of determination and something almost vulnerable as he drums his fingers against his leg.

My heart pounds a powerful beat. The guy I had a crush on, is standing right in front of me, asking me to fake-marry him. For a moment, it's almost surreal. But as much as I care about his mom, I just can't do it. I don't think I have what it takes to get over him a second time.

"I'm sorry, Oliver. As much as I love your mom, I can't."

His shoulders sag, and for a moment, he looks defeated. But he quickly pulls himself together, standing up and offering me a small smile. "I understand. I'll let you go. Goodnight, Karley."

"Goodnight." I'm relieved he agrees.

I watch him leave, and as soon as the door clicks shut behind him, I rush to lock it, leaning against the wood to catch my breath. My heart is still pounding, my mind spinning. I should be relieved that he's gone, but I'm not.

There's only one thing that will calm me down right now... painting.

I grab a blank easel, set up my paints, and begin. The only way to get Oliver out of my head is to lose myself in something I love more.

CHAPTER 9

KARLEY

THANK GOD, IT'S FRIDAY so I could finally sleep in. I'm stretched out on the sofa, sipping my coffee and watching a new show, my mind drifting back to the property. I've put some earnest money down, but I still need to figure out where to get the rest before the thirty-day window is up. My phone rings, interrupting my thoughts.

I glance at the screen and recognize Hugh's number. My pulse quickens as I answer. "Hello?"

"Hi, Karley, it's Hugh. How are you?"

I sit up, trying to sound casual. "I'm good, and you?"

"Yeah, I'm good too. I'm calling to let you know there's been more inquiries about the property."

My stomach drops, and I grip the phone tighter. "Oh, really?"

"Are you still interested in buying it?"

"Yes, of course." I hadn't expected this call so soon. "I'll have the money soon." Even as I make the promise, my mind runs through my lack of options. This house means everything to me, and I can't let it slip away.

There's a pause, and it makes my stomach uneasy.

"I can hold off for another week, but that's it," he finally says. I can hear the unspoken pressure behind his words.

"A week? Not the thirty days we discussed?" My voice comes out higher than I intended. My plan was based on that timeline. Selling my paintings should cover the amount I'm short.

"I'm sorry, but the offer is too good for the owners to turn down."

"I'll have the money." I clench my jaw, determination covering the panic threatening to surface. *Maybe I could get another job?*

"This week?" he repeats, the words sounding more like a question than an answer, as if I could somehow push it off a little longer.

"Yes."

"Okay, good," he says, relief softening his voice. I can tell he wants this sale as much as I want the house, just for a different reason. "Call me when you're ready to come in and make the offer."

"I will." I try to sound confident, but it comes out high, as if I'm trying to convince myself more than him.

"All right, have a nice weekend, Karley."

"Bye." I hang up with a shaky hand, staring at the phone. I have a week. I open my banking app hoping for a miracle, but the balance hasn't changed. The bank won't lend me the money I need. My freelance income is too inconsistent. And my credit score isn't high enough for this type of loan. I don't know what to do. Asking Declan is out of the question. He'll insist on "fixing" everything, smothering me with his help while reminding me how I can't manage on my own. I drop the phone on the coffee table and bury my face in my hands, feeling tears forming. But I refuse to let them fall. I can figure this out.

When I finally sit back up, I scroll through the TV until I spot something under "Continue Watching." It's the series I started with Oliver.

The guy who wants to marry me, and offered me money to do it. Could I ask him for enough to buy a house? No. That would be using him. But then again, isn't his proposal a transaction? He gets the gallery, I get money.

A flicker of hope fills my chest. Maybe I could go through with it... marry him for a short time, get the house, and then move on. If I keep it transactional, I won't grow feelings.

What other choice do I have right now?

I grab my phone again, find his number, and before I can talk myself out of it, I call.

He doesn't answer, but I hear his smooth, raspy voice-mail. I don't leave a message. I hang up, my cheeks burning with embarrassment even though no one witnessed my moment of desperation, and decide to call Evelyn instead. She picks up after a few rings.

"Hey, it's early," she croaks.

"It's ten."

"And some people like to sleep in," she groans. "What's up?" she asks, sounding more awake now.

I take a deep breath, composing myself. Evelyn's always been the impulsive one, the friend who bought a one-way ticket to New York after a bad break-up. Normally, I'm the cautious one who talks her down, but today, I need her crazy ideas, because I only have a week to find this money.

"I need help. The real estate company called about the house. They said someone else is interested, and I have a week to buy it."

"And you had to tell them you couldn't afford it." Her tone is gentle and sympathetic.

"Well, not exactly..."

"What did you do?"

I consciously grimace as I confess. "Maybe I told a little white lie."

She hisses. "Where are you going to get the money from?"

"I have an idea." My gut knots as the words leave my mouth. Saying it out loud to her will make it real, and may turn it from a thought into an actual plan I might follow through with.

She snorts. "Selling an organ only works when you're dead."

I wrinkle my nose, even though she can't see me. "Ew gross, Evelyn."

"I'm serious. How else are you getting the money in a week?"

I hesitate, my throat tight. I gather my courage because this is the moment that once I say it, I can't take it back.

"I could..." I start but then stop. "What if I..." I take a deep breath and finally push the words out. "Marry Oliver Lincoln."

"Sorry, what?" she screeches so loudly, I have to pull the phone away from my ear.

Not exactly the response I was hoping for, but at least it's not disapproval. The shock in her voice mirrors my own initial reaction to Oliver's proposal. Bringing the phone back to my ear to talk, I continue, "He offered, and I told him no originally, but now I'm thinking about it."

"Okay, rewind, and tell me everything."

I do, and I find myself remembering Oliver's kindness, respect, and strictly business demeanor about the arrangement. It sounds more reasonable and yet absurd the second time. Am I talking myself into this, or out of it?

Once she's caught up, she sighs, and I brace myself for her reply. "I say do it. He's so hot. There are worse things than pretending to be a billionaire's fake wife."

Her support sends a wave of relief through me. I'm not completely crazy for considering this.

"But what are the negatives?"

I have thought of my own... *What if Warne finds out? What if he changes the terms? What if I meet someone I actually want to marry while I'm legally tied to him?*

"You'd have to marry and live with an insanely hot guy. Possibly kiss and hold hands with him."

There's no chance of us kissing because he doesn't like me that way, and I'm not going to try again.

I laugh. "I'd drive him nuts if we lived together."

"It's short-term," she encourages.

"He said that. A few months, and then I could move out into my own house." I can picture the sun beaming through the kitchen window, a garden I could maintain, and something permanent. Something that's mine. The thought sends a flutter of longing through my chest that almost drowns out the anxiety about Oliver's arrangement.

She hums. "Now that sounds good."

I'm interrupted by the sound of another call coming through. I check the screen, and my heart lurches when I see his name.

"I gotta go, he's on the other line," I rush out.

"Alright, see you later and you can fill me in."

I hang up and answer his call.

"Karley?"

"Is that what you'd call me if I was your wife?" I ask, trying to sound playful, but there's a quiver in my voice.

"You aren't my wife."

"But if I was?" I ask.

"I'd answer straight away."

I'd be that important?

"Good to know."

"Does this mean you've changed your mind?"

My chest aches with longing as I picture the house I want as if I'm there again. "You said any amount, right?"

"Whatever you need, it's yours."

I scrunch up my face in a wince. "Say, 1.5 million dollars?" If I'm getting married, I want him to buy the house so I never have to stress about money again.

"You got it."

He'll give me the money for the house.

Am I really doing this?

I ignore the butterflies in my stomach and say, "I don't need that much, but close."

"I'll transfer whatever you need."

Am I actually going to agree to this?

Fuck it. "Okay."

"Can you come to my office?" he asks, excitement barely contained beneath his professional tone. "We'll go over the terms, and I'll transfer you the money."

Just the thought of us alone in a room ties my stomach in knots. I need space to think clearly, and it would be easier with people around. "Does it have to be your office?"

"I'd prefer it. It's safer to discuss our arrangement."

Duh.

"What time?"

"Could you come this morning? I have meetings in the afternoon."

I peer down at my sweats, knowing I'll have to change. "That works."

"I'll text you the address. Call me when you arrive, and I'll meet you at the front. I can give you a tour."

"Okay, I'll see you soon." My voice is steady, but inside, I'm a mess. This could solve everything or complicate my life beyond repair.

I'm about to hang up when he speaks. "Karley."

"Yeah?"

"Thank you."

I'm standing outside the address he texted me. I take a deep breath, letting the sun warm my face. What is it about him that has me so flustered? I need to treat this like a business transaction, but my heart doesn't know how to stop pounding. I've been to this gallery before, but never to his office, and for some reason, it feels more personal.

The door swings open before I can overthink it. My breath catches.

It's Oliver, in another tight designer suit. A pale cream one this time, with a white shirt unbuttoned at the top and no tie. His brown hair is slightly tousled, and as I bring my eyes back to his face, he flashes a crooked grin. "Hey!"

His energy is infectious, I'll admit. He's always been the loyal, hardworking, and determined Lincoln. And undeniably handsome...

"Hi."

"Come in."

I follow him up the stairs, trying to focus on anything but him. The gallery is filled with bright light streaming in through the skylights and big windows. The statues and artwork are a mix of modern and classic. The scent of paper and ink washes over me, warm and inviting.

I'm completely lost in the surroundings when his hand touches my arm, bringing me back to reality and leaving a tingle in its place.

"Sorry, I didn't mean to startle you."

"I was just admiring the art. It's beautiful." Every piece has its own spotlight, perfectly arranged to draw your attention to it. "Are you planning to do something similar in the new gallery?" I ask. The color palette of ivory white, blush beige, and bronze is subtle, elegant, yet striking.

"I want the new place to have a similar look, but with a touch of something different. I'm just not sure what that will be yet."

I nod. Imagining my paintings in a place like this makes my chest tighten with a mix of hope and dread. The fear of people mocking me or tearing my art apart makes me feel vulnerable.

"Karley?"

I shake my head, snapping out of my past, realizing I missed what he was saying. "Sorry, what?"

"Nothing important," he says with a slight smile, his tone gentle. "Come on, let's go to my office."

I follow him down the hall and into a large room, which is not at all what I expected. It's just as inviting, with deep navy, black, white, and soft gray tones. The painted artwork on the walls stands out, a mix of large and small pieces, with a beautiful framed canvas of flowers that matches the office perfectly. My gaze lands on one painting hung on a wall of its own.

"It's beautiful, isn't it?"

I feel his eyes on me before I turn to see him watching my reaction.

"Yeah," I murmur, still taking it all in. A rush of something intimate fills me in a way I wasn't prepared for, bringing a strange connection to this space, and to him.

"Do you want to sit on the sofa or at the desk?"

I glance at both. The sofa feels too intimate. "At the desk. Easier for taking notes."

"Good idea," he says with a small nod. There's a professional confidence in his posture now, but I catch the tap of his fingers against his desk. Maybe he's not as completely at ease as he appears. "Want a drink?"

I want to say yes, but I have work later in the day so I better not. "No, I'm good, thank you."

"Okay." He settles into his sleek, black leather chair.

I take a seat, forcing myself to focus on the task and not on him. "So, how is this going to work?"

He leans forward. "Let me transfer the money first."

"No contract?" I ask, raising an eyebrow.

He looks up, meeting my eyes. His gaze assesses me with an intensity that makes my skin prickle. There's something almost challenging in his expression, as if he's wondering just how much I trust him, or perhaps how much I trust myself. "No, I trust you. Unless you'd feel more comfortable with a contract, then I'd be happy to draw one up."

I shake my head. "No, I'm just asking."

"You don't seem like someone who backs down from a challenge."

On the outside, maybe. Inside, I'm hiding so much. All the times I've pretended to be braver than I felt, like right now, sitting across from him. Although we haven't been close because our relationship centers around Declan, I find it comforting that he trusts me. Which I suppose is good since I'm about to become his wife.

He turns back to his computer, then asks for my bank details. My fingers hover over my phone, suddenly aware of what I'm doing... giving him financial information with nothing but a verbal agreement. The reality twists in my stomach. If this goes wrong, I'll have nothing to fall back on, no proof, no protection, just his word against mine. But then again, that house, the kids...

"What do you need the money for?" he asks casually, but there's a hint of curiosity in it.

I pause, considering how much to say. Declan doesn't even know I've looked at houses, but if I want the money...

"A house."

He nods, no further questions, but I don't miss the flicker of wonder in his eyes.

"I think buying property is a smart move. Is there something you want to tell me?"

"No."

"How much is the house?"

"1.2 million," I say, trying to keep myself steady. Even saying it out loud makes me sweat. Maybe I should've just asked for the $50,000 I need for the down payment, but this is marriage so I need something big in return.

He nods thoughtfully, then looks at me with that easy smile. "I'll give you a bit extra. You'll need to buy things during our time together, like evening gowns. I don't expect you to pay for those."

I bite my tongue, resisting the urge to argue. Normally, I would, but he's right. If I'm going to play the part of a billionaire's girlfriend, I'll need the designer clothes, makeup, and hair to match. I'm supposed to be myself while transforming my appearance to fit a wealthy wife. It feels like a contradiction because I've always prided myself on authenticity over appearances.

"What should I say I do for a job?" I ask, tilting my head slightly. I brace for his answer, expecting to be either an art consultant or gallery director, something that wouldn't embarrass him.

"Tell them you're in school and you work at Sip N' Paint."

"That doesn't bother you?"

He raises an eyebrow. "Fake or not, I'd never expect you to be someone you're not."

I'm momentarily caught off guard by the sincerity in his voice. "Good to know," I say quietly, feeling my cheeks flush.

He turns to his computer, taps on his keyboard, then shifts back to face me. "The transfer is done. Check your account."

I pull out my phone, log in, and see the money there, just like he promised. Relief floods me, though my hands are still shaky as I put the phone away, hiding them in my lap.

A tear falls, and I quickly swat it away.

"Are you okay?" he asks, reaching over to touch my arm.

The warmth of his fingers against my skin sends a tingle down my spine. It feels too intimate for what this is supposed to be. I pull back slightly.

"All good. Let's just move on," I say, leaning back, causing his hand to disconnect. "What are the rules?"

He pulls his hand to the desk, his brow furrowed as he leans forward. "There's a few," he begins, his tone shifting to something more serious. "First, my mother can't know about the fake marriage. She can know we're dating, but that's it."

"Okay, hang on, I might just take notes." I open the notes app on my phone, suddenly feeling overwhelmed. His mother? I hadn't considered we'd be lying to her. Lying to Warne is one thing, but deceiving his mother feels wrong.

He waits until I stop typing on my phone and looks up.

"Second, as soon as the gallery is transferred to me, we'll file for annulment."

I type that next.

"Third, we fly to Vegas tomorrow and return on Sunday."

My fingers freeze mid-type. "Tomorrow?" The word escapes me louder than I intended. "As in, twenty-four hours from now?"

This isn't hypothetical anymore; it's actually happening. My brother would not only be furious I was flying to Vegas to marry his best friend for money, but disappointed in me. He may have agreed to the fake marriage, but this isn't that...

Before I type that, I remember something important for this to happen. "We'll need a witness."

"Cora, my assistant. She'll have to know about our wedding anyway."

I blink rapidly, trying to process all the information he's telling me. *How will I explain a sudden Vegas trip to everyone? What should I pack for a wedding I never planned to have? How will I keep this lie up for months?*

He exhales through his nose, eyes flicking away before meeting mine again. "Who do you trust to tell about this?"

"My best friend, Evelyn, and Amber." I'll be calling Amber as soon as I leave here. I can already picture her wide-eyed shock, followed by questions and then approval.

I watch him, waiting for a reaction, but he just nods again, his face unreadable.

"Okay," he replies. "Also, you'll have to come to dinners and events with me, act like a couple, and we need to live together."

I nod, trying to keep my composure, even though my stomach does a little flip. Luckily, Evelyn mentioned the possibility of us living together, so at least I've had time to consider that option. But her saying it versus him saying it sends blood rushing to my ears. This isn't just paperwork and bank transfers. It's a complete temporary life change.

"And nicknames might help."

I blink, surprised by his suggestion. "Nicknames?"

He shrugs, looking at me with a small smirk. "Yeah. Something to make it feel more real." His smile widens just a touch. "Maybe something fun. I can come up with something."

And even though I came here with the idea that this is a transaction between us, I worry what all this proximity will do to us... Or should I say, do to me. But it's also more than that. I could lose my independence and possibly even the house. Leaving me both heartbroken and humiliated.

My hands tremble, and I hide them under the desk. The air in the room seems too thick to breathe properly; the walls closing in. I'm trying to hold it together, but I need some fresh air.

"Is that all?"

"Yes, my dear fiancée," he says, his lips curling into a playful grin. "Tomorrow, I'll pick you up. We'll pick out wedding rings and head to Vegas."

I nod, forcing a smile. My heart pounds with a strange mix of excitement and apprehension. For him, this is all effortless, like breathing. But me? I'm stepping into a world I'm not sure I belong in. But I'll play the part... Whatever it takes to get that house.

My rule for this trip? No drinking. I can't afford to lose control with him... *again.*

CHAPTER 10

OLIVER

I REVIEW THE PROPOSAL for an upcoming auction piece on my computer. I'm picky about what I choose... Originality, inclusivity, and texture matter to me. Some have thick, bold brushstrokes; others are smooth and flat but still pull me in. It's not just about how it looks. It's about how it makes me feel.

My desk phone rings. "Cora?" I say when I answer.

"Ray is on the phone," she explains.

I sit up straighter. "Thanks. Transfer him now."

"Mr. Lincoln," his young voice greets me quietly.

"Ray, do you have some good news for me?"

There's only one reason he'd be calling.

"I have a new painting from the anonymous artist."

I glance at my Rolex. I've been distracted and unable to focus since Karley left. "I'll be there shortly."

I hang up and finish reviewing the proposal before heading over to Cora's desk. "Hi, I need a few things done urgently."

"Yes, sir," she replies, turning her full attention to me.

"I'll be at The Lincoln School of Art to pick up a painting. And this weekend, I'm heading to Vegas." I'm really doing this. Rushing into a fake marriage, which, until recently, was only a hopeful plan.

Her eyes widen, curiosity etched on her face. "You are?"

I clear my throat. "I'm getting married this weekend."

Her hands freeze over her keyboard. She stares at me, mouth parted, clearly stunned. "Married? This weekend?" She shakes her head slightly. "Mr. Lincoln, I've managed your calendar for years, and I didn't know you were seeing anyone seriously."

"It's complicated. But right now, I need you to arrange a private appointment at Winston's Jeweler, book the jet, and handle accommodations with a return flight on Sunday."

She clasps her hands and her smile widens. "And who is it?"

My lips naturally curl as I think of my blonde, feisty fiancée. "Karley Maddox."

"Oh, you two have known each other forever. I saw the way you looked at each other when she came in. I'm so happy for you."

It couldn't have been from me. Sure, she's stunning, but I don't look at her any differently than anyone else. And she couldn't have read anything in Karley's eyes other than annoyance. When she looked at the gallery, her eyes lit up, but toward me, they dimmed. But I don't ask Cora to clarify because all I care about is that we look like a real couple.

"And I need you to come and be a witness." Cora keeps my professional life running smoothly, so dragging her into my personal life crosses a boundary I've always maintained. Still, I have no choice. I need someone I can trust.

She blinks in surprise as her hand touches her scarf around her neck. "Um..."

"I'll cover everything for you and your family. Make it a weekend trip on me. I just need you to sign as a witness."

She's married with two kids. Paying for a holiday is the least I can do, considering I'm dropping this on her last minute.

"And to get photos," she adds. "But... why isn't your family going?"

"I don't have time to go into the details right now. I need to meet with Ray, but I'll brief you on everything when I return."

"What about dinner?" she asks.

My mind immediately flashes back to the other night, quietly sitting with Karley on the sofa, eating toast.

"No, I'll handle it."

Karley is different. She doesn't care for fancy dinners or over-the-top gestures. Simple things make her smile, and I plan to show her how grateful I am for what she's doing for me. The money was easy to transfer, but making her happy is more important. Which is an unfamiliar feeling for me. In business, in relationships, even with family, I've always controlled my emotions, so this urge to care for Karley is strange. It's not just because of the favor she's doing for me, though that matters. It's the way she carries so much without ever asking for help, like she's afraid to need anyone. Maybe it's guilt, or maybe it's something else... but there's a strong pull to take care of her that I can't shake. I want to be the reason she feels like the world isn't always taking from her.

"Book the Bellagio as the accommodation," I instruct. Remembering the Fine Art Gallery they have there.

"Okay, anything else?"

I shake my head, stepping away from her desk. "Nothing for now, but I'll call if I need anything else. Otherwise, I'll see you in Vegas tomorrow." Unease swirls in my chest, so much depends on this working for not only me but for Karley too.

"Yes, sir," Cora calls back.

I walk out of my building and get into the car, making my way to buy another painting.

I approach Declan and Karley's brown brick condo, already anticipating the inevitable brotherly warning from Declan, as if I haven't heard it before. He's going away to

Florida to view the new house this weekend, so we didn't have to tell him about Vegas. If he knew about our trip, he'd insist on coming along, or worse, try to talk Karley out of it.

"Hey, man," I call out as he opens the door.

"Hi," he replies, stepping aside to let me in.

His brow furrows as he looks me over. My outfit is a simple black t-shirt, blue jeans, and shoes. It doesn't scream, *we're going to Vegas to get married*, but he's definitely assessing me.

I step inside, and my eyes immediately dart to the black suitcase by the door before shifting back to him.

The temperature in the room drops when his icy eyes gaze at me.

"She said you two are going to live together?"

A lump forms in my throat, unprepared for this conversation, and so I say the first thing that pops into my head. "Yeah, we need to for a short while. She'll be in one of the spare rooms. We're grabbing the rest of her stuff this weekend."

Declan runs his hand through his hair. "The more I think about it, the more I don't like this."

"It's only for a few weeks. After that, she'll be free to move out into her own place," I reassure him, even though I don't have a specific end date.

He nods. "I'm glad she's taking your money to buy property. It makes me feel better knowing she won't be renting."

"Can you stop talking about me as if I can't hear you?" Karley's voice cuts in.

I see her at the door, in light gray sweats, white Chucks, her hair up, and a big frown that hides her blue eyes. Something unexpected aches in my chest at the sight of her. I have to swallow a laugh as I watch her grab her suitcase with a huff as she enters the room, pausing beside her brother. As I grab the case to take it to the car, I expect her to throw her independence at me, but I'm grateful she accepts my help. When I try to move it and struggle, I see why.

What the fuck has she got in there... Weapons?

"Declan, I'll be fine," she says, patting her brother on the chest. "Oliver won't let anything happen to me. And if he does, I give you full permission to kill him." She turns her head and winks at me.

I chuckle softly.

"Focus on your relationship and your new house with Armani," she tells him. "I'm planning to visit during the holidays, so you better get a room ready for me." Karley opens the door.

"Fine. I'll talk to you tomorrow," he says, his arms folded across his chest.

With a quick nod, she heads off to the car without looking back.

I dip my chin and head out the door, dragging her case.

The driver takes her suitcase, and she slides into the back seat. I climb in next to her.

"Are you ready?" I ask. This isn't how I'd imagined my wedding day: sitting beside my best friend's sister who barely acknowledges me, both of us tense with uncertainty.

"Not one bit," she replies.

I can't have her back out, so I get her focused on what she wants.

"But when you're sitting in your mortgage-free dream house, will you be okay with this?" I raise an eyebrow at her.

"I won't care about any of this," she says, and something heavy settles in my stomach. It's clear she doesn't see this as a real wedding, and neither do I. Except, I think about how traditional my parents and grandparents were—married first, then kids. Even though this isn't real, there's a part of me that feels guilty for not doing it the right way. But I'll make it up to them with my next marriage, and they'll never have to know about this one. I've already planned that when the time comes for annulment, I'll ensure the records are sealed.

A few minutes later, we're on our way to Winston's.

"You're actually going to waste money on a real ring?" she asks, side-eyeing me.

"I can't exactly get you a Ring Pop." I smirk.

"I wouldn't be opposed to a cherry one," she replies her expression matching mine.

A small laugh escapes me. "No. If this is going to be believable, I'm buying you a nice ring."

"Will you want it back afterward?"

I hadn't considered the ring beyond getting one that looks convincing. The idea of asking for it back doesn't sit well with me after what she's doing for me. The car rolls to a stop. I unbuckle and twist my body to face her. "No, it's yours. So, pick a design you like."

She shakes her head, peering at the shop through the car window with a sigh. "This is such a waste of money."

"Nothing I do for you will ever be a waste, so get over it and get your sexy ass out of the car so I can get a fiancée," I say, gently nudging her with a grin.

The driver gets out first, and before he can reach her door, I step out on my side. I circle around the back of the car, reaching her door just as the driver opens it. I hold my hand open for Karley. She takes it without hesitation, and for a moment, my heart skips a beat. But then she quickly drops my hand, and I run it through my hair, confused by the reaction.

What the fuck was that?

"You don't have to do all of this. It's not official yet."

I lean my head close to her ear, watching her throat move as she swallows. "What if I enjoy practicing my role as husband?"

She lightly shoves me away and rolls her eyes playfully. "I wonder what I'll have to put up with when we're actually married."

Before I can stop myself, I wink and respond, "You have no idea..."

I can see the wheels turning in her head as if she's going to ask me something as we step inside, but Grant Winston interrupts us. "Mr. Lincoln. The one I have yet to meet," he says, a reminder of how single I still am as everyone else in my family had their wedding bands made by him. He's around sixty, with gray hair and a short black beard peppered with more gray. He wears a navy suit that keeps him looking professional and yet approachable.

"Hi, Mr. Winston, thanks for having us on such short notice." I reach out to shake his hand.

"It's good to see you again." He clasps my hand briefly, then turns his attention to Karley.

"This is my fiancée, Karley." The word *fiancée* feels foreign yet natural for a lie that's only hours old.

Karley smiles as she takes in the surroundings.

It's just the three of us here, so it's quiet, but with all the lights on, the shop sparkles. Floor-to-ceiling glass cases display diamonds and gemstones so flawless they don't look real; each piece resting on velvet like it's royalty. Crystal chandeliers hang overhead, casting soft, golden reflections across the marble floors. The walls are a deep, rich navy, making the jewelry pop like stars against the night sky.

Mr. Winston works alone, always has. Not because he can't afford help; he could hire an entire staff if he wanted, but because no one else meets his standards. Every piece in here has passed through his hands, shaped by his expert eye. "So, you're here for something available to take now?" he asks. "Cora explained—"

"I don't think Cora has explained..." I interrupt. "This is not to be mentioned to anyone from my family."

Winston's eyes widen. "Why is that?"

"We're eloping," I say, matter-of-factly.

Karley remains unusually quiet, and when I glance at her from the corner of my eye, she looks rigid, her hands still at her sides. Immediately turning to her, I whisper, "Are you okay?"

"I didn't want to interrupt you," she says, trying to wave me off, but she doesn't seem like herself. Quieter...

I turn back to Mr. Winston. "I'd pay extra for you to keep this just between us until I'm ready to announce it to the family."

"Not necessary," he assures me. "So, who would like to start?" His eyes dart between mine and Karley's.

I suddenly realize I'll need to choose a ring too. I've been so focused on Karley that I didn't even think about myself. *What would I like?*

I turn to Karley, asking, "Do you want me to go first?"

She nods. Her face has paled. Maybe watching me choose something first will ease her nervousness.

"I didn't have anything specific in mind," I admit to Mr. Winston. "I wouldn't even know where to begin. This is all new to me."

He turns around. "Let's start with something simple and classic. For men, I have gold, platinum, and black."

I turn to Karley. "What do you think?"

She looks up at me, her eyes bright and wide. "I don't know. Whatever you prefer."

I'd hoped she might have an opinion; her detachment makes me uneasy.

We follow Winston over to the glass cabinets. I pull out an emerald velvet chair for Karley, and she sits, nodding her thanks. I take my seat next to her.

He pulls out a selection. "We should start by choosing a color," he suggests. "Then we can decide on a design."

"Okay," I mumble as this all becomes very real.

Winston pulls out a gold band, so I slip it on my left finger. It feels cold and strange.

I shake my head. "I don't like this color on me. It just doesn't feel right."

"Well, let's try the black next," Mr. Winston offers.

I hand back the gold band and slip on the black. Again, it doesn't feel or look quite right. Part of me wants to pick anything and be done with it. After all, this is all just for show. But then I worry that others will notice and question our relationship. "No, I don't like this color either."

"Picky much," Karley teases under her breath.

I shift my gaze to find her grinning.

"I bet you'll be worse, *wife*," I tease back.

Mr. Winston clears his throat. "The last option would be platinum."

"I never pictured you as a platinum guy," Karley remarks.

"I'm full of surprises," I reply, earning a classic eye roll from her. I grin as I take off the black band and slip on the platinum one. It looks good on my hand... feels like it belongs there. "Yeah, I like the platinum."

"Would you like any design? Maybe stones?" Mr. Winston asks.

I look down at the display, at the different platinum rings. There are so many designs, but I can't decide without knowing what Karley's going to choose. For some reason, I want them to match. Even though I'll only be wearing the band for the short term.

"Why don't we figure out Karley's choice first and come back to mine?" I suggest, handing the band back. "But I think a plain platinum band will suit me the best."

"Yes, Mr. Lincoln," Mr. Winston says, putting the other bands back.

I lean in close to her ear, getting a good inhale of her sweet apple shampoo. "You ready?"

"Get out of here," she mumbles, pushing my shoulder back gently as she stands. "This ought to be fun," she adds sarcastically.

I rise, and we follow Mr. Winston, who's holding the ring I chose, to another area of the shop. He settles behind another glass display of rings. I pull out a chair for Karley, and she sits, this time her body settling more easily.

"So, what do you think?" Mr. Winston asks.

"I always thought I'd go for gold," she admits, tilting her head slightly, as if she's thought about this before. A twinge of guilt hits me, knowing she's probably thinking about her real wedding, the one she probably dreamed about since childhood.

"Well, why don't we start by ruling out the ones you don't like?" Mr. Winston suggests.

She nods, and he picks out a rose gold band.

She slips it onto her left finger, and I catch a glimpse of her freshly painted, clear-polished nails. I'm suddenly transfixed by how perfect an engagement ring looks on her delicate hand.

Chapter 11

Karley

I'm holding my hand out, inspecting the rose gold engagement ring. My fingers tremble with nervousness, and I wonder if Oliver notices. He doesn't say anything, so I hope he hasn't.

Having such a delicate and expensive ring on my hand feels heavy and foreign.

"The rose gold suits you," Oliver says, his words pulling my gaze away from the sparkling ring and to his face. His eyes are slightly widened, and the hint of a smile plays at the corners of his mouth.

I'm a bit surprised, but I agree. "Yes, I didn't think I'd like it."

"Well, let's keep going and try different colors," Mr. Winston encourages, holding out a platinum ring.

I slip off the rose gold, immediately missing its warmth against my skin, and try the plain platinum band. It feels colder and more clinical. "I think it matches yours better,"

I say to Oliver, glancing down at where the ring sat on his hand, before looking back up to meet his gaze.

He shakes his head. "It doesn't have to match mine. I'll match you. I just want you to find a ring you love."

Warmth spreads in my chest at his unexpected consideration. It's such a nice gesture... letting me choose, rather than forcing coordination.

"Karley, let's try on some other options in rose gold, and I'll figure out how to tie them together," Mr. Winston offers, glancing at me, then over to Oliver, who nods.

"I really like the rose gold with the Platinum," I say, my hands steadier as I hand the ring back. Now that I've tried two on, I feel more confident exploring different styles. "Do you have any other designs you'd recommend?"

"Tell me about yourself. What do you like? What do you do? It might help me recommend a style," Mr. Winston says.

How much should I share? Will Mr. Winston look at me differently once he knows I'm not from this world?

"I study art, painting specifically, and I work at a paint studio on the side," I reply confidently. No need to apologize for who I am.

He smiles. "Do you like colors?"

"Yes."

"Would you be open to a colored stone?"

"A colored stone?" I repeat, as if I've never thought about it before. "That could be interesting,"

Mr. Winston brings out a selection of platinum rings with emeralds, sapphires, and rubies, as well as the same in rose gold. My eyes scan over each, drawn to a few. Even though this is feeling very real, I know I'll only have this ring for a short time and never wear it again.

Oliver shuffles closer, his shoulder nearly touching mine. I find myself oddly comforted by his nearness.

"Which colors stand out to you?" Mr. Winston asks.

"To be honest, I love them all," I admit, unable to choose.

Oliver laughs. "As pretty as these rings would look on each finger of yours, let's save them for anniversaries."

I pause, my smile faltering just slightly. "Anniversaries?" I echo, trying to keep my voice light. "You do remember this isn't real, right?"

He shrugs, totally unbothered. "Real or not, people are still going to expect the part. Might as well get used to saying things like that."

I laugh, mostly to ease the knot tightening in my chest. "I didn't think it'd be this hard."

"We're not in a rush," Oliver says, and I appreciate that he's trying to make this easier for me, even though it contradicts everything about our whirlwind arrangement.

I try on an emerald first, but it doesn't feel quite right. The green stone is beautiful, but too formal and not me. The moment I slide the next one onto my finger, my breath catches. "I like the rose gold with the ruby. It's pretty," I say, wiggling my finger around.

"We also have some pink stones, if you'd like," Mr. Winston offers.

"I don't see myself with pink. It feels too... modern," I say.

Next, I try sapphire. I slip it on, and my heart swells. I stare at it, feeling a warm rush pulse through me. "I love this."

"Let me see," Oliver asks, gently taking my hand and inspecting it.

His touch makes my body temperature rise. "Yeah. I do too. The blue looks good on you," he adds, and I can hear the softness in his voice.

"This feels like your ring." Mr. Winston says. "I'll bring out a few with similar styles, then we can pick a matching band."

"There's more?" I gasp. What else could there be?

"Oh yes," Mr. Winston says. "We'll narrow it down further, choose a shape, then decide on the wedding band. And if he's going with platinum, it'll match perfectly. If the rings you choose don't quite fit, I can give you a placeholder and keep you updated on when the custom one will be ready." After trying a few more, I find the one that I love. A 6.50 carat blue sapphire halo ring set in platinum. The stone sparkles, and I can't help but smile at how perfect it looks. "This is it," I say, slipping it off and handing it to Mr. Winston, who grins and starts packing it up.

"You're not going to get something like this for yourself?" I ask, arching an eyebrow at Oliver.

He points to the plain platinum band he liked earlier. "I think I'll skip the colored stone and let yours stand out."

I laugh, nudging him playfully. "Oh, so I'm the attention-seeker now?" The thought of people noticing the ring sends a flutter of anxiety through me. I'll have to get used to explaining this sudden relationship.

"Absolutely." He smirks.

I snap a photo of the rings and send it to Amber, remembering my phone conversation with her this morning when I told her I was getting fake married to Oliver. As expected, she told me to be careful, but she supports me. Her response was, *"If anyone can make this crazy plan work, it's you."*

Mr. Winston boxes up our rings. "Anything else?"

"What about a pair of earrings?" Oliver asks me with a wry smile.

I shake my head. "No, we're good. Let's go to Vegas before I change my mind."

We arrive on the tarmac outside his jet, and I do a double take. It's stark white against the gray concrete, "Lincoln"

emblazed in navy-blue lettering on the side. A uniformed attendant stands at the bottom of the stairs. I've never been on a private plane before, and it feels insane that this is just how he travels, like it's as ordinary to him as catching the subway. It makes me wonder what other things money has turned into casual details in his life; things that would feel unimaginable in mine.

"You ready?" he asks, getting out of the car and holding his hand out for me.

I step out of the car, grabbing his outstretched hand. He closes his door, and I start to move around to the back of the car to grab my bag, but he shakes his head. "They'll put it on the plane for us. We can head inside."

"This is insane," I mumble, the words hidden by the roar of the engines nearby and the steady wind sweeping across the tarmac.

I follow him up the stairs into the jet and stop mid-stride to take in the plane's interior. Everything is a creamy white leather with polished black trim, bright and spacious. The air smells faintly of vanilla, making it feel strangely cozy yet undeniably luxurious.

"Where do I sit?" I ask, standing in the middle, looking around at the numerous chairs, expecting he has a particular spot.

"Wherever you want," he says.

I take a middle seat near the window, assuming he'll sit across the aisle from me. But instead, he chooses the seat directly opposite, and his long legs almost bump into mine. As soon as he sits and buckles in, there's a small gap between us, and I intend to keep it that way.

Taking out my phone, I snap a few pictures and send them to Evelyn before putting it away. Oliver is typing on his phone too, so I keep my eyes out the window, watching the bags being loaded. Excitement and nerves churn in my stomach at how much closer we are to getting married. I'm interrupted by an unfamiliar woman's voice. "Hi, can I get you anything?"

I glance at the brunette hostess with a warm smile, out-lined in bright red. For a second, I wonder if he's slept with her, but I push those thoughts away. He's been extremely nice and respectful. I know it seems silly to most, but the thing is that I just can't take any more rejection. It's easier to just stay behind my protective wall than risk that again, but this time together is new. I have to find a way to make this work, at least for the sake of his mom. I've never spent this much alone time with him, and the more time that passes, the more I see how wrong it was of me to assume he belongs in that douchebag category.

During the flight, Oliver alternates between working on his laptop and making casual conversation. He asks about work, school, and my favorite artists. I eat sushi and a brownie that I wash down with a soda. My eyes grow heavy after the huge meal. I drift off with the smooth motion of the jet, exhausted from the day.

I don't know how long I'm out before I wake from a nightmare... my mom snapping and then throwing out my pencils. A touch on my shoulder and a whisper of my name in my ear makes me shudder and blink open my eyes. I instantly perk up, my heart racing as I look around, remembering where I am, and that this isn't, in fact, a dream.

"We're here," Oliver says. I'm actually getting married today. My fingers tighten around the armrest, knuckles turning white as the moment I get off this plane, I know it's happening in a matter of hours.

When I don't move, he speaks again, as if he thinks I didn't hear him. "Time to get off the plane."

"Great," I murmur. "Let's get married."

He clears his throat. "No second thoughts, right?"

"No second thoughts, but this is not how I thought I'd get married," I admit, standing up and stretching my back. The admission feels oddly vulnerable, like I'm revealing more of myself than I intended.

"How did you think you were going to get married?"

I drop my arms to my sides again and look at him. His expression is genuinely curious, head tilted slightly, his usual polished confidence replaced with something more approachable. "I'm not sure. I suppose I imagined it in a church and maybe even a party afterward."

"I never pictured you as the traditional type."

His words sting. Just because I didn't grow up with anything traditional doesn't mean I wouldn't want it now. "Why do you think that?"

"You're quiet, artistic, and... don't take this the wrong way, different," he says, leaning forward. "In a good way."

I nod. "That doesn't mean I dreamed about Elvis officiating my vows."

"Hey, you chose him."

I laugh, remembering telling him during our flight, but not thinking it would happen. "I didn't think you'd be able to pull it off in a few hours. This is as dysfunctional as it gets, so why not have a story to go with it?"

"Exactly. If we're doing this crazy shit together, let's promise to at least have fun." He stretches his hand out.

I look between his palm and his face. He wants to shake on it. My muscles coil. This is what it is, a transaction, not a fairytale. "Deal. Now let's go get married." I shake his hand quickly, knowing there's no way I'll change my mind. I need the money for the house. I smile at the hostess, but she only gives me a half one back before smiling at Oliver like a love-sick puppy. I guess I'll have to get used to that for the next few months. He's handsome and charming. Women will want him, which gets me thinking of something we didn't discuss, but we need to.

"As part of our marriage, we aren't seeing anyone else, right?" His jaw tightens as he speaks, "No."

His reaction surprises me, and I find myself needing clarity. "And this includes... casual partners?"

His face morphs into amusement. "Are you offering?"

He's teasing me because he knows my brother wouldn't allow it. Declan's warned Oliver in front of me. It would risk his friendship, and I don't want to ruin that.

"No chance. I'm just checking we're on the same page."

He leans in really close and whispers, "If I want to get off, I have my hands."

A shiver runs down my spine as his warm breath tickles my skin. A hot image flashes through my mind, but there's no way I'm letting him know I'm picturing him naked. Instead, I wince and say, "TMI. Let's get on with this before I lose my nerve."

Spinning on my heel, I move toward the exit, stepping carefully onto the metal staircase, my hand gripping the warm railing. From halfway down, I take in Las Vegas. Beyond the tarmac, the strip rises in the distance, and mountains frame the background. As I reach the bottom step, I'm hit by the Vegas heat. I immediately regret not wearing shorts and a top instead of my sweats. But they were comfy, which is probably why I fell asleep on the plane.

I spot another black car waiting for us. Oliver opens the door for me, which surprises me because it seems genuine rather than a performance, and we slip inside.

"Where are we staying?" I ask once I'm buckled inside.

"The Bellagio."

I recall the details from the Google search I did earlier, and it's luxurious. Travel was never something I allowed myself to dream about when I was younger. When you're bouncing between foster homes, you don't waste time imagining far-off places; you're too busy hoping the next house isn't worse than the last. Dreams felt useless. Even after I found good parents, the habit stuck. It felt safer to keep my hopes small and within reach.

As we drive through the streets, I look out the window, feeling like I've stepped into another world. It's better than the pictures online. In the midday sun, the city feels alive, every building and sign practically glowing. Neon lights and gigantic billboards surround us, there are huge screens showing ads for performers and shows, and even from here, I catch glimpses of fountains shooting up by the hotel doors.

Traffic crawls along, giving me time to scan the sidewalks, which are packed with tourists, street performers, and vendors. My eyes flick from one extravagant hotel to the next, each more surreal than the last, and I try to soak it all up.

"Have you been here before?" I ask, still captivated by the world outside the window.

"Once, for work," he says. "Why do you ask?"

"Just making conversation."

He doesn't ask about my travels, and it doesn't bother me. I know he's aware I haven't been anywhere.

We arrive at the hotel, and I find myself speechless. The Bellagio is grand, with soft beige and cream tones, arched windows, a curved façade, and lush landscaping. But the best feature has to be the lake in front. I remember reading about the shows at the fountain at night and how captivating they are. I didn't realize last night that this would be where we would be staying, but now I'm hoping our room will have a view of it.

I wait for him to climb out, and before I can do the same, Oliver is there, offering his hand. We walk inside, where I'm struck by the lobby's extraordinary ceiling made up of a garden of hand-blown glass flowers in vibrant colors. I welcome the air conditioning on my damp skin as I crane my neck, taking in all the details.

As we move to the front reception, I notice the same white and beige colors, glossy beige tiles, and patterned rugs with splashes of green cushions and artwork.

We're called up, and the attendant, a polished man in his fifties with a perfectly fitted suit, greets us. "Mr. and Mrs. Lincoln." My mouth opens to correct him, but I quickly shut it. In just a few hours, Lincoln will be my last name. Surprisingly, it doesn't make me feel uneasy.

I'm in a foggy daze as we follow the attendant to the elevator and head straight to the top floor.

As we exit on the top floor, the attendant opens the room door, and I follow, my jaw dropping. The suite is stunning, with the same color tones as downstairs but on a much bigger scale. I slowly walk around, barely listening as the attendant rattles off instructions. I hope Oliver is paying attention because I'm too distracted. The far wall is all glass, revealing a panoramic view of the Vegas Strip. The fountain below is mid-dance, each burst of water lit from beneath. I walk closer, pressing my hand lightly to the window, awestruck. From up here, the chaos of the city looks almost magical, like something out of a dream.

A rustle behind me draws my gaze back inside, I walk to the closest bedroom and that's when I see it.

"Congratulations" is spelled out in red rose petals on a massive white duvet king bed that dominates the room.

Everything is so over the top, I'm getting dizzy as I continue walking through the suite. There are multiple bedrooms, TVs, bathrooms, a huge kitchen, and a lounge. But on the positive, we don't have to share a room. I'm not ready to share a bed with Oliver.

The attendant leaves, and after the most chaotic day of my life, we're finally alone.

I turn to him, catching him in an unguarded moment as he runs his hand through his hair, saying the first thing that pops into my head. "This seems a bit excessive for one night."

"You deserve a nice place for our wedding night," he says, his eyes locked on mine as he steps toward me.

I swallow, a lump forming in my throat. "What time are we getting married?"

He checks his watch. "In exactly four hours."

Great... The blood drains to my feet. I grab a water bottle from the fridge, not caring if it's overpriced, and drink half in one go.

"I know how you feel."

I look up at him, taking in his relaxed posture as he leans against the wall, and mumble, "I doubt that."

"I'm serious. Do you think I was thinking about getting married any time soon?" He runs a hand over his jaw.

I shrug. "I don't know. We don't really hang out for me to know much about you."

"Well, you will now."

Heat rises to my cheeks. I look around. If he went to all this trouble, I can't imagine what the wedding will look like. I walk to the cream fabric sofa, ready to relax and watch TV when there's a knock on the door. "Are you expecting someone?" I ask. He's messing around on his phone.

"Yes," he says, but doesn't elaborate as he answers the door. My ears prick up when I hear female voices.

What is this? More wedding preparations? Hotel staff?

Who knows with Oliver. I smooth my clothes nervously.

"Oh, you must be Karley," one of the two women who've walked in says like we're old friends.

"Uh, yeah," I reply, giving her a tight smile.

Who is she? I hope he's not expecting her to be my bridesmaid. I would've told him to fly Evelyn out if I had known.

"We're here to get you ready," she says with a sympathetic smile. Obviously reading my confused expression.

"Get me ready?" I ask, trying to understand why he's going to all this trouble for a fake marriage.

Oliver steps in front of me, placing his hands on my shoulders. "They're here to help with your hair, makeup, and dress."

I exhale. "I've never had my makeup professionally done before."

"Well, enjoy. I'll meet you downstairs."

"Okay," I say, a little shakily. "But where will you get ready?"

"I've planned to meet Cora."

"Where is she staying?"

"She chose the Mandala Bay for her kids. It's more family-friendly."

His hands drop from my body, and I want to protest. His touch had been comforting in all this craziness. Then he strides to the door and leaves the penthouse suite. As soon as the door clicks shut, the women immediately start telling me what to do, including urging me to have an everything shower. They instruct me to exfoliate, shave, and moisturize.

This preparation seems like a lot for a wedding night that won't exist. I know that they don't know about our arrangement, so I just follow their instructions.

After I've prepared every part of my body and come out in a robe, the hair and makeup artists get to work. The makeup artist adds bronze shadows to make my eyes pop, and then finishes with a rosy lip stain to keep my request of a natural but polished look. Meanwhile, the hairstylist transforms my usual messy hair into a classy bun.

"Will he like it?" I ask before I can stop myself. Why should I care what Oliver thinks? This isn't real. Yet I find myself anxious for his approval anyway.

When I turn to the mirror, I gasp, barely recognizing myself. I'm amazed at how pretty I look. It's me, but flaw-less.

The makeup artist hands me a lacy baby blue lingerie set. They told me it was for the something blue aspect of getting married. Which is a sweet gesture, regardless of this being a fake marriage.

I have a sinking feeling. I need to know. "Who chose this for me?" I ask in a shaky voice.

Please don't say Oliver.

"Mr. Lincoln, of course," the hairdresser says with a sweet laugh.

I close my eyes as I let the words settle.

Oliver chose this for me?

The idea of it is jarring, yet I find myself curious. Will it fit? Why did he choose this specifically? Was it another necessary prop, or did he actually think about how it would look on me?

I head to the bedroom and slip it on. When I'm dressed, I move slowly to the full-length mirror, admiring the way it accentuates my curves, showing off my hourglass figure. I gulp down air as I stare at myself. I look sexy. Surely, he isn't expecting to see it.

A knock at the bedroom door startles me. "Come in," I call, covering myself up with the robe.

"I have your dress." The stylist walks in, and I gasp.

CHAPTER 12

OLIVER

"I CAN'T BELIEVE I'M doing this," I say on the phone to my brother, Jeremy. I'm dressed in my wedding suit, pacing the pavement on the ground floor of the Bellagio. I called Jeremy yesterday and filled him in on the wedding because I needed someone to confide in.

"I wouldn't say I'm happy about it, but I support you."

"I'm not trapping her in to this. She's willing to do it," I say, guilt tightening around my throat.

"I didn't say she wasn't, but you threw money at her."

I rub my forehead with my other hand. "I know, but she deserves her own place. She works hard."

"I'm not saying she doesn't deserve it, but I worry this is going to end badly."

I frown as I dodge people coming into the hotel. "I'll make sure it doesn't. And what's going on with you? How are the wedding preparations coming along?"

He's getting married in a few weeks, and his bachelor party is next weekend.

"Yeah, everything is set. You didn't let Evan throw you a bachelor party."

As he says it, my heart squeezes. Not for my bachelor party, but for Karley. Have I taken away her chance at having a bachelorette? But this is all fake. When she remarries, she can have one... My stomach knots weirdly again at the thought.

With a sigh, I stop pacing the sidewalk as movement catches my eye. I look up and freeze, all thoughts vanishing as my breath catches in my throat.

"You there?" my brother asks in my ear.

"Yeah." I clear my throat. "But I've got to go." Karley walks toward me, giving me time to let my eyes drift slowly over her.

Her white high heels make her legs seem longer. Her white dress, silk and flowy, slips effortlessly over her hourglass figure. The thin straps make her look delicate, and the dress compliments her complexion. Her hair is in a low bun, and by the time I take in her red lips and natural makeup, it's hard for me to breathe.

I've never seen her look like this. I have to swallow hard and refocus.

As I bring my gaze up to hers, my lips twist into an easy grin. "You are breathtaking."

"Do you think so?" She smooths her hands over the dress.

"You look like my wife," I reply with a wink, surprising myself with how right the words feel coming out of my mouth; how much I mean them despite this arrangement.

She smiles, a blush blooming across her cheeks. Her eyes gaze over my suit. "You clean up alright, too."

I tip my head back and chuckle, warmth spreading through my chest at her approval. "It's a nice way to compliment me. I thought I looked rather handsome."

She shakes her head with a grin. "Let's get married."

"Hang on," I say, a sudden impulse taking hold that I can't entirely explain to myself. "You're missing something." She looks down, scanning the floor like there's a problem with her dress.

I drop to one knee. Her eyes widen, her face pales, and her mouth falls open until she covers it with her hands, a gasp muffled behind them. I smile, enjoying the moment of catching her by surprise. There's something strangely satisfying about seeing her speechless.

I hold out the open box from Winston's toward her, the ring she chose sparkling up at her.

"What are you doing?" she finally asks, dropping her hands and darting her eyes around.

"Karley," I say, ignoring the strange flutter in my chest. Even knowing this is all for show, there's something about saying these words that feels important. "Will you do me the honor and be my wife?"

"Yes. But why?" she says under her breath as I take the ring from the box. "Oh my God, people are staring."

"It's okay. Just give me your hand," I say. She initially fights me before allowing me to slip the engagement ring onto her finger. The ring we chose together. God, it looks perfect against her freshly painted, clear nails. Her hands are just as hot and clammy as mine. I know it's hot out today, with the sun blazing down on us. But this isn't the weather's fault.

"You can get up now," she whispers. I purposely stand extra slowly, just to annoy her, because even though I know she doesn't like the attention, I think she's more than deserving to have everyone see her in this moment. She's stunning, but more than that, I want everyone to know she's mine... even if it's fake.

I don't miss the way she admires the ring on her left hand for a second. "It really is beautiful. This is such a waste."

"Why's it a waste?" I ask. Something about seeing it on her finger feels right, not wasteful at all.

"Because it's too beautiful to just be an everyday ring," she mumbles.

"Sell it then, put it toward your house." The thought of her removing it, of someone else wearing the ring I placed on her finger, creates an unexpected tightness in my chest.

She looks up at me, then at the ring.

She sighs. "I don't think I could sell it either."

I smile softly, relieved by her answer in a way I'm not ready to think about. "Do whatever you want with it, but we should get going now."

"Alright, alright," she says, and we move to the car. I open the door for her, watching as she gathers the bottom of her dress with her hands.

"Need help?" I offer my arm for support.

She nods, accepting my help as she gets into her seat. I lean in closer to help arrange her dress, catching a hint of her perfume, something sweet and delicate.

After closing the door, I walk around to my side, using those few seconds to breathe. When I slip into the seat beside her, the car feels smaller. Her dress takes up space between us, yet I'm aware of how close we are.

After she buckles in, I notice her leg bouncing nervously, her fingers twisting together in her lap. Without thinking, I place my hand gently on her thigh, just above her knee, hoping to calm her. Her head twists to me, and I flash her a reassuring smile. She surprises me by letting me leave my hand there, rather than shoving it off.

The drive to the Graceland Wedding Chapel is short, only about ten minutes. We could've walked, but I didn't want her walking in heels with extra eyes on her. She'd hate the attention, and I can't afford to let anything get in the way of us marrying today.

"Cora is meeting us there," I remind her. She stares out the window until the car stops. I remove my hand from her and slip out, my heart beating fast.

Is this nerves? Anticipation? Something else entirely?

I quickly dust my sweaty palms on my pants before grabbing her hand. I interlock our fingers on our way to the door.

We're about to head inside the white chapel trimmed with blue, when I spot Cora coming out with some flowers. My shoulders drop with a mix of relief and gratitude. I didn't want it to feel like I hadn't thought of everything, so I made sure Cora took care of the important pieces. I can also see the veil sitting in Cora's hand, and for some reason, the idea of lifting it off Karley's face makes everything feel real.

"You made it," Cora calls out, hurrying toward us with a bright smile. She waves at Karley first, then turns to give me a quick hug. "Everything's ready inside."

Karley and Cora exchange excited whispers as they admire each other's outfits, and I find myself watching Karley's bashful expression.

As they talk about what we're about to do, their words hit me. I'm going to have to kiss her. My heart just about beats right out of my chest.

I need to breathe. I excuse myself, gasping for air, leaving her with Cora. As I step inside for a moment alone, it all hits me at once. I close my eyes and imagine the gallery, my mom's face, all of her students' pieces, including Karley's, on display. When I picture Karley's work, I think bold, bright, and intricate paintings. They deserve a head start, and this is how I can help them.

I reopen my eyes, taking in the beige and white décor. At the front of the chapel, I find the Elvis impersonator waiting on the small brown stage. I head over to meet him, and we exchange quick hellos. He looks ridiculous, and I'd never have chosen him, but Karley deserved to pick one ridiculous thing out of this entire crazy arrangement. If she wants to go full Vegas, I'm here for it.

"Clair de Lune" starts. One of my mother's favorites, a piece I've heard countless times. I'm staring at the doors as they open. The soft tone of the music, plus her standing at the other end, makes emotion clog my throat. She heads toward me, looking so different with the veil down and a bouquet in her hands. *I am getting married. She's going to be my wife.*

Even with the air conditioner blowing cool air, my back heats beneath my suit. I worry I'm going to be a sweaty mess by the end of this. I take slow, deep breaths, watching her walk toward me.

There's something different about seeing her this way, moving toward me, compared to when I first saw her outside the hotel. This feels significant. And in this light, she's absolutely stunning.

I can see her chest rise and fall; she's just as nervous as I am, which helps me calm down a bit. As she comes closer, I see her eyes are misty, and I smile, watching her try to blink it away.

"Hey," I whisper as she reaches me. "You okay?"

"I'm fine. It's just... the veil."

My eyes flick to Cora, who narrows her eyes at me, silently telling me to leave it.

Karley passes the bouquet to Cora, and I take Karley's hands in mine. She stands directly in front of me, both of our gazes on Elvis. My heart is pounding, and I concentrate on breathing, scared I might pass out.

I can only assume she's feeling the same way.

The ceremony begins, and the whole time, I can only hear the loud beating of my heart.

Then, we're asked to exchange vows. The moment feels surreal, as if the weight of everything, the promises, the future, is suddenly pressing down on me all at once. As I look at her, the way her eyes shine, my nerves settle, replaced by something deeper, something real.

I take a deep breath, recalling the words I wrote on the plane. They come out slower than I expect. "Karley, thank you for taking this journey with me. I couldn't imagine it with anyone else. I promise to listen to you, to support you in every dream, and to protect you through every challenge. I vow to stand by you, not just in the easy moments, but in the ones that truly matter, and to grow alongside you with love and understanding."

She clears her throat, looking down at our joined hands before lifting her eyes to me. They're glassy. I didn't mean to make her sad with my vows. I just wanted something from the heart.

"Oliver, I never in a million years thought we'd end up here today, standing before each other like this. But here we are. I promise to help you through the tough times, to support you when you need it the most, and to care for you with all my heart."

Her words hit me with unexpected force. Something about hearing her say my name like that, with such sincerity in her voice, makes my breath catch.

As I slide her wedding band on her finger, I watch as her eyes soften, and for a moment, everything outside of this room vanishes. It's just the two of us, making this promise to each other.

When she slips the ring on my finger, I stare at it for a second. I take her hand in mine, and her finger touches the wedding band, spinning it slightly.

His words sound muffled and distant, but I don't miss my cue to say, "I do."

She says it too, her voice trembling just a little, and it makes my chest tighten.

"I now present you as husband and wife." Then, with a bright grin and a wink, Elvis says, "It's time to kiss your bride."

I step forward, my heart racing as I reach for the edge of her veil. Lifting the delicate fabric, I reveal her face like a present. Lips slightly parted, she's breathing heavily, her eyes drifting closed, waiting for me to kiss her. I don't overthink it. I lean forward, closing the distance between us. The moment my lips touch hers, my heart slows. I relax into it, my hand cupping her cheek, but then she pulls back quickly. I blink, confused.

She glances over at Elvis, but I'm focused on her flushed cheeks. I wonder if she didn't feel that spark between us.

Cora cheers and Karley's hand tightens in mine. We turn to face her, posing nicely as she snaps some pictures, and in that moment it feels real.

Hand in hand, we walk down the aisle together, my heart racing, knowing we're now husband and wife.

"This is fucking bizarre," I whisper to her as we walk out of the chapel. "Can't wait to get changed out of this suit."

She laughs, her head tilting to look up at me. "I thought you were going to stay in that for the whole day."

"You're kidding, right? I'm not staying in this. Imagine the looks I'd get."

She squeezes my hand. "It's okay. You don't have to pretend you love me now." Her words land heavy, leaving a hollow feeling in my chest.

We still have appearances to maintain for a while, but that has little to do with why I want to keep holding her hand. Cora steps over and we take a picture with us three before I say thank you and goodbye and she heads off to rejoin her family.

"So, what's the plan?" Karley asks when we're alone again.

"Let's get back so we can get changed, and then we can do something you want to do. I only have one thing planned for tonight, but I wanted to see if there's anything you had in mind."

Her eyebrows lift. "That sounds unusually nice coming from you."

"Hey, I can be nice."

As we head to the car, a few people congratulate us, and I notice her tight smile. I pull her closer, and her head burrows into me. The feeling of her nestled against me causes a sense of protectiveness I hadn't anticipated. When we climb into the car, her shoulders drop, and she lets out a deep breath.

We make it back to the hotel after ten minutes, and there are a couple more congratulations as we head through the lobby. During the elevator ride, I wonder about what comes next, and even in here, it's a balance of sharing space while maintaining boundaries.

Once we're in the safety of the penthouse, she kicks off her heels.

I laugh. "Those looked uncomfortable."

"They were," she admits. "Heels are horrid, which is why you never see me in them."

I nod, thinking back to when the last time I saw her dressed up. It was at my gallery party. She'd worn a black dress and silver heels, her hair pulled back, highlighting her high cheekbones and full lips. I remember being struck by the transformation and how confident she looked moving through the crowd. "True, only on special occasions. But I can't deny you look good in them."

She leans in slightly. "I'll save the heels for when I really want to impress you. Now, where are we headed next? So I know what to change into."

"Something comfortable," I recommend. "Like jeans, Chucks, and a sweater."

"Now you're speaking my language," she says, moving to her room. I watch her go, finding myself hating the thought of her hanging up the dress and the ceremony becoming just a memory.

I quickly change, throwing on jeans, a t-shirt, and some casual shoes. As I button my jeans, I wonder if this counts as our first date. As I step out of the bedroom and into the main room, I'm still lost in that thought. Just as I'm about to sit on the sofa, I hear her footsteps approaching.

She's wearing exactly what I suggested, her usual style. I smile. "Ready?"

"Yep," she replies, and we head to the elevator. Taking her out, showing her Las Vegas, spending time together suddenly feels like the most natural thing in the world.

Inside the elevator, I'm unsure whether to grab her hand, but there's no need to pretend here, so I keep my hand in my pocket while she holds on to her purse.

Once we reach the ground floor, I place my hand lightly on the small of her back, guiding her through the crowded lobby toward the exit. She leans slightly into my touch as we pass the other hotel guests. The private car arrives, and we get inside without a sound. The driver, already pre-booked, knows exactly where to go.

It's getting darker, and I know the view ahead is going to be stunning. But we haven't eaten for a while, so I grab the snacks I had the driver arrange for us to munch on during the ride. Inside, there's assorted cheeses, crackers, chocolates, fruit, and a bottle of sparkling water.

We snack and chat as the city lights begin to glow around us. Just as she finishes a bite of chocolate, the car pulls to a stop, and she gasps. "Are we actually going on a helicopter over the Strip?"

I nod, grinning. "Let's go."

She jumps out of the car before I can even reach her door.

I laugh, teasing, "Excited, huh?"

"I've never been in a helicopter."

I forgot she hasn't, but I figured she'd love seeing the strip at night. I haven't seen the strip at night either, so I listen carefully to the instructions as we're shown to the helicopter. Asking a couple of questions to mask my own nervousness. I requested a private tour, so it's just us. After the safety briefing, the pilot keeps us entertained until we're inside.

Our thighs touch in the tight space. There's a current of electricity between us that makes my skin tingle. She gives me one of those big, excited smiles. In the close quarters, I catch a hint of her scent, which is sweet and sugary, making it difficult to focus on anything but her presence beside me. As the helicopter takes off, she grips my thigh, her fingers digging in slightly, making me jerk a little. I slide my hand into hers, interlocking our fingers, letting her squeeze it tightly. Her hand feels so small, yet comforting.

She keeps holding on, eyes glued to the view outside the window. The ride is smooth as we climb higher, and the pilot starts pointing out landmarks. "Look... There's the Bellagio fountains!" she shouts over the headset, pointing eagerly at the bursts of water dancing in perfect sync to music we can't hear from up here. I hadn't expected her to be so enthusiastic. She doesn't stop there, her finger darting to the Eiffel Tower at Paris Las Vegas, then to the bright beam shooting into the sky from the Luxor.

Her excitement is infectious, spilling over with every landmark she spots. She talks about how tiny everything looks, how the Strip feels endless from up here, like it could stretch right into forever. I just smile, letting her energy wash over me, not saying much, because watching her, completely captivated, eyes sparkling with wonder, is somehow better than the view.

"Hey." I lean closer so she can hear me through the headset. "Let's get a picture?"

She turns to me with another bright smile and nods, sliding closer until our shoulders press together. I pull out my phone and snap a photo of us, wanting to capture this moment with her.

We land after forty-five minutes of being in the air and, honestly, I could've stayed up there all night.

I get out and then carefully help her shaky legs step down, but before we head off, the pilot offers to take a photo of us in front of the helicopter. Pride washes through me at having chosen something she so clearly enjoyed.

We stand together, smiling. Her arm slips around my waist, and I wrap mine around hers. I don't think she even realizes she's done it. But as she leans in close, I savor it, feeling unexpectedly calm and comfortable.

I'm tempted to kiss her. We look at each other, and I smile at seeing the flush on her cheeks. "Where to next?" she asks.

I've already got the next stop planned: the "O" Cirque du Soleil show. I've tried to pack as many experiences in as possible, wanting her to enjoy every bit of this. But as we get back into the car, I find myself wishing we had more alone time. As I scroll through the photos we just took, I pause on one of just the two of us. I'm struck by how natural we look together.

"We actually look like a real couple."

She elbows my ribs. "Get over yourself. I was just happy to be in a helicopter. You just caught me at a good time," she teases.

"Oh, so it wasn't my charming personality?" I raise an eyebrow. "Just the helicopter ride?"

"Exactly," she deadpans, then breaks into a smile that crinkles the corners of her eyes.

The shared joke turns into laughter between us. And God, it feels good. I can't remember the last time I laughed like this.

Soon, we arrive at the show's venue. When she spots the signs, her eyes widen, and she grabs my arm. I find myself leaning into her excitement once more as we join the line at the entrance. "Being your wife might not be so bad if you keep doing stuff like this," she says as we approach the ticket counter. Hearing her call herself my wife sends an unexpected thrill through me.

I hand our tickets to the usher, who tears the stubs and points us toward the main lobby. "Not that I want you spending money on me... but I've always wanted to see this."

There's a catch in her voice, and I realize she didn't know I paid attention to what she likes. We follow the crowd through the grand entrance hall, passing by merchandise stands and promotional posters.

"Have you been to this show?" she asks, peering up at me with genuine interest as we navigate through the growing crowd toward the theater doors.

I shake my head. "I've seen Cirque du Soleil, but not this one."

She eyes me mischievously. "Another thing you haven't experienced."

The theater buzzes as an usher checks our ticket stubs again and directs us down the aisle. Karley takes in everything, the big stage, massive water tank, the performers already moving through the audience. I find myself watching her reactions more than the surroundings, savoring each smile. We grab a program from our attendant and stop at the private concession stand for premium ticket holders for some popcorn and candy, then settle into our plush, slightly wider seats with the unobstructed, perfect view of the stage.

"These seats are amazing, front and center, but I'd expect nothing else from you." She smirks.

"Only the best for my wife."

The lights dim, soft music begins, and an announcement informs the room that the show is about to start. I force my gaze away from her, though it takes more willpower than it should. There's something magnetic about her today.

It's spectacular; the kind of experience that sweeps you up entirely, and the show flies by. Throughout the performance, we lean toward each other to whisper observations. And at one point, I slip my arm around her without thinking. She doesn't pull away, instead settling against me as if we've sat this way before.

When it ends, she turns to me. "That was even better than I dreamed."

"It's definitely close to being my favorite," I say as we follow the huge crowd out. Her arm loops through mine as people surround us, and the casual touch sends a warmth through me.

"Which is your favorite?" she asks, leaning toward me with curiosity in her eyes.

"The Mystere."

"Why?"

"It's more of a classic experience with clowns and acrobatics," I explain, gesturing with my hands to mimic a tumbling motion.

"I don't like clowns," she mutters, wrinkling her nose.

This revelation catches me by surprise. After all these years of knowing her, I'd never learned this about her.

"You are scared of something?" I tease.

Her chin lifts to look at me. "Yes. My real parents always dressed up as clowns for Halloween."

She visibly shivers, so I peel her arm out of mine so I can wrap my arm around her. Her body fits perfectly against mine.

"I promise not to scare you with clowns."

"Good. Because if you do, I'll pay you back even harder," she says playfully.

Our walk is slow once we get outside. It's been a huge twenty-four hours, and I could call it a night, but I don't think I'm ready for this night to end. I hope to at least talk more or watch TV on the sofa.

"So... where to next?" she asks, somehow still bursting with energy.

I laugh, realizing I hadn't planned this far. "Well, we're in Vegas, right?"

"Yeah!"

"How about a rooftop bar?" I suggest. "There's one at Mandalay Bay with amazing views, music, and vibes. I've been there with Harvey once."

"Two young Lincolns on the loose."

I chuckle, knowing she's right; we were the menaces out of the four of us.

"I'd like to say Harvey was worse. Now he's about to get married, so I think his reign of terror is over."

I find myself comparing our situations. His upcoming wedding and my already completed one. The weight of my wedding band still feels foreign on my finger, a constant reminder that I'm Karley's husband now, even if it's only temporary.

We arrive at the bar. The space is filled with low couches, ambient lighting, and a fantastic view of the city.

"What would you like?" I ask.

"Surprise me."

I order us drinks and make sure we're seated in the VIP section. It doesn't take long when you're willing to pay whatever it takes to be in one. I just don't want us crammed into the main area of the club. I want us to be able to continue talking; I want to know more about her.

We're up on the rooftop bar, and she's sipping on her mojito while I take in the view, the music thumping softly around us.

She leans in to talk in my ear. "I think your mom's going to love the gallery when you get it."

Her breath tickles my jaw, causing the muscle to pulse.

"I hope so. It's crazy, having money, but still feeling like you can't get the one thing that actually means something to someone else," I admit. That was way more honest than I intended to be, but she makes it easy to drop my usual walls. She looks at me like she's holding back words.

"It's strange," she says finally, looking out into the crowd before her eyes return to mine. "You're not the same person I thought you were."

I tilt my head, both intrigued and slightly unsettled by her observation. Have I changed, or has she just never seen the real me before? "What do you mean?"

She sets her glass down, taking a breath before bringing her gaze back to me. "You just always seem so confident. Seeing you admit you are scared you can't have something... it surprised me."

My grin widens at her honesty, but something in my chest tightens. "Of course that would excite you." Our eyes lock for a moment longer than necessary, and I feel an unexpected pull toward her.

"Honestly, though, you're not what I pictured." She fiddles with her empty glass, rolling it between her palms. "You pay attention and..." she hesitates, glancing away for a second, "you're not flirting with everyone like I expected." There's a hint of relief in her voice that makes me wonder what she's been worried about all this time.

A sharp disappointment hits me that she would think I'd be chasing other women while with her, even if our relationship is fake. Does she really think so little of me? Or is it my reputation? Either way, I find myself wanting to prove her wrong... Not just for this arrangement, but because suddenly it matters what she thinks of me.

I reach across the table, my fingers lightly brushing against her hand. "I may not be perfect, Karley, but when I commit to something, or someone, I'm all in." The intensity of my own statement surprises me, and I pull back slightly, caught off guard.

She looks at my hand, then back to my face, as if she's searching for something. The moment hangs between us, charged with unspoken questions.

"Want another?" I ask, finishing mine with a last gulp, my voice gentler than intended. But I don't break eye contact, silently letting her know that whatever this is between us, fake marriage or not, it matters to me.

"Yes." She nods, but yawns, looking as tired as I feel. "But after that, I think I'll be ready for bed."

The mention of bed sends my thoughts in a direction they shouldn't go: images of her curled beside me, her hair spread across a pillow... wearing that blue lingerie set I picked out for her. I quickly redirect my thoughts, knowing I can't act on them.

"Same," I reply as I wave down the server.

"What time's our flight tomorrow?"

They come and pour us another. "Morning. But as soon as we land, we have to move the rest of your stuff into my house."

"Oh, great." She rolls her eyes, taking a sip of her new drink. "And when my brother's back, he's going to show up, over-analyzing everything and laying down ground rules."

I give her a playful nudge. "I'll be there, so it'll be two against one. But let's hope he doesn't make it back from Florida in time."

"I hope not. The whole fatherly figure thing drives me nuts. I'm looking forward to getting some distance."

"I've organized a truck and some movers, so we don't have to do it ourselves, but we have to be there to direct them."

She squints at me. "How did you find time to organize all of this?"

"Cora helps."

"So I should be thanking her." She smirks.

"Probably," I murmur, taking another sip so we can go soon.

She wiggles her eyebrows at me. "You'd better hide all your mess and get rid of any old girlfriend stuff. Your wife is moving in."

I hold her gaze, strangely pleased by the idea of her things in my place. "I don't have any other girls' stuff at my house."

She gives me a curious look. "Oliver, can I ask you something?"

"Yes. Of course."

"Why haven't you had any serious girlfriends?"

Her question surprises me, my temple throbbing, but I answer truthfully. "Because I'm focused on the galleries. I don't make much time for relationships."

She takes another sip, eyeing me. "Hmm."

"What?"

"Nothing," she mumbles.

I groan. "I hate it when women say 'nothing.' It always means you're thinking of something you don't want to say."

She laughs softly. "No, really, I'm just surprised by your answer."

"Well, what about you?" I ask, raising an eyebrow, genuinely curious. "Where's your boyfriend?"

A slight blush rises to her cheeks, maybe from the drinks. "I don't have time with work and studying. Plus, now I'm focusing on getting my own place, which, thanks to you, I'll finally have. Maybe now I'll have time for a boyfriend."

I sit up straighter, my jaw clenching at the thought. "Well, you're going to be married to me for a couple of months, so I guess you won't need one for now."

We finish our drinks in silence, but when she yawns again, it causes me to yawn in response. I stand and hold out my hand. "Come on, wifey," I say, smiling. "Let's get you to bed."

"We're not sleeping together," she says, rising and slipping her hand in mine.

I chuckle, though there's a flicker of disappointment I'm not ready to acknowledge. I wonder what it would be like if this were a real honeymoon.

"I know, relax."

We leave the club, holding hands, which causes a warmth that I'm becoming addicted to.

In the elevator, back at the hotel, I find myself drawing her closer. We enter the penthouse, and I pause at the entry to her room. Part of me wants to suggest tea, TV, or another conversation, anything to postpone the moment we have to separate. Instead, I simply say, "Goodnight, wife."

"Goodnight, husband." Her smile is soft, almost shy. There's no sarcasm, just contentment. She moves to her bedroom door and closes it behind her, and I walk to my room.

Lying in bed, I twist the wedding band around my finger, barely realizing I've kept it on. But this is the problem; a part of me is becoming intrigued by her in a way I've never allowed myself to before, even though it's fake. I must remember she's only being nice because of the arrangement, the money for her house. But still, I think of her smile tonight. She seemed genuinely happy... Was it because of me?

As I close my eyes, I see her walking down the aisle to me, and my last thought before I drift off is how easily I could've kissed her for hours.

CHAPTER 13

KARLEY

"WHY DO YOU SIT on the counter?" Oliver asks from behind me.

I turn my head, watching him enter the kitchen of the hotel suite. But then I almost choke on my coffee when I notice he's not wearing a shirt.

My cheeks heat as I dart my eyes away from his toned body and stare at my cup. The reality of our situation hits me... We're actually married. Yesterday's ceremony still feels like a dream, and waking up in this suite together makes everything more real.

"I like to drink my coffee in peace," I say.

When I cautiously glance up, he's flashing me a grin that does funny things to my stomach. His blue eyes crinkle at the corners, and I can't help noticing how relaxed he seems with this whole arrangement. "And I'm the opposite. I love to talk in the mornings."

I roll my eyes and mutter into the cup, trying to hide the smile tugging at my lips. "It's going to be a long marriage."

This is temporary, I remind myself. A business deal with an expiration date.

He leans in a little closer. "You'll miss me when you get your peace back, I guarantee you."

"I doubt that." I bring my gaze to the window to avoid looking at him, but not before he catches the flicker of amusement in my eyes.

"Are you hungry?" he asks as he bangs cupboards and drawers. It pulls my attention away from the window and onto him. He's looking around for something.

"Yeah, are we going to grab breakfast?"

He closes a drawer and looks up at me, his blue eyes brighter today. "Well, I had another idea."

I laugh. "Of course you did." And because he's facing me, I can't miss how his shoulders are broad, round, and toned. I can see just a dusting of hair on his chest. His black sweatpants hang low, so I catch sight of his hipbones.

He moves in front of me to stand between my legs, and my breath catches. Before I have a chance to ask what he's doing, he grabs my hips and moves me effortlessly in his arms to another part of the counter. My heart is thumping, but he looks completely unfazed. Meanwhile, my skin's still tingling where he touched me.

"Here it is." He holds up a booklet, which I guess is room service. Something I haven't experienced before, and suddenly the thought excites me.

He holds it out to me, and I take it from his hands, his ring catching the light. My heart swells at the sight… He didn't take it off.

I didn't either.

I shake my head and focus. Lowering the cup, I scan the menu as he still stands in front of me. My eyes widen at the prices. Twenty dollars for pancakes? I debate between playing it safe with something familiar or taking the opportunity to splurge.

"Do you know what you want?" he asks.

"Pancakes sound good."

As he calls up our food, I finish my coffee and then slip off the counter.

"So before we head off, I was thinking we could go check out a gallery here in the hotel?"

"Planning to buy something?" I ask, putting the cup in the sink and keeping my gaze firmly on my task to avoid looking at his naked chest.

"Maybe, if I see something I like."

His morning voice is a little huskier. I can feel it on my skin. I make the mistake of looking at him. *God, his abs*. You could grate a cheese block on them. But I bring my focus back to his words, wondering what it's like having people buying your pieces as they walk into a gallery. It would be a surreal moment.

"I'll shower and pack up while we wait for breakfast." I walk out of the kitchen, needing to get some distance between us. My heart is beating too fast, and I'm not sure if it's from attraction or panic. Either way, being alone with a half-naked Oliver feels like playing with fire. I need a moment to remember this isn't real; that I'm not supposed to notice how his eyes follow me or how easily he lifted me off that counter.

I shower, pack my bag, and then hear a knock at the door. Room service is here.

When Oliver opens the door, I barely contain my excitement at the sight of the silver trays being wheeled in. The server arranges everything on the dining table with an effort that makes me feel like royalty.

"This is amazing," I whisper after the server leaves.

Oliver looks genuinely pleased by my reaction. "Dig in before it gets cold."

We eat quickly, but I savor every bite.

"That was incredible," I say as I finish the last strawberry. "Almost worth getting fake married for."

Oliver laughs. "Just wait until you see the gallery. The Bellagio has one of the best collections in Vegas."

Once we've checked out and our bags are stored with the concierge, we make our way toward the gallery. As we approach the Bellagio Gallery of Fine Art, I notice how the entrance stands apart from the casino's glitz. There's an understated elegance to the façade, with clean lines and soft lighting. Oliver walks close beside me, not quite touching, but I can feel the warmth radiating from him.

When we reach a narrow corridor, his hand finds the small of my back, guiding me forward. The gentle pressure sends a shiver up my spine that I try desperately to ignore. Once we arrive inside, I'm struck by the calm and elegant atmosphere, with soft lighting and perfectly spaced displays. The marble floors and muted tones set a peaceful backdrop for the bold, detailed art on the walls.

"I wanted to show you this place," Oliver says quietly. "There's something special about how they organize each exhibition... They understand that art needs room to breathe, to speak to the viewer."

I glance at him, surprised by the passion in his voice. "You really love this, don't you? It's not just business for you."

"Never has been," he admits with a small smile. "The business part came second. I fell in love with art long before I thought about selling it."

Each piece feels intentional, telling a story or capturing a moment with raw energy. It's so different from what I'm used to back home. Some pieces are bright and abstract, while others, dark and realistic, but they all seem to pull you into another world.

I stop in front of a painting. It's of a woman standing alone in the middle of a crowded street, her face turned upward, though no one around her seems to notice. The colors are muted, mostly grays and blues, but there's a light shining on her face.

I can't look away. Something about her expression resonates deeply with me. I've spent so much of my life feeling invisible, yet still searching for my own light.

"This one speaks to you," Oliver says softly.

I nod, not trusting my voice. How long have I been standing here?

When I finally tear my gaze away from the painting to look at him, he's closer than I expected, his eyes warm with something I can't name. "We should probably keep moving. There's a lot more to see."

We continue through the gallery, occasionally brushing against each other. I find myself both avoiding and seeking these accidental touches.

After we've seen everything, lingering longer than I expected, we make our way toward the exit.

"I'm surprised you didn't buy anything," I say as we step back into the hotel's main corridor.

Oliver runs a hand through his hair, expression thoughtful. "There were a couple I liked, but I just... know when it's right. It's like a feeling. You look at a piece, and it moves you," he replies.

Does my art do that to people? Does it make them feel something? I'd like to think my art brings happiness. My work is feminine, mostly flowers in watercolor, though I've done birds here and there. But flowers are what feel right to me.

"All set to go home?" he asks.

"Yeah." I smile, though there's a flutter of nervousness in my stomach. Going home means starting this marriage for real—no more hotel bubble, just the daily reality of pretending to be Oliver's wife. "You'll have to show me this mansion I'll be 'enjoying' now."

"It won't be so bad," he teases.

"I've lived in worse places, trust me," I say. "It's been…a journey."

The air gets a bit heavy, and I see a flash of something in his gaze. Concern? About what I've just hinted at. But instead of pushing, he just softens his voice. "I'll try to make it as comfortable as possible. But don't get any ideas about taking the main bedroom."

His playful energy instantly lifts me. "Why not? I might like it better than the guest room."

"No chance. That's mine. You can have any room. But I'm keeping mine."

"How desperate are you for the gallery?" I ask, lifting my eyebrow.

His jaw drops. "You wouldn't."

I wink. "I'll decide when we get there."

"Evil," he murmurs.

I hide my smile, enjoying the way we've fallen into this. Almost like a game between friends.

On the plane, I settle into my seat, more relaxed this time. The same pilot and flight attendant welcome us, and I gaze out the window, thinking about what comes next.

Before I know it, we're back and in his car, heading toward my place. I run through what I have to do: what to pack, what to throw out, how to organize my new life without losing myself in Oliver's world.

"Why don't I just meet you there?"

He glances at me curiously. "The movers will handle everything. That's why I hired them."

"I know, but there are some things I'd rather pack myself," I explain, thinking about my sketchbooks, art supplies, and old journals, specifically the ones where I've written about him.

"No, I'll help direct the movers. And as my wife, you could use my driver."

"To work and school? I don't need a driver for that," I say, laughing. "When I'm with you, fine, but I don't need the driver every day."

He sighs. "Alright, but will you at least take one of my cars?"

"Oh, really? Does that include the Aston Martin?" I grin, remembering the sleek car I'd admired from afar.

He shrugs. "Sure, take it."

The deal doesn't sound so bad now. Live in a massive house, drive a fancy car, wear a pretty ring, and dress up occasionally as his "wife." There are worse things in life. It's not like I'll fall in love with him.

When we get to my place, Oliver directs the movers while I pack my personal things into boxes. I don't have much, because growing up in foster care taught me to keep only what matters most, like my paint brushes. Especially the ones Amber and Wren gave me. When they adopted me and found out I loved to paint, they took me to an art store. That day changed my life. I started to feel happy again. Those brushes and palettes mean the world to me, and I'll always hold them close.

After a little while, the movers start moving the boxes to the truck. It doesn't take long; my entire life fits into just nine boxes. I direct them, one by one, feeling like I'm taking a big step forward. Oliver watches the movers and gives me space, even though he offered to help.

How did he know I needed that? I'm starting to see a different side of him. Not a rich man barking orders, but someone who reads the room and offers soft reassurances.

But what will happen when we get to his place? Earlier, I was playing about taking his bedroom, but now it'll be my first time seeing Oliver's house, his personal space. My brother's been there a million times, but I haven't, and it feels new, like unexplored territory.

The truck is packed up, and I climb into Oliver's car, where he guides me through the turns. It's only ten minutes from where I was living, but it might as well be another planet. We pull into a private garage. He drives slowly, allowing me to take in his place. A four-story beige limestone mansion that towers over everything around it. The large, arched windows, the dark wood and glass double doors. It's a complete world apart from my place with Declan.

Stepping out, I notice the other cars parked beside us. A red Ferrari and the familiar black Aston Martin. Evelyn's going to lose her mind when she hears about all this. She'll beg me for a ride in that Aston. The thought of myself behind the wheel of either vehicle seems crazy, like playing dress-up in someone else's life. Would I ever feel comfortable driving something worth more than most people's homes?

"What's with the smile?"

Shifting my gaze from the cars to his, my smile fades, suddenly self-conscious. "Nothing."

He nudges me with a grin. "You were looking at the Aston. Don't lie, you're excited to drive it."

I roll my eyes. "Let's just meet the truck so I can pick a room."

"You actually sound excited."

"Wishful thinking." Part of me is terrified and the other buzzes with anticipation. "Now show me my new room before the truck gets here."

His face widens, and I realize what he's thinking, but before I can correct myself he speaks. "I'm paying them. They won't mind waiting until we're ready."

We step into Oliver's house, and I freeze in place. My eyes sweep over the entryway. It's grand, with every wall arched and clad in artwork, warm cream tones softened by dark wood accents. The air is thick with a faint scent of fresh pine, and something warm like wood.

Oliver walks ahead, veering to the right as we enter a formal living room. "Honestly," he says, sounding almost embarrassed. "I never use this room. It's more for show."

I've heard of rooms like this, but actually seeing one is surreal. Cream sofas, a massive fireplace, and arched windows flood the space with natural light... more than I'd imagined for his place. A large, ancient rug with muted mosaics and grays stretches across the dark wooden floors, giving the room a cozy, timeless charm.

His kitchen, visible from here, features sleek white marble counters with dark wood cabinetry. I take in the faded cream rugs with intricate patterns and the assortment of paintings in vibrant, varied styles lining the walls. His taste leans heavily toward floral art, which surprises me. I try to imagine myself here with a morning coffee at that island.

We step back into the hallway and down toward another room. "Is this your room?" I ask softly, feeling a strange hesitancy, like I'm crossing a boundary.

"Yes, it's mine," he says, watching me.

The bedroom is enormous. Three times the size of my old one. Tall ceilings, cream walls with delicate detailing, more arched windows letting in soft light. My gaze falls on a dark green and gold tree painting framed in gold above the bed. I've never seen artwork quite like it, but it's beautiful. The bedding is neat, all in cream, with layered, luxurious pillows. I find myself wondering what it would be like to wake up here with sunlight filtering through those custom drapes, but then I quickly push it away.

He points to the bathroom and closet. "Feel free to look around."

I hesitate, not wanting to invade his personal space. "Maybe just show me my room?"

He cocks his eyebrow. "You're not taking it?"

I scrunch up my nose, trying to hide the fact it smells and feels too much like him that I wouldn't sleep well in it. "No. You probably fart and leave marks in there."

He laughs. "No marks, but I can't say I'm not human. But if you wanted it, I'd happily give it to you."

"No, this is your personal space. I was only kidding about taking it over." Part of me wants to stay here and learn more about the private Oliver that exists in this space. But another part recognizes the danger in that curiosity.

We continue along the main hallway, passing through a vast living area that opens into the kitchen and dining room. More dark wood, warm creams, and iron chandeliers. The back windows let in natural light, but the kitchen feels cozier, almost shadowed compared to the other rooms. It's different from any kitchen I've seen.

"I actually use this living room," he says, grinning. "This is where I watch TV when I'm home."

I move to join him on the rug. "Oh, good," I say. "Then we can pick up on that show we're watching. You haven't watched episode three without me, have you?"

He shakes his head. "No, I've resisted. No point if you're not watching with me. Plus, I made a promise that I plan to keep."

His words linger, sending an unexpected flutter through me, but I push the feeling aside. "Come on, I need to see my room so I can get the movers set up."

We walk upstairs, and I'm grateful for the space. Having separate levels will give me the breathing room I need. He shows me down a hall lined with spare bedrooms, each with tall ceilings, cream walls, and their own variations of the same artful, unique style. Every room has its own character, with different colors in the cushions and throws, and a unique piece of artwork above each headboard.

I stop in one room, captivated by a large painting of a flowering tree. It's beautiful, filled with pink blossoms, and something about it feels like a sign. "I think this is the one," I say, stepping in and lying down on the bed, melting into the plush mattress. "Oh," I sigh, half to myself. "This is heaven."

"Looks like someone's found their room."

I open my eyes to find Oliver leaning against the door frame, watching me with an amused expression that softens into something warmer as our eyes meet.

He takes a step toward me, just as his phone pings with a notification of someone at the door. Oliver clears his throat. "I'll get that," he says, heading off.

As much as I don't want to move, I force myself up before the movers catch me sprawled across the bed. I glance into the adjoining bathroom and closet, marveling at the space. The closet is much bigger than my old one. More than enough room for my stuff.

I hear heavy footsteps and voices approaching, so I step back into the bedroom. The movers file in, taking directions from me as I point out where everything should go.

Just then, my phone buzzes. Declan. I move out to the hallway, with Oliver following. "Hi."

"Hey, just thought I'd check in," he says, a bit stiffly. "I'm at the airport now."

I swallow the lump that's formed in my throat from the guilt. What will he think when he finds out I've married Oliver for real? "Well, I won't be home tonight." I glance at Oliver, who's arching an eyebrow in curiosity.

My brother's voice drops, sounding weary. "Maybe we can meet up later?"

Oliver catches my gaze and mouths, *invite him for dinner.*

I fight the urge to roll my eyes, but I know if Declan sees me safe and happy, he'll be fine with this arrangement.

"Would you want to come over for dinner next week?" I ask.

Oliver nods as he gestures to the kitchen, whispering, *make it a family dinner, Armani included.*

My eyes widen at the suggestion. Inviting Armani changes everything... It makes this feel like a real family gathering, not just an awkward catch-up with my brother.

"Uh, sure. Let's do it," Declan says finally. "I have to go, sorry, I'll call you tomorrow."

When I hang up, a sudden, awkward tension settles over me.

Oliver looks at me. "Make sure Evelyn comes too."

I nod as I process having everyone together in one room. I'm going to choose to look at this as an exciting dinner, because it'll be fun to have all of my loved ones eating together, which leads me to say, "And I'll ask Amber and Wren. I know they'll want to see where I'm living, too." Yes, this will be good. Right?

Oliver rubs the back of his neck, tilting his head as he looks at me. "Meeting the parents."

"Yeah, but you usually do it before you tie the knot."

CHAPTER 14

KARLEY

THE MOVERS LEAVE, AND everything's finally put away. I sit on the edge of my new bed, taking a deep breath, about to call my adopted parents to invite them over, knowing they'll be happy to visit to check on me and meet Oliver. I'm unlocking my phone when Oliver gently knocks on the door.

"Hey, roomie. How are you settling in?" He leans against the door frame, looking more relaxed than I've ever seen him. His hair slightly disheveled, like he's been running his hands through it, and there's a softness to his expression that makes my heart flutter traitorously.

"I've been here for two minutes," I say with a half-smile. "I'll need a bit more time to answer that."

He chuckles, lifting off the door frame to pace the room for a moment before stopping in front of me, holding out a set of keys. "Here are the keys to the Aston, the house, anything else you might need."

My mouth parts as I look up at him, surprised by the gesture. There's something so trusting about it, handing over access to everything he owns. He jingles them, so I walk up to take them, feeling the weight of each one. There's something strangely comforting in this small moment. Like I'm stepping into a new chapter, even if it feels unfamiliar.

"Sunday nights, I usually go to my grams' for dinner," he says, scratching the back of his head. "Would you like to come?"

Warmth spreads through my chest at the invitation. It's unexpected, and I'm happy at the thought of being included, but just as quickly, the warmth is replaced by a heavy feeling. I don't know if I can sit across from his family, especially his mom, the woman I admire so much, and pretend that everything's normal. Seeing her passing the halls at school is enough; sitting down to dinner feels like too much, too soon. "But... your family doesn't know about our arrangement."

"I can bring a friend," he says, offering a soft smile.

"Thanks, Oliver, but it's been a long weekend. Meeting all your family is... a lot for me right now," I admit gently.

He nods, looking thoughtful. "I didn't think about that. Sorry."

"It's alright." I manage a reassuring smile. "I just need a little time to settle in."

"Promise you'll wait for me to watch episode three?" he asks, raising an eyebrow, trying to lighten the mood.

A grin slips onto my face. "Deal."

"I won't be late."

"Stay as long as you want," I reply softly, as he turns to leave. "I'll be here."

His footsteps take the stairs, and the door opens and closes, leaving me in his house alone.

I quickly call my adopted parents, and then I take the chance to explore without his watchful eyes. The main floor is big, polished, and filled with fully furnished rooms, where many feature art pieces where you'd expect beds. *He really does love art*, I think, smiling slightly. There's something comforting about that. I understand him a little more now, and maybe, in some small way, he gets me too.

At the top floor, I find a bright office with an incredible view of the skyline that pulls me in. The sun beams down through the large window, illuminating his desk, bookshelves, and drafting table. I turn and then freeze.

There is... *my* painting, one of my first, the one I'd done back at his mom's school. A large pink peony with two big bumble bees. Does he realize it's mine? No, because I don't sign it. The idea of putting my name on a piece of work still paralyzes me. My heart pounds as I stare at it, hanging on the wall opposite his desk, where he would see it every day. A part of me was already in his home unknowingly, and warmth seeps into my chest at the thought.

My stomach growls. With one last look at my painting, I head downstairs to the kitchen, running my hand over the smooth marble counter, admiring all the high-end appliances. I grab a packet of chocolate chip cookies that I brought with me, pour myself some milk, warm it up, and sit with them.

The taste of the cookies brings me back to my adopted parents and the way they used to ease my anxieties with milk and cookies. I wonder if he ever feels alone in this big house... The thought sticks with me. The clink of my wedding ring against the mug pulls me back to reality. If you'd told me six months ago I'd marry him, I'd be overjoyed. But this isn't real; it's an arrangement that benefits us both.

Finishing up the snack, I put the cup in the dishwasher and head to the living room. I sit on the sofa, and as I turn on the TV to a makeover show, making me think about the house I'm about to buy, I get a text message.

> **Oliver:** *You better not be watching that show without me.*

I smile, glancing around as if he might be watching before texting back.

Me: *No, I'm waiting for you. Stop in-terrupting my peace.* ☒

My stomach flips; it's a lie, but also somehow true. There's a strange comfort in this house, yet it stirs up old memories of empty rooms and cold nights. I settle back, focusing on the present, the soft cushions beneath me, the expensive throw blanket in my hands, and the roof above me that won't suddenly disappear.

When one episode finishes, I scroll to find another renovation show. I'm ten minutes into that episode when I hear the front door open.

I sit up, brushing off my lap, feeling like an intruder.

He comes into the room, his cheeks slightly flushed and his hair messy from the cool evening air.

"Did you miss me?" He shrugs off his jacket.

I bite the inside of my cheek to prevent a big, stupid smile at his playfulness.

"You were gone for just over an hour, barely enough time to watch a movie." I try to keep my tone light, but I can feel the heat creeping up my neck, and from the way his eyes glint, I know he sees it.

"I had someone to get home to tonight," he says as he walks closer to me.

My heart skips, but I remind myself, *he's just here to watch the TV show, nothing more.*

"I brought you something." He holds up food on a plate. "My grams' banana cream pie."

I stare at the plate, feeling touched. He thought of me while he was with his family. Brought this back like I belonged somehow. I've never had anything like that before. I get up to join him in the kitchen, expecting to eat it there, but he motions for us to head to the sofa with the plates. "Come on, I've been dying to watch the next episode." He nudges me over.

I return to my spot on the sofa. Yes, I'm claiming this part of the sofa as mine. He hands me a plate, and I dig in, savoring the sugary taste. Settling in beside me, he grabs the remote to start the next episode of our show.

We watch in comfortable silence, both focused on the show as I enjoy dessert. When I finish, I put the plate on the coffee table, feeling full. Without warning, he grabs the throw and tucks it around me. His hands brush against the outside of my thighs, hips, and then waist. It feels nice to be cared for, even in this small way. When he's finished, I give him a shy smile.

To my surprise, he sits closer. I think about moving away to keep a careful distance, but the warmth of him beside me is comforting, and I'm tired of always being guarded. Just for tonight, I allow myself this.

I try to concentrate on the episode, but I'm annoyed when my mind keeps drifting to his side against mine. I breathe in, letting myself feel it, a small comfort I didn't realize I needed. When was the last time I let myself relax around a guy, accept their touch, and give in to my desire? *A long time...*

As the episode ends, I glance over and see his head resting next to mine. This suddenly feels too close to something I might want and can't have. Gently, I push the blanket off and stand up. "Alright. I'm off to bed. I have school and work tomorrow."

He sits up, stretching his arms above his head. "Yeah, I'll be up early for a workout and then heading to work. I might not catch you before I leave."

"That's okay. I'll be fine without you."

He nods, but there's something in his gaze, like he's trying to read me. It reminds me of how Declan looks at me sometimes, trying to figure out if I'm really okay or just pretending to be.

"Don't be like my brother," I say, trying to keep it playful as I walk off.

"I'm not looking at you like you're my sister," he murmurs, low enough that I almost miss it. My heart stumbles over itself as I make a beeline for the stairs and head to my room, his words replaying in my head, making it impossible to shake the flustered feeling they leave behind.

I get up, the cool air hitting my skin as I shuffle toward the kitchen. My oversized t-shirt falls just above my knees, and my thong is the only other thing on my body. I need a drink. Something cold. My feet barely make a sound on the wood floor as I cross the dimly lit living room, the silence broken only by the hum of the fridge. I open the door, reaching for the glass, but before I can fill it, his voice, rough and unexpected, cuts through the quiet.

"I couldn't sleep either."

I freeze, my heart slamming into my ribs. My hand trembles as I grip the glass, and he steps out from the shadowed corner of the kitchen, his figure still half lost in the dimness. But I can make out the mess of his hair, the slight tug of his jaw as he watches me. His eyes are heavy-lidded, hooded with sleep, or maybe something else, and they lock onto mine with a force that makes my chest tighten.

I blink, fighting the sudden dizziness, and for a second, I think I must be dreaming. His presence feels too real, too electric.

"I just needed a drink." I force the words through a scratchy throat, trying to hold on to some normalcy. My voice feels raw, barely there.

The space between us feels charged, an invisible pull that I can feel in my bones. My mouth's dry. I swallow, almost painfully, but my lips betray me as they instinctively part, taking in the sight of him. He's so fucking beautiful, it's almost painful to look at.

His eyebrows raise slightly, his lips curling into something like amusement, and I realize, to my horror, that I've said that out loud. I want to die.

"I could say the same about you."

My breath catches in my throat as he takes a step closer. His gaze never leaves mine, the weight of it pressing on me, making it impossible to look anywhere else. My chest rises and falls with every shallow breath and, suddenly, it feels like there's not enough air in the room.

Just a taste. My pulse thrums in my ears, the ache between my legs undeniable. It's too much now, his warmth wrapping around me. I want him. I ache for him.

He's standing so close now, toe to toe, the heat of his body radiating toward me, and my skin hums in response. His fingers graze my cheek so gently, I feel it like a jolt to my system. Slowly, as if testing the limits, his hand slides under my chin, tilting my head back, forcing me to meet his gaze.

"What woke you up?" he whispers, but it lands like a command.

I swallow, my throat tight with something I can't name. "Just a nightmare. Nothing. Really. Just my stupid past."

The words are a lie, but I can't seem to stop them from spilling out. I keep my eyes on him, feeling the soft burn of his fingers as they trail down the length of my throat, brushing over the skin beneath the neck of my t-shirt. The feeling spreads throughout my body, tightening my chest, my breath hitching.

I wish I was wearing his t-shirt, *I think, my body betraying me with the thought.*

"Maybe I should give one to you," he says, with an edge I can't quite place.

God, what is he doing to me?

He's still holding my chin, his thumb now brushing over my pulse. I can't stop myself from shuddering. His touch is like fire, gentle but scorching, like he's mapping out every inch of me.

I breathe in. But it feels like I'm suffocating.

I shouldn't want this. I shouldn't want him. I don't have the strength to fight it, but I know I should. The words are there, on the tip of my tongue, but they won't come.

He teases, leaning in, just close enough that I can feel his breath on my skin.

"You want me."

I nod; a silent admission. And that's the moment it breaks everything I've held back, every little piece of control I had slipping away. I want him, all of him. And he knows it.

"I've always wanted you."

My eyes close as he continues spilling words I've been desperate to hear. "I've wanted you since that party. Do you know how hard it was to push you away?"

"Are you gonna push me away now?" I breathe out a challenge, desperately wanting him to prove me wrong.

"Fuck no, I've wanted you for too long."

And then, his lips are on mine, taking my breath away. It's a violent rush of teeth, lips, and tongue as we immediately consume each other. "Fuck," he mumbles into my mouth between kisses.

I should stop... This is going to be messy in the morning, but worse, I'll be left heartbroken when he admits he made a mistake.

But my mind replays the words I've craved for years. I've wanted you since that party. Do you know how hard it was to push you away?

My core aches. I'm wet, hungry, and I can't stop my fingers from moving across his chest, touching everything like I'll never have it again. His hot skin, soft hair, the ripples of his strong chest, I drag my fingers down each bump of muscle until I reach his boxers.

"Karley, touch me," he commands.

"Only if you touch me too."

His fingers skim the top of my thigh, lifting my t-shirt, and as his hand slips under my cotton thong, grazing the wet heat between my legs, I quiver.

As he sinks two fingers in, I have to really concentrate and push through the moan to touch him. My fingers slip beneath his waistband, touching his hard cock.

He groans before bringing his lips back to mine. The gentleness catches me off guard. This isn't a calculated kiss like the chapel, but something raw that makes my legs weak and my walls begin to crumble.

I arch into his hand, craving more.

"So fucking wet," he says.

"So hard," I breathe.

"All for you."

My eyes involuntarily roll back in my head and my legs wobble. I'm struggling to hold myself up as my orgasm builds. I grip his shoulders with one hand and stroke him with the other. He's growing thicker in my hands. I feel pre-cum on my fingers, so I use it to rub him.

He jerks in my hand. "Fuck, yes."

His two fingers inside me move faster, rubbing along my front wall. I gasp for air as I almost beg for him to let me go when he says more words I've been dying to hear.

"Come for me," he demands. "Give yourself to me. I'll look after you."

My back lifts as the orgasm washes over me, and I cry out, hearing him call me beautiful.

The next morning, after an eventful night of wet dreaming, my hand reaches out to the nightstand, where something catches my eye. A paper bag, a coffee cup, and a folded note. The coffee is still warm when I take a sip. Inside the bag is a bagel sandwich wrapped in foil. I unfold the note and can't help but smile.

Brought you breakfast. Hubby xo

My cheeks warm at the signature.

The rest of the day passes in a blur of classes and avoiding Evelyn's questions.

"You look different," she kept saying, studying my face. *"Something happened."*

I told her about the new living arrangements, the house, and cars. The subtle touches and long looks replayed in my mind all day. By afternoon, I'm exhausted from pretending they hadn't shaken me.

Now back at Oliver's, I open the cupboard and look inside to find something to make for dinner. I scrunch up my nose, disgusted as I pick up something that has the word "fermented" written on it.

The air shifts behind me, and I know it's him before he speaks. "I don't hide dead bodies in there."

I snort, pulling back out of the cupboard to glance over my shoulder, spearing him with a look. My pulse quickens at the sight of him still in his work clothes. Dark pants, a white shirt buttoned down with the sleeves rolled up. "I'm not looking for your dirty secrets. I'm looking for food."

He steps closer. I straighten, suddenly aware of how small the kitchen feels with him in it.

"There're heaps of food."

I raise my eyebrow. "Is that why you left me a store-bought breakfast bagel sandwich and a coffee?"

He opens and closes his mouth as his eyes dance with amusement.

"I'll head to the store. Is there anything in particular you want for dinner?" I ask, smiling as I close the pantry door.

He tilts his head with a deep scowl. "What food do you need?"

I shrug. "Normal things, like pasta, cereal, milk, fish, rice, and snacks."

His eyes flick to the closed cupboard, then back to me. "I have that."

"It's okay. I want to grab a few other things anyway." I brush past him to my purse. He doesn't move, so my body skims his.

"I'll come with you."

I wave him off as I sling the bag on my shoulder. "It's okay. I'll be back shortly."

I don't need to spend more alone time with him. The sexy dream I had of him last night is enough to tell me I need some space. He's clearly getting in my head.

"No, I've got nothing else to do."

Really? I suck in a breath as he grabs his keys and gives me no choice, heading to his Aston Martin.

"How was your day?" he asks, breaking the silence as he opens the door, holding it open for me to climb in.

"Good," I answer automatically, like I usually do when my brother asks me, knowing he doesn't really want to know; he just feels the need to ask, to make sure nothing bad happened.

He closes the door as I buckle in, and he climbs into the driver's seat. "What was good about it?"

I look over at him, his eyes on the road as we drive out of his lot.

But he glances over at me with a soft expression, and it makes my stomach flutter weirdly.

"It was fun. We had to draw the start of something, then the teacher sent us out to grab a drink. When we returned, she mixed up the canvases and told us to finish the drawing."

The challenge of picking up where someone else left off, of finding the balance between their vision and mine, was exactly what I needed.

"That actually does sound fun. What did you draw?"

I smile as I stare out the car window, watching the people pass on the sidewalk, wondering why we didn't walk, but also grateful I can get home and eat faster as my stomach churns in on itself. "A side-view picture of a woman."

"Did you find out who had whose?" He parks the car in the busy parking lot.

"Yeah, we did." Stepping out, the cool air whips around my arms, and I regret not bringing a sweater; the cami isn't enough. I briskly walk to the entrance as he follows.

I move to the shopping cart, and he veers toward the basket.

I laugh. "We need a cart."

His eyebrow lifts higher as he strides to me, taking the cart, our hands briefly touching and sending that spark through me again. "I thought you said we only need a few things."

"We do, but I just like pushing a cart around," I say as I direct him to the first aisle.

We walk side by side, my eyes scanning for things I like.

I'm a fussy eater, so I need comfort foods or meals that feel familiar.

I throw in sugary cereal, but he picks up the package, turning it to the side to read the label.

"Do you even know how to pronounce the ingredients?" He tosses it in the cart.

"Hey, be careful," I scold, shaking my head.

He stares at the box like it's poison. "The ingredient list is a mile long and the main ones are sugar and food dye."

I nod proudly. "Exactly. The perfect comfort food."

He ignores me and snatches a box off the shelf, comes back to me, and holds it out for me.

I take it, reading its ingredients, ancient grains, and flaxseed and chia clusters.

"This is better."

I squint at the box. "This is rabbit food."

He sniffs his nose in the air. "That's because rabbits have excellent taste."

Eyebrow raised, I point at his chest. "You're really walking around here calling me out when you're eating rabbit food?"

He looks at me, straight faced. "Rabbits would never touch those refined sugar treats."

I hold the box up, smirking. "I'll stick to this for now, but throw that in the cart if you want it for you."

Turning, I head to the next aisle to grab some instant noodles, thinking that would be a great choice for tonight's dinner.

He's grumbling something about processed food, but I'm already walking away to grab snacks.

My arms are full of different chip bags.

His face is sour as he eyes them.

"Stop judging me." I lower the bags into the trolly, spotting his organic selection of foods. Kale, apples, broccoli, potatoes, meat, and something fermented in a jar.

"Too late." His eyes drop, and he leans in, picking up a family bag of sour cream and onion chips. "This is what you call food?"

I mock gasp as I snatch the bag, clutching it to my chest and patting it like a newborn baby. "Food? These are the most delicious life-saving snacks."

"If your life depends on processed foods, maybe reevaluate your choices."

I lower the bag gently into the cart. "Don't start with me, Mr. Organic." Rolling my eyes, I pick up a bag of quinoa. "You know who eats this? People who pretend to like it."

He snorts a laugh as his eyes lock with mine. A silent battle, but there's something that makes my toes curl inside my shoes. A flicker of heat... Or am I imagining it?

"You say that now." His voice pulls me back to our argument. "But when your blood sugar crashes from all that processed shit, you'll be begging for my quinoa salad."

I wave him off and grab a packet of mac and cheese. "If it takes me having a blood sugar crash to eat quinoa, just let me go."

We make our way to the produce. I go to the red apples that are on sale, grabbing five and dropping them in a bag.

"These look good. See, I can do healthy." I wink at him.

Before I put the last one in, he grabs my hand and takes the apple from me to hold it up, the light catching on the skin. "They're coated in wax and pesticides."

I meet his pinched face with a smirk. "They're coated in deliciousness. Plus, nothing a wash can't fix."

He grabs one from the shelf, holding it up in the air like a gem. "This is an apple. One free of wax and pesticides." He bites into it like a TV commercial, and I'm a little transfixed as juice trickles out of his mouth, but his tongue swipes it up quickly.

Daring me to try it, he holds it out for me. Because I want to prove him wrong, I take a bite and chew it slowly, glaring at him. "It tastes the same, but mine isn't triple the price."

He leans in, eyes narrowed. "You just don't have a refined palate."

My hand lands on my chest in mock horror. "Okay, fancy pants. Next, you'll be trying to tell me to drink sparkling water."

He grins. "Actually, I drink Kombucha."

I throw my hands up with a giggle. "Oh, well, that explains everything." I spin around, ready to check out. "I'm done with your organic, quinoa, kombucha, fermented self. I'm ready to go home. You coming?"

"Did you try my fermented tea or yogurt?" His footsteps follow behind.

"Hell no," I reply, not looking back as I head to the empty register, but as I do, I reach for more peanut butter. I grab the generic brand, and he goes for the organic.

"This one," I say.

"Not happening," he argues, shaking his head.

"I saw it first," I argue, gripping the jar tighter in my fingers.

"We can get both."

"That's a waste."

"They say marriage is all about compromise."

"Fine," I say with a huff, putting my peanut butter jar in the cart.

"See? Compromise. I win."

I'll show him who wins. Glaring at him, I grab the marshmallow fluff off the shelf and some cookies and put them in the cart. His jaw works, and I expect a comeback at my petty response.

"And I win," I say triumphantly, straightening my spine.

He cocks an eyebrow. "What will you do with that stuff?"

"I'm going to eat it and think of you with every bite." I smirk.

His eyes glint as they lock on mine. "Be careful," he warns. "You might start craving me too."

I already do, but I don't tell him that. "I'd rather crave rabbit food."

He steps closer, the teasing in his voice is gone and replaced by an edge. "Keep telling yourself that."

My heart skips; just once. I hate that he knows what I'm feeling. I spin the cart around with way more force than necessary, walking off with my head high, calling over my shoulder without looking back. "Last one to the checkout pays."

"Don't start what you can't finish, wife."

We are side by side at the checkout, unloading our crazy haul of groceries onto the conveyor belt, organic kale next to rainbow cereal, two peanut butter, apples, instant noodles, fermented foods, quinoa next to marshmallow fluff. It's utter chaos, like us.

When I turn, I catch him watching me. There's something soft in his gaze that makes my skin warm.

"What?" I ask.

He shrugs. "Nothing."

I glance at him for a moment longer than I should before I roll my eyes, turning back to the groceries, muttering, "Weirdo."

He speaks under his breath so the cashier can't hear him. "Yeah. You too." A smile tugs at my lips despite my efforts to hide it.

As we exit the store with our bags, it's raining heavily. I'm not scared of a bit of rain, so I begin walking into the thick of it to get to the car.

But the wind picks up, and I struggle to see in front of me. I spot an awning and make a beeline for it.

My cami is sticking to my body, but I have a bag close to my chest. His white top clings to his muscles like a second skin. His forearms glisten from water. I look away to stop myself from staring at him as I wait for the storm to pass.

"Fucking hell," he spits.

I adjust the bags in my arms, and one of them bursts open, the contents going in different directions. Cursing,

I rush to grab them, but he snatches my wrist just as I'm about to take a step.

"Don't," he says.

I freeze. My heart skips a beat at the unexpected touch. I look at him, my hair sticking to my face. His blue eyes are intense, and his jaw is set in a way that suggests he's not going to back down.

"I'll be quick," I say.

He holds my gaze for a second, his thumb brushing gently over my wrist where he's holding me. The rain beats down harder.

"You're not going out there," he says. "I'll go."

I look down at his hand and then back up to his face. "I'm fine." I need to prove I can handle this myself. It's a small thing, but it matters. I've been taking care of myself for so long that accepting help, even for something trivial, feels like surrendering a piece of my independence.

I try to pull away, but he doesn't let go. Instead, he steps closer. "Please don't."

His eyes drop to my cami, then flick back up to my face, and there's a darkness there that makes me shiver in the best way.

I swallow roughly, trying to regain some composure, but the pull between us is undeniable now.

"You're really bossy for a guy who spent twenty minutes picking out overpriced apples."

His lips curve into a smile, but there's something deeper in his expression now. "And you're really stubborn for a woman who's about to catch a cold over sugar."

He doesn't move back, his hand still gently holding my wrist, though he's aware of how close we are. His thumb absently traces a small circle against my skin, sending an electric current up my arm.

I look up at him, my eyes searching his face, and what I see makes my breath catch. The usual guarded confidence is gone, replaced by something vulnerable. His eyes have softened at the corners, pupils dilated against the blue. There's a slight furrow between his eyebrows, not of frustration but of restraint, like he's fighting an internal battle. His lips are slightly parted, and the muscle in his jaw twitches. For a split second, the distance between us seems to shrink. The playful barrier has cracked, leaving something raw in its place.

"You're making this weird," I finally whisper.

He swallows, his fingers tightening around my arm just slightly, enough to make my skin tingle.

"I'm not trying to make it weird. Just..." He pauses.

"I can do it. Stop trying to be my hero." I try to sound casual despite the confusing flutter in my chest.

He lets out a breath, a small chuckle breaking the intensity of the moment.

"Okay, okay. I'll hold the bags. You go."

He steps back slightly, releasing my wrist but lingering close.

A small, relieved laugh slips from my lips, even though my pulse is still racing. "I'll make this quick."

He nods as his lips curve up.

I sprint out into the rain. My feet slip slightly on the wet pavement, but I catch myself and keep going, refusing to give up.

I reach the cookie package just as it begins to slide toward the gutter. My cold, wet fingers close around it just in time. I hold it up like a trophy, the rain pouring down on my face.

"Got it," I yell, but my breaths come faster. My heartbeat is a little more erratic from the chase. I scan the concrete, spot both peanut butters and kale, and snatch them up.

When I turn to head back, I'm startled to find Oliver still standing under the awning... He listened to me, and that sends an expected warmth through me despite the cold rain.

I'm out of breath, and my soaked clothes cling to me in a way that makes me feel naked. He watches me, his clothes wet too, his abs visible through his shirt, and the way the rain beads on his skin makes me want to lick him all over. When I'm back under the awning, my focus stays on the food, but he's looking at me differently. There's something in his eyes, something that wasn't there before. It makes my pulse spike. I find myself shifting slightly, a subtle motion I can't quite explain.

He's a little hesitant, the teasing smile from earlier fading.

"You really risked your life for those?" He says it almost absently, his voice rougher than it should be.

My heart skips again, but I can't tell if it's from the run or something else. I smile, shaking the water from my hair.

"For the record, I saved your food, too." I glance at his groceries, his precious kale and peanut butter still intact.

All of a sudden, rain falls harder.

He pulls me gently back toward the awning, my body now pressed against his as I stumble slightly. We're close... so close. I can feel his warmth against me. His hand is still wrapped around me, but it feels like something more.

"You risked hypothermia for that?" He gestures at the dripping packages.

I sniff, hugging the cookies to my chest. "They're delicious."

As we stand, the humor fades. He looks at me, water dripping from my hair and face.

"You really don't care, do you?" he rasps.

I frown, glancing up at him, unsure of how to handle the shift. I try to shake it off with a laugh. "Care about what?"

"About what you eat, what you spend money on. You just... go for whatever's easiest and cheapest."

My smile drops a bit and I straighten as it hits me in the stomach. "Not all of us grew up with the luxury of being picky. Sometimes you take what you can get."

He falters. "I didn't mean—" he starts.

"Yeah, you did." I brush past him, ready to get out of here.

He hesitates, then follows me into the rain, the bags still in his arms. "Wait."

I keep walking, muttering, "Just drop it, okay?"

He stops me with a hand on my arm, his voice firm but not unkind. "That's not what I meant."

I turn to face him, the rain causing my hair to stick to my face. "Then what did you mean?"

He looks at me, something unspoken passing between us. Finally, he sighs. "I just... You deserve better."

My expression softens at his unexpected sincerity, but I quickly cover it with sarcasm. "So, what, kale is supposed to fix my life?"

He smirks faintly, his hand still on my arm. "Maybe not. But it pains me to think that you've had to struggle."

I pull away gently, shaking my head. "There's so many kids who grew up without, not just me."

He watches me for a beat, then shrugs lightly. "Yeah, but I'm not standing here with them. I'm standing here with you."

I turn and walk to his car, mulling over his words. *You deserve better.* Maybe trying his fancy kale wouldn't be the worst thing in the world. Not because I think it'll magically improve my life, but because there's something touching about his concern. And I'm curious about the things that matter to him.

As we get to the trunk, I finally break the silence, realizing I was childish with my outburst, and I want to bring back the peace between us.

"You know... I might try kale. Just once."

He grins. "See? I'm rubbing off on you."

I glance at him sideways, fighting back a smile as I playfully bump his arm with mine. "Don't push your luck."

He closes the trunk, and we climb into the car. Memories spill from my lips as we settle inside, and I keep my eyes forward, watching the rain hit the glass. "We didn't really get storms like this in the foster homes. The roof would leak even if it was just drizzling. I used to pray it wouldn't rain, just so my bed stayed dry."

He pauses, twisting to look at me. "You never told me that."

I shrug, trying to brush it off. "Not really the type of thing you bring up, is it?"

A tingle sweeps up the back of my neck and across my face as soon as the words leave my mouth. I don't know why I shared that. Something about him is making me slip up, and I'm not sure if I'm grateful or terrified. I risk a glance at him, expecting pity, but find only quiet understanding in his eyes.

"Thank you," he says simply, starting the car. "For telling me more about your past."

We drive in silence for a few minutes, but it's not uncomfortable. The rain starts to ease up, but the moment still lingers between us.

At home, we gather the bags and walk inside. I smirk. "I'll make dinner. But only if you promise not to lecture me about kale."

He pauses at the island, giving me a sidelong glance. "Sold."

I hide my glee, knowing he's about to eat the most processed instant noodles, and I'll make him love every second of it.

CHAPTER 15

KARLEY

As I step out of Hugh's office, my heart pounds. I put down a payment on the house... *My house*. After months of dreaming, of saving every penny, it's finally happening, thanks to this fake arrangement with Oliver.

My phone buzzes in my hand. Speaking of Oliver...

> **Oliver:** *Do you have time to teach me how to paint? I want a lesson.*

> **Me:** *Why? You know your mom could give you professional lessons.*

> **Oliver:** *She's busy and I would prefer my wife.*

My fingers hover over the screen, my stomach doing a little flip. There's something unexpectedly sweet about him choosing me. Like he actually wants me there.

> **Oliver:** *It'll make for good social pics. Warne will see them.*

I can almost see him typing that second message quickly, as if he needed to justify the first one to himself as much as to me. Sometimes it's too easy to forget this is all for show.

> **Me:** *Could you come by Tills tonight before my 6pm class starts?*

> **Oliver:** *I'll be there. Do you need me to bring anything?*

I hesitate, then decide to share my news. It feels important that he knows since he's the reason it's happening at all.

> **Me:** *No, but I just paid the down payment on the house. It's really happening.*

There's a brief pause before his reply comes through.

> **Oliver:** *Congratulations!*

I stare at the word longer than I should, tucking my phone away before I can overthink anything, and then head to work.

The hours crawl by, and before I know it, it's nearly five in the evening. I'm already at the studio, the light outside starting to shift.

I set up a station and lay out all the tools he might need, checking everything twice. I tap my finger on the edge of the table, wondering if there's something I've forgotten, but a knock at the door pulls me out of my thoughts.

I open it to find him standing there in his work uniform.

"Didn't have time to change," he answers my silent question as he steps through the door and heads straight to the small easel on the table.

"You better focus if you don't want to get paint on that suit." I close the door and watch as he sits down.

"If I'm as careful with the paint as you are with your instructions," he says with a wry smile, "I'm sure I'll walk out of here without having to throw away this suit."

My mouth drops, and a small, pained noise leaves my mouth. "You wouldn't throw it away."

He shrugs. "My cleaner has tried before, but the paint won't come out."

"I could get it out at home." My lips slam shut.

We lock eyes, and it's like an elephant in the room. *Home...*

"What will I do when you leave?" he says, playfully poking my arm. The thought of walking away from this house, from him, creates an unexpected hollowness in my chest.

"Find my replacement," I joke, but it dies on my tongue when he speaks.

His expression shifts into something more vulnerable. "You're irreplaceable."

Is this still part of our act, or something else? If I let myself believe it's the latter, it would make leaving so much harder when the time comes.

I pretend his words didn't make me shudder and focus on the task; otherwise, we'll run late.

"I've chosen a painting for you to save time," I say, turning to face the setup.

"Is it easy? I need easy," he says from behind me.

I twist to face him, lifting my eyebrow. "Oliver, when the hell have you taken the easy option?"

He points to the floor. "Now. I need to be good at art."

"Everyone is good at art."

He crosses his arms. "Not according to Warne."

"Art isn't about perfection; it's about feeling." I walk to the canvas I've prepared on the easel in the corner of the classroom, where I've sketched the outline of a tree similar to the one hanging in his bedroom. He walks over to get a better look. "How does that make you feel?"

"It makes me feel like everything's going to be okay." He straightens, and I face him with a small smile.

My heart is trying to jump out of my chest. Not from anxiety or fear, but from the realization that Oliver might be seeing me in a way few people ever have.

"Good." I clasp my hands together to hold back my excitement.

He exhales heavily, looking around at the brushes. "Tell me where to start."

I point to the chair. "Take a seat, and I'll explain."

He does and so do I. Then, grabbing the pencil, I hand it to him. "I would outline the tree first."

He takes the pencil, and just as I think he's going to begin, he lowers it and twists to look at me. "I can't have you watching me. It's adding too much pressure."

"Alright, I'll start setting up for the class. Would that make you more comfortable?" I've always hated when people hover while I paint; the pressure and judgment. But another part of me is curious to see his process.

"Yes. Thank you." He brings the pencil up, and the scratching along the paper has a calming effect on me. I move around every now and then, glancing over to see him. Finding his lips parted, head close to the paper, and his eyebrows pinched. I snap a picture for him before returning to my task.

"Done," he announces a little while later. I walk over to check it out, and he's done a pretty good job.

I give him a genuine smile. "Nice. Now it's time to paint." I point to the tray full of different colored paint.

"You can stay for this if you want," he says so quietly I almost miss it.

Of course I want to see, so I quickly take my seat before he changes his mind and watch him dip the brush into the green paint. I get lost in his strokes, and I don't know how much time passes, but when he's done, I feel like I was suddenly woken up from a trance. The tree is technically not perfect, but there's heart in it. I take a picture of his work and then one with him and the painting. Then he snaps a picture of us with the art to put online for Mr. Warne to see.

"Can I take it home?" He looks at the canvas, then back at me, his eyes searching, as if my answer matters.

I lean my elbow on the table, holding my head in my hand, feeling content in this shared moment. "Yeah, you can. Just be careful for a few hours while it dries."

"Noted, thanks."

We lock eyes, and the room feels hotter. His blue gaze burns brighter, neither of us looking away.

"I better finish getting ready," I breathe out, suddenly aware that the class will arrive soon. I stand, but just as I turn, his fingers curl around my wrist, pulling me back gently so I land in his lap, my heart racing immediately.

Our eyes lock. His face is inches from mine, his breath warm on my lips. I'm aware of how little time we have before people arrive, but right now, I don't care.

"Fuck, Karley," he mutters, as if he's in pain.

"What?" I whisper.

He grabs my chin and brings his lips to mine, capturing my gasp into his mouth. The first touch sends electricity through me. When his tongue meets mine, tasting of mint, I melt against him.

I slide my hands into his hair and pull him closer. His hands move to my hips. Things are escalating, and there's no way to stop myself. I've wanted him for so long, and it's even better than any dream I've had. We're crossing a line we can't uncross, and it complicates our arrangement in ways I'm not ready to think about. His mouth controls the pace, which is slow yet strong. I follow it easily.

The chatter of the group outside jerks me out of his lap and into reality. *What was I thinking?* I almost trip over his leg, trying to straighten myself. I knock a few paintbrushes on the floor, and when I lean down to grab them, my hands fumble picking them up and a brush grazes my cheek.

He chuckles as he rises from the chair. Breathless, I shoot him a look that says *shut up*.

Flustered, I move to the door and open it, so he can leave and the group can come in. He follows, and I look at the door frame, hoping to avoid his eyes. Too scared to see regret in them. My breath hitches when he steps closer, his hand touching my face, bringing my eyes to his. What I see staring back makes my knees buckle. A longing fire. One that matches my own.

I realize he kissed me. He initiated it. What does that mean, and where does that leave us?

"Come here," he says, his voice pulling me out of my thoughts and back to the present.

My eyebrows pinch as I step closer to him.

"You have paint here." His hand grabs the back of my head as his thumb rubs along my cheek. I swallow roughly, his smell cocooning me and making me melt with its familiarity.

My lips are parted, but no words leave them.

He leans forward, capturing my lips in an all too brief kiss, and then winks at me before leaving with his painting.

I watch the second group of the night head out one by one, their laughter lingering in the distance, and with a sigh, I grab a rag and start wiping down the table. But my mind is miles away, replaying tonight's kiss with Oliver. I can't hold it in any longer; I need to talk to someone. Pulling out my phone, I dial Evelyn's number.

She picks up after the first ring. "Hey? I'm at work. What's up?"

My palm flies to my forehead. "I'm sorry, I can let you go," I say, though I can hear the desperation in my voice.

"No, it's okay," she says quickly. "I've got five."

I take a deep breath, barely able to contain my excitement. "Oliver kissed me."

There's a split-second pause. Then she lets out a short laugh. "Karley! I said quick, but don't skip details. How did this happen?"

I laugh, sinking into the chair Oliver was in just a few hours ago. My hand brushes over the table where his fingers had rested, and a warm thrill runs up my spine. "He asked me to give him a painting lesson. He needs to show the gallery owner he doesn't just pretend to like art."

Evelyn chuckles. "I'm a little lost, but keep going. I want to get to the good bit."

"Well..." I say, my cheeks growing warm, "we were sitting next to each other while he painted, and then...I got up to walk away. That's when he grabbed my wrist and pulled me into his lap."

"Oooh," she whispers. "And then you kissed him?"

"No, that's the thing," I whisper, as if speaking it out loud would somehow lessen the magic. "He kissed me."

"That's amazing, Karley. I'm so happy for you."

"Relax," I say, trying to keep my voice steady, but the grin spreading on my face betrays me. "It was just a kiss."

"Uh-huh. And... how was it?"

I close my eyes as memories flood back, the heat, the intensity, the feel of his lips on mine. How was it?

Hot.

Sensual.

Addictive.

Passionate.

"Everything I hoped for," I whisper.

"Damn, girl!" She laughs. "Can you imagine if he'd been a sloppy mess? Imagine your crush kissing like a frog?"

I wince, laughing. "Ugh, gross. But he was nothing like that. It was... perfect."

"So..." she says slyly. "Are you going home to him now? What's going to happen next?"

My heart pounds at the thought of stepping back into the house, finding him waiting up for me, the possibility of feeling his lips on mine again. Nerves swarm my stomach. "I don't know."

"Do what feels comfortable," she says. "But I better get back to work before I get fired."

"Thanks for risking your job for me," I say, my heart full.

"For you, anytime."

I hang up and finish cleaning, my mind replaying our kiss. As I head out, I quickly call Amber and check in.

Just calm down, I tell myself as I park the car and get out, stomach twisting as I ready myself to go inside. I take steadying breaths with each step closer to the house, then push the door open, half-expecting to see him waiting.

But as I step in, the hallway is dark. No light peeks out from his room, the entire house is silent. My heart sinks, heavy and cold. He's... gone to bed?

I stand there, my excitement plummeting into something hollow. I replay our kiss once again, every touch, every glance, and wonder if it meant something different to him. Maybe I was just an itch that needs scratching, a moment of weakness, and I was just... there.

Without another thought, I storm upstairs, my footsteps heavy, each step a beat of anger and hurt. I walk into my room, shut the door, and sit on the edge of the bed, too furious to cry.

CHAPTER 16

KARLEY

THE DOORBELL CHIMES AND I set down the financial paperwork I've been reading for my house.

Oliver's been gone all day. This morning, his breakfast note left me both relieved and disappointed.

> *Off to Jeremy's bachelor party. Try not to have*
> *too much fun without me. Call me if you need*
> *me. And no watching our show until I return.*
> *Hubby xo*

I open the door, and Evelyn steps inside, eyes wide. "Are you kidding me?"

I laugh, closing the door behind her. I probably had the same reaction when I first saw his place.

Her gaze darts around. The herringbone timber floors, the dark wood, the high ceilings.

"Okay, this place is insane," she whispers, eyes still moving. "Have you ever been here before?"

I shake my head. "Nope. First time."

Evelyn pauses in the long entryway, looking around like she's in a museum. "He always came to your place. Kind of makes you wonder why, doesn't it?"

I shrug, but the question hits differently now that I've been alone in his house. It's quiet, empty... lonely.

She grabs my arm, eyes bright with a grin. "What if he had a secret crush on you and came over just to see you?"

I laugh, swatting her hand away. "Please. He came to see my brother, not me. So don't even put that idea in your head."

She raises an eyebrow. "Okay, Mrs. Lincoln."

I groan. "Come on, stop making up stories, and let's go look around."

As we walk through, she glances over. "Has he texted since he left?"

"Maybe," I admit, shrugging. "He just checked in earlier, making sure I'm not trashing the place."

"What did you say?"

"I told him I'm hosting a party and destroying his house."

She bursts out laughing. "No way!"

"Oh, yes, I did." I show her the text, and she laughs even harder. Oliver hasn't responded yet, so I put my phone away and take her on the tour.

When we reach his office, Evelyn stops dead in her tracks, her mouth falling open when she spots my painting on the wall.

"Wait, is that yours?" She moves closer.

"It is."

She peers over her shoulder at me with a raised eyebrow. "And he has it displayed in his office? Karley, do you know what this means? He's had your work this whole time."

"It's probably just something his mom gave him."

She turns to face me. "In his private office? Nobody keeps art they don't love in their workspace."

I open and close my mouth, unable to find the right words. Lucky for me, she gets distracted by a medical book on his shelf.

By the time we're back in the living room, Evelyn flops onto the sofa. "I think I need a nap after that."

"I know, it's crazy. I've never seen a house like this," I say, looking around. "It doesn't feel real."

Evelyn nods, eyes shining. "And those arched window s... I mean, wow. Have you ever seen ceilings this tall?"

"Never." I laugh.

She perks up. "Hey, we didn't snoop in his room!"

"No way," I say, shaking my head and crossing my arms. "I don't want him going through my stuff, so I won't go through his. I saw it briefly. Trust me, that's enough."

She huffs. "Fine, but have you told him they're yours?"

I shake my head vehemently. "No, and I'm not telling him." I feel a twinge of anxiety just thinking about it.

She gives me a reassuring look. "That's fine. I won't say anything."

I sigh, uncrossing my arms. "Thanks. I just can't... It's hard to explain, but the thought of people knowing who I am makes me freeze. I just can't handle it."

Sensing my discomfort, she nudges me gently. "So, how's work?"

"Nice change of subject," I say, smirking.

"Oh my God, I almost forgot to tell you what happened last night." She sits up straighter. "This woman in her forties, totally put together, Chanel bag, perfect hair, comes to the front desk, asking for her husband's room key. Says she's surprising him for their anniversary."

I wince. "Oh no."

"Oh yes," Evelyn nods. "So protocol says I need to call the room, but she begged me not to spoil the surprise. She was so sweet about it that—"

"You didn't."

"I did! I gave her the key," she groans, covering her face with her hands. "Twenty-five minutes later, security calls down because there's a disturbance on the sixth floor."

"Let me guess, no anniversary surprise?" I ask, pretending to be shocked.

"Not unless you count the surprise of finding your husband with his twenty-something assistant," Evelyn says.

"By the time I got up there, she'd already thrown the ice bucket and all his clothes off the balcony, and was in the process of destroying his laptop with the hotel phone."

I burst out laughing. "No way."

"The poor security was standing there, lost for words. The husband was trying to cover himself with a pillow while the assistant was hiding in the bathroom."

"What did you do?"

"What could I do? I just stood there, saying, Ma'am, please put the phone down, while secretly thinking, *Get him, girl.*"

I'm laughing so hard my stomach hurts. "Did you get in trouble?"

"Yeah, the manager wrote me up for not following protocol, but then the wife comes over, totally calm now, hands me a hundred-dollar tip and says, 'Thank you for the anniversary gift of freedom."

"Wow, that's insane," I say, shaking my head.

"On the bright side, the woman broke a piece of art from the hotel, and I offered to replace it with one of mine," she says with a wink. "Free marketing."

I tap the side of my head. "Smart thinking. We poor folks have to get creative."

My phone chimes and Evelyn leans over. "Is that him?"

I shrug, but my pulse rises at the possibility. Grabbing my phone from the coffee table, I see his name. "Yes. He's asking for a picture of the house."

She smirks, pointing. "Send him one of the room. Really sell the 'mess' you're making."

I nod, loving her idea, snapping a photo and sending it without a caption.

He replies immediately.

> **Oliver:** *Never pictured you to be a liar.*

> **Me:** *You really wouldn't care if I trashed your house?*

> **Oliver:** *Of course I'd care, but I know you wouldn't do it. Plus, I'd be offended if you partied without me.*

> **Me:** *I forgot that you are a party guy.*

> **Oliver:** *Was! I'm a married man now.*

I feel a twinge of satisfaction at his response.

> **Me:** *Good to know. How's the trip going?*

> **Oliver:** *It's actually great. I'm spending time with my dad, brothers, and*

> **friends. We haven't done anything like this since we were kids.**

> **Me:** *Then I won't keep you. Have fun.*

> **Oliver:** *Actually, I'm already in bed.*

> **Me:** *Shouldn't you be out partying it up?*

I can't help the skepticism in my response. After all the worry and anger I've felt, his tame behavior seems almost suspicious.

He sends me a photo of the TV in his room, mirroring what I'd done to him earlier.

> **Me:** *Well, if you're bored, can't your brothers entertain you?*

> **Oliver:** *I think I've had enough of them. I'm ready to come home.*

> **Me:** *What time do you fly out tomorrow?*

My insides vibrate at the thought of him coming home. I'm surprised by how conflicted I feel. Part of me still wants to hold on to my anger, but another part misses him more than I care to admit.

> **Oliver:** *Why, trying to figure out how much time you have to clean up the house?*

Me: *Not at all. I'll be sure to leave you a mess.*

> **Oliver:** *I think the plan is to be home in the afternoon. But I need to tell you, we've got a double date Saturday with Dan Warne and his wife.*

Me: *Wait, what? Since when?*

> **Oliver:** *Sorry, I've been meaning to tell you.*

Me: *So... where is it?*

> **Oliver:** *Golf first, then lunch. Nothing fancy, I promise.*

Me: *Easy for you to say. You actually know how to play.*

> **Oliver:** *I can teach you.*

CHAPTER 17

OLIVER

I WAKE UP FEELING surprisingly refreshed, knowing it's my last day here. It's Saturday, and as I climb out of bed and walk to the window, I can't deny how breathtaking the view of this private island is. So far, we've had meals prepared by top chefs, listened to a live band one night, and spent our days jet skiing, deep-sea fishing, diving——and even unwinding at a beachside cigar bar.

For the final few hours today, Harvey and I are taking over, as Evan was in charge, but the girls have gone a little wild.

On Nova's social media, there's one shot that shows Chelsea laughing with a drink in hand, her hair wild from dancing, and her friends crowding around her in the background. Another photo features Nova, her hand raised like a cheerleader, urging the crowd on with a big grin as the party goes into full swing. The captions are full of playful challenges, like "Let's take this up a notch" and "Who's ready for round two?"

I've seen enough pictures of Nova, Chelsea, and the girls having fun that I urge us to turn it up. So, today will be a James Bond-themed event... including tuxedos, casino games, and luxury speedboats. Looking at those photos, I can't help but think Karley would fit right in with them since she has the same energy.

Then my phone rings. It's Liam. I ignore it and then a text comes through; it's a photo of him and Warne at the golf course. I didn't realize they'd still play without me. When I called to tell Mr. Warne I married Karley, he was thrilled. It made me feel like I'm miles ahead, but I know I can't relax until the gallery's in my name. I'd hoped the bachelor party might delay the golf game. But of course, Liam went out of his way to make sure it still happened. I don't respond. I'm too annoyed, and I should focus on being with family today.

Harvey and Jeremy are the only ones who know what's going on with Karley. I needed someone to confide in, especially after I kissed her. When I'm around others, I keep my ring in my pocket. I couldn't bring myself to tell Evan because he's like a second dad. He'd just lecture me about responsibility and how I need to think things through before acting, so I keep it between Harvey, Jeremy, and me. Being the two youngest, we naturally bonded more than with our older brothers, Jeremy and Evan. And since Harvey met Jemima, who's expecting, he's softened. He just wants me to be happy, like him.

There's a knock at my door. I quickly put my phone away and open it to see the boys, all dressed up in sharp James Bond suits. "Coming or what?" Richard, my friend, asks with a goofy grin.

"Give me a second; I just woke up." I laugh, running my hand through my hair.

"Well, hurry up! We're starting early," he says before walking off.

I walk into the house and kick off my shoes, hearing a faint noise that makes me smirk. The TV's on, so she must be watching something.

When I enter the living room, I stop and grin at the sight of her curled up on the sofa, a blanket wrapped around her, eyes closed. She looks peaceful, beautiful...

I inch closer, squatting in front of her, covering her with the blanket, then brushing her hair away from her face and tucking it behind her ear. There's a tiny trail of drool on the cushion that catches my eye, and a deep chuckle bubbles out of me.

She jerks awake, practically launching herself off the sofa, eyes darting around before they land on me with a mix of confusion and irritation.

"Hey, you're back." She wipes at her mouth, sitting up. Her face is bare, no makeup, just freckles scattered across her cheeks, her hair messy from the nap. She finally looks up at me, her eyes bright under the light.

"I am." I rise, smirking, move to the kitchen, grab a glass of water, down two Tylenol, and settle on the sofa. Grabbing the remote, I flick through the channels.

"Did you want to watch the next episode of *Nobody Wants This*?"

"Already watched it."

"You didn't."

A soft laugh escapes her. "Gotcha."

"You had me there for a second," I say, eyes narrowed playfully. "Now come on, let's binge this."

She curls up beside me, leaving a little space between us. "Did you have fun?"

"I did. Thanks. It was good to hang out with them, just us, no work, with nothing but time," I say, watching her expression soften. "Spending one-on-one time with each of my brothers was something I didn't realize I needed. I wouldn't say we've drifted apart, exactly, but life keeps us all so busy. Even at Sunday dinners, we're mostly there for Grams. But this trip... it gave us a chance to really reconnect."

"I get that," she says quietly, her fingers fidgeting with the edge of the blanket. "Sometimes you don't realize how much you've missed someone until you finally slow down and really talk to them again."

"Yeah. You're right. I think I needed that trip more than I thought." I pause, holding her gaze. "And maybe I needed this too."

She smiles faintly. "Yeah... me too."

I settle back beside her, pressing play on the next episode. "Let's see if you can stay awake for the whole thing."

She elbows me gently. "I've had my nap... I'm good. You're the one who looks ready to crash."

My lips lift into a small smile. "Just don't give me the blanket."

She laughs, shaking her head. "I hear excuses."

"Excuses?" I snort. "Please, I've got stamina for days."

As the words leave my mouth, her eyes widen briefly before returning to normal. I catch that reaction and feel a flicker of heat in my chest, knowing exactly where her mind went. I try not to smirk.

"Stamina?" she teases, throwing a corner of the blanket over me. "Better?"

I pull more over me. "Much better. Just don't be surprised if I outlast you."

We share a smile, a silent dare to see who's really going to make it through this episode.

CHAPTER 18

KARLEY

A FEW HOURS LATER, I blink my eyes open, disoriented for a moment in the darkness. As my vision clears, I realize he's lying on top of me, his head on my stomach, feeling the rise and fall of his breath against me.

My heart skips a beat. When did I fall asleep like this? I lift my head slowly, careful not to wake him, but a part of me doesn't want to move. Lying here, surrounded by his warmth, feels safe in a way I'm not used to.

But I can't stay like this. This isn't real. I have to keep reminding myself of that. Gently, I shift, trying to slip away without waking him, but his grip tightens around me.

"Hey," he mumbles, his voice raspy as it rumbles against my belly, sending an involuntary shiver up my spine.

"Hi," I manage to say, giving him a little shove. "Come on, get up. I can't feel my legs."

More like I'm feeling way too much with him wrapped around me like this.

He smirks, barely lifting his head. "Guess I'm just that comfortable, huh?"

"More like you're crushing me," I say, trying to keep my voice steady as I wriggle free.

He chuckles, finally rolling off and stretching lazily. "Don't act like you didn't enjoy it."

"In your dreams." I fight a grin as I toss the blanket at him and head for my room. "You're not as charming as you think."

"Is that right?" he teases, catching the blanket. "Guess I'll have to work on that, then."

The next morning, I wake drenched in sweat and my heart pounding. I need a drink of water. The nightmares have come back, the same one as always. I'm a little kid again, watching my parents tear up my paintings, telling me how shitty they are and how nobody would ever want them.

There's no way I can ignore it, so I get up and tiptoe down the stairs and through the hall to check the time. It's five a.m. I make my way to the kitchen, but I falter at the sound of water running. He's showering. The bathroom is filled with steam. My breath catches as I peek in—he's naked. I swallow down the moan that wants to escape as I watch the water trail down his perfectly lean back, muscles tense, one hand pressed against the white tiles and the other between his thick thighs. He makes a sound, a soft grunt, and I bite my lip to stop a whimper from slipping, feeling the heat rise within me. His arm movements quicken and his ass muscles contract. I know I shouldn't be here, but it's like a scene out of my fantasies. He grunts something incoherent, and reality pulls me back. I retreat quietly, heading to the kitchen, my heart pounding in my ears. Grabbing a glass of water, I hurry to my room, pretending I never saw a thing.

The next time I come down, he's already gone. But I walk to the counter, looking forward to my new favorite comfort food, along with my note. Today's is:

> *If this doesn't win me 'Husband of the Year,'*
> *I'm filing a complaint.*

It's Saturday morning, which means we have golf with Dan Warne and his wife.

Taking a deep breath, I roll my shoulders back and head down the stairs.

"Good morning," I say, surprised to see him in the kitchen in sweats. He glances over his shoulder with a casual smile, something I don't get to see very often. "What's cooking?"

"Eggs," he replies, flipping something in the pan. "No bagel today. I figured I'd poison you with my food."

I roll my eyes at his joke. It's lame, but it's like his notes; it's something that I've found myself bouncing out of bed for.

"Need any help?" I try to sound relaxed, even as my heart beats a little faster. I walk closer to him.

"Nope, I've got it. Just make yourself comfortable."

It's nice having someone cook for me. I turn and sit on the stool at the island. "So, what's the plan for today?" I ask, trying to keep the anxiety out of my voice. I'm nervous about meeting these important people in Oliver's life, worried I'll say something wrong and ruin his business relationship with Mr. Warne.

"We're meeting the Warnes at the golf course at ten," he says.

I lean my arms on the counter, watching him cook. The muscles in his back shift beneath his fitted t-shirt as he moves between the pan of eggs and a second pan, where bacon crisps perfectly. The kitchen smells amazing. "You realize I've never played golf, right?"

He turns to look at me with a smile. "I'll help you. Don't worry. As long as we pretend to be madly in love, we'll be fine."

"Alright." I laugh, though my nerves haven't entirely left. I wonder if we can pull this off, pretending to be in love when we've spent the days avoiding talking about the kiss. Will we need to hold hands? Will Mr. Warne expect to see affection between us? The strange part is, I don't think it'll be that hard to act like I'm falling for Oliver. That's what scares me the most.

He turns back, finishing cooking, and soon, he places a plate in front of me. "Want some juice or coffee?" he asks, pulling me out of my thoughts.

"Coffee, please." I watch him make it, waiting for him to join me before I start eating. He sits down beside me, and the silence is surprisingly comfortable.

"Do you want to do anything afterward?" he asks between bites. "Or did you have something planned already?"

I pause eating to answer, touched by the thoughtfulness of his offer. It's a small thing, but it shows he's considering my needs even after our "business" is done. "Actually, I need to fill in forms for my new house tonight."

"Okay," he says, setting down his utensils and leaning forward slightly. "I can help." There's something unexpectedly eager in his tone, as if the prospect of mundane tasks with me appeals to him more than whatever glamorous alternative he might have planned.

Once we're finished eating, I head upstairs to get dressed, wondering what exactly one wears to impress rich golf people. After searching online for 'women's golf attire,' I settle on a skirt and a light t-shirt, perfect for the warm day ahead. I'm nervous about meeting the Warne's, but also curious. These people hold the keys to Oliver's future, and now, by extension, mine too. I wonder if I'll be able to read their reactions to me... *to us.* Will they believe we actually married for love?

I'm dressed and walking down the stairs when I see him on the phone. The moment he notices me, his face lights up.

Is this okay? I mouth as I stand in front of him.

He mouths back. *More than okay.*

I feel a blush rising, but try to brush it off as he wraps up his call.

"You look perfect. They're going to love it. You look like a pro," he says with a grin as we head to the door.

My stomach does a little flip at his compliment. I know it's for show, part of our act, but the warmth in his eyes seems genuine. I try not to read too much into it.

"Well, I bet I don't swing like one," I reply. "But I'll do my best to make you look bad."

He chuckles as he locks it behind us. "I wouldn't expect anything less."

Golfing isn't an activity I'd normally choose, but Wren used to play with his friends occasionally. I'd always preferred to stay behind, alone painting or with Amber.

"How about I drive us there? No driver. It'll look more... married."

"Yeah, good idea," I say as it dawns on me. "Do clubs even fit in your car? And do I have clubs?"

"I got you a set. But if you don't like them, we can get others," he says as we get to his red car and he opens the door for me.

"Don't worry. It's not like I'm planning to make this a regular thing." I give him a small, teasing smile, brushing off the seriousness as I slip into the seat.

"You might surprise yourself," he says, pausing at my door. "Golf's actually a good outlet. You might enjoy it."

"We'll see." The words come out lighter than the thoughts behind them. I wonder how many more of these outings we'll have together before our arrangement runs its course. Once Oliver secures his deal with Mr. Warne, will there be any reason for us to keep up with this charade? It's strange to think that, soon enough, this could all be over... The late nights watching our favorite show, the breakfast bagels and notes, the shared quiet moments. I push the thought away, unsure why it leaves me feeling hollow.

He closes the door and, shockingly, the clubs actually do fit. The interior is just as stunning as I'd imagined, with leather seats and perfectly coordinated colors. I've never been one for fancy cars, but if I were in his position, maybe I'd go all out too.

I settle into my seat. "So, let me get this straight. We play golf, act like a couple, and that's it?"

"Pretty much. We'll probably play nine holes and then have lunch with them."

"So, what does his wife do?" I ask, trying to gather as much information as possible before this meeting. The more I know about these people, the better prepared I'll be to navigate conversations without revealing our arrangement.

"Honestly, I think Eden worked in administration for him, but I'm not sure anymore."

I give him an *are you serious* look. "You're trying to impress the guy, and you don't know what his wife does?"

He shrugs, keeping his eyes on the road. "I know the important stuff. He's married, has kids. I think she worked in admin, but I don't know her hobbies or anything."

Shaking my head, I laugh softly. "Alright, I'll just fake it till I make it." I imagine myself smiling through awkward conversations, complimenting Eden's outfit, and finding something we might have in common. I'll have to be careful not to slip up about our relationship timeline, and I'll need to look at Oliver with the right amount of affection. Not too much to seem fake, but enough to be convincing. At least the golf part gives us something to focus on besides conversation.

We're there in less than twenty minutes. I quickly spot the sign for Liberty National Golf Club.

As we pull up, the resort comes into view. Lush green grass, immaculate trees, it all screams wealth. Suddenly, nerves twist in my stomach, and I wonder if I can really pull this off... or should I say, *we*.

We walk side by side to the entrance, our hands not quite touching, though close enough that anyone watching might expect us to reach for each other at any moment. I glance around, realizing we don't have our clubs. "Do we need to bring them in?" I lean into Oliver and whisper so no one else can hear.

"They'll take care of it," he says.

I nod, trying to relax. His hand brushes mine, and I flinch, momentarily forgetting we're supposed to be acting like a couple. Taking a breath, I unclench my hand and let him slip his fingers through mine. My heart speeds up as we walk in, passing women with perfect makeup, manicured nails, and designer golf clothes. They look like they belong in a fashion magazine, the kind who make you feel underdressed in an instant. I can only imagine what Eden is going to be like.

Oliver walks us up to a guy with dark gray hair, a silver beard, and black-framed glasses. A woman in navy pants and a white polo shirt stands beside him. Her polished yet soft features make my shoulders relax a little, giving me hope she might be easy to talk to.

The man's gray eyes light up. "Hi, Oliver and Karley. Thanks for joining us." He shakes Oliver's hand.

I disconnect my hand from Oliver's to shake his. "Thanks for inviting me today."

"What happened to your hand, dear?" Eden gasps, her dainty polished nails covering her lips but not touching her lipstick.

I look down, noticing my stained nail beds. "Paint."

"Paint?" Eden echoes, her hand dropping away from her mouth.

Mr. Warne grins. "Karley is a painter," he tells Eden.

"She is," Oliver adds, looking proud.

My chest flutters at the way he says it. Not as an afterthought, but like it's something special about me.

"Why haven't I seen your work?" Oliver leans down and whispers in my ear, his scruff skimming my jaw and his breath tickling my ear sending goosebumps to rise on my skin.

"You will," I breathe through the lie.

I could've come clean and said, *You have my paintings hanging in both of your offices,* but the realization of that makes me dizzy.

"Professionally?" Eden asks, tilting her head.

"I'm going to school at the moment."

"Where?" Mr. Warne asks, his face lighting up.

I hesitate for a split second, wondering if this is some kind of test. Would the wrong answer hurt Oliver's chances? I'm not sure how much they already know about me, or us, and whether my response needs to match some story Oliver had already told them.

"My mom's school," Oliver interrupts.

"Of course, learning from the best. You should try," Mr. Warne says to his wife with hopeful eyes, grabbing her waist and pulling her in to kiss her cheek.

She shakes her head and pats his chest. "I won't have the time or energy with the treatment starting soon."

The air surrounding us suddenly turns cold. At first, I thought it was from the conversation, but then I hear a familiar voice call out, "There you are," and it makes me turn to stone. Liam.

CHAPTER 19

KARLEY

HE'S DRESSED IN BLACK pants and a green polo, his brown hair swept back and his cold brown eyes staring right at me.

He walks up with his girlfriend. Her hair is blonde too, but hers is more platinum than mine, and longer. It compliments her blue eyes. She's in a fancy green golf dress that matches Liam's polo.

Oliver's hand tightens in mine. "Liam," he says through a tight jaw.

"Hello, hello, couldn't let you have all the fun," Liam says with the biggest fucking smirk that you want to slap off.

"I didn't realize you were joining us today," Oliver says, stepping away from Liam. "The tee time was scheduled for four people."

"Dan invited us," Liam replies smoothly. "And of course, I couldn't resist."

Something about the calculated way he's looking between Oliver and me makes me uncomfortable.

"I want to introduce you to my girlfriend, Paige," Liam says. "It's getting serious."

His words sound performative, like he's putting on a show rather than sharing good news. I wonder if this is part of whatever strange dynamic exists between him and Oliver.

"Hi, Paige." I smile. "I'm Karley."

"My wife," Oliver says in a dark tone, his hands wrapping my middle as he pulls me close.

Paige's face glows. "It's lovely to meet you."

"Have you played golf before?" I ask. If I'm going to spend the next few hours with this woman while our partners compete for Mr. Warne's attention, it would help to have something to talk about.

"Yes, last week, but I'm not very good." Paige giggles.

"It's okay. I'm sure to be hopeless," I say, waving a hand.

"The lunch and spa make it worth it," Eden interjects with a wink.

I like her. Actually, both ladies seem nice. There's a pang of guilt, though, since these women are being genuine, while I'm playing a role. I push the feeling aside, reminding myself why we're doing this.

It's just Liam... The way his eyes zone in on Oliver makes me shiver.

But when I look at Oliver, his gaze is on me.

This is why I get so confused. He looks at me with a fire, that I feel deep in my core but I can't trust it. Not after everything.

"Okay, let's get started. We need the extra time, otherwise, we'll miss the lunch reservation, and it sounds like that's all the ladies want," Mr. Warne jokes, but kisses Eden on the cheek again, and I melt at the affection.

"You know me too well." Eden smiles lovingly at him.

Oliver links his hand with mine as we follow them. His palm is warm, our fingers interlacing naturally.

"Why are people moving the bags for us?" I whisper so only Oliver can hear, surprised by what seems like unnecessary service.

He brings his lips to my ear. I ignore the closeness and listen to his words. "That's part of Dan's package."

I blink slowly, trying to comprehend all this extra stuff they can get because they have money. *The power they have...*

I hang back, waiting for my turn, which unfortunately isn't that long. Eden hits the ball with ease. I'm surprised, because I'd assumed she was more of a social golfer like me, here mostly for the lunch afterward. Now I feel even more out of my depth.

Paige takes a few goes before hitting the ball. I notice Liam getting frustrated beside me, giving her instructions in a huff. I glance at Mr. Warne, noticing his slight frown as he watches Liam's behavior. I wonder if Oliver will get frustrated with me.

Now it's my turn, and I look at Oliver, who gives me an encouraging smile.

"What club do I pick?"

He hands me one, standing close. "This is a driver. Perfect for beginners." Positioning himself behind me, he gently guides my arms into the correct stance.

"Keep your eye on the ball, not where you want it to go," he whispers softly against my ear. "And don't try to smash it. Just a smooth, easy swing."

I step up to the ball, and he tells me to relax. Yeah, sure, that's easier for him to say; he knows what the fuck he's doing, whereas I've never played, and I have them all watching and waiting.

I swing the club hard, and because my hands are so sweaty, the club slips out and hits a tree. Gasping, my hands cover my mouth. The roar of laughter behind me makes me relax a little, but I'm still mortified.

Turning to Oliver, I expect to see disappointment, but he's doubled over. When he straightens, he's misty eyed and red faced.

"Stop laughing at me."

"Sorry, *Petal*," he says, walking over and handing me a new club before going back to watch me with the others.

I suck in a breath at his nickname for me and try to focus on the ball, but of course, it rattles me more, and I hit the grass.

"I don't know if I can do this," I say quietly when I swing again and move a piece of grass. I want to die inside. This perfect, expensive grass is now damaged because of me. My throat tightens, and I struggle to breathe.

I'm staring at the big dirt hole, wondering what to do. I'm so lost in thought that I don't hear Oliver walk up. It's only the heat of his body, the clean smell of his aftershave, and his voice that wraps around me like a hug.

"Stop doubting yourself. Don't let fear win. Use your courage." His body slips behind me, my back flush against his chest as he wraps his arms around me and covers my hands over the club. If he thinks I'm able to do this with him standing so close, he's got another thing coming.

"I've got it," I say.

"I know, but this is perfect for our show."

My heart squeezes painfully. I swallow, looking out in my peripheral vision, noticing all their eyes on me.

All for show.

My eyes burn from hurt and anger. I'd begun to imagine moments like this could be real between us. Standing in his embrace, I suddenly picture myself back at the house, alone in my room while he's out living his real life when our arrangement ends, and I'm packing to leave. What am I doing, letting myself get attached? This is a business deal, not a love story. It switches something in me. I picture my-self in my new house and start questioning my reasoning. Taking a deep breath, I focus on the ball and let him guide me.

We hit the ball, and it sails forward. "I did it," I cry, surprised at my own excitement over something so small. His warm body leaves me, and I'm a mix of pleased and sad. Paige and Eden clap, and Mr. Warne says, "Good job."

It's Mr. Warne's turn again. I'm standing with the others as Oliver slips his arm around my waist. I lean into him without thinking and peer up at him. His gaze remains straight ahead, focused on Mr. Warne, but he turns slightly and winks at me.

Mr. Warne hits the ball far, and he turns with a smile that grows as soon as he spots his wife. Moving to Eden, he kisses her softly, whispering something that makes her laugh. The easy affection between them stirs something in me.

As we walk the course, following our balls, reality crash-es back. Once this agreement is up, what happens then? I'll still be at his mother's school. Declan will still be his best friend. Our lives are tangled in ways I hadn't fully considered before. A clean break might be impossible.

We finish the nine-hole game in three hours, thanks to my inexperience with every swing. Despite my initial embarrassment, I found myself enjoying the afternoon a lot more than I expected. Paige struggled too, which made me feel less alone. Though Oliver kept his competitive edge with Mr. Warne and Liam, he never once showed frustration, unlike Liam, whose patience with Paige had clearly worn thin.

The clubhouse gives us the most surreal backdrop of the New York City skyline and the iconic Statue of Liberty. As we walk farther in, I'm in awe. This place exudes sophistication, with glass walls and sleek furniture perfectly set up to enhance the view. Inside, we pass private lounges and head into a first-class dining room. I follow like a little lost puppy, holding Oliver's hand for guidance.

We arrive at the table, where Oliver pulls out a chair for me before taking his seat beside me. Eden sits across from me with her husband at her side, while Paige and Liam take the remaining seats. As soon as we settle in, the service begins. A white napkin is laid across my lap, water is poured, and I'm asked if I'd like a drink. The girls order wine and the boys order scotch. I order a soda and Oliver orders the same. I lean into him. "You can have a scotch to blend in."

He moves his mouth to my ear. "No. I don't need a drink to have a good time." He squeezes my thigh. "I'm in good company."

"Or good free entertainment?" I raise an eyebrow, and my lips lift, remembering all my mistakes on the golf course.

"Both. I hope you had a good time."

I smile at his warm eyes, getting lost in them. It suddenly feels like it's just us here. "I did, aside from being embarrassed by how bad I was. It was fun."

He leans closer. "Don't be embarrassed, we were all bad once."

I roll my eyes playfully, leaning back, touched by his attempt to make me feel better. "Yeah, right."

"No, I'm serious. Once I forgot to put the cart in park, and it rolled downhill and into a pond."

I giggle, covering my mouth.

"I had a squirrel once take my ball and run off with it," Mr. Warne adds, pulling my gaze to him, having forgotten we should be engaging with them.

"My ball hit a tree once, ricocheted off a second tree, and ended up in another golfer's cart," Liam adds. Something feels performative about it, like he's sharing the story to fit in, rather than genuinely connecting.

The light chatter of the restaurant buzzes softly around us, accompanied by the clink of utensils and soft laughter from other tables.

Eden swirls her drink thoughtfully, casting a sly glance at her husband.

"I would say don't wear white," Eden says, a mischievous glint in her eyes. Her gaze flickers to Mr. Warne, and a knowing smile passes between them. "I slipped on the grass once, and received some interesting looks while walking to the restaurant." Her eyes roll dramatically, and a giggle escapes her lips as she sweeps her gaze around the table.

I find myself warming to her even more. Despite her obvious wealth and status, there's something refreshingly unpretentious about Eden. She doesn't take herself too seriously, and I appreciate how she's trying to make me feel better about my own mishaps.

Oliver's hand rests on my thigh, his thumb tracing small circles. His warmth seeps through the fabric of my skirt, grounding me as I lean into him. "You're not alone," he says softly, his voice low and reassuring.

Feeling a bit of the tension ease from my shoulders, I flash him a genuine smile.

I want to return the favor, remembering something Oliver told me about Mr. Warne's teasing remarks about him "pretending to enjoy art." An idea forms in my mind, and I decide to share a story that will help Oliver's case while maintaining our cover.

"Dan, you should see how good Oliver is at painting," I announce suddenly, earning a sharp intake of breath from Oliver. His surprise ripples through me, but I press on, undeterred.

Mr. Warne's bushy gray eyebrows shoot up, curiosity dancing across his face. "I didn't realize you painted," he says, his tone genuinely intrigued.

"I d—" Oliver begins, but the words dissolve into a strangled yelp when I squeeze his thigh... or at least what I thought was his thigh, but is actually his cock. His sudden noise draws every eye at the table. My stomach plummets when I realize my mistake.

Oliver leans forward, his face flushed, breathing deeply as I quickly release him.

"Are you okay?" Liam asks, amused. He sits close enough to have noticed everything, and the glimmer in his eyes confirms it.

"He's just embarrassed and doesn't like to talk about it," I say quickly, shooting Oliver a glance to ensure he's alright. He meets my gaze, a mix of amusement and disbelief written all over his features, but he says nothing, allowing me to steer the conversation back on track.

I pull out my phone and scroll through the photos.

"What did you paint?" Liam snorts, clearly trying to stifle his laughter.

"It was a tree with blossoms," I reply, ignoring him as I swipe. Finally, I find the photo and hand the phone to Mr. Warne. His keen eyes narrow on the image and says he saw it online, but Eden gasps.

"Wow, Oliver, it's beautiful," she says.

I smile, letting my pride show. "He's really talented."

Oliver leans in. "Having a good teacher helps," he murmurs before pressing a kiss to my cheek. The gentle gesture sends a flush of heat over my skin, leaving me momentarily breathless.

"I might need some lessons," Liam chimes in.

My stomach tightens at his tone; there's something un-nerving in the way he's looking at me.

"I can give you a referral," I reply coolly.

"I want you." His smirk deepens, and Oliver's hand tightens slightly on my leg. I glance at Paige, who seems to have checked out of the conversation, staring at her phone beneath the table. Her disinterest in Liam's flirting makes me wonder if this is normal behavior for him.

"Unfortunately, she's not available," Oliver says, his eyes narrowing into sharp slits as he glares at Liam.

"Boys," Mr. Warne interjects enough to silence them both. "Enough."

Eden, sensing the tension, lightens the mood. "Maybe you should sell your paintings, Oliver," she says.

"He should and try different classes," I add quickly, eager to shift focus. The tension between Oliver and Liam feels like it could snap at any moment. "I didn't know I loved watercolor—" I stop short, suddenly remembering no one here knows the full truth about me.

"So you can learn different things?" Paige asks.

"Yeah, there's heaps," I reply, my smile returning. "Drawing, painting, sculpture, printmaking..."

"Do you do them all?" Mr. Warne asks, his gaze steady on mine.

I shake my head softly, letting out a small laugh. "Not anymore. I focus on drawing and painting."

We are interrupted by the waiter. Oliver takes the opportunity to whisper, "Thanks."

We enjoy our meals: small dishes that look like art on a plate. I have no idea what they're called. I just ordered exactly what Eden did, figuring she'd choose something good. The food looks nothing like anything I've eaten before. Tiny dots of colorful sauce, chicken placed on top, with little green herbs sprinkled around like delicate decorations. Each bite feels like a surprise, more like a fancy experiment than a regular meal. I take my time, savoring every piece until my plate is clean.

"Are you ready?" Eden looks at me and Paige.

I tilt my head.

"It's spa time."

Paige darts out of her chair so fast she doesn't finish her meal. The eagerness in her movement makes me wonder if she's been waiting for an escape from this tense lunch all along. Eden follows.

I rise, and as I'm about to step away from the table, Oliver's hand grabs my wrist and brings me to him.

"You forgot something." He gently pulls me to him, bringing his lips into an unexpected sweet kiss.

My toes curl. He pulls away, leaving me gasping, and a little disorientated. "Now you can go." He winks, knowing exactly what he's done.

Eden gushes at how cute we are as I walk beside her and Paige. I've lost my words and can only mumble in agreement.

CHAPTER 20

KARLEY

THE SOOTHING SCENTS OF lavender and eucalyptus greet us as we step inside the spa. Soft, ambient music plays in the background, blending seamlessly with the gentle murmur of the staff. The lighting is soft and calming, reflecting off the polished marble countertops and plush seating.

Eden whispers something to the receptionist before turning back to us. "We're going to have a massage before we meet at the lounge."

I hesitate, a sudden wave of anxiety washing over me.

"Liam paid for yours," Eden says to Paige before turning to me. "And Oliver paid for yours."

"He did?" I ask, blinking in surprise.

Eden tilts her head, confusion flickering across her face. "He's your husband."

I stammer, trying to recover quickly. "Of course. He just didn't mention that he already took care of it." My fingers toy with the rings on my hand, hoping my fumbling excuse is enough to cover the slip.

Fortunately, the spa staff appear just in time to call our names, guiding us to private rooms. I follow a woman down a hallway. My shoulders tense as we enter the treatment room.

This is my first time in a spa, and the unfamiliar luxury makes me feel like an impostor. The room is dimly lit, with heated stone floors and a plush massage table draped in crisp white linens.

The massage begins, and the tension in my muscles melts away, though my mind remains restless. My thoughts flick between Oliver, the embarrassing incident at the table, Oliver's unexpected generosity, and the mountain of stuff I need to organize for the house. It isn't until the final ten minutes that I finally let go and drift into relaxation.

After the massage, I redress and wander into the lounge area. Eden is already seated, her legs crossed elegantly as she sips her tea with a satisfied smile.

"That was amazing," I say as I sink into the seat beside her, rolling my shoulders. The tension from the past week feels like a distant memory, my body lighter than it has been in ages.

Eden leans in, her eyes sparkling with mischief. "It's the best part of golf," she whispers with a wink.

I laugh softly, shaking my head. "So that's why you play."

Her smirk deepens as she eases back. "Yep."

I lean back against the chair, letting my head rest for a moment as a sigh escapes me. "I could get used to this."

The words leave my lips almost too easily, and the momentary indulgence feels foreign but tempting. This isn't my life. My mind begins to shift back to all the things I need to do.

Like the new house. I'll be knee-deep in setting it up soon, and there's still so much to do. My thoughts spiral to how licensing a home for family meetups is way more complicated than I expected. It's not just about having an extra bedroom.

First, I need to complete mandatory training classes about childcare and trauma. Then there's a ton of paperwork, like background checks for everyone in the household, FBI screenings, child abuse registry checks. My home has to pass a super strict safety inspection with working smoke detectors, locked cabinets, emergency plans. The state will investigate everything... My finances, my references, my entire life. It's intense. The whole process could take months, but it's designed to make sure kids are going to a truly safe environment.

I make a mental note to follow up on the process as soon as possible.

The extra money I've managed to keep thanks to Oliver can help speed things up. It's a small relief.

"You're miles away," Eden teases.

I smile, though it feels a little forced. "Just thinking about everything I need to do."

She hums thoughtfully. "Don't get too lost in it. Worry about it later."

Paige nods in agreement from the plush chair beside me, her feet soaking in a small basin of rose-scented water. "That's what spa days are for. Turning off your brain."

Her words linger in the back of my mind, a gentle reminder to relax and breathe. For now, I let the soothing music bring me back into the present.

"We should do this more often." Paige sighs, stretching out.

But all too soon, our time is up. I change back into my clothes and prepare to leave. The lingering scent of relaxation clings to my skin, but the peace I'd found inside is already slipping away. Eden is deep in conversation with someone she knows, her laughter light and carefree. Paige disappeared into the bathroom a few moments ago, leaving me to find Oliver on my own.

Rounding a corner, I collide with what feels like a brick wall, stumbling back slightly before glancing up. My heart drops as I meet Liam's hard, piercing gaze.

"You and Oliver aren't real," he says. The venom in his voice feels like a slap. I take a step to the side, attempting to move around him, but he shifts to block me.

I square my shoulders, crossing my arms over my chest as my heart races. "Yes, we are," I reply firmly.

Liam's lips curl into a sneer. "So it's just a coincidence that Dan mentioned one of us should settle down, and suddenly, Oliver's married? That doesn't add up."

I shrug, forcing a nonchalant expression. "Maybe you should focus on your own life. You're way too invested in ours." I try to sidestep him again, but his hand darts out, gripping my arm firmly.

"I'm going to figure this out," he says.

Anger flares in my chest as I yank my arm free, my voice steady despite the unease tightening my stomach. "Let me go before I tell my husband."

He laughs, a hollow, chilling sound that makes my skin crawl. The unease turns to outright fear as I push past him, practically sprinting down the hallway.

When I see Oliver waiting by the reception desk, a relaxed grin on his face, relief washes over me. But as soon as he spots my expression, his smile vanishes, replaced by concern.

"What happened, Petal?" he asks, pulling me into his arms. His embrace is warm, strong, and grounding, exactly what I need after Liam's unsettling words.

I melt into him, letting the tension seep out of my body. My arms wrap around his waist, and I press myself closer, burying my face against his chest. His scent, a mix of cedarwood and something distinctly him, fills my senses and helps steady my nerves.

"Liam," I mutter, my voice muffled against his chest. "He gave me a warning."

Oliver stiffens, his body taut with anger. He tilts his head back to look down at me, his eyes blazing. "He what?"

I shake my head quickly, tightening my hold on him. "It's fine. Forget about him," I say, though my voice wavers. I don't want him to let go just yet. For once, I allow myself to lean into someone else's strength, even if it feels dangerously vulnerable.

His hands smooth up and down my back in soothing strokes, the rhythm calming my ragged breathing. I focus on the steady beat of his heart, letting it settle me, as his chin rests lightly on the top of my head.

After a few moments, I take a deep breath and step back, though part of me doesn't want to. His hands linger on my waist as he studies me, his piercing eyes searching my face.

"You okay?" he asks gently.

Our eyes lock, and for a second, the world around us fades away. But I feel too raw, too exposed. I need to pull myself together before I fall even further into something I know I can't keep.

"Yeah," I say with a small nod, forcing a smile. "I'm good. What's next?"

He narrows his eyes slightly, clearly not convinced, but he doesn't push. Instead, he reaches for my hand, linking his fingers with mine. The simple gesture feels more intimate than it should.

"It's time to go," he says, offering me the reassurance I desperately need.

I nod. Paige and Eden are back. Across the lobby, I spot Liam talking to Mr. Warne, his expression tense. My stomach twists as I wonder what he's saying; if he's sharing his accusations about Oliver and me.

I've never wanted Oliver to get something more in my life, so I do something stupid... I lift onto my tiptoes, grab Oliver's face, bring my lips to his, and I let go. I kiss him like I've always wanted to. His mouth is already slightly parted, so I take advantage and sweep my tongue in and passionately kiss him. His hands move to my lower back, pulling me flush to his body as his tongue tangles with mine.

The room fizzles out, and all I feel, taste, and smell is him. I tentatively bite his lower lip, and he moans. We're lost in our own world as we kiss and explore.

A sudden clearing of a throat startles me. I spin around, my cheeks instantly heating as I realize everyone is staring. My gaze lands on Liam, his jaw tight and his eyes narrowed. My lips curl into a smug grin. *Take that, Liam.*

Mr. Warne steps forward, his warm smile easing some of the tension. "We're heading off. Thanks for joining us today. You should come out with us again sometime."

I untangle myself from Oliver and offer my hand. Mr. Warne shakes it firmly, then turns to Oliver with a playful wink. "She's amazing. You're a lucky man, Oliver."

Oliver's gaze meets mine, sincerity shining in his eyes, as he replies, "I am."

The words feel like sparks skimming across my skin, leaving a trail of heat in their wake.

We exchange goodbyes with the group, and I give Eden a quick hug. "Thanks for including me today."

She squeezes my shoulder with a smile that says she understands more than she lets on. Paige offers a wave.

The farewell with Liam is particularly strained. He extends his hand, and I force myself to take it, maintaining eye contact as we shake briefly. I keep my smile firmly in place. No way am I letting him see how much he got under my skin earlier.

As Oliver and I walk hand in hand to his car, a strange warmth settles over me. It's been years since I held a man's hand like this. We've held hands a few times since the arrangement began, but this feels different, like this isn't just for show anymore.

As we reach the car, Oliver's phone rings. He glances at me, his brow furrowing slightly. "Do you mind if I take this? I tried calling her earlier, but she didn't answer."

I nod, curiosity flickering. *Her?*

Settling into the soft leather seat, I buckle up and let my head rest against the window as Oliver presses accept via Bluetooth.

"Hey, Grams," he says softly.

A smile tugs at my lips as I look out at the scenery. The lingering relaxation from the massage and tea wraps around me like a cocoon.

"I heard you're not coming on Sunday." His grandmother's voice crackles through the phone. "Are you okay? I haven't seen you much."

"I'm sorry," Oliver replies with an apologetic chuckle. "I have an important dinner."

I know he means dinner with my family and Evelyn.

"It better not be for work," she fires back.

I bite my lip, holding back a laugh. She's giving him a proper scolding, and it's... adorable.

"It's not," he assures her, shaking his head with a grin that makes me frown slightly. *What's so funny?*

"So, it's a woman," she presses.

I hold my breath, waiting for his answer. His eyes flick to mine, and he drops to a quiet, almost shy tone. "Yes."

"I couldn't hear you. Speak up, Oliver. Where are you?"

I bite the inside of my cheek to stop myself from laughing. She's relentless and reminds me of how much I missed having grandparents growing up.

"Sorry, I'm in the car. I just left the golf course," he explains patiently.

"Well, I'll let you go for now," she says after a moment. "But call me later. We need to discuss this woman."

"Alright, Grams. I love you," he says.

"Love you too, Oliver."

She hangs up, and we spend the rest of the drive in comfortable silence, my mind replaying the day's events.

Climbing out of the car after we pull into the driveway, I glance at Oliver, feeling an unexpected softness toward him. Hearing him tell his grandmother he loves her melts something inside me. I hadn't anticipated this side of him, the one who cares deeply for others, including showing kindness toward me. Each gesture has been changing my initial opinion of him... He isn't the selfish, rich playboy I assumed he was.

"I get the feeling she's going to grill you about me."

He laughs, running a hand through his hair. "Oh, she will. She'll have my ass hanging out by the end of it."

His grin is so infectious that I laugh, the tension from earlier fading into the background.

As we step inside, the familiar warmth of the house wraps around me like a comforting embrace. Dropping my bag onto the kitchen counter, I kick off my shoes and stretch out my arms. "Thank you for booking me a massage at the spa."

Oliver's lips quirk into a crooked grin, his eyes sparkling with mischief. "You're welcome. Though, if you want to return the favor, just try to be gentle next time."

I squint at him, unsure what he's implying until it clicks. My cheeks heat instantly. "I'm not putting my hands on you."

"But you did," he teases, his grin widening into a full-blown smirk. "I'll admit, I was a little surprised. But if I'm being honest, I didn't hate the bold move."

His words strike a nerve, and my face flushes hotter. Gritting my teeth, I walk past him, shaking my head and muttering, "Not to get rejected again."

I turn, but only take a few steps before I feel his hand wrap around my wrist, stopping me in my tracks. His grip isn't tight, but it's firm enough to spin me back toward him. His expression is unreadable, his gaze sharp and questioning.

"What did you just say?" he asks.

I stare at him, my heart thudding loudly. There's no one here to witness this moment, no audience for the roles we're supposed to play. It's just us. And for once, I speak honestly. "You would push me away. You've done it before."

His eyebrows knit together, and he steps closer. I back up until my spine presses against the counter. The cool surface does nothing to ground me; it only adds to the heat of his presence.

"Is that what you think?" he asks.

Heavy and loaded, his question hangs in the air between us. I meet his gaze, searching for a hint of what he's thinking, but his expression remains unreadable. My breathing quickens, my pulse hammering as I try to find the courage to answer him... or the strength to look away.

CHAPTER 21

OLIVER

"It's what I know," she says, arching an eyebrow. Her chest rises and falls quickly, giving away just how much she wants me.

"What makes you so sure?" I stare down into her blue hypnotizing eyes.

I'm walking on thin ice after the earlier accidental touch of my cock and kiss.

She juts her chin up. "You've turned me down."

"When?" I ask, trying to recall when she's been this forward, and I turned her away... My mind immediately jumps to that night at the studio when I'd kissed her, felt that same electricity, but then left abruptly. I'd been in bed by the time she got home, deliberately avoiding her. Then I headed to Jeremy's bachelor party. But surely, that hadn't been what she meant? That hadn't been her making a move, that was me losing control.

Her chin drops, and her eyes shift away. I hate not being able to see her eyes, so I grab her chin and tilt her head back, bringing her pretty eyes back to me.

She exhales. "At Declan's party."

My eyebrows pinch, and when I remember that night, I shake my head.

She sucks in a breath and closes her eyes briefly. When they flutter open and pain stares back at me, and I blurt out the truth. "I couldn't touch you. But it doesn't mean I haven't wanted to."

She snorts, eyes rolling. "Sure."

A growl slips out of me, and I grab her waist to pull her to me. For weeks, I've been fighting this attraction, telling myself it would complicate everything, or worse, hurt her somehow. But seeing the disbelief in her eyes breaks my last thread of restraint. "I'll happily show you just how much I've wanted you."

Her mouth parts, ready to say something else, but she stares up at me, begging me to prove her right. I don't let her speak. My other hand reaches up to hold her neck, and I lean down. She sucks in a sharp breath as I press my lips to hers in a desperate kiss.

She thinks I've never wanted her—how fucking wrong she was. It's the opposite. I've wanted her, but never allowed myself to cross the line. Plus, she acted like she hated me, but now I know it's because I turned her down. I couldn't show her then, but I sure as fuck can do it now.

Except the memory of Declan's face flashes in my mind. The promise I made him... that I wouldn't touch her. Breaking that promise means betraying one of the few people who's had my back through everything. But with her body so close to mine, I'm finding it hard to remember why that promise seemed so important.

I absorb the way she tastes, and how sweet she smells, giving her everything of me in this moment. The noises she makes are a mix of plea and pleasure. With no audience, I take in the fact I'm kissing her without worrying about anything except how much I want this. Fuck, I want her. Her hand grabs my neck to pull me closer, as if I'm already not close enough.

Her body melts into mine, my feet on the outside of hers, our heads shifting angles to get deeper, our pace less frantic the more we kiss, both of us slowing down to savor each other. I want her to know what exactly she's doing to me. We explore each other with our hands and mouths. My hand skims the back of her right thigh and hitches it up. Her eyes snap open, wide and feral as she gasps for air. I lower her leg, letting her catch her breath. My own is labored; my heart is beating so hard. She's a great kisser. I haven't found someone who matches my rhythm. But we are so in sync with her pressure, soft but hard when needed.

"Believe me yet?"

"Shut up and kiss me again." She grabs me by the back of the neck and pulls me down. This time, I don't stop. I grab the backs of her thighs and lift her onto the counter. She spreads her legs, and I stand between them. Now, with her at the same height, my hips line up with hers. My hands shift to her cheeks, my thumbs dusting over them and angling her face to kiss her deeper.

My heart is poured into this kiss, trying to show her how I've longed for her but never let myself dream.

Fuck, the amount of times I've stroked myself, I'm surprised it still works.

But now I get the real thing and she's better than I ever imagined. I can't stop breathing in her air; she's intoxicating. My hand slips gently over her cheekbones, down to her shoulders, and to her waist.

"You're better than I imagined," she groans, and my chest swells at her confession.

It amps me up more.

I move my kisses down over her jaw, to her ear, and then down her neck, biting and sucking as her head tips backward, giving me more access.

"Oliver-r," she whimpers.

The sound is like music to my ears.

I bring my lips to hers again, but this time hovering to whisper, "You're so beautiful."

Her hands grab my shoulders, and when her nails dig into me, not wanting me to stop, I growl against her mouth and shift my bodyweight forward. Her legs grip my hips tighter. She trembles, moaning my name again, and her nails are definitely going to leave marks.

I pull back to breathe against her swollen lips. "I knew you'd be sweet."

"How?"

"Your attitude is a wall, and underneath, there's a sweetness begging to be freed."

She swivels her hips, causing friction between us, and my body responds instantly. My cock hardens further, and a groan escapes from deep in my chest. At the same time, she runs her tongue along the seam of my lips. "You always try to keep things so controlled," she whispers against my mouth. "Right fucking now, I want you to lose it."

"You have no idea how many times I've thought about fucking you."

I rock my hips to grind myself against her, the clothes making me uncomfortable as I grow harder.

"Fuck, Karley, I need you."

I touch her breast over her clothes. She arches her back and pushes herself into my hand. At the same time, I bring my mouth to her neck, kissing and dragging my teeth over her skin, drawing a sexy groan from her lips. Her breasts are the perfect handful.

She was made for me.

I need more.

I pull back, and her eyes flutter open. Grabbing her impatiently, I push her skirt down. Her shirt gapes, showing me her purple bra, and I dip my head and kiss her stomach up to her breasts.

One hand stays on her waist, and the other pushes the bra below so I can kiss her skin. She smells like caramel, making my mouth water.

I lick my lips, take one of her nipples, and roll my tongue around her tight bud. Her hands sink deep into my hair, holding me to her.

After giving that one attention, I kiss and nibble my way to the other and give it the same treatment.

Her hips rock, begging for more. I grip her waist tighter, trying to steady her movements, or I'll lose what little control I have left.

"I could get used to this. You, lying on my counter, all ready for me."

I touch her pussy over the delicate fabric covering it. She cries out, her head tipping back.

A deep rumble leaves my chest. "So wet."

I loop my fingers through the string and pull her thong down over her legs until they're on the floor. She leans up on her elbows and spreads her knees. My cock jumps at the sight, and a wave of disbelief washes over me... She wants this, wants me, as desperately as I want her.

I lift one foot on the counter and then the other. She hisses when I skim my hand along her thigh, my lips following, kissing higher and higher until I meet her wet pussy.

I peer up and see her mouth parted as her breasts rise and fall, her blue eyes locked on mine. I lick my lips. "I've always wondered what you'd taste like."

Her mouth moves, probably to argue, but I steal her breath the moment my tongue slides along her pussy. The taste of her hits me hard. Her body shakes under my palms. She's fucking perfect.

Her eyes flutter as she struggles to keep herself up and watch me. I want to unravel her. Make her feel so good no one would compare.

My gaze follows the path of my hands as they move to her pussy. I rub her clit in a slow circle as I bring my mouth down to her and lick her again. Forcing myself to ignore my cock, I focus on her pleasure.

I continue a lazy and firm rub on her swollen clit. Her breath hitches.

"What do you want, Karley?"

She mumbles something I can't understand. I lick her again. "Tell me."

"More."

"You want to come, don't you?"

I rub her clit faster, my own breath catching at the sight of her pleasure.

I do what I've been so desperate to do—slip a finger into her wet pussy. The tight, velvet heat surrounding my finger nearly makes me groan. She squirms, hips pressing toward me, fucking my finger, and I get off on it.

"Oliver," she pants.

"Karley, is all this mess for me?"

I insert a second finger, and she clamps down on me. "Yes-s."

At first, I'm slow and steady, but when I hit her G-spot, and she whimpers, I pick up the pace.

"Fuck, Oliver."

She's making a mess, and I fucking love it. "I'm going to make you come now, and then I'm going to fuck you, and make you come again."

"Yes..." She trails off when I bring my lips down to her clit and suck hard as I keep fingering her. Her whole body convulses, and she comes hard, moaning my name louder than I've ever heard before. There's something intoxicating about watching her come undone and knowing I'm the one who did it. Now I need to do it again, but this time with my dick.

CHAPTER 22

KARLEY

OLIVER PULLS HIS MOUTH from me, and I melt into the counter. Lying on my back, gentle kisses press on my pussy and up onto my lower stomach. My legs wrap around his waist as I let myself recover from the intensity of my orgasm. I can't believe we've crossed this line, this invisible boundary we've been dancing around for weeks. There's no going back now. This could ruin everything we've built or transform it into something real.

He wants to fuck me on this counter, and I want that too. At this height, I can feel his erection behind his pants.

He presses soft kisses up over my breasts, causing me to shiver as he touches my sensitive nipples.

"You're so beautiful when you come."

His words make me flush.

As he kisses up to my neck, I flop my head to the opposite side, enjoying his soft lips on my skin.

Trailing them over my jaw, he meets my lips, where we kiss passionately. Our tongues tangle, and I taste myself on him. The intimacy shocks me. And when we pull apart, there's a look of need in his eyes that makes my body come alive.

He steps away, and I look at his muscled back as he removes his pants and pulls out a condom. I'm entranced, watching him bring it to his mouth and ripping it open with his teeth. It's erotic.

As our eyes hold each other's, his hands grab my hips and drag me down so I'm on the edge.

"You enjoying the view?" He lifts an eyebrow.

I bite down on my lip and nod, my heart hammering against my ribs. After all this time, all the fantasies, the stolen glances, the aching, he's finally here, with me.

He rolls the condom onto his erection and comes to stand between my legs as I part them wide.

"You want to be fucked hard, don't you, Petal?"

"Yes. Please."

He growls. "God, you giving in like this is just as sexy as your sassy mouth."

He grabs my hips tightly, and I wrap my legs around his back, locking my ankles. His cock is *so* close to my pussy.

Before I can beg him to fuck me, he enters the tip of his cock inside me. I opened myself to him when I told him I wanted him. Now I surrender completely.

My hands grab his forearms to hold on, and he slides in farther, sending ripples of pleasure-pain up my spine, and I concentrate on breathing to allow my body to take him.

He takes it slow, but his pinched expression tells me he's restraining himself for my sake.

He groans, "Fuck." When he's all the way in, the fullness is overwhelming. He gives me a second to adjust, but then his hands tighten to hold me in place as he pulls out and thrusts in hard again.

The cold counter feels nice against the heat burning up inside me as he fucks me ruthlessly.

My body bounces with every slam, but his firm hold on me doesn't allow me to get too far from him. I peer up from under my lashes to see his gaze on our bodies coming together. This isn't just physical either. The risk of losing him terrifies me, but the thought of never knowing what this feels like would have haunted me forever.

He must feel my eyes on him because he looks up and gives me a crooked grin. "You should see how good we look."

I try to speak, but I can only moan. A second orgasm is coming on. But I'm desperate to come with him.

"You take me so well, Karley."

My grip on his forearms slips with perspiration. His confidence and knowing what my body needs right now is impressive. He gives it to me, and I try to meet every thrust.

"Oliver," I breathe a warning that I'm close to the edge.

But he doesn't stop, he keeps the pace and adds a finger to my clit. "Come for me."

I close my eyes and let go. My body pulses as I shatter around him, panting at the same time he grunts my name, and his body stills. The tight grip he has on my thigh loosens as his cock jerks inside me. His orgasm hits him at the same time. His body folds over mine, and I soak up the feeling, amazed at what just happened between us. The fact that I could make him lose control like this fills me with pride.

Minutes pass as we catch our breath, neither of us wanting to move. My hands wrap around his shoulders, holding him to me, my legs around him, and he stays inside. What happens when this moment ends? Will he pull away, make some excuse, pretending this was just physical?

But eventually, he leans back, his hands on either side of my body, a smirk on his face.

"What?" I ask.

He shakes his head. "The first time I have you and I fuck you in the kitchen."

"I'm not complaining," I say, though a flicker of uncertainty passes through me. Is he regretting it, wishing we'd done this properly? I search his face for clues. "You acted like you just couldn't wait."

"I couldn't. I fucking couldn't wait a second longer."

His gaze roams my body before his eyes meet mine with a knowing look, and I push at his chest.

My eyes hold his as he leans in. "I wanted you too."

"Well," he manages to say, a small smile tugging at his lips, "now that we're married, you're mine."

"Possessive much?" I laugh.

He brushes a strand of hair from my face with a grin. "Says the woman who's been wanting me longer."

I shove his shoulder playfully. "No need to rub it in."

"I'm not rubbing it in," he says softly, looking down. "I just wish I'd handled it differently."

"I don't know... I think it's better now. We actually got to know each other first."

He sighs. "Yeah... we did." His gaze lingers on mine, something tender in it. "Maybe that's what makes this feel so good right now."

Before I can say more, he discards the condom before coming back, lifting me effortlessly, pulling a startled squeal from my chest. I laugh as he carries me down the hall, holding me like I weigh nothing. He lays me down on his bed, his gaze never leaving mine as he kisses me, and everything else fades away. His arms wrap around me, strong and steady, holding me to this moment. I melt into him, feeling safe, wanted, and cherished in a way I never have before. As I curl into his side, I close my eyes, hoping with everything in me that when I wake, he'll still be here. That this is real.

CHAPTER 23

KARLEY

"I HAVE AN IDEA. Let's go out," he says, sitting up with me still in his arms. I twist in his embrace, my brow furrowed in confusion. Here I was, thinking I was about to fall asleep, but the excitement in his eyes tells me there's something else going on.

"What idea? Where are we going?" I ask, watching him closely.

"Come on, let's get ready. I have a surprise for you." He tugs my hands gently, his excitement infectious.

"What am I wearing?" I ask, a little amused by his sudden energy.

"That's my girl." He grins. "Anything you're comfortable walking around in."

I slide the blankets off, my feet brushing against the cool wooden floor as I swing my legs over the edge of the bed. Before I can step out of the room, his voice stops me.

"We need to move your clothes in here."

I freeze, turning toward him with a raised eyebrow. "You have no room for them."

I don't own much, never have. But Oliver? He has everything. A wardrobe full of suits, shoes, and shirts. All perfectly pressed and folded. His life is organized in a way mine never was. I saw it myself when I explored the house.

"I'll make room."

"It's only upstairs." I shrug, not thinking much of it.

He steps toward me, his hands resting gently on my waist as he gazes down at me, his eyes both soft and intense. "I want to make sure you're all the way in. No half foot out the door, waiting to run when our arrangement is up."

My lips part, but I can't find the words. He's right. He's completely right. Something flutters in my chest: surprise, hope, fear. I hadn't expected this from him.

"If you make room, I'll move my stuff," I offer, despite the swelling in my chest. "Is that proof enough?"

He doesn't answer right away. His thumbs brush slow circles against my sides, grounding me. "It's a start. But I need more than just your stuff here. I need *you* here."

The words hang between us, heavier than I expect.

"So, what are you asking for?" I whisper.

"I'm asking if this is real for you," he says, swallowing roughly. "I want to know if you're willing to date?"

Feeling the gravity of his words pulling me closer, it's hard to take a full breath. "This is real for me too," I whisper back, my chest tight with everything I feel. "I don't want to go anywhere. I want to be here... with you."

The confession leaves me feeling strangely exposed.

His breath catches slightly, and then he pulls me closer, his forehead resting against mine. "Then let's stop pretending this is temporary. Let's not just be convenient for each other. Let's be real. Whatever you want to call it, just as long as it's us."

I nod, my heart racing. "Okay. Us."

It feels terrifying and freeing all at once. But mostly? It feels right. A shadow of worry crosses my mind as I think about Declan and what he would think about this. Would he see this as a betrayal or understand that something real has grown between us?

I rise onto my toes, my lips meeting him in a kiss that's both tender and eager. "Are you sure you want to leave?"

A deep laugh rumbles from his chest as his hands tighten around my waist, pulling me closer. I can feel the beat of his heart against mine, steady and comforting. "You make me want to never leave. But I promise to date you first."

"And you have to do it right now?" I laugh, feeling the heat between us, but also the sweetness of the moment.

"Yes." He grins, nodding. "Now go get ready. I'll meet you in the kitchen."

I huff playfully, turning away as I head up the stairs. As I climb, I feel like I'm floating. I pull on a pair of blue jeans, slip into my Chucks, tug a long-sleeve white top over my head, and then a light blue sweater for warmth. Grabbing my purse, I head back down. I don't bother with makeup and my hair's looking surprisingly good today, so I leave it as it is.

When I reach the kitchen, Oliver's tapping on his phone, but he stops as soon as I walk in, his eyes lighting up with a smile. "Ready?"

I nod, excitement bubbling inside me. "Where are we going? It's eight o'clock at night."

He flashes me a mischievous grin and opens the front door for me. I walk outside and climb inside the waiting car, trying to suppress my curiosity. I've always been the type to demand answers immediately, but there's something sweet about letting him surprise me.

"You'll have to wait and see," he teases, squeezing my hand.

"Damn it," I mutter under my breath, but the smile on my face betrays my excitement.

"We're at stop one anyway," he says, his voice full of anticipation.

The car comes to a stop. I glance out the window, my breath catching in my throat. We're parked in front of Hudson Yards Vessel, the striking, honeycomb-like structure of bronze-colored steel and concrete glowing under the city lights.

"Are we going to climb the stairs?" I ask, trying to calculate how many flights it has. Sixteen stories... This could be a workout.

"No." He chuckles. "We're doing an art scavenger hunt."

I blink. "Are you kidding?"

He shakes his head, a warm smile spreading across his face. "No. I want to make up for lost time, make new happy memories with you."

My heart swells with gratitude as I lean in and kiss him.

"Okay, photo time," he says, snapping a shot of the Vessel from an angle, the light playing off the metal. Then he pulls me into a selfie, our bodies close, my head resting on his chest as we hug each other tight.

"Where to next?" I ask.

"I promise we're almost there." His hand slips into mine as we walk down the sidewalk.

We stroll side by side, my heart racing with each step, until we reach the High Line. It's over a mile-long elevated park that runs from Hudson Yards to the Meatpacking District, and as we wander along, I am in awe of the rotating art installations.

We pause in front of a large sculpture, and I ask a passerby to take our photo. As we stand there, the sound of an interactive audio installation suddenly bursts to life.

"That scared the daylights out of me." I laugh, my heart still pounding.

"Look over there," he says, motioning toward a vibrant video art display on a nearby building. The colors pulse and shift across the screen, almost alive in the night, glowing against the dark backdrop of the city.

"The next stop is Chelsea to explore the galleries," he says, glancing at his watch. "I know they're closed at this time of night, but we can peer in the windows. The lighting hits the artwork differently at night. Which one do you want to check out?" he asks.

He doesn't even need to list them. I already know the major ones, and out of them all, there's one I've been dying to see.

"Gagosian Gallery."

"Good choice. Ten minutes, and we'll be there," he replies, a content smile on his face.

True to his word, we're there in no time. I stand in front of the large glass windows of the gallery, peering inside. The oversized sculptures and bold contemporary pieces are illuminated in the most stunning way, glowing softly in the dark night. It's as if the gallery was made to be seen at night.

The oversized orange Balloon Dog by Jeff Koons immediately grabs my attention. I stand beside Oliver, staring up at it, completely captivated by its playful, childlike nature.

"It really taps into that feeling of innocence, doesn't it?" I say softly. "Like it's meant to remind us of the simple joy of a kid with a balloon at a birthday party."

I remember the surprise birthday party Amber and Wren threw me when they found out I'd never had one. They hired a balloon artist, and the dog was white, but seeing this massive orange version of it now makes me smile, bringing back all the happiness from that moment.

"Yeah, exactly," Oliver says, his eyes soft. "I wonder if kids still love balloons like that? Do people still hire balloon artists?"

"No idea." I laugh. "But I love how they've set it up so we can see it at night."

"It's incredible, isn't it?" he says, his arm brushing mine as we stand there.

"What about your gallery?" I ask, nudging him gently.

"You know what? That's a brilliant idea."

He pulls out his phone, snapping a quick photo of the Balloon Dog, then turns it toward us for a selfie.

After a few more moments spent admiring the art, Oliver checks his watch. "We need to keep moving," he says, his tone light but urgent.

It's just after nine, and before I can ask where we're heading next, he speaks again.

"This is the best date ever."

"How many dates have you been on?" I tease, my stomach twisting nervously as I try to ignore the unease crawling inside me.

"You answer first," he says, clearly amused.

"No, I asked first," I reply quickly. "I don't care, Oliver. I promise. You're with me now."

He looks down at the concrete, thinking for a moment, before meeting my eyes again. "None since I was in my twenties. But none of them were like this."

I smack his arm playfully. "Sure, sure."

"I'm serious," he says, pulling me to a stop in front of the gallery. His hand runs through my hair, soft and tender. "I've never had this kind of connection before."

I know exactly what he means. The way my heart races whenever he's near, the way I can't stop smiling when he looks at me, or how my stomach flutters when he kisses me. I've never experienced anything like this either.

We walk toward the Meatpacking District, where vibrant street art is splashed across every surface. We stop to snap photos of three different pieces, but one mural in particular catches my eye. The Love Letter Mural by James Goldcrown. It's a massive, spray-painted heart, full of intricate patterns and rich colors.

"At night, the colors really pop against the buildings." I've been here before but never seen it like this. The city lights make it seem alive. I feel the love radiating from the piece, almost like it's speaking to me.

I hold on to Oliver a little tighter, feeling the positive energy around us. The cool breeze ruffles my hair, and the crisp scent of the city at night feels almost magical.

We stop to take a photo in front of the mural, and I squeeze his hand, feeling so happy, so full.

"Where to next?" I ask, my excitement bubbling up again.

"You'll see in five minutes," he says, grinning. We walk hand in hand to the subway.

"I can't believe I'm on the subway with you," I say with a laugh.

"Why?" Oliver asks, clearly amused.

"You just... seem too cool for this," I admit, trying to find a polite way to say it.

"You mean too rich?" he teases.

"Yeah," I say sheepishly.

"I have been on the subway, but rarely do it now." He shrugs. "But I want to experience everything with you."

He pulls out his phone, snapping a picture of me standing on the subway. I'm not self-conscious at all. Then I pull him close and kiss him as he takes another shot of the two of us together.

"I'm so glad you pushed me to leave the bed tonight," I admit. "This has been incredible."

"It has, hasn't it?" Oliver agrees. "I've loved every second of it."

"I'm tired, though." I yawn.

"Our ride's waiting at the end," he says, taking my hand as we step off the subway.

We exit the subway and find ourselves in Washington Square Park, in the heart of Greenwich Village. The park is alive with energy, street performers, live music, dancers, and poetry readings. Oliver pulls out money and tips each performer, and my heart swells at his generosity.

We stop in front of a sketch artist. He's an older man with wire-rimmed glasses. His easel displays completed portraits of couples, families, and animals. Oliver asks him to sketch us. I bounce on my heels, thrilled by the idea of having this memory captured.

We sit close on the little bench in front of the easel. I try to hold still, but I keep glancing at Oliver, who's fighting a grin every time I shift. The artist barely looks up as his pencil moves swiftly across the page, like he's done this a thousand times.

When he finally turns the sketch around, I light up.

"I love it," I say, brushing my fingers over the edge.

Oliver nods in agreement, handing the man cash. "Can you roll it up for us?"

The artist obliges, slipping the paper into a cardboard tube and capping it off. Oliver tucks it under his arm like it's something precious.

It kind of is.

We make our way to our next stop, the Little Italy Mural in Manhattan. The mural is a stunning, colorful piece, full of pizza, pasta, Italian landscapes, and portraits of famous figures from the community.

I read the signatures on the mural, impressed by how brave the artists are for putting their work on public display. Before Oliver and the arrangement, it's something I've always admired, and I hope one day I'll be brave enough to do the same on a bigger scale than the school shop. I'm getting stronger, but I'm not quite there yet. *But I will be.*

"Let's grab a picture before the final stop," Oliver says, pulling me out of my thoughts.

"Sounds good," I reply, still on a high from the night, unable to stop smiling.

We walk down the street, and I spot Morgenstern's Finest Ice Cream.

"This is the final stop?" I ask, a grin forming on my face as I squeeze his hand tighter.

"Yes. I take it you've been here before?"

"Not often, but once. And the matcha ice cream was incredible."

We enter the shop. The sweet, creamy scent of waffle cones and freshly churned ice cream wraps around me instantly. The interior is minimalist, with sleek counters and bright color pops against walls. Behind the glass display, sits rows of different flavored ice creams.

"I don't even know where to start," I murmur, scanning the names.

"Try this one." He hands me a sample spoon the lady hands him. "You'll like it."

I hesitate, then take the tiny spoon from his hand, our fingers brushing a second too long. His eyes don't leave mine as I taste it, a rich chocolate with a hint of sea salt.

"Mmm," I say, licking my lips. "That's dangerously good."

"Right?" He leans in a little too close. "Here, try this one too." Asking for another scoop in a different flavor of chocolate chip cookie dough, he offers it straight to my mouth this time.

I don't even think, I just lean forward and take the bite, letting his thumb brush my lower lip as he pulls the spoon away.

"Okay, now you have to try mine," I say, a little breathless, turning to ask for a sample of salted caramel pretzel. He meets my gaze, his lips curving as he leans in and lets me feed him.

"You're right," he says, his voice lower now. "It's going to be too hard to choose, so I say we get a scoop of all three."

I nod, grinning.

A few minutes later, we're outside with a single over-filled cup between us. We take turns with the spoon, laughing as we flick through the photos from the night.

I yawn, feeling the exhaustion finally catch up with me.

"Let's get you home. I organized a car," he says, helping me to my feet.

In the car, I snuggle up beside him, curling into his side, our fingers intertwined. His thumb brushes slow circles across the back of my hand, causing a flutter in my stomach.

The drive is peaceful, the city lights blurring past the windows as we talk about our favorite moments of the night.

We arrive at home and head inside his place.

He closes the door behind us, then leans against it, eyes locked on mine. "Can we pick up where we left off?"

I arch an eyebrow, slowly turning to face him fully. "Now you want to?"

He steps closer, his hands flexing at his sides like he's holding himself back. "Please," he rasps, gaze raking over me. "Don't make me beg."

I take a teasing step back. "I think I need to hear you say it."

His jaw tightens, and then... he does. "I want you. I've wanted you for so damn long. I don't care how long it takes. I'll beg all night if that's what it takes."

An ache grows as I close the distance, brushing my fingers along the hem of my shirt.

"Well then," I whisper, lips closer to his, "start begging."

His breath hitches, hands fisting, and when I finally start to undress under his smoldering gaze, everything else disappears.

CHAPTER 24

KARLEY

"WHERE DO YOU THINK you're going?" Oliver rumbles through the quiet of the room.

I pause mid-step, caught in the act of sneaking away to the bathroom. As I glance over my shoulder, my breath hitches at the sight of him. The soft morning sunlight filters through the half-drawn curtains, spilling golden light across the bed. It illuminates the toned lines of his relaxed, naked body, the disheveled mess of his dark hair, the faint shadow of stubble on his jaw. He looks incredibly sexy, like something out of a dream.

His eyes soften as they meet mine, a lazy smirk tugging at his lips. "Come back here," he murmurs, his outstretched hand inviting me closer.

"Give me two minutes. I'll be right back."

When I return, he's still lying there, waiting, the sheets low across his hips. I crawl back into bed and let his arms wrap around me, holding me in a way that feels both safe and dangerous all at once.

"That's better," he says against my hair.

I nestle into him, inhaling his woodsy scent. The soft tickle of his chest hair brushes against my cheek, and I sigh in contentment, momentarily forgetting the outside world.

"What are your plans today?" I ask.

He hums, the vibrations rolling deep through his chest. "I have one idea," he replies before he flips me onto my back, pinning me beneath him.

My pulse quickens, every nerve in my body sparking to life under his heated gaze. His proximity is intoxicating, and I find myself lost in his eyes.

"Oliver," I begin, attempting to steer the conversation, even as a smile plays on my lips.

"Are you turning me down?" he teases, his tone mock-wounded, but his grin entirely wicked.

"No," I say with an exaggerated roll of my eyes. "But I was hoping you'd come with me to check out the house I bought."

His expression shifts, his eyes widening slightly. "Of course, I'll come."

"We need to get ready soon."

"I just need a minute with you." Then, without any warning, he closes the space between us, silencing my thoughts with a kiss.

I hang up from the New York State Office of Children and Family Services as we pull up in front of the house. My dream of creating a family visitation center is slowly becoming real.

Climbing out of the car, I turn to him, my heart pounding. This moment feels monumental, and yet I'm terrified of sharing too much. In only a few weeks, it's mine.

We stand side by side on the sidewalk. I peer up at him, trying to read his face. His expression thoughtful, eyebrows slightly drawn together as he takes in the property.

"Well?" I ask, breaking the silence. "What do you think?"

He studies the house, his eyes looking over every detail before his lips curl into a teasing smirk. "It's charming," he finally says. "And big."

Nudging him playfully, I roll my eyes. "You're the one to talk about big houses."

He chuckles. "Fair point. But it's been nice sharing mine lately."

"Sharing it with who?" I tease.

His arms slip around my waist from behind, pulling me close. "You. Only you," he whispers, his lips brushing the curve of my neck.

Warmth blooms in my chest as I place my hands over his, chasing away my earlier nerves.

"Tell me your plans for this place." He rests his chin on my shoulder. "What do you want to change?"

I hesitate, the weight of my plans suddenly feeling heavier. But with his arms around me, I find the courage to share. "This house isn't for me," I begin. "It's for foster kids. A place where they can spend time with their biological families, somewhere safe."

He stays silent, encouraging me to continue.

"Growing up, not being able to see Declan often was... hard. Harder on him, though."

"I think he's just more vocal about it." His words hit me with force. I'm surprised that he saw what I've spent years denying, but also relieved that someone finally understands. Declan always wore his hurt on the outside, the anger and frustration visible. I buried mine, to seem like I was coping. But Oliver sees through that.

Oliver turns me to face him, his gaze searching mine. I'm unable to hide now, and I'm sure it's written on, not only my face, but in my eyes how much that rings true. "You don't have to be tough with me," he says. "You can trust me."

"Trust doesn't come easily for me," I admit quietly.

"How can I earn it?" The sincerity in his eyes makes words fall from my lips.

"Share something real with me," I say. "Something that makes me feel like I'm not the only one letting my guard down."

He exhales slowly, staring at his hands. "Everyone sees this successful guy who has it all figured out. The truth is... I still feel like that kid who was given the galleries from his mom. Every meeting, every deal, there's this voice in my head, saying they'll figure out I don't belong. That I'm not good enough. So I keep people at arm's length... It's easier than letting someone close enough to confirm what I'm afraid of."

"But my brother said—" I begin, my eyebrows lifting in surprise at the contradiction between the Oliver I thought I knew and the one being revealed to me now.

He cuts me off with a sad smile. "The playboy thing? It's a convenient mask. Keep it light, keep it casual, never stay long enough for anyone to see past the façade."

This sounds too good to be true. I ignore the way my heart swells and wait for clarification. I'm not special. Just your average girl wanting security and, lately, because of him... love and affection.

"Why haven't you been in a serious relationship?"

"Because who'd want the real me when the fake version is so much more impressive?" He runs a hand through his hair. "Plus, in my experience, money attracts the wrong kind of attention."

His words land like a stone in my chest, and I feel a sudden chill. "But this arrangement was for a business deal."

He shakes his head. "A house that you'll use for struggling kids isn't the same. You're not asking for fancy dinners, shopping sprees..."

I peer down at my rings, knowing they are the only lavish gifts I own. "I'd rather paint or be at home."

His hand lifts my chin, forcing me to meet his gaze. "You're different. What you're doing here, with this house, proves that."

I shake my head as fear of being abandoned again threatens to overtake me. "I'm scared," I whisper.

"Then let's continue to take it slow," he says softly. He turns me so he's holding me again. We stay like this, staring at the house for a while longer.

A few hours later, the warm scent of herbs and roasting chicken fills the kitchen. It's quiet except for the chopping of vegetables. Oliver stands beside me at the counter, sleeves rolled up, slicing carrots with precision. I brush past him to grab garlic, and my hand grazes his. A fleeting touch that sends a thrill up my spine. My cheeks flush, and I quickly turn back to my cutting board, pretending to be focused on mincing the clove. But I can feel his eyes on me.

"You've been quiet. Are you okay?"

"I'm focused," I reply without looking up, though my pulse quickens as he steps nearer.

"Focused?" he teases. "You've chopped that garlic into dust."

Heat floods my face as I realize he's right. I laugh as I sweep the tiny pieces into a bowl. "Just trying to make sure it's perfect."

His phone chimes with a notification of someone at the door, so he moves away with a soft chuckle. I can't tell if it's at my expense or because he finds this endearing.

Evelyn enters behind Oliver, her eyes lighting up when she sees me. "Karley!" she squeals, moving to give me a big hug. As she pulls back, her sharp eyes immediately take in the scene. She arches an eyebrow but says nothing, heading for the fridge to cool the bottle of white wine she's brought with her. My stomach twists with the urge to tell her everything about last night, the way Oliver completely unraveled me. But the timing hasn't been right, and besides, Oliver has barely left my side since the moment we woke up.

Not that I'm complaining.

"How can I help?" Evelyn offers as she watches Oliver return to the kitchen.

The door chimes again. "Could you grab that?" Oliver asks.

She smiles and heads to open the door.

He shifts closer to me, reaching over to pluck the tray from the counter. His arm brushes mine, lingering just enough to make me catch my breath.

"You okay?" he asks.

I glance up at him, momentarily lost in the soft intensity of his piercing gaze. His question feels like he's asking more than he's letting on.

"Yeah," I reply, steadier than I expected. "Just... preoccupied."

His smirk returns, but there's a flicker of something deeper in his expression. "Good," he says softly. "Stay that way. It makes this easier."

I don't have time to unpack what he means, because the sound of heavy footsteps announces the arrival of the family. The room fills with laughter and voices, breaking the sexual tension around us.

Their familiar faces brighten the room, and I move in for a quick hug. "Hi," I greet Wren and Amber when they step into the kitchen.

"Hey," they chime back, both smiling warmly. Amber's sharp eyes flick briefly to Oliver, and I can tell she's assessing him in her own way.

Oliver, ever the charmer, steps forward with his hand extended. "Hi. Nice to meet you both," he says, firmly shaking first Amber's hand, then Wren's with a warm smile. His eyes drift to the bundle of white fluff nestled in Wren's arms. "And who's this guy?" Oliver asks, leaning down slightly to get a better look at the dog.

"This is Rufus," Wren replies, his voice full of affection.

I reach out to pat Rufus's soft fur, cooing at him. Oliver follows suit, his larger hand brushing the top of Rufus's head. The dog seems content, at least for a moment, before wiggling excitedly out of Wren's grasp.

Oliver pours wine for Evelyn, Amber, and me, and cracks open beers for himself and Wren. The gesture is so effortless, so natural.

As we all settle into the rhythm of cooking and conversation, I glance at Oliver, catching the faintest hint of a smile as he works.

Just as I'm about to take Amber and Wren on a tour of the house. Rufus, now free, lunges at Oliver's leg with determination.

"Rufus!" Wren's voice cuts sharply through the room.

But Rufus, undeterred, clings to Oliver's leg and humps.

"Rufus, stop!" Wren commands again, his tone more urgent.

Oliver freezes, his face going pale as his hands hover awkwardly at his sides. His normally composed expression is replaced by one of utter disbelief as Rufus continues his embarrassing display.

I can't hold back the giggle that bubbles up. "Looks like you've got an admirer."

Oliver's eyes narrow as he shoots me a pointed look. "I have plenty of admirers," he quips, his tone suggestive, the double meaning unmistakable.

Heat rises in my cheeks, creeping up my neck, and I quickly look away.

"I'm so sorry," Wren says, scooping Rufus up with an apologetic wince. "He's started doing this lately. I have no idea why."

"It's fine," Oliver says, the corner of his mouth twitching as if he's fighting a smile.

I try to smooth over the moment as I motion for Wren and Amber. "Let's start the tour before Declan and Armani get here."

Wren nods, holding Rufus as if to prevent another incident. The group begins to move toward the entryway, but before I can follow, a firm hand wraps around my waist.

Oliver's breath warms my ear as he leans in, his voice a low rumble. "I can't wait to have you all to myself later."

Twisting around, I push lightly against his chest, my pulse racing. "We should stop before they come back."

With a teasing smirk, his arms stay wrapped around me. "You're my wife," he says simply, his tone both playful and possessive. "Hugging you is one of my favorite things."

I inhale sharply, knowing there's no winning this. Instead, I manage a weak glare before slipping out of his grasp and following the others up the stairs.

The tour is brief but lively, filled with Amber's observations and Wren's occasional teasing. I make sure to avoid the room with my painting on the wall, in fear that Amber will tell Oliver that it's mine. I still haven't told him about my art because my painting feels like one of the few things that's truly mine, untouched by our arrangement. I'm feeling closer to sharing that piece of myself... Just not today.

As we head back down from the top level, muffled voices drift up from the front hall.

Declan and Armani have arrived.

The moment I see Declan, an unexpected warmth fills my chest. I step forward and wrap him and Armani in a tight hug.

"Hey," I say.

"Karley," Declan replies, his tone as steady as ever.

As I pull back, my eyes flick between them, soaking in the familiar comfort of my brother and Amarni, who has become like family to me. I've truly missed them. Having some distance has been good for us. I no longer feel smothered. I'm genuinely happy to see him.

Declan studies me, his eyes narrowing. "What's with that look on your face?"

"I'm happy to have all my favorite people in one room." I wave a hand around the kitchen, and Armani grabs it mid-air, her eyes lighting up.

"Look at your rings," Armani squeals.

Evelyn and Amber rush over. I glance down at my hand, realizing I've grown so used to the wedding rings that they no longer feel foreign. Somehow, they've become a part of me.

"Oh my God, they're gorgeous," Amber gushes, holding my hand under the light.

Armani and Evelyn take turns admiring the sapphire, their delight making me blush.

"Isn't this a little over the top for something that isn't even real?" Declan says, his voice dipping into that familiar skeptical tone. I struggle to keep my expression neutral, even as something inside me protests. His old habits die hard, apparently.

I glance at Oliver, curious and a little anxious about how he'll handle my brother's bluntness.

"You know she wasn't going to get anything less than what she deserves," he says with a wink, just as his phone rings.

He mouths, *It's Dan*, and steps away to take the call. I smile. Mr. Warne knowing about our family dinner definitely helps sell our marriage.

Declan's gaze shifts back to me, his expression unreadable. I press my lips together and turn to Armani with a grin. "What about you? What kind of ring would you want?"

She lights up at the question, her hand fluttering to her chest. As she begins describing her dream ring, I make a mental note. My brother loves hard and fast, and when the time comes for him to propose, I want to make sure he gets it right.

Later, we're all seated around Oliver's long wooden dining table. The spread is social media worthy: golden roast chicken, roasted vegetables glistening with olive oil, cornbread, creamy mashed potatoes, and a crisp Caesar salad.

The hum of conversation fills the room. Just as I'm settling into the comfort of the moment, Declan cuts through it like a knife. "So, when are you annulling the marriage?"

The room falls silent, tension thickening in the air. My stomach drops and heat rushes to my face.

I peek up at Oliver from under my lashes, silently begging him to take this one. I don't want to answer. Oliver and I had a discussion about dating, but I don't feel like being lectured by Declan today. I just want to stay in this bubble I've been living in for a little bit longer.

"We haven't secured the gallery yet."

Amber, always the practical one, jumps in. "Is there any news on it?"

"Not yet," Oliver replies. "But he seems to be happy with Karley and me, so I'm hopeful."

"You'll get it," I say, wanting to offer him even the smallest reassurance. I've seen how hard he works, how much pressure he puts on himself to live up to expectations.

Oliver's blue eyes lock onto mine, and for a moment, the rest of the room fades away. The longing in his gaze is almost overwhelming, and I feel it in the pit of my stomach.

He smiles softly. "We will."

Evelyn leans back in her chair, a sly smile playing on her lips. "You two are a little too good at faking it."

Her words stir something in me. I realize I need to tell her about last night... now. With Declan's blunt reminder of our arrangement, I need someone to talk to before I explode with all these conflicting feelings. I lean toward her, whispering, "Come help me with dessert?"

She shoots me a giddy expression and follows me into the kitchen. As I grab the peach cobbler from the oven, she gets the vanilla ice cream from the freezer.

"We hooked up last night." The words tumble out in a breath before I can stop them.

Evelyn nearly drops the ice cream. "Okay, I need details," she whispers, leaning in closer with wide eyes. "Was it everything you hoped for?"

My face breaks into the widest grin. "Better. And he said he wants to date me."

Evelyn freezes. "You're kidding."

I shake my head, my grin only growing.

"I'm so happy for you." Giving me a half hug, she pulls back, her eyes sparkling with excitement. "It's been a long time coming."

"Thanks," I reply, as nerves flutter in my stomach.

"But wait, what about the whole arrangement thing?" she whisper-shouts, nudging me with her elbow.

"I don't know, exactly."

Evelyn waves it off. "That's okay. Take it one day at a time."

Oliver comes into the kitchen to help, ending our conversation. We serve the dessert, returning to the table just as the conversation shifts to the news. But even as I settle back into the group, my mind lingers on Oliver and the way everyone's so at ease. Now that Declan has gotten off the topic of my and his best friend's relationship status, we're actually a family. He is my husband. I catch his eye across the table. That quiet, knowing smile of his is aimed my way, and I wonder if he can read my mind.

An hour later, as I walk Evelyn out, I pause, the soft glow of the porch light casting long shadows across his incredible yard. I can hear the laughter of the group inside, but I need a moment alone with her, away from prying ears. The cool night air wraps around us, and I take a deep breath before speaking. "Thanks for coming."

"Of course. It was a lot of fun," Evelyn replies, smiling as she pulls her jacket tighter against the evening chill.

She turns, but I take a step toward her, my hand lightly gripping her arm to keep her from leaving. "I need help telling him about me being the artist of those paintings he owns."

Evelyn raises an eyebrow, curiosity sparking in her eyes. "You want to make it special?"

I nod, my heart picking up speed. "I'm nervous to tell him."

She leans in a little. "Why? He's going to freak out when you tell him."

I bite my lip, looking down at my hands. "That's what I'm afraid of. What if this changes everything between us when we're just figuring things out?"

Would he just like me for my art? And not me as a person?

"He'll be ecstatic. Not only does he have a beautiful wife, but she also happens to be a brilliant painter."

I look back up. Her words hit me in a way I wasn't expecting. I'm so lucky to have a good friend in my life. "It takes one to know one."

Evelyn waves her hand dismissively in the air, grinning. "Oh, thanks."

"I want to do it in a romantic way. I don't want to just blurt it out."

She looks at me thoughtfully, tapping her chin. "Hmm, what about you organize a date night next weekend? Go away somewhere... private?"

"I like that idea. Maybe one of those A-framed cabins in the woods..."

Evelyn scrunches her face in horror, stepping back a little. "A cabin in the woods? Where bears can eat you? Not romantic."

I laugh, rolling my eyes. "You're so dramatic. It's about snuggling up by the fire and listening to the sounds of nature."

She shakes her head, her soft laughter filling the air. "You and I have different tastes. I was thinking warm, relaxing... Maybe something with a spa?"

I smile, imagining how nice that would be, but I'm set on the cabin idea. "But I can't do it next weekend."

"Why not?" Evelyn asks, her brow furrowing.

"I just need more time to plan everything. I want it to be perfect."

Evelyn nods in approval. "Make sure you tell me the name of the place and check if it has service. Don't want to be stranded without a signal."

I'm touched by how much she cares. "I will."

She narrows her eyes at me. "And read the reviews. Otherwise, I will."

"Okay, okay. Thanks again for everything."

With one last smile, she walks toward her ride, but I stand there for a moment, letting the cool night air settle around me. The thought of telling Oliver about not only my art, but my identity, which is a part of me he doesn't know yet, fills me with anticipation. But I know after my supportive chat with Evelyn that, in a few weeks, I can make it happen.

Amber, Wren, and Rufus head out next. Declan and Armani are the last to leave, and Oliver is talking at the door, so I excuse myself and head up for a quick shower. When I step out, I find Oliver standing in the bedroom, dark eyes roaming my naked body. He's unmoving, and his attention has goosebumps rising on my skin. The pure desire etched into his face makes me step closer to him until my toes touch his. "Like what you see?"

"Fuck, yeah."

My heart races as I drop to my knees, peering up at him with a smirk.

"Look at you, so pretty on your knees for me," he says, removing his sweater.

He's in a black t-shirt and black pants, his erection pressing hard against his zipper. But he doesn't make a move to kick off his shoes or remove any clothing.

I reach up and cup him over his pants, feeling his reaction beneath my palm. "Someone's excited," I whisper, a playful smile tugging at my lips.

His nostrils flare as his thumb traces slowly over my parted mouth. "Only for you," he murmurs, voice rough with desire. "Show me how much you want this too."

I lift higher on my knees and reach for his button and zipper, undoing them quickly.

His hands hang by his sides for now, but I make it a mission to have him so out of control he has them buried in my hair.

Pushing his pants and briefs down to his ankles, his cock stands heavy and thick in front of my face. I swallow hard at the sight of pre-cum. I'm so ready for it. Ready for him.

His hand clenches by his side. "Fuck. Petal, the way you're staring... It's fucking killing me."

Knowing he's already feral for this makes me squirm with need.

I grab him around his base and open my mouth to lick the head, bringing that salty pre-cum onto my tongue.

He hums, and his eyes roll. "So good." His praise sends a thrill through me, a rush of pleasure, knowing I can make him feel this way.

I keep my eyes on him as I lick him again, only slower this time. A noise vibrates from his chest. I do it again and again like a lollipop. My own breathing quickens as I work. When his cock is glistening with my saliva, I cover his tip with my mouth and suck.

"Yeah, just like that," he hisses and grabs the back of my head, curling his fingers into my hair. The pressure of his hand guiding me sends a shiver down my spine.

His other hand pushes the hair back from my face. The friction makes my eyes flutter and his darken with desire.

He looks like he's holding back from fucking my face.

"So fucking good."

I squeeze him tighter, suck him harder, and when my hand reaches up to touch his balls, he curses. "My darling wife, if you don't get off now, I'll come in your hot little mouth." Hearing him call me his darling wife makes my heart stutter. A deep ache builds inside me that has me pressing my thighs together as I hold his eye contact and suck harder.

"Karley, fuck!" he cries out, and I whimper with my own desperation. But I don't stop, keeping my eyes on him as he thickens even more in my mouth.

Knowing he's close, I go faster, and his balls tighten in my hands at the same time.

His breathing is rapid, but it's when his eyes close and his head tips back that hot bursts explode in my mouth. I keep swallowing until he stops jerking, and a wave of satisfaction flows through me. His muscles soften, his hand uncurls in my hair, and he smooths it down before crouching and lifting me to my feet. His lopsided grin and flushed face are incredibly tender.

"You, my wife, are incredible. Now it's my turn to be a good husband and let you come on my dick."

I shift restlessly against him. "God, yes."

My mouth crashes onto his, and his lips move with soft passion as he walks me backward. When the backs of my legs hit the mattress, I pause. He lifts his lips from mine, breathing labored, his body perspiring. I watch my hands as they roam his hot body.

"Turn around, hands on the bed, feet stay on the floor."

I don't bother asking about his plans because his cock is fully erect and ready again.

Turning around, I bend over, placing my palms flat on the mattress.

I hear the sound of ripping foil. He must be putting a condom on.

Then I feel his hand on my ass cheeks, squeezing gently, before he reaches around and touches my breast, tweaking my nipple. The sharp sensation shoots straight to my core. My back arches as he lays a kiss on my back. "Ready, Petal?"

"Please, Oliver."

"Spread your legs wider."

As I move my legs farther apart, Oliver drags his fingers from my clit to my entrance, and I shudder with need. "Is this all from sucking my dick?"

I hum, the touch on my pussy making me forget how to speak.

"Lean down on your elbows."

I drop down, feeling the tip of him at my pussy, and I clench, the anticipation too much.

He glides his tip up and down through my wetness, teasing me before he finally presses his thick cock slowly inside. We both groan. His hands hold my hips as he continues stretching me until he's all the way in. I feel incredibly full. He pauses, waiting for me to adjust to his size. I pulse around him at the intrusion, sucking in deep breaths of air.

"You take me so well."

I moan. His hot, delicious words only add to my arousal.

"You ready?"

I nod, barely able to speak.

"Words," he demands roughly.

"Yes," I breathe. "Fuck me, Oliver."

"God," he growls. "I'll never get sick of you begging for it."

He pulls out just enough to make me ache, then slams back into me. My breath catches.

I grip the sheets with white-knuckled force as he sets a pace that's as punishing as it is perfect.

"This angle is so much deeper. Do you feel that?"

"Yes," I whimper, overwhelmed.

His grip on my hips tightens, thumbs digging into my skin. Leaning over me, his mouth brushes along my spine. His rough stubble grazes my back, and it's almost too much. My legs tremble under the intensity of it all.

"Oliver," I gasp, voice cracking.

"Hold on," he pants. "Almost there."

I moan, knowing I can't hold on much longer. The sounds of our skin slapping together and his grunting makes my orgasm consume so much quicker this time.

"I'm going to..."

"Come for me, wife."

That word. *Wife*. Hits me harder than anything else.

"Fuck," he grunts.

I lose it. I cry out his name as his fingers dig into my skin. He thrusts hard into me one more time and then pauses, his cock jerking inside of me. We come together exactly like husband and wife.

CHAPTER 25

OLIVER

I PULL UP OUTSIDE Jeremy's house; the headlights cutting through the dusk as I park. It's poker night, and while I haven't made it here much recently, with Karley working, I've decided to show up. Being home alone has lost its appeal now that she occupies my bed.

As we walk into Jeremy's den, cards are shuffling, ice cubes clink against glasses, and chatter bounces off the walls. The others are already here, Evan, Harvey, Lukas, and Richard. They're all seated at the table like they've been there forever.

"Hey," I say, sliding into my usual seat. "I'd say sorry I'm late, but I'm right on time." I tap the face of my Rolex. "What's the deal? None of you want to be at home tonight?"

"No," Evan quips. "It's the opposite. We want to play, win, and get the hell back home."

For the first time, I feel a rush of agreement with Evan's thought. Usually, I'd be the one pushing to extend our fun, but tonight, all I can think about is getting back to Karley.

"Then let's get to it," I reply, cracking my knuckles like I'm a professional poker player, even though they all know I'm not. I actually suck compared to them.

We settle into the game, each in our so-called "lucky spots." Lukas insists his seat gives him "the winning energy," which usually means he's the first to lose.

I glance around as the cards are dealt. "What'd I miss?"

Before anyone answers, there's a loud pop. A spray of beer spills all over Richard's lap. He stares down in shock.

"First casualty of the night!" Lukas laughs, holding up his can in a mock toast.

Richard glares at us as he grabs a handful of napkins. "This is sabotage! Someone shook my fucking beer."

Jeremy, failing miserably at looking innocent, leans back with a smug grin. "Don't blame the beer. Blame your inability to open it like a normal person."

"Next time, drink the good shit, and it won't happen," Evan mumbles.

As the laughter dies down, my phone lights up beside me. A grin tugs my lips before I can catch myself. I reach for the phone as Harvey leans over, peering at the screen like an overgrown teenager.

"Wifey?" he asks, grinning like the Cheshire Cat.

The rest of the table joins in, chiming, "Wifey's calling!" in unison.

I grab my phone and stand, rolling my eyes as I head out of the den. "I'll deal with you idiots when I get back."

In the quiet of Jeremy's living room, I answer. "Hey."

"Hi," Karley's soft voice comes through. "Sorry, are you busy?"

"Not for you. What's up?"

"My group canceled, so I'm home. Do you want me to cook you dinner?"

"How about I bring something home instead?" I suggest, as poker suddenly seems less important.

She sighs with something that sounds like half-relief. "That sounds amazing."

"What do you feel like?"

"Whatever."

I smile. "Okay, I just need a few. I'm at Jeremy's."

"You don't need to leave. I can order delivery."

"No," I say firmly. "I'll pick it up. I need you."

I've never been the type to admit needing anyone, but with Karley, it's true. I brace myself for the inevitable teasing from the guys, but at this moment, I find I don't care.

There's a pause on the line, and then a quiet, "I need you too."

Her words hit me hard as I say goodbye and hang up. She's still hesitant in the relationship, but when she opens up, it feels like a big step forward. It's going to take a long time to earn her trust.

Movement in the corner of my eye catches my attention. Jeremy's fiancée, Nova, enters the room with a warm smile.

"Hi, Oliver. Sorry, I couldn't help but overhear."

"It's okay," I reply, gesturing for her to join me. "I'm going to have to face those idiots in there soon. It might be nice to talk to someone sane first."

She sits across from me. "So... you have a girl at home?"

A stupid grin spreads across my face. "Yeah."

Her smile grows. "Is it serious?"

I tread carefully, knowing they all don't know about the marriage and gallery. I can't risk it getting out. "At first, it wasn't..."

Nova raises an eyebrow, leaning in with playful curiosity. "At first, it wasn't... but?"

Chuckling, I scratch the back of my neck. "But now, it's... complicated. Good complicated."

Her grin widens. "Good complicated sounds serious to me."

I shrug, trying to play it cool, though the thought of Karley makes my chest tighten in a way I can't breathe. "Let's just say, she's important."

Nova studies me for a moment, then tilts her head with a knowing smile. "You look different. Happier. Whoever she is, she's clearly good for you."

I laugh and shake my head. "Let's hope the guys don't figure that out. They'll never let me hear the end of it."

"Don't worry," Nova says with a wink. "Your secret's safe with me... for now."

Before I can respond, the door to the den bursts open, and Jeremy sticks his head out, grinning like the devil.

"Oi, Oliver. Are you spilling secrets out here? Nova's probably grilling you isn't she?"

Nova waves him off with mock irritation. "Go back to your cards, Remy. Let us talk in peace."

He smirks, but retreats, leaving the door slightly ajar.

Nova leans closer, her expression softening. "You know, you deserve this. Happiness, I mean. I don't know much about her, but if she's making you smile like that, then hold on to her."

Her words catch me off guard, and I nod. "Thanks, Nova. That means a lot."

"Now go," she says, standing and shooing me toward the den. "Before they come out here and start interrogating both of us."

Before I can do exactly that, my phone buzzes again. It's Ray from the school shop, calling about a painting of the anonymous artist's being ready for pick-up. The excitement is contagious, and I promise him I'll have Cora pick it up ASAP.

When I return to the den, I'm practically buzzing.

"He's got the look, boys," Harvey says with a grin.

"Shut the fuck up," I reply, packing up. "I just got off the phone with the school shop. Another painting came in."

Harvey smirks. "Stop avoiding the topic. Unless she works at the school?"

"No. I talked to my girlfriend first," I say.

That stops them. Richard whistles.

"I couldn't let you boys have all the fun," I say nonchalantly.

"Who is she?" Evan asks, eyeing me over his drink.

I hesitate, anticipating their shock and disbelief when they realize it's Declan's sister. "Karley."

A glass clinks hard against the table. "You're kidding, right?" Evan says.

"Nope. Dead serious."

"What about Declan?" Lukas chimes in. "He'll have your balls."

I shrug. "He doesn't know."

Jeremy leans back, smirking. "This is going to be fun to watch."

I shake my head as my thoughts drift back to Karley. They can tease all they want, but I've got exactly what I want.

Soon, I need to have a conversation with Declan before he moves to Florida. We're friends, and I want to make it known Karley and I aren't faking our relationship anymore. I'm not sure how he'll react. I didn't want to tell him last night with everyone around. This conversation needs to happen one-on-one.

I drain my glass before saying goodbye, thinking how not long ago I wanted what all my brothers had, yet I did it better. I got married first...

CHAPTER 26

OLIVER

THE PHONE RINGS JUST as I'm reviewing the quarterly numbers. Dan Warne. My heart rate picks up slightly as I answer.

"Oliver. Are you and that lovely wife of yours free tomorrow night?"

I glance at my calendar, already knowing I'll clear anything that might be there. "We are. What did you have in mind?"

"Just an intimate dinner with friends. Nothing formal. At the gallery, around six?" There's a casualness in his words, but I know better than to treat any invitation from Dan Warne as informal.

"We'll be there."

"Excellent. I look forward to catching up with you again."

"Can't wait. See you at six tomorrow."

The next night, I'm standing in the kitchen, flicking through my phone while waiting for Karley to finish changing. A picture makes me straighten. Liam's getting ready, too. Perfect. The prick scored an invite. Fucking great. Maybe tonight's the night Mr. Warne finally announces who's getting the gallery, and I won't have to deal with Liam's smug grin ever again.

The sound of heels clicking on the floor snaps my head away from my phone. There she is.

Her black dress has a high neckline and falls modestly to mid-length, but then she moves, and the thigh-high slit on the left side catches my attention. My throat goes dry, and I almost choke on my tongue.

"You look incredible, Petal," I manage to say, slipping my phone in my pocket as I step toward her with my hands out.

She places her palms in mine. Her makeup is flawless, her face radiant, but the way her eyes flick to the floor and back up tells me she's blushing.

"Thanks for arranging the girls to help me," she says softly, glancing back toward the bedroom, where the stylist and makeup artist from our wedding day are packing up. I'd flown them here to help Karley feel more comfortable tonight.

"I wanted to make your life easier."

"It helped. There's no way I'd look this good without them."

"I beg to differ. You always look good."

She smiles, and I notice the way her cheeks lift, her confidence shining through. "Thanks."

There's a quiet pride in watching her confidence grow, knowing I had some small part in it.

"The shoes are a nice touch." Slipping my hands to her lower back, I pull her closer. The added height from her black stilettos brings her just close enough to my level.

"I'm hoping not to break my neck in them," she jokes.

"I won't let that happen." I brush a stray strand of hair behind her ear. "Though if you trip, we're making it a scene. Maybe I'll fake a tumble too... Really sell it."

She grins. "Oh, and have Dan thinking we're both hopeless? Sounds like a solid plan."

"Exactly. If we're going down, we're going down in style."

"Speaking of style..." She steps back and gives me a once-over. "You look good."

I smirk, stepping back and giving a small spin. "Careful, Petal. Complimenting me this much might make me think you're smitten."

"Oh, I am. But don't think I didn't catch you almost choking when I walked out."

"Almost?" I tease. "I'm still recovering."

She shakes her head, laughing as the hairstylist and makeup artist quietly gather their things and head out, and I nod in appreciation.

"Are you ready?" I ask, slipping my hand into hers.

She gives my fingers a soft squeeze, her smile soft but determined. "Yes. Let's charm them so they can give you this gallery."

I raise an eyebrow, gesturing toward the door. "Let's get out of here. And remember, if you fall, aim for Liam."

Laughing, she shakes her head. "You're impossible."

"Impossible to resist," I shoot back, leading her out the door.

The car comes to a stop in front of The Warne Gallery, and I slip out, the cool evening air brushing against my face. My palm feels clammy, an unfamiliar sensation that irritates me. I'm not the type of person who gets nervous about business deals. Yet here I am, discreetly wiping my palm against my black pants before holding it out for Karley. She steps out gracefully, her hand slipping into mine.

We take the steps to the gallery entrance, the glow of warm lights illuminating the sidewalk. My heart pounds, each step bringing me closer to what could be the night everything changes. If I play my cards right, this gallery will finally have my name above the door.

The Lincoln Gallery.

And it's not just the business acquisition that matters, there's Karley too. This arrangement between us has grown into something I never expected, something I'm not ready to lose.

"Mr. and Mrs. Lincoln," the doorman greets us, his tone polite and welcoming.

Karley's fingers squeeze mine lightly. I glance down at her. Her lips curve into a sly smile, the kind that makes my pulse race for an entirely different reason.

Hearing that title doesn't scare me the way I thought it might. If anything, I fucking love it. But what about her? Did the squeeze mean she liked it too? Her expression gives little away.

The doorman ushers us in, and as we step into the softly lit space, I lean down to murmur in her ear. "Mrs. Lincoln. God, I love the fucking sound of that."

Her body shivers slightly, and the reaction gives me my answer. But this time, the possessive rush inside me is stronger than ever before.

The gallery's interior is stunning, exuding understated elegance. A long wooden table dominates the room, surrounded by chairs and lit by the warm flicker of candlelight. Gentle amber lighting highlights the art on the walls, each piece perfectly curated, creating a calming atmosphere. The faint strains of instrumental music fill the space, soft enough to soothe, with just enough volume to mask the echo and our footsteps on the polished concrete floor.

For the first time tonight, my nerves begin to settle. The anticipation remains, but with Karley beside me, her presence grounding me, I feel like I can handle anything.

We approach the table, where Dan and Eden stand to greet us. I scan Mr. Warne's face for any hint about tonight's purpose, but his expression gives nothing away. Their smiles are wide and welcoming, genuine warmth radiating from them.

"Oliver, Karley, welcome!" Mr. Warne says, shaking my hand firmly while Eden leans in for a cheek kiss.

Karley mirrors the greeting.

As I glance around the table, I take in the unfamiliar faces. There are more guests than I'd anticipated... Dan and Eden's friends, no doubt. But my gaze quickly lands on two I recognize: Liam and Paige.

Liam is already seated in a black suit, leaning back in his chair like he owns the place. Of course, he got here early, probably to position himself as Mr. Warne's favorite. Asshat.

I briefly nod to the table, playing nice for now. Karley, ever the picture of grace, kisses Paige on the cheek and, of course, extends a friendly greeting to Liam.

I, however, can't bring myself to shake his hand. Instead, I opt for a curt nod, my jaw tightening. She's a better person than I am, that's for sure.

We slide into the last two available seats, side by side. As I settle into my chair, I take a deep breath, stealing a quick glance at Karley. She meets my eyes, and for a moment, her lips twitch with the hint of a smile.

Yeah, I've got this. With her, I'm unstoppable.

Karley leans in, her caramel-sweet scent enveloping me, her breath brushing warm against my cheek. The candlelight brightens her eyes, making them dance with curiosity. "What's this?" she asks quietly.

"Truffle gnocchi," I murmur, turning my head. The proximity startles me... My lips are just a whisper away from hers. Her gaze lingers on mine, unspoken words swirling between us before she turns back to her plate.

"I like gnocchi," she said, picking up her fork. "So, I'm sure I'll like this."

She takes a small bite, her expression unreadable at first, until a faint sound from the back of her throat draws my attention. Amusement tugs at my lips. "Not a fan?" I ask, biting back a laugh.

Karley shakes her head slowly, her expression slipping into an exaggerated smile that doesn't fool me. She swallows, wincing slightly, and then reaches for her wine, chasing the taste away with a long sip.

I chuckle, leaning in close enough to bring my lips to the shell of her ear and whisper, "Want to know a secret? I hate truffle."

Her head shoots up, whipping toward me, her eyes narrowing into an accusing glare. "You could've told me."

Laughter bubbles out of me, and I lean back. "Where's the fun in that? Watching you try to mask the horror was perfection."

"Mean," she mutters, but her laugh betrays her. Her elbow bumps mine as she pushes her plate aside.

Her nose scrunches adorably. "See, that's the difference. My parents cooked pasta, tacos, fish... Meanwhile, you were probably raised on oysters and truffles."

I grin. "Wrong. We didn't eat that stuff unless we were at some restaurant, party, or gallery opening."

I picture taking her to Sunday dinner at Grams' to show her the home-cooked meals we had growing up.

The light-hearted tone wavers for a moment. A question hangs on the tip of my tongue, one I'd danced around before but never dared to ask. Tonight, though, it feels like the right time.

Before I speak again, a friend of Mr. Warne's pulls me into a conversation about recent market trends. I nod along, offering advice while glancing at Karley, who's engrossed in conversation with Paige and Eden. She laughs at something Eden says, looking completely at ease despite her earlier nervousness.

We finish dinner, and as the servers clear our plates, there's a small break before dessert.

Karley leans close to me. "Would you like to check out the new art?"

"Lead the way," I say, standing and offering her my hand.

She slips hers into mine, her fingers warm and sure. Together, we wander through the gallery, our hands interlocked as we examine the intricate strokes of paint and the emotion captured in each piece.

"For someone who never wears heels," I say, "you're doing amazing."

"Don't get your hopes up," she says with a quirked eyebrow, touching my chest. "This isn't becoming a thing."

I lean closer, my voice dropping. "What if I end up buying the gallery? Will you wear them for opening night?"

"Only for opening night," she replies with a smirk.

"Deal." I move my lips to her ear. "Because I am going to get it."

She playfully rolls her eyes as her smile grows. "So cocky."

"And you love it," I quip, earning a laugh that lights up her entire face.

The moment is interrupted by the soft chime of a bell as the waiter approaches. "Dessert is served."

"Time to retake our seats," I say, leading her back. There's a reluctance in me to break this private moment we've created. Walking beside her, my hand in hers, feels natural and not just playing the part of husband and wife. The reason for tonight doesn't seem quite as important as it did when we first arrived.

As the sound of silverware hitting glass hushes the room, Mr. Warne rises from his chair, his eyes sweeping the crowd. "I'd like to make a toast."

Everyone turns toward him. My hand instinctively slips onto Karley's thigh, and she interlaces her fingers with mine.

Mr. Warne's voice carries over the quiet. "As most of you know, I've owned this gallery since I was young. I won't bore you with numbers because, frankly, I don't want you figuring out how old I am."

Laughter ripples throughout the space, including my own, though mine comes from a place of tension rather than amusement. I catch Liam smiling across the table. We both know what's coming. My grip on Karley's hand tightens as I brace myself for Mr. Warne's next words.

"But life has a funny way of telling you when it's time for change." His gaze drops to his wife, Eden, who smiles up at him with quiet encouragement.

"My sweet wife and I have decided it's time to sell this gallery and retire. Truthfully, I'm scared. But with her by my side, I know life will be anything but dull."

"I love you," Eden whispers, her voice carrying through the silence.

Mr. Warne's voice thickens with emotion. "This gallery isn't just a place; it's my heart. I wanted to pass it on to someone who would cherish it as much as I have. And so, I'd like to announce that the new owner will be... Oliver Lincoln."

Applause erupts around me. My heart is erratic. After years of work, countless late nights, and ruthless dedication, it's finally happening. This gallery will be mine. Karley gasps beside me, pulling me into a tight hug. "Looks like I'll be wearing these heels again sooner than I thought—"

"Hang on." Liam's sharp voice interrupts, rising from his seat and pointing a finger at me. "They don't deserve it."

A cold dread spreads through me.

Silence takes over the celebratory moment, tension thickening the air. Mr. Warne's brow furrows, unimpressed. "Why?"

"They're not even really married," Liam spits, crossing his arms.

My stomach is in knots as I try to find a way out of this. Everything we've worked for, including me and Karley, is unraveling. I force myself to remain calm, though my heart is shrinking. "Come on, don't be bitter now."

"They only got married for the gallery. They'll split the second the ink dries on the deal."

A storm brews in my chest, my mind spinning. But I'd be damned if I let him ruin this for Karley and me.

My hands move with purpose, pulling my phone from my pocket. The screen lights up as I find the photo of our marriage certificate. "You're wrong." I flip the screen around, the image glowing in the dim light of the gallery, the proof for everyone to see. I glance quickly at Karley, trying to make sure she's okay.

Liam doesn't flinch. "Well, congratulations," he sneers. "But let's not pretend. You only did it to get the gallery, and the second it's yours, you'll break up."

"Where's your evidence?" I snap.

Liam smirks, leaning back as if he's already won. "If you were so in love and so real, how did you not know the artist, Blue Lotus... is your *wife*?"

The room collectively gasps, whispers spreading like wildfire. Dan and Eden exchange wide-eyed looks of disbelief.

My chest tightens as the words hit me like a freight train. I look to Karley, my stomach twisting. She's silent, her head bowed, her gaze fixed on the table. Her fingers grip the napkin in her lap, knuckles white.

I reach out, gently tipping her chin up with my fingers. Her eyes meet mine, shimmering with unshed tears. There it is... confirmation. No. *No fucking way.* My mouth opens, but no words come.

"That's right. They're frauds." Liam's accusation cuts through the tension like a blade.

The world tilts. My pulse pounds wildly, trying to catch up with my thoughts. There's too much to process...too much to feel. But before I can say a word, Karley rises abruptly, her chair scraping against the floor.

"Excuse me," she murmurs, her voice breaking as she walks away, shoulders stiff and head held high.

I push my chair back to follow, but Eden's hand on my arm stops me. "Let me," she says softly.

I hesitate, every instinct screaming at me to go to her, but Mr. Warne steps in, his firm grip on my shoulder anchoring me. "Give her a moment," he says. "Come with me."

Reluctantly, I let him guide me to the side; the gallery buzzing with hushed murmurs behind us.

"Explain," Mr. Warne demands, his tone low but urgent. "Everything. Now."

The words spill out of me, unfiltered and raw. "Karley's my best friend's sister. I knew she loved art, so when you mentioned the gallery and the marriage stipulation, I thought she'd be perfect. We went to Vegas and got married. At first, it was just a plan, but... the more time we spent together, the more real it became. We fell for each other. We're together. I swear." As the words leave my lips, I realize I don't care if Mr. Warne believes me or not. My eyes search the room for Karley, concern for her above everything else. I need to make sure she's okay.

Mr. Warne studies me, his expression unreadable. "And the paintings? How did you not know?"

I drag a hand through my hair, frustration coursing through me. "I don't know. She never said a word. She kept it from me."

Images of Karley's eyes when she talks about trust, the vulnerability about her past, the way she gradually opened up to me... She wouldn't keep something this big without a reason. "But she's not the type to betray me," I add, more to myself than to him. "Trust is everything to her. There has to be a reason."

Mr. Warne watches me for a long moment before nodding. "Do you love her?"

The question catches me off guard, but my answer is immediate, without hesitation. "Yes. I do. More than anything."

"Then you'd better run after her and tell her," Mr. Warne says firmly, a flicker of a smile breaking through his seriousness. "Because she just left."

I whip around, my eyes darting toward the gallery's entrance. Sure enough, through the glass doors, I see her disappearing into the night.

Mr. Warne's hand on my arm pulls me back for one last moment. "You've got the gallery," he says quietly. "Now, go get your woman."

His words push me forward. I don't care about the shouts from Liam or the commotion behind me. All I see is her running, dress clinging to her in the rain.

The world blurs as I burst through the doors, the cool night like a slap. The rain is coming down harder now, soaking through my shirt as I scan the street.

She's ahead, her pace unsteady, her arms wrapped around herself against the chill.

"Karley!" I call out, my heart pounding.

She doesn't stop, doesn't turn. But I won't let her go, not like this. Not tonight.

I break into a sprint, the rain splashing around my feet, determination driving me forward.

I have to catch her. I have to fix this.

Chapter 27

Karley

I didn't get the chance to tell him. There was no time. Between work, school, and being pulled in a million directions, I haven't had a moment to breathe, let alone tell him I'm the artist. And every time we're alone, the conversation shifts, dissolving into laughter, teasing... sex.

How could I tell him? How do you fit something so big into such small moments?

I had a plan, but now... it's too late. The truth is out for everyone to see. My identity is exposed, my art vulnerable. The humiliation is crushing. My mind goes back to that moment when I was seven, standing in the living room, clutching a drawing of our family—Mom, Dad, Declan, and me. I'd spent ages on it. I was so proud of it. My dad's sneer, the sound of paper ripping, and my mom's laughter echo in my ears.

I can't stop shaking, and every breath feels like knives. I run, my tears turning streetlights into blurry streaks.

Keep going, I tell myself. *Just keep going.*

But the tears won't stop. The tears keep coming, weighing me down until my legs feel heavy. I don't stop running until my heel catches on something, and I go down hard.

My knee scrapes against the rough pavement, but I barely feel the impact over the ache in my chest. I don't move. I hunch over, curling into myself as sobs rack my body.

I cry for every memory I've locked away, every hurt I've swallowed down, and every moment I've felt like I wasn't enough.

The cold water soaks my hair, sticking it to my face. My mascara is surely running, dark streaks mixing with tears on my cheeks. I can't bring myself to care.

I curl my arms around my knees, rocking slightly as the rain falls harder, a steady rhythm that drowns out the noise in my head but not the ache in my chest.

"Karley!"

Oliver's voice slices through the rain, tinged with fear. My breath catches as heavy footsteps pound against the wet pavement, growing closer.

And then, arms wrap around me, strong and familiar. "I've got you, Petal." He's breathless, his words warm against my ear, filled with relief, not anger. I break apart at the sound, fresh sobs shaking my body as I bury my face in his chest.

He isn't mad. How can he not be mad? I've ruined everything... Cost him his gallery and exposed us both.

But he holds me tighter, one hand cradling the back of my head, the other pulling me closer, as if to shield me from the rain, the world, my own self-loathing.

"Come on," he murmurs against my hair, his voice steady. "Let me get you home."

Home.

The word sinks into me, filling the hollow ache in my chest. Home. A place where you feel safe. And God, I feel safe here, in his arms. *With him.*

I nod weakly, unable to form words. There's no fight left in me, no resistance to give. I want to go home with him. I want to curl up in the space we've built together.

I want to tell him.

I want to explain everything, to apologize until he understands. Until he forgives me, if he can.

Oliver scoops me into his arms, his strength carrying me like a shield. My body goes limp in his embrace. I let my head rest against his shoulder, feeling the steady rhythm of his heartbeat beneath my ear. His arms tighten around me, as if he's afraid I'll slip through his fingers, as if I might disappear.

But how could I fall? Not when I have him. Not when he's holding me so close, with such care, like I'm the most important thing in his world.

His breath brushes against my skin as he adjusts his grip, lifting me higher, and I clutch him tighter, my hands threading around the back of his neck. I bury my face against his warmth, inhaling the scent of him. He's here. He's real.

The words he whispers in my ear are a gentle promise. "Petal, I've got you."

It's not just reassurance. It's spoken with such sincerity that it makes me breathless. He says it like he would do anything to protect me, and I believe him completely. Right now, I trust him more than anything.

He doesn't put me down. Instead, he holds me close, shifting as he opens the car door and carefully slides inside, settling us both into the back seat. I stay wrapped in his arms, my head still resting on his shoulder, feeling the warmth of his body, the steady rise and fall of his chest beneath me.

"Sir, your—" The driver's voice falters, his words dying on his tongue.

"Drive. Home. Now." Oliver's command is laced with an edge I've never heard before, not from him.

There's a wobble in his tone, something raw and vulnerable beneath the authority. It catches me off guard, making my heartbeat spike.

The car moves slowly through the rain-soaked streets. I close my eyes, trying to focus on the sound of his heartbeat. It's the only thing I can cling to. I breathe with it, each pulse settling my racing thoughts, calming the tremble in my body. I let myself surrender to the security of his embrace.

In this moment, all I need is him.

As soon as we stop, Oliver gets out of the car and is carrying me toward the house. My head rests on his shoulder, my body too heavy, too drained to resist. I want to tell him to put me down, that I can walk, but I can't. The words won't come and, honestly, I don't think I could stand on my own.

He carries me inside. The familiar scent of his home wraps around me like a fragile thread of comfort. It smells like wood and safety. I don't know where he's taking me until the sound of running water reaches my ears.

I open my mouth to ask, but the razor blades in my throat won't let me speak. He doesn't let go, doesn't say a word, just holds me close like I might slip through his fingers if he loosens his grip. Tears sting my eyes again, falling freely.

Why isn't he angry? Why isn't he trying to fix the disaster I caused? I've probably ruined everything for him. The gallery, his plans, all gone... and yet he's here, holding me like I'm the only thing that matters.

The sound of the shower grows louder as he steps inside with me still in his arms. The water spills over us, soaking through my cocktail dress and his suit in seconds. But he doesn't let go. He doesn't hesitate.

My sobs return, shaking me as the heat of the water seeps through my skin. His hand brushes my hair back from my face, gently tucking the wet strands behind my ears. I squeeze my eyes shut, too ashamed to meet his gaze, too scared of what he might see in mine. I feel like a kid again, unraveling and wild.

The soft press of his lips on my eyelid startles me. Then he mirrors the kiss on the other lid. My breath hitches, the touch so tender it makes my chest ache. He tips my chin up. His lips find mine.

It's a whisper of a kiss at first, but it ignites something deep inside me. I clutch his soaked jacket lapels, pulling him closer, holding on like he's the only thing keeping me afloat. The shame, the fear, the overwhelming mess of it all fades under his touch, leaving only the raw need to feel him, to be near him.

As the water cascades over us, his arms stay steady, holding me like I'm fragile but unbreakable all at once. And for the first time, I feel it too. Little Karley, the girl who used to cry alone, convinced she wasn't worth the care, finally has someone. Someone who doesn't let go. Someone who stays.

We stay like this—the water pouring over us—until my tears finally run dry. Slowly, with the utmost care, Oliver moves. He loosens his grip around my waist and carefully lowers me until my feet touch the shower floor. His hands remain steady on my hips until I find my balance, water streaming down between us as I stand before him. His hand then brushes over my shoulder, trailing down to the zipper of my dress.

I barely register the sound of it sliding down, the fabric loosening against my soaked skin. His fingers glide along my back, skimming the bare, wet surface with a touch so soft it almost breaks me all over again. When he pushes the straps from my shoulders, the dress slips down to my hips.

I tip my head back and force my eyes open, my movements sluggish but deliberate. His face comes into focus, the dark strands of his hair plastered to his forehead, water trickling down his sharp jawline. He looks like something out of a dream, but it's his expression that roots me.

His blue eyes are wide and hold me still. They shine with a quiet kind of devotion that steals the breath I thought I'd lost entirely. I reach up with trembling fingers and brush the wet hair off his forehead. My hand lingers, as if taking every second in.

Oliver doesn't speak, doesn't rush. His hands return to the damp fabric clinging to my hips, pushing it away with a light touch that stings more than any of the pain I've been holding on to. His unhurried care sends a shiver down my spine, not from desire, but from the overwhelming realization that this moment isn't about passion or lust. This is something deeper, something sacred. It's him seeing my pain and holding it with me, letting me know I don't have to carry it alone.

If I thought I understood my love for him before, I was wrong. This moment, here, with him, this is true love. It's in the way he cares for me when I can't care for myself. In the way he reminds me, without words, that I'm worth loving, worth supporting, worth being seen.

And just like that, the walls I've spent years building around my heart crumble. Washed away by the water streaming down the drain. I stand there, stripped of everything, my dress, my pain, my fear, but not alone. Never alone with Oliver.

He picks up the shampoo bottle, squeezing a small amount into his palm. "Turn around," he says softly. He gently works the shampoo through my hair. His fingers dig into my scalp, massaging away the tension pounding in my temples. When he rinses it out, he follows with conditioner, with the same tenderness, as if each stroke of his fingers is meant to reassure me that I'm safe.

Once my hair is rinsed clean, I turn around, and he removes his own soaked clothes, adding them to the pile of damp fabric gathering in the corner of the shower. For all the space in his luxurious, oversized shower, we stand so close, it feels like we're in a world of our own, where the heat of his body brushes against mine.

He washes himself in quick movements before shutting off the water. The loss of warmth is instant; the bathroom filled with steam but not enough to hide the chill of the air. Without a word, he grabs a plush towel, wrapping it securely around me. He helps me step out of the shower, steadying me with firm hands as I dry off.

Leaving me for a brief moment, he disappears into his walk-in closet and returns with one of his t-shirts. It's soft and gray, worn just enough to be comfortable. It smells faintly of him, a mix of wood and something clean I can't quite name.

"Your clothes are upstairs," he explains, holding out the shirt. He's already dressed in a pair of boxers, his skin still damp from the shower. The small, lopsided grin he's wearing as I pull his shirt over my head is all I need to warm me. He likes seeing me in his clothes, and it makes the corner of my mouth twitch despite the exhaustion weighing me down.

"Come on, Petal, let's go to bed."

He pulls back the covers and slides beneath them, patting the empty space beside him. I climb in and snuggle close. My head rests on his chest, his heartbeat a steady rhythm in my ear. With my arm draped across his stomach, the warmth of his body eases the last bit of tension still clinging to me.

His hand moves to my back, his fingers tracing soothing patterns over the fabric of his shirt. The gentle motion, paired with the steady rise and fall of his breathing, makes my eyelids grow heavier with each passing second.

Just as I'm about to give in to the exhaustion, I think I hear him whisper, "I love you."

The words are softly spoken, almost too quiet to catch. I can't tell if they're real or just a product of my wishful thinking. As sleep takes over, I let the words rest in my heart. They're enough to help me drift off, utterly spent, but no longer alone.

Chapter 28

Karley

The next morning, I wake in his arms and choose to stay perfectly still, savoring the quiet, the way his fingers grip my waist even as he sleeps.

I tilt my head to look up at him. His dark lashes rest against his cheeks, his face relaxed, boyish even, in the morning light. A small smile tugs at my lips as I reach up, gently cupping his cheek.

His eyes flutter open, those piercing blue eyes locking onto mine. A lazy grin spreads across his face.

"Morning, Petal," he murmurs, rough and sleepy.

"Morning," I whisper back, feeling the corners of my lips curve up.

"How are you feeling?"

The question brings back the heaviness in my chest. "Better," I admit hoarsely. "But I need something to drink. My throat's sore."

Reluctantly, we untangle from each other, the warmth of his body lingering as we move to the kitchen. I'm bracing for the inevitable conversation we need to have. He'll want an explanation. A weight settles in my gut as I remember the look on his face when Liam revealed my secret. I grab a bottle of water from the fridge and tilt it back, gulping it down in one go. The coolness soothes my throat, but my mind is already spinning with thoughts of what's to come.

He makes coffee, the rich aroma filling the air.

I sit at the counter, watching him move around with a casual ease that makes my heart skip. He's shirtless, his hair still messy from sleep, and I wonder how he can look so effortlessly perfect.

Once he pours two mugs of coffee, he slides one across the counter toward me with a playful smirk. "Coffee for my girl."

I smile as I take the mug, the warmth seeping into my hands as I take a sip. The moment feels light, easy, but the question weighing on my mind refuses to stay silent.

"What's going to happen with the gallery?" I ask quietly, my gaze fixed on the steam coming from my coffee before looking back up.

Oliver freezes for a moment, then sets his mug down and steps closer. "Mr. Warne gave me the gallery."

My head snaps up, disbelief flooding me. "What? How?"

He rounds the island in a few strides, his hand lifting to cradle my face. The affection in his touch steals my breath as his gaze locks onto mine.

"He knew we weren't fake," Oliver says. "Yeah, the marriage was fast, but he could see it, Karley. He saw how much we love each other."

Love. He said it so naturally. And after all this time guarding my heart, of expecting disappointment, hearing him say that with confidence means he's not walking away from me.

"He did?"

"Yes." His eyes soften as his thumb dusts my cheek. "Karley, I love you. I love you so incredibly much."

The words hit me like a tidal wave. My heart clenches, tears pricking at the corners of my eyes. But this time, they aren't from pain, they're from relief, from pure joy.

"I love you too," I manage as I throw my arms around him, holding on tight.

He hugs me back, his grip firm. "Not as much as I love you," he murmurs, pulling back just enough to meet my eyes. "I can't believe all this time I was searching for you, and you were right there in front of me."

A grin breaks across my face. "I nearly died when I saw it in your office."

Laughing softly, he rests his forehead against mine. "That room's getting an upgrade. I want your paintings everywhere, Karley." And for the first time, knowing he knows... knowing everyone knows... I feel okay.

An idea sparks in me, making my stomach flutter. "I want to paint us something new. Something special. In that arch shape you have in your room."

His smile widens, his eyes full of adoration. "I'll get you anything you need. I'll turn a whole room into a studio if you want. You should be painting. And when the gallery opens, it'll be ours, every painting, every student, everything. We'll do it together."

New hope fills my chest. I lean up, kissing him, pouring every ounce of love and gratitude I feel into it. This moment, this man, is my future. And for the first time in forever, I am ready to embrace it.

Chapter 29

Oliver

Declan sits across from me in my den, leaning back in the armchair, a beer bottle dangling loosely from his hand. My leg bounces as I try to steady myself, the low hum of the television the only sound between us.

Karley and Armani are out shopping, prepping for the gallery opening next month. With the house quiet, now feels like the right time to finally say it. I take a deep breath and just go for it.

"I wanted to let you know that Karley and I are dating."

His jaw tightens, and for a second, I brace for the lecture. But instead of exploding, he nods slowly. "I figured."

I blink. "You figured? How?"

He shrugs, leaning forward to set his beer on the coffee table. "The last couple of times I've been here, you've been acting differently around her."

"Different how?"

"Borderline I want to smack your head in for looking at her kind of differently," he says with a smirk, though there's a hint of seriousness in his voice.

A laugh escapes me, easing some of the tension in my chest. "Yeah, I'm not going to apologize for that. I've never felt like this about anyone before."

The humor fades from his face, replaced by something more serious. "Just don't hurt her, Oliver. She's been through enough already."

"I won't," I say firmly, locking eyes with him. "I care about her, Declan. I'm telling all my family tonight, and the ones who haven't met her will at the gallery opening."

He nods as his expression softens a little. "That's a good move. Ease her into it. Your family's a lot to handle."

Another laugh slips out as I imagine the chaotic storm Karley's about to walk into. "Yeah, I know. But she can handle it. She's stronger than most people realize."

Declan picks up his beer again, studying me for a moment. "Alright," he says finally. "If you're serious about her, and it sounds like you are, you've got my support. Just don't make me regret it."

"You won't," I promise, the words coming easily.

A few hours later, I'm walking up the familiar steps to Grams' house, my nerves buzzing. I called everyone here to tell them about Karley and me, and now I can hear their voices inside, but it's louder than I expected.

Saylor, Grams' housekeeper, greets me with a warm smile as I step through the door. "Oliver, they're all inside."

"Thanks, Saylor," I say, my pulse quickening as I head down the hallway.

The living room buzzes with noise. Entering the room, I take in all the people. Besides my family, I spot a few extras: Nova, Jemima, Chad, and Chelsea. My brother's partners and son. Their presence surprises me, but works in my favor. I won't have to repeat myself.

"Nice to see you all on time," I announce, stepping farther into the room.

I make my way to Grams first, her face lighting up when she sees me. She looks better today, her cheeks flushed with color, and her emerald-green checkered dress with a white cardigan neat as ever. I lean down, pressing a light kiss to her cheek, careful not to be too rough.

After greeting her, I move to Mom and Dad. Mom smiles as I kiss her cheek. Dad shakes my hand firmly before I make my way around the room.

"Will you play basketball with us?" Chad pipes up. Chad is my brother Harvey's stepson.

I glance at Harvey, raising an eyebrow. "Basketball?"

Harvey grins and shrugs casually. "I promised him we'd play a friendly game."

I snort. "Friendly? I don't think we've ever played a friendly game of basketball."

Growing up, Harvey and I were always at each other's throats when it came to competition—sports, jobs, even girls. If there was a way to win, we went all in.

"Even Pop is playing," Chad says, his excitement contagious.

I look at Dad, my eyebrows shooting up. "You're playing?"

He ruffles Chad's blond hair with a soft smile. "Yeah, I don't want to miss out."

I glance at Harvey again, noting the ease in his expression. He doesn't even flinch at Chad calling our dad, "Pop."

It's sweet, really, and the way Mom and Dad beam at Chad warms my chest. He's fit into the family so effortlessly, and seeing how much they adore him just reinforces how special he is. For a moment, the thought of Karley being part of this family makes me smile. She's going to be just fine. Karley is working today. She tried to get out of it, but couldn't.

The living room buzzes with low chatter and the occasional laugh, but Jeremy cuts through it all, leaning forward in his chair. "So, other than a family game of basketball, why are we here, Oliver?"

I stand, shifting my weight as I try to steady myself. "Well, now that I have you all here, I have a couple of announcements."

The room quiets instantly, all eyes on me.

"I got married." I let the words hang in the air.

A few gasps echo around the room. One of them is definitely Grams, her frail hands pressing to her chest as she stares at me, wide-eyed. The excitement in her eyes is impossible to miss, but so is the shock. Guilt twists my stomach. Maybe I should've told her first.

"You what?" Dad says, his brows shooting up like he's not sure he heard me right.

"Oh my God," Mom murmurs, her hands covering her mouth.

"When did this happen?" Dad asks.

"Recently," I say. "We didn't tell anyone at first because... well, we wanted to keep it just us for a while."

Gram beams. "Are you happy?"

"I am," I say softly.

Jeremy whistles low. "Damn. Married before me. Didn't see that coming."

"I'm gonna need some wedding photos," Mom adds with a laugh. "Or at least a date for the reception I assume you didn't throw."

"Don't worry," I say. "I'm planning something. You'll all be there."

Grams' eyes are filled with tears now. "I can't wait to meet her. And you better bring her to Sunday dinner next week. No excuses."

I nod, heart swelling. "I will."

"And that's not all..." I continue before someone speaks, turning to face Mom. I step toward her, taking her hands gently and coaxing her to stand. She rises slowly, looking around the room, clearly trying to process my words.

"Oliver?" she asks, her voice soft but cautious.

I reach into my pocket to pull out a small key. Holding it up, it dangles between us.

"I bought Warne Gallery," I say, watching her expression, closely waiting for her reaction.

Her eyes widen, her hands trembling slightly in mine. "What? How?"

"Mr. Warne sold it to me," I explain. "But I didn't buy it for myself. I bought it for you."

"For me?" she repeats, her voice barely above a whisper.

I nod, squeezing her hands. "It's now called *The Lincoln Gallery*. I want it to be a space for your students to showcase their work. A place where their talent can shine."

Grams stands and shuffles closer with her walker, her face glowing with pride. "Oh, Oliver, that's so sweet,"

"The first opening is in a month," I tell them, glancing around at everyone. "I'd love it if you could all be there."

Tears spill down Mom's cheeks as she pulls me into a tight hug. "I'm so proud of you," she whispers. "Thank you for doing this, for them."

Dad raises an eyebrow, curiosity flickering in his eyes. "Hold on. You haven't told us who your wife is yet."

I smile as the rest of them lean in, waiting. "It's Karley."

Mom's eyes widen, and she tilts her head. "Karley Maddox?"

Grams frowns as her gaze bounces between us. "Who's Karley Maddox?"

"She's Declan's sister," Mom explains, her tone laced with surprise. "And one of my students."

There's a ripple of murmurs, but I'm not finished. "And one more thing," I say, letting a smirk tug at the corner of my mouth. Karley won't mind me revealing this to my family. "I've found the anonymous painter I've been raving about."

Mom's lips twitch with a knowing smile. "And?"

"It's Karley,"

"No fucking way!" Jeremy blurts out, leaning forward in disbelief.

"Jeremy," Grams scolds, glaring at him. "Watch your language."

"Sorry, Grams," he mutters, face flushed.

Grams waves him off and focuses back on me. "How did you figure it out?"

"I didn't. I was told, but I'm going to guess Mom already knew."

Mom shrugs, making it clear she's been keeping this secret for a while. "I have access to the gallery's security cameras and the students' work."

I groan, running a hand over my face. "Why didn't I think of that? Or why didn't my guys figure it out?"

Mom grins. "Because I paid them not to. Karley is special, Oliver. Exposing her before she was ready would've been wrong."

I nod as I hug her again. "Thank you."

Mom pulls back, patting my hand, her tears drying as she smiles. "You're welcome. Now, let's make this gallery opening something to remember."

The local court buzzes with the energy of a family basketball game, the sound of sneakers squeaking against the concrete, and the occasional shout echoing in the cool air. On one side, it's Dad, Harvey, and Chad. On the other, Evan, Jeremy, and me. The competition is intense, as it always is when we're all together.

During a water break, I lean against the edge of the court, catching my breath. Evan walks over, his bottle in hand, and settles beside me.

"Congratulations," he says casually, wiping his forehead. "I'm not surprised, though."

I glance at him, raising an eyebrow. "No?"

He shakes his head as a faint smirk plays on his lips. "Not at all. You've known each other for a few years."

"I didn't see her coming," I admit, running a hand through my damp hair. "I wish I'd noticed her sooner." *Really noticed her.*

Evan shrugs, taking a swig of water. "Maybe, but you wouldn't be here if you had. Timing's everything, Oliver."

He's right, though the thought stings a little. If I'd seen Karley for who she truly was back then, maybe things would've been different. Feels like I've already missed so much time with her.

"So, she's living with you now?" Evan asks with a tilt of his head.

"Yeah," I say, nodding. "We did things a little backward."

Before he can reply, Harvey's voice cuts through the air, loud and impatient.

"Are you guys done over there? We've got a game to finish," he shouts, tossing the ball in my direction.

The ball hurtles toward me, but I effortlessly snatch it out of the air with one hand, smirking.

"Relax, Harvey," I call back, spinning the ball in my fingers. "I'm ready to school you."

Chad cheers from across the court, his enthusiasm contagious as he claps his hands and calls out for Harvey to bring it. Evan chuckles beside me, clapping a hand on my shoulder before jogging back into position.

The game is on.

CHAPTER 30

KARLEY

A MONTH LATER, I step into the house I purchased... the one I thought I'd live out the back of after my arrangement with Oliver ended. Well, the joke's on me, because I won't be staying here.

I move through the open space, carrying a box packed with furniture to build. The bane of anyone's existence, especially when they don't come with an Allen key.

"Where's this one going?" Wren asks from behind me, Rufus trailing along beside him, his nails scratching on the floor. Oliver had a meeting today about the gallery, so Amber and Wren are here helping me.

"The front room," I reply, shifting the box slightly to get a better grip before heading toward the main living area.

Amber joins me, her arms already full of smaller boxes. The house isn't ready for kids and families yet... Not officially. The permit is taking forever, and I know I'll have to be patient. For now, all I can do is set up and prepare, room by room.

Amber sets her boxes down beside me. "Need help?"

"Always," I say with a smile. Together, we tackle one of the furniture kits—a TV console. I glance toward the other room, where I can hear Wren working on something, and I bet he'll finish his piece before we're even halfway through.

As Amber and I sort through the pieces, I sigh. "Thanks for helping me with this."

She glances up, her warm smile reassuring. "Anytime. We're so proud of you."

Her words make me pause, my hands freezing midair. I look up at her, her expression calm and sincere.

"Even though I had to marry to get it?" I joke, though there's a twinge of self-consciousness.

Amber laughs softly. "It takes a clever woman to do what she needs to for her dream. You didn't give up. That's all that matters."

"I could have easily given up," I whisper.

"But you didn't," Amber says firmly. "And as much as you claimed to hate him, I could always see the light in your eyes whenever you talked about him."

My head snaps up at that. "I was obvious, wasn't I?"

Her eyes sparkle. "Not to him."

I groan, shaking my head. "How? I don't know how he didn't see it."

"Maybe he had it in his head that you were like a sister to him," she says with a playful shrug.

The thought makes me grimace, my stomach flipping at the idea. "I never looked at him like a brother."

Amber laughs and nudges my shoulder. "Yeah, I didn't think so. But it's different now."

"I've always liked him," I admit.

Her hand covers mine, giving me a gentle squeeze. "I love that your story is unconventional. It reminds me of my own journey."

They tried for years to have kids, doctor after doctor, test after test, hoping something would work. But nothing did. Eventually, they applied to be foster parents.

I feel so lucky they chose me. They show up for me, every day, in all the little ways that matter. They didn't just make room in their home. They made room in their lives and in their hearts.

I pause, my chest tightening. "I'm sorry you couldn't have kids."

Amber smiles. "I'm not."

I frown. "You're not?"

She shakes her head. "No, because if I had, I wouldn't have gotten you."

My chest aches with emotion. Her eyes glisten, and my own vision blurs as tears prick at the edges.

"I'm the one who's grateful," I choke out. "I don't think you'll ever understand how much it meant to me that you... chose me."

Her smile deepens as she takes her hands from mine but shuffles closer. "I do understand. Watching you work so hard, and now, seeing you in love and chasing your dreams... It's everything to us."

Blinking back the tears threatening to spill over, I swallow hard. "Can I ask you something?"

"Of course," she says.

I glance down at the box in front of us, gathering the courage to say the words that have been on my mind lately. I just don't want to let her down. "I don't think I want kids."

The silence stretches between us. I feel my heartbeat in my throat as I slowly lift my eyes to hers.

"Then don't have them," she says simply.

"But what if Oliver wants them?" The worry slips out before I can stop it. We haven't had that conversation yet. He's been busy with the gallery, and I've been finalizing the house.

"What if he doesn't?"

"I don't know..." I tuck my hair behind my ear, feeling the weight of uncertainty pressing down on me.

Amber touches my arms and looks straight into my eyes. "This is your life. Talk to him. Tell him what you told me and see what he says."

I nod, her advice sinking in.

"Let's finish this," she says, moving her hands back to the wood. Both of us focus back on the console. We work in silence for a bit before Wren comes in to help us finish assembling the piece.

The door swings open. My heart lifts as Oliver steps inside, his sexy and powerful presence commanding attention. Especially in his light gray work suit.

He moves with ease, his smile lighting up the room as he greets Amber with a shake of her hand. "Hi, Amber."

Then he turns to Wren, shaking his hand too. "Wren."

Rufus leaps at Oliver, latching onto his leg, and enthusiastically humps him. *Again.*

I burst out laughing, the craziness of the moment too much to contain.

"Rufus!" Wren scolds, his face bright red.

Oliver, ever the good sport, chuckles as he picks Rufus up. "It's fine. I guess it's better than him biting my dick off."

Wren's lips twitch, and he lets out a reluctant laugh. "Yes, well, that would make it hard to have kids."

The words make my heart squeeze, but after my talk with Amber, I know it's time. I don't want to wait in case it's a dealbreaker for him.

Oliver steps over to me, his eyes heated as he leans down and kisses me softly. "Hi, Petal."

I glance over at Amber and Wren. They stand together, their expressions soft and full of warmth. Amber's hands are over her chest, her eyes glowing with pride.

"We'll leave you two," Amber says with a smile. "But we'll see you Saturday."

The thought fills me with joy. Saturday. The opening of Oliver's gallery. My art will be there for everyone to see.

"Let me know if you need help," Wren offers with a wink at Oliver, then takes Rufus from Oliver's arms.

The moment the door closes, Oliver locks it, and my pulse quickens.

"I need my wife," Oliver murmurs.

"Do you now?" I say, a grin spreading across my face.

"Yes," he growls and steps closer. "It's been six hours. And I've thought about you the whole morning. Every meeting. Every moment."

I let out a soft laugh. "I'd say I'm sorry."

"I should make you say it," he mutters, his lips brushing against mine.

"It's not going to happen," I whisper.

"Want to make a bet?" he asks.

He just smiles wickedly at me, walking me backward so my back hits the door, his hands beside my head on the wood caging me in.

I grab his tie, trying to undo it.

"I like it when you show me how much you want me," he says.

Likewise, which is why I'm trying to remove his clothes. He hasn't stopped showing me he wants me, and I want to return the favor.

I tug it, but it's still not undone.

He slips into my life so easily. He's perfect with my family. I couldn't have asked for anyone better.

Pulling his tie free, I let it slip onto the floor. "You want me to fuck you right here? Against the door?"

Undoing the buttons on his shirt next, I couldn't imagine moving. "Yes."

"My wife is so fucking needy for my cock."

I slip the white shirt off his shoulders so it falls to the floor. "Shut up and fuck me." Taking the bottom of my top, I pull it over my head, tossing it on the floor.

His tongue darts out to wet his bottom lip. "Karley."

"What?" I ask innocently, watching his eyes drop down my body.

He stares at my chest. "So beautiful."

I reach around and unclip my bra, and the black cotton drops to my feet.

His right hand reaches out to palm my breast, the other still beside my head. I moan as he squeezes it, and then rolls my nipple until I'm desperate for him.

Eyes flaring with appreciation, he dips his head, takes my nipple into his mouth, and sucks hard. My pussy clenches at the sensation.

"Fuck," I cry out, slamming my head back, my eyes close.

He stops sucking, and I'm about to protest until I feel his warm breath across my skin to the other breast repeating the same pattern. My body quivers with the pressure building between my thighs. When he's finished sucking my nipple, I'm rolling my hips into the air, in need of friction. His hand lowers to my pants.

"These look cute, but will look better on the floor."

"I won't stop you."

He quickly pops the button, unzipping me, before pushing them over my hips. I shimmy, helping them glide down to the ground and kick them aside.

Now I stand in only a cotton black thong.

"I'm so fucking hard. You're so beautiful."

My hands move to his button and zipper. Eager to see him hard for me.

I push his pants and briefs down together. He kicks off his shoes before his pants and briefs are gone. He stands there heavy, thick, and leaking of pre-cum. All for me.

My tongue darts out, licking the seam of my lips. He's beautiful. I can never get my fill.

His hands move to me, and I think he'll remove my thong, but instead his hand slips beneath them, skimming my clit. I buck at the touch.

"Oliver, fuck!"

"Mmm... my name on your lips kills me."

He does it again, causing my back to arch again.

But instead of just grazing my clit, he dips two fingers inside of me. The tight thrust all the way in makes me cry out. "Oliver-r!"

"God, you're perfect."

He doesn't stop pumping his fingers. My body collapses against the door, and luckily, he holds me up with one hand. The other is buried in my thong.

"So fucking wet for me."

I try to speak, but it comes out as a moan.

I'm so close.

He keeps up the same pace. I clench around his thick fingers. I'm about to come. He brings me to the edge, but then swiftly pulls out.

My eyes snap open, my gaze ping-ponging between his two heated blues, trying to figure out why he's stopped. "What are you doing?"

He runs his fingers over my lips. I smell myself on him and shiver.

"I want my wife to apologize for making me unable to think straight."

"Sorry," I rush out.

He chuckles. "I've never heard you apologize quicker in my life."

"Shut up and let me come."

"With pleasure," he says with a mischievous look. "But taste how intoxicating you are first."

He puts his finger into my mouth, and I hesitate, but then suck it, tasting the sweet and tangy mix of myself. Withdrawing his finger, he grabs my thong, ripping it from my body. Discarding the fabric onto the floor.

Grabbing his pants, he pulls out a condom and rolls it on. It sends a thrill up my spine, loving how desperate he is to be inside me.

He grips my thighs and lifts me, my back against the cold wood, the tip of him at my hot entrance.

"You ready?" he asks.

"Yes, husband, please fuck me,"

I want to be fucked raw and passionate right now. Unhinged even better.

"Fuck, I love that," he rasps as he thrusts in one motion, sliding through me.

I cry out at the fullness, loving the way we fit perfectly, like a puzzle.

Holding his arms, I whimper as he rocks his hips, thrusting harder every time. His thick erection is growing.

"I can't get enough of you. Luckily, you're already my wife, otherwise I'd ask you to marry me."

"My husband," I moan.

"My wife," he says with the most delicious guttural groan. His arms bulge with each thrust. His pumps get faster. I know he must be close. I want to come together, so I relax and let my body feel the sensation. On the next few thrusts, my body clenches and I cry out his name, and he goes still as he jerks.

His head falls to the crook of my neck. The sounds of him pushed me over the edge and they still turn me on, even after an orgasm. Neither of us move, not wanting to end this.

I soak in his hot skin and heavy wood aftershave, letting it wrap around me like a warm blanket.

After a minute, Oliver peels his head away and looks down at me lovingly.

"Fuck, that was incredible."

I bite the inside of my cheek, nodding.

He slowly helps my legs down, and I take a second. Then I look over to get dressed, but my thong is ruined. "I'll have to go home wearing no thong."

"I don't see a problem with that."

I roll my eyes. "Of course you don't."

"I'll buy you new ones."

"It doesn't help me now."

He laughs. "I'll order them over the phone and get my driver to pick up the package."

I'd argue, but I need to clean up the mess from the furniture assembling, and by the time I do that, he'll have dropped them off.

"Thanks."

"Don't thank me yet. I'll rip them off again when we get home."

"Insatiable."

He leans forward and kisses me hard. "No, just in love."

I smile softly. "I love you too." I pause, taking a deep breath. "But I need to talk to you about something." If I don't say it now, while I have the courage, I'm afraid I never will.

A groan escapes him as he leans back, running a hand through his hair. "This can't be good."

My heart pounds as I walk into the living room, sinking into the sofa and curling my legs beneath me. The soft fabric soothes me, but it doesn't stop the nerves tightening my chest. He follows me, sitting beside me, his body turned toward mine.

"I need to tell you something," I begin, feeling shaky. "It might change our future."

His eyes widen slightly, but the shift is so quick I almost miss it. "Okay..." He's calm, but there's a flicker of unease as he watches me.

I prop my head on my hand, and his fingers find my arm, tracing slow, comforting circles. It's a small gesture, as if he needs to touch me whenever we're close. Usually, it calms me. Today, it makes my throat thicken. *What if this changes everything?*

"I don't think I want to have kids," I finally blurt out.

He nods slowly, his expression thoughtful. "That's okay."

I shake my head. "No, I mean... like, ever."

His fingers pause, the warmth of his touch still lingering on my skin. His silence feels heavier than I expected.

"Oh."

The word hangs between us, and I can't bear to meet his eyes, so I look away. "I get it. You want them. I thought this would be a dealbreaker."

"It's not."

His response is quiet, but certain. My head snaps up, searching his face for any trace of hesitation. "No?"

He shifts closer, his knees brushing mine. "No," he says again, firmer this time. "I've thought about it, more than I've ever admitted. And the truth is... I was never set on having kids. Not really. I just assumed I would, because that's what people do. But it's not something I've dreamed about. You're the thing I've dreamed about."

His words wash over me slowly, sinking in bit by bit.

"I want you," he says, his voice softer now. "If you don't want kids, then I'm okay with that. You're the only thing that matters. I don't want to lose you."

Cupping my face, his thumb brushes my cheek with a tenderness that pulls something inside me.

"I don't want to lose you either," I say through a tremble. "But this... This is a big decision."

He leans in, his forehead almost touching mine. "I know," he says gently. "And I'm glad you care enough to make sure I've thought about it. But I have. All I want is you. There's no one else for me, Petal. You're it."

Chapter 31

Karley

"Do you really have to blindfold me?" I ask, eyeing the navy fabric in Oliver's hands.

"Don't you trust me, Petal?" He smirks, and it's doing nothing to calm my nerves.

I let out an exaggerated sigh and turn around. "Of course I trust you. But I wanted to see the gallery steps with your name on them."

"Our name," he corrects, slipping the fabric over my eyes. His fingers brush against my hair as he secures the blindfold, and then he takes my hand, lacing our fingers together. "I promise you'll see it tonight, but first, there's something I need to show you."

I can only see faint outlines through the fabric, but the ground beneath my feet feels steady as we take the steps. Soft instrumental music greets us when we step inside, and the familiar scent of fresh paint fills the air. The combination of sounds and smell is comforting, yet it makes me more impatient.

I tug lightly at his hand. "Can I take this off yet?"

"Patience," he whispers.

The anticipation builds tight in my chest with each step, my heart thudding faster as we stop.

"Are you ready?" he asks, his breath brushing against my skin, leaving a trail of goosebumps.

"Yes! Just hurry up!" I say as I shift on my heels.

His chuckle is deep and rich. As he carefully lifts the blindfold, he ensures my hair and makeup remain intact. There, front and center in the gallery, is my painting, highlighted in warm spotlights.

"Oliver..." My hand flies to my mouth, muffling the sob threatening to escape. "Oh my God."

"You deserve to be seen, Petal."

The nickname, ridiculous as it is, feels perfect. As much as I've tried to be tough and guarded, I've always longed for a love as delicate and beautiful as a flower petal.

"Thank you," I whisper.

"I love your new signature," he says, gesturing to the bottom right corner of the canvas where my name, *Karley Lincoln*, is written in blue. "There's something incredible about seeing *Lincoln* in your work. I'm so proud of you."

The painting is a vibrant bouquet of blue lotuses in varying stages of bloom, which feels like my life on display. Closed buds represent my fear as a child, while the open flowers show the freedom I've fought so hard to claim.

"I thought it was time to stop hiding," I admit, my eyes never leaving the painting. "But I didn't expect to be the one in the spotlight."

"You shouldn't have to hide your talent," he says.

I reach for his hand, squeezing it as I smile. "Show me around before everyone else gets here."

Leading me through the gallery, he explains that every piece of art on display is by a student. I beam with pride, knowing how much this night means to him... and to them.

We pause in front of a familiar painting, and my chest swells. "This one's Evelyn's," I say, pointing to a detailed design of a hospital. "We joke that she manifests working there because all her paintings are of hospitals."

Oliver chuckles. "It's impressive. She's talented."

"Hi, guys! Sorry to interrupt, but The New York Press is here," Cora says, her emerald-green dress shimmering under the gallery lights.

"Thanks, Cora," Oliver replies before she turns to me with a smile.

"I love your dress, Karley," she says, eyeing the delicate floral embroidery that decorates my olive-green long-sleeved dress.

"Thank you. You look amazing too," I reply, and she blushes before excusing herself.

"I'll keep walking around if you want to meet the photographers," I offer.

"No, you're coming with me," Oliver insists. "They're here for the full story, and I made sure to get personal images too." I blink at him in disbelief.

At the entrance, we meet Evan and his fiancée, Chelsea. Oliver's hand settles firmly on my waist as he introduces me.

"Evan, Chelsea, meet my wife, Karley."

"Hi," I say warmly, shaking Chelsea's hand.

"Evan tells me you paint?" Chelsea asks, her brown eyes sparkling under her bangs.

"Yes—"

"She's the one in the front," Oliver cuts in, pride radiating from him.

Chelsea gapes at him. "Wow. You're incredible."

Callum, the photographer, steps forward with his camera. "Can we get a picture of you next to your painting?"

"Sure." I step beside the canvas. The flashes make me self-conscious, but I relax when Oliver joins me, pulling me close.

I lean into him, savoring the moment. This photo will be a reminder of how far I've come, from a scared, uncertain girl to a woman who has embraced her art, her worth, and love.

"I love you," I say, turning to look at him.

His grin is slow and full of warmth. "Not as much as I love you," he whispers as he brushes a kiss against my lips.

The camera clicks again, capturing the moment just as a familiar voice cuts through.

"Get a room!"

I laugh as I turn to see Harvey walking in, a familiar stunning pregnant woman on his arm. Her navy gown hugs her bump elegantly.

I watch them for a moment, before I'm introduced to Jeremy and his fiancée, Nova. Oliver places a warm hand on my back.

"Are you excited to get married next week?" I ask.

Nova glances at Jeremy, her sleek bun catching the soft light of the gallery. "Very excited, thank you. You'll be joining us, right?"

"Yes," Oliver replies confidently.

"Am I now?" I shoot him a side-eye, arching an eyebrow.

Nova giggles behind her hand. "Did he forget to tell you?"

"Yes," I say, looking at Oliver.

"We've been busy," he says smoothly, as if that excuses everything.

"Too many details," Jeremy chimes in with a knowing chuckle, clearly used to Oliver's behavior.

I smile at Nova, taking in her radiant red dress that contrasts beautifully with the gallery's neutral tones. "Well, I'm looking forward to it."

She beams back at me, but before we can chat further, the photographer interrupts, ushering us into position for group photos.

As we arrange ourselves, Oliver's mom, dad, and grandmother walk in. Eliza, Oliver's mom, doesn't hesitate to make her way toward me, her face glowing with warmth.

"I can't believe you're part of my family. I'm so lucky," she whispers as she wraps me in a big hug. *Family*. I'm the lucky one, and I open my mouth to tell her that, but the room suddenly feels small making it hard to breathe.

Oliver steps up beside us, pride evident in his expression. His presence immediately settles me down. "Mom knew you were the artist I was looking for."

"No way! And you didn't tell him?" I ask, looking at Eliza.

She smiles softly, a hint of mischief in her eyes. "It was your secret to share. I wanted to protect you."

Despite my efforts to keep my emotions in check, I feel a lump forming in my throat. I sniff, trying to hold it together. "Thank you."

She pulls me into another tight hug, her embrace comforting and maternal. Out of the corner of my eye, I notice Oliver's eyes glistening as he watches his mom.

Then his grandmother steps forward, her arm looped through Sebastian's, Oliver's father. She's stunning, her white hair styled elegantly and her navy collared dress exuding sophistication. Her sharp, playful eyes meet mine as she speaks.

"I want to meet the beautiful, talented addition to the family," she says, her voice warm and welcoming.

I feel heat rush to my cheeks as I smile. "Hi."

"I'm Iris," she introduces herself.

"It's so nice to meet you," I reply sincerely.

"I'm surprised my teddy bear-loving grandson has found love. I'm so glad to see all my boys growing up," she says with a small grin.

"Teddy bear?" I ask,

Iris's grin widens as she nods. "Oh, yes. He carried that brown teddy bear everywhere and swore he'd never outgrow it."

Oliver clears his throat. "She hasn't met Teddy yet. It's in a box at my house."

I laugh. "Now I have to meet Teddy."

Oliver groans softly, but Iris waves it off and turns her full attention back to me. Her tone shifts, becoming more serious. "Karley, I was wondering if you'd paint something for me?"

My heart expands at the request, excitement bubbling inside me. "I'd love to. What did you have in mind?"

"My garden is full of flowers," she says. "I'd love for you to capture it."

I hesitate for a moment at the fact she's asking me to paint something personal to her. Actually seeking out my art. I'm so touched that she really likes my work that much. "I've never painted an entire garden before."

"You don't have to," she reassures me. "Just choose a part of it. Whatever inspires you."

"I'd be happy to. Maybe I could come by early, before Sunday dinner one week?"

"That sounds wonderful," Iris says, her smile turning playful again. "Thanks for having me tonight, and I hope my grandson is taking good care of you."

I laugh softly, sneaking a glance at Oliver. "Oh, he is."

Oliver's hand tightens slightly on my waist, and when I meet his gaze, there's a knowing glint in his eyes that sends a shiver down my spine.

He more than looks after me... in ways I never imagined.

When Amber and Wren arrive, they pause to take in the space, their expressions a mix of awe and admiration. A rush of warmth fills me as I watch them, my heart swelling with gratitude.

"Sorry, if you'll excuse me," I say to Iris with a smile. "I need to say hello to my family."

"Of course, dear," Iris replies, her smile as warm as ever. "I'll see you later."

"Thanks for coming," I add, giving her arm a gentle squeeze before making my way toward them.

"Hi," I say, hugging them.

Amber and Wren are already scanning the gallery, their eyes landing on my painting. Amber nudges Wren, and I can see the pride written across both their faces.

"Can you believe this is my painting?" I ask, gesturing toward the canvas displayed prominently under the lights. I'm surprised how comfortable I am about this now.

Amber turns to me, her eyes shining. "Of course we can. We're just so glad Oliver has helped you see what we've seen all along."

Wren nods, his smile full of warmth. "You've worked so hard for this, Karley. It's about time the world sees how talented you are."

Their words make my throat tighten, but I manage a smile. "Thank you."

"Yeah, you deserve all this and more, sis," Declan adds.

I shift my gaze to him and Armani. She stands tall beside him, her usual composed demeanor softened by a genuine smile.

"Hi," I say to them, my grin widening as I hug them. It feels so good to have them here with me.

Before I can say anything more, Callum steps forward, camera in hand. "Let's get a group photo," he suggests, motioning for us to gather together.

We huddle close, arms around each other as Callum takes a photo.

Just as we're starting to pull apart, Evelyn strides into the gallery, her energy instantly lighting up the room.

I walk straight up and pull her into a tight hug.

"Look at your painting," she says, grinning from ear to ear. "It's exactly where it should be."

"Thanks. But I want to show you something." Taking her by the hand, we weave through the crowd until we stop in front of her painting. Evelyn's eyes widen. She freezes for a moment before letting out an ear-piercing screech.

"No fucking way!" she squeals, before realizing we're inside.

Laughing, I watch her expression shift from shock to pure joy. "This is so fucking cool," she says, practically bouncing on her toes. "I need a photo. I'm tagging the hospital. They have to see this."

I smile, loving her passion and hustle. If that hospital doesn't take her after this, I'll personally make sure they regret it. "Here, give me your phone," I say, holding out my hand.

She hands it over, and I snap a few shots of her posing confidently next to her painting. Her pride is written all over her face. Once I give her the phone back, she immediately uploads one of the photos, tagging the hospital like it's her mission.

As she finishes, she tucks her phone away and turns to me with a softer, more thoughtful expression. "So..." Her voice is quieter now. "How have you been?"

"Goo—" A sudden tapping sound draws my attention. I turn toward the front of the room, where the soft hum of conversation quiets. Oliver stands at the center of the gallery with a microphone in hand, his tall frame commanding the room. I'm surprised to see him there. He didn't tell me he was doing a speech.

"Excuse me," he begins, his deep, steady voice filling the space effortlessly. "Thank you all for coming tonight. This event isn't just special for me, it's life-changing for these students. Their talent has left me speechless, and I wanted to create a space that honors their work and gives it the attention it deserves."

Around us, guests stand scattered around the room, wine glasses in hand, eyes trained on the makeshift stage. A few teachers from the art school linger near the back, nodding along. Some donors and family members are gathered closer to the front, dressed elegantly, the clink of ice in their glasses the only occasional interruption.

And then there are the students, the real stars of the night, clustered together with hopeful eyes. Their artwork lines the walls behind him, bold and beautiful. Each piece is a reflection of something deeply personal, now on display for everyone to see.

I glance at one girl in a green wrap dress near the corner, her eyes glassy with disbelief. Like she still can't quite believe she belongs here. And maybe that's the magic of it... Tonight, we all do.

"I hope you'll take the time to truly experience each piece. Not just glance at them, but feel them. And please, share their work. Take photos, talk about what you see tonight. Some of these students might want to stay anonymous, but that would be a shame. Art is meant to connect, to evoke emotion, and they deserve to know the impact they're having. But they can't unless we help spread the word."

A wave of soft murmurs flows through the crowd. His voice shifts, growing softer as his gaze locks onto mine. My heart swells from his kind words.

"I also want to thank the people who make everything in my life possible. My parents, my brothers, my Grams... and my wife."

The room goes silent for a beat, then erupts into cheers and applause so loud it feels like the walls might shake. My heart skips. His eyes are still on me, and I can see the depth of his emotion, raw and unguarded. "Can you please join me up here?"

I glance around, nerves fluttering in my chest. But when I meet his gaze again, he gives me a small nod, a silent reassurance. My legs feel shaky, but I walk up the steps, taking my time. When I'm close enough, Oliver reaches out. I grab his hand, steadying myself in his grip. He pulls me in for a kiss.

I can hear Evelyn's familiar holler cutting through the noise. It makes me laugh.

The cheers get louder, but all I feel is the tender warmth of his lips.

He pulls back slightly before he speaks into the mic. "There's something I want to redo," he says, his eyes sparkling with mischief.

Confused, I tilt my head. "Redo?"

"I want to renew our vows. This time, in front of everyone we love."

The room erupts again, cheers and clapping echoing through the space. My heart feels like it might burst.

"The first time, it was just us," he says softly, turning fully to face me. "But I want the people who support us to witness this. To witness us."

Oliver squeezes my hand and begins his vows. Every word is a promise, a reminder of the life we're building together. By the time he finishes, I'm barely holding it together.

He hands me the mic and a piece of paper—my vows from Vegas. I glance down at the familiar words and take a deep breath, reading each one aloud. I tremble, but I push through, speaking from the heart.

Oliver pulls me into another kiss, and the crowd roars.

As we stand there, wrapped in each other and surrounded by the people who mean the most, I know without a doubt that this is forever love.

Epilogue

Karley

Ten months later

I stretch in the bed, fingers brushing against cool sheets. The spot where Oliver should be is empty. A hint of disappointment tugs at me until the smell of fresh coffee and the faint tang of salt fill the air. My heart lifts. With a lazy grin, I flip the blanket off and swing my legs over the edge of the bed. The dark wood is cool beneath my feet.

After a quick stop in the bathroom, I open the door to see Oliver walking in, wearing just boxers, a wooden tray balanced carefully in his hands. Steam rises from a cup of coffee, the bright orange of fresh-squeezed juice catching my eye. A plate with a toasted bagel sits in the center like a prize.

"Get in bed, Petal," he says, his eyes crinkling with warmth. "I made you breakfast."

My heart does that silly little flip it's been doing since the day we met. Climbing back in, I nestle into the pillows, watching as he places the tray over my legs with careful precision. "How did I get so lucky?" I ask, looking up at him with genuine awe.

The flush on his face is instant. It spreads from his cheeks to the tips of his ears, softening his sharp features. His hair is a tousled mess, free from the product he usually uses to tame it. He looks younger this way, so much so, that for a moment, I'm tempted to ditch breakfast altogether. But today is too busy to give in to that urge.

"So... you think I've earned Husband of the Year this time?" He smirks.

I grin, nodding. "You already did. Did you eat?"

He sits on the edge of the bed, hands resting on his thighs. "Yeah, I had to taste it. Quality control." He shoots me a wink. "I'm gonna shower. You'll be okay?"

I hum, picking up the glass of orange juice. The cool sweetness hits my tongue, and the bits of pulp surprise me. Lowering the glass, I squint at it suspiciously before eyeing him. "Did you make this yourself?"

"Of course," he replies, chest puffing slightly. "You can taste the difference, can't you?"

His face is so serious, eyebrows slightly raised, lips pressed together in a firm line, that I have to bite the inside of my cheek to keep from laughing. He's too cute, and I'd never tell him I can't taste the difference. Not today.

We've had our fair share of battles in the grocery store, though. Most of the time, I just go alone. I'll buy his organic, pesticide-free, fermented foods, but I'll also grab my sugary treats. We've learned to mix and match. There are even nights where dinner is peanut butter toast on the sofa while binge-watching our favorite shows.

He leans in and kisses my forehead before heading to the bathroom. Moments later, the sound of the shower running fills the air. I'm halfway through my bagel when I notice a small, folded note tucked under the edge of the plate. I unfold the paper, already smiling before I've even read it.

No punchline today. Just a simple I love you, Petal. Love your (actual, real-life) husband
xo.

I read it twice, pressing my lips together to keep from grinning too wide. My heart swells with that aching, sweet kind of love that makes you feel like you're exactly where you're supposed to be. I tuck the note into the drawer of my nightstand, where all his letters are stored. One day, I'll turn them into art. A piece to hang in this house, our home.

I'm about to get out of bed, but I pause, lifting the tray off my lap, setting it aside. Bagel still in hand, I wander over to the bathroom doorway. He's under the stream of water, head tipped back, droplets sliding over the contours of his back and shoulders. The sight makes me pause.

He must sense my attention on him because he turns, eyes locking on me. "Is it good?" he asks, nodding toward the bagel.

I let my gaze sweep over him, slow and deliberate. My tongue skims my bottom lip, catching the crumbs. "Delicious."

His eyes narrow, and a wicked grin spreads across his face. "Get in here."

I arch an eyebrow, bringing the bagel to my mouth for another bite, chewing slowly, savoring it. "Make me."

He's out of the shower in a heartbeat, water dripping from every inch of him. Before I can react, he's in front of me, snatching the bagel from my hand and tossing it onto the tray. His arms wrap around me, his grin turning feral as he lifts me up and over his shoulder. Laughter bubbles out of me, but it's cut short when he rips the oversized t-shirt from my body, the cool air against my skin sending a shiver down my spine.

The next few moments blur as his hands skim across my skin, the rough scratch of stubble against my neck, the breathless sound of my name on his lips. He's not gentle, and I don't want him to be. Every move is a claim, every touch a reminder that I'm his and he's mine.

A few hours later, we arrive at the house to open the door for its first day. I once thought it would be mine, but now it's something so much bigger. A place for families to meet up. **Lotus Connections.** The name feels perfect. Each petal of a lotus connected to the center, just like the people who will find their way here.

I step onto the porch with Amber, Wren, and Rufus, taking in the sight of the navy door welcoming everyone in. Inside, the smell of fresh flowers mixes with the faint scent of lavender candles we lit this morning. The soft hum of calming music plays in the background. Every room is decorated with care. Soft, cozy furniture, and walls covered with art from local children. It feels like home with color and comfort, and it's exactly what I envisioned.

The licensed social workers, security personnel, family support specialists, child life specialists, and maintenance staff were all handpicked and meticulously trained. Which wouldn't have been possible without the Lincolns. At first, accepting their help felt like swallowing glass, but Oliver's gentle persistence wore me down. *"We're married,"* he would remind me. *"Helping you is helping us."* Every time he said it, the walls around my pride crumbled a little more. And as I move through the house with a buzz of excitement and confidence, I'm glad I listened. I paid for what I could with my own money from selling paintings and the shifts I still take at Till's Sip N' Paint. I'm there less now, though; my days split between school, work, home, and here. Somehow, it all balances itself out, though I'm still learning to lean on Oliver, just as he leans on me.

We've made plans to travel, including returning to Vegas on our one-year anniversary. Vegas gave me a taste of art and history, and now I crave more. More of the world.

Today, a few families are scheduled to visit, and nerves twist in my stomach. I smooth down the front of my pale blue dress, my hands shaking just slightly. What if they don't like it? What if this place doesn't feel like the safe haven I dreamed it would be?

Oliver catches my eye from across the room, flashing me a reassuring smile. He's leaning casually against the doorway, watching me with that look. The one that says he believes in me, even when I don't completely believe in myself.

You've got this, Petal, he mouths, as if he's reading my mind.

I take a deep breath, nodding once, and step forward as the first family arrives. Today isn't just about an open house; it's about opening hearts.

Amber stands to my left. On my right, Wren holds Rufus, stroking his fur. Ever since Wren started insisting on carrying Rufus, he's been on his best behavior. No more leg-humping Oliver, though I can't blame him. Oliver's hard to resist.

We're ready. I'm ready. This is just the beginning.

As we're cleaning up for the day, the familiar chime of the front door signals another visitor.

Evan strides in first, his grin sharp and mischievous. Behind him follows a man I've only seen in old photos Oliver has shown me from the boys growing up. The guy's taller than Evan, with sharp cheekbones and an easy smile that seems to belong on a billboard. His sleeves are rolled up, revealing forearms smudged with dirt.

"Look who it is," Evan announces to Oliver, slinging an arm around the man's shoulders. "Doctor Derek Pierce."

He holds out his hand. "Derek."

"Karley."

"Nice place," he says, nodding toward a framed drawing of sunflowers done by one of the local kids. "You've got an eye for art too."

"Don't be fooled," Oliver cuts in, walking up to join us, giving Derek a man hug. "She's got an eye for every-thing." He pulls away from Derek to stand beside me. A hand lands lightly on my back, his fingers trailing for just a second too long to be casual.

"Still a charmer, huh?" Derek says as his gaze flick between us with a knowing smirk. "Guess some things never change."

"Like how you two used to pretend to hate each other?" Evan's voice is pure tease as he leans against the counter, eyes dancing with amusement.

We glance at each other, the corner of Oliver's mouth tugging upward at the same time Evan's does. Their eyes meet for a brief moment of our shared memory, unspoken but fully understood.

"Yeah, good times," Oliver says with a grin.

"So..." Derek says, rubbing the back of his neck. "Evan told me that you may be interested in some of my pieces before I move to Pulse Point." His eyes shift to Oliver, eyebrows raised, like he's giving him the first pick.

"Interested?" Oliver tilts his head, letting a slow smile spread across my face. "I'd be crazy not to be."

The End.

THE BILLION DOLLAR CHRISTMAS

GRAMS/IRIS

I SHIFT THE CANDLE to the center of the table, careful to not put out its flame. The smell of peppermint fills the air, blending with the soft sound of Christmas carols playing in the background.

Gripping my walker, I slowly straighten, taking a moment to admire the work of the crew I hired to set everything up. Twinkling Christmas lights line the mantel, garlands of greenery drape gracefully over doorways, and the long dining table, once a dream, now stands ready with place settings for all my loved ones, minus my beloved husband who died of a heart attack ten years ago. The tablecloth is a soft cream, embroidered with golden snowflakes that catch the light just right. It's beautiful. It's everything I've hoped for, but can't do on my own anymore. Hosting these parties was always my pride and joy, but it's too much for me now. The crew's help is a blessing, and I'm thankful for them and for my housekeeper, Saylor.

Saylor moves around the kitchen like she's been doing it forever, her hands always busy. The counters are packed with dishes, roasted turkey, creamy mashed potatoes, green beans, and trays of cookies sprinkled with sugar like fresh snow. She cleans as she goes, her soft humming mixing with the sound of Christmas carols playing low in the background. I told her she could have the whole day off to be with her family, but she waved me off with a smile, saying, *"The Lincolns are my second family."* It's not often you find loyalty like that. Having her here makes the day feel more complete.

Family means everything to me. It always has, but since I was told I have breast cancer, time feels different. Every minute feels important, like a gift I can't waste. I want to soak it all in, including the laughter, the conversations, and even the quiet moments. None of it feels small anymore. Life isn't promised. I don't know how much time I have left, and that thought stays with me every day.

My son, Sebastian, is my greatest blessing. He comes by every day, checking in like it's just part of his routine. When I look at him, I see the boy he was and the man he's become. I worry about how he'll handle things when I'm gone. I've talked to Eliza, his wife, about it. She listens with so much patience. I've told her a hundred times she's the daughter I never had, and I mean it every time. My son did well with her. They're raising my four grandsons with so much love.

The doorbell rings, its sound cutting through the music. I check my small gold watch, expecting Sebastian. When I walk over and open it, I'm met by Jeremy and his fiancée, Nova.

Nova's dark curls bounce as she leans forward, her brown eyes lighting up as she scans the front yard. "Your house looks spectacular," she says, taking in the carefully manicured garden and the soft glow of fairy lights along the path.

I grin and step aside to let them in. "I'd love to take credit, but I had a lot of help." I wink, and she smiles back.

Jeremy leans in and presses a quick kiss to my cheek; the faint scent of his woodsy cologne lingering in the air. Nova follows behind him, closing the door softly.

"Are we the first ones here?" Jeremy asks, his eyes scanning the house as he pulls his jacket off and hangs it on the polished brass hook near the door.

Both of them are in blue jeans and sweaters.

Nova shrugs out of her coat, a deep green wool number, and hands it to Jeremy. He takes it without a second thought and hangs it up beside his.

"You know you're always the first, Remy," I tease, leaning against the door frame, a playful smile on my face.

Jeremy's grin stretches wider, dimples appearing on his cheeks. "Well, someone's gotta make sure you're ready."

Nova chuckles softly as she smooths the front of her sweater and looks around. Her eyes catch the flicker of candlelight in the foyer and the Christmas decorations neatly arranged in the house. "It all looks amazing, though. You've really outdone yourself."

I feel a flush of pride at her words. "Thanks. I just hope the others appreciate it as much as you two do."

"Don't worry," Jeremy says with a wink, slinging an arm around Nova's shoulders. "We'll set the tone."

As we walk through the house, I turn to Nova. "How's your dad?"

"He's good. I'll join them for dinner with Jeremy after here," she replies, her voice warm but tired, as though balancing everything with grace.

"That's nice, dear."

"What about you?" Nova asks, her gaze turning to me. Her curiosity is genuine and inviting.

I smile, and the warmth in her tone makes it easy to be honest. "Good, thank you. I'm seeing another Christmas, but this one feels different. Special. It's got a little extra something. And seeing my house filled with a long table like this has been a dream of mine for years." My eyes drift over the room where the table is now set, shining under the soft light of the chandelier. I feel a swell of pride in my chest.

We move into the dining and living area. The light from the fireplace casts a cozy warmth over everything.

"Grams, this is huge. I hope it hasn't been too much for you," Jeremy says, his voice filled with concern as he surveys the room, his brow furrowing.

"Do you think your father would've allowed this?"

Jeremy lets out a soft chuckle and shakes his head. "No. He wouldn't have. Not even close."

"Exactly," I say, smiling. "Sit down while we wait for the others." I know I need to sit too. I'm a little tired, my feet aching from all the preparation, but it's worth it. This is everything I've worked for.

"Where's Dad?" Jeremy asks as he glances around.

"He went home to have a shower. He should be back soon." I look at both of them, sitting side by side on the opposite sofa. Their closeness reminds me of what it was like when love felt so simple. I miss my husband, especially now, when I need his strength. One of the things I'm most looking forward to on the other side is being reunited with him.

"Do you want a drink while you wait?" I ask, my gaze flicking between the two of them. They look comfortable together, their hands occasionally brushing as they talk. They suit each other perfectly.

"No, we're fine," they say in unison.

Then, the doorbell rings again.

"I'll get it," Jeremy says, rising from the couch. I give him a soft nod, grateful not to have to walk so far. I watch as he makes his way to the sofa, his long strides quick and confident.

I glance at Nova, the light catching the gold flecks in her hazel eyes. She meets my gaze for a second, a small smile tugging at the corner of her mouth, then her eyes drop to her left hand. The round-cut diamond on her finger sparkles.

She's getting married next weekend.

What I thought would've been my first grandson getting married, but my grandson Oliver had other plans. He and his fiancée eloped in Vegas, leaving the family surprised and me slightly disappointed in missing such a special moment.

He set up a nice gallery ceremony, but it didn't have the same magic as a wedding organized by the bride. Moments like these feel special; little treasures I'm lucky to witness. "How are you feeling about the wedding?"

Nova's teeth graze her bottom lip as she lets out a breath just shy of a sigh. "Nervous," she admits, tucking a strand of brown hair behind her ear.

"That's normal, dear." I lean forward with a knowing smile. "Wait until the big day. You'll be running to the bathroom every five minutes."

Her eyes widen in playful horror. "It's already started," she says with a half-laugh, tapping her fingers on the edge of the sofa.

"What's already started?" Jeremy's voice cuts in as he walks into the room. His footsteps come closer, his brows lift with curiosity. Behind him, Evan and Chelsea walk in, arms full of brightly wrapped presents. Their hands are linked, fingers laced together, while their free hands balance the pile of gifts.

"Nothing," Nova says, flashing me a quick wink, her eyes crinkling.

"The table looks amazing," Chelsea says, her dark eyes going wide as she takes in the spread. Her gaze lands on the gold reindeer figurines lined up down the center, their glittery antlers catching the light. Her smile softens. "These remind me of Mom's. She always had little reindeer like this."

She rubs her bangs back into place with slow, deliberate movements, like she's soaking in the moment.

"You're driving there after this, right?" I ask, tilting my head toward her as I smooth the front of my dress.

"Yeah," Chelsea replies, shifting the weight of the presents in her arms. "Mom's making her famous pecan pie, so we're not missing that."

Her family is in Connecticut, but I've met them; they are kind people.

"We won't run over time," I say, trying to ease any concerns. "We'll eat, open presents, and have you all on your way to your other families."

"There's no rush, really," Chelsea adds, waving a hand dismissively, her smile warm.

I nod, satisfied, and pat the cushion beside me. "Sit down while we wait for the others." My hips ache as I ease back into the sofa, the familiar throb settling into my bones. I've been on my feet too long today, but I'd do it all over again for moments like this.

Jeremy lowers himself onto the sofa, his long legs stretching out like he's claimed the whole space. He slouches back, comfortable as ever. Evan and Chelsea sit beside him.

"Where's Dad?" Evan asks, glancing toward the front door like he expects him to walk in any second.

"He went home to shower," I say, smoothing my hands over my dress. "Should be back soon." I glance between the two of them, my gaze lingering longer than I mean to.

"Did you want a drink while you wait?" I offer.

Evan shakes his head, and Chelsea mirrors him, both of them too settled to move. I glance toward the window, my fingers curling over the arm of the chair as heavy footsteps draw my attention away from the garden.

Sebastian enters without pressing the doorbell. He's followed by Eliza, who's nearly hidden by the biggest bag of gifts I've ever seen.

But I love how they spoil my grandkids. Kids are never too old for gifts.

I force myself up from the sofa to greet them as they step inside, each offering a quick, "Hi."

The others rise too, with warm hellos and laughter. Amongst the loud voices, Sebastian moves with quiet purpose, carrying all the presents to the tree and arranging them with the precision of someone who takes pride in the little things. It reminds me of when he was little, and he lined up all his toy cars.

The quick sound of light footsteps pulls me out of memory lane, and I don't even have to look to know it's Chad. Sure enough, he steps in, followed by my grandson, Harvey, and his beautiful pregnant fiancée.

Chad's wearing a crisp white shirt tucked into smart dress pants, and for a moment, my heart softens at the sight. He's a perfect mini version of Harvey, right down to the slicked-back blond hair.

Without hesitation, Chad darts around the room, his energy like a burst of light. When he reaches me, he throws his arms around me in a hug so strong it nearly knocks me off balance. I wobble, but I catch myself against the arm of the sofa just in time, laughing as I steady us both.

"Look at your tree. It touches the roof," Chad exclaims, his eyes wide with awe.

"And it's real," I whisper, leaning down with a grin. "Go on, smell it."

He shoots me a skeptical look, his nose scrunching like I just suggested something ridiculous. But curiosity wins, and he steps closer, giving the branches a small sniff. His eyes go wide like he's just discovered a secret world.

"Whoa."

"Nice, right?" I say, nudging him with my elbow.

He shakes his head. "Not really... but it's cool."

Jemima walks over. "Do you mind if I sit?"

"Not at all. I'll join you," I reply, grateful for the excuse to rest a little longer.

Harvey approaches next, leaning down to kiss my cheek. "Hi, Grams."

"Hi," I say softly.

He kisses Jemima on the head. "Do you need anything, buttercup?"

Smiling, she shakes her head.

Harvey glances toward me. "I'm going to show Chad the garden, if you don't mind."

I meet his eyes and give a small nod. "No, go ahead. When you get back, lunch will be served."

He smiles, nods, then strides over to Chad, whispering something in his ear. He holds out his hand, and together, they head toward the back, joined by Evan, Chelsea, Nova, and Jeremy, leaving me in the quiet of the living room with Jemima, Sebastian, and Eliza.

"Mom, what happened?" Sebastian asks, stepping away from the tree with a frown, his gaze locked on me.

I glance around, puzzled. "What?"

Scowl deepening, he points at my right wrist.

I lower my hand to my lap, trying to hide the mark. "It's nothing."

I brush it off, hoping he'll drop it. I know if I explain, he'll just start asking more questions.

"It didn't look like nothing," he mutters, standing in front of me now, arms crossed.

"I argued with the baking tin," I say quickly, trying to keep it light.

"You could've had someone else bake the pie."

I narrow my eyes at him. "I'm not giving up baking, son," I reply, my voice final.

I turn my arm, revealing the red burn from the hot tin.

"It's fine," I add. "I'll pop some cream on it, and it'll be gone by morning." I stand up from the sofa and head to the bathroom.

A few moments later, I return to find Sebastian sitting across from me, watching as Jemima carefully smears a generous amount of white cream over the burn, sealing it with a bandage.

"Happy?" I raise an eyebrow at him, amused.

"Hmm," he mumbles, his expression unreadable.

Just then, a soft throat is cleared. "Sorry to interrupt, but would you like me to serve?"

"Yes, please," I reply, my smile warm as I glance at Saylor.

"I'll tell the others to come in," Jemima says before I can protest, already heading toward the door.

As everyone starts to trickle back in, I glance at the wall clock, noting the time.

"Does anyone know where Oliver is?" I ask, my gaze flicking to the clock once more. I'd planned to start lunch at noon, and now it's already a quarter past.

"No, but let's start without him," Sebastian suggests, his tone nonchalant. I don't argue; I like sticking to a routine, especially when it comes to meals.

I push myself up from the walker, steadying myself by gripping the arm of the sofa.

"Mom, take a seat, and I'll bring you a plate," Sebastian says, ever the caretaker.

"Thanks," I reply, not bothering to argue. Part of me thinks he enjoys fussing over me a bit too much.

I settle at the head of the table, feeling the warmth of the gathering surrounding me. Saylor pours me a glass of eggnog I prepared earlier, the creamy liquid settling as I watch.

"Grams, how much bourbon is in this?" Harvey announces, eyeing hisglass suspiciously.

"Enough to give you some chest hair," I say with a wink, amused by his cautious tone.

"What's bourbon?" Chad asks as he reaches for Harvey's glass.

"Not for you, bud," Harvey replies quickly, pulling the glass out of reach.

"Why not?" Chad protests, his eyebrows pinching together.

"Adults drink it," Jemima explains calmly.

I smirk around my drink, savoring the familiar flavor.

"How about some cold milk?" I offer, looking at Chad.

His face lights up, and he beams at me, the joy in his eyes making it impossible not to smile back.

Saylor stands and heads to the kitchen, grabbing a glass of milk for him before sitting down beside me at the table. If she's missing her family lunch, then she'll join ours.

Everyone digs in, the clink of silverware and soft chatter filling the room. I take a moment to soak it all in, my gaze shifting from face to face. This is how it's meant to be, my house full of life and noise. It's different now; it used to be eight of us, back when my husband was alive. But now, it's grown bigger, louder, and filled with more love than I thought possible.

I start eating my turkey, enjoying every bite, and by the time I'm halfway through, I hear the sound of the door opening.

"Look what the cat brought in," Jeremy says with a smirk, glancing toward the door where Oliver and his wife, Karley, step inside.

I push my chair back to rise, but Sebastian's hand gently rests on mine. "No, Mom. Stay there. They can come to you."

I nod, but the urge to greet them is too strong, and I push my chair out anyway, standing just enough to offer a warm welcome.

Karley is wearing a soft green sweater that highlights her striking blue eyes. She steps forward with a nervous smile, and I extend my hand. "Nice to see you again, Karley."

She shakes it, her smile growing a bit. "You too."

"Please, take a seat." I gesture to the empty spot beside me. "We'll have a meal warmed up for you."

"I'm sorry we're late," she says, her face flushed with embarrassment, and I don't ask why. I was young once, and some things are written clearly on your face.

Oliver, standing behind her, looks guilty as well. "It's my fault, Grams," he says softly.

I smile at him, my heart light. "It's alright, darling. You're here now."

Everyone settles into their seats, the warmth of the room wrapping around us like a comforting blanket. I lean over to Saylor, lowering my voice just enough to keep it between us.

"Could you grab a photo, please?"

She nods, her smile softening. "Yes, ma'am."

Rising from the table, she clears her throat. "Excuse me for a moment, everyone. Could we grab a quick photo?"

The room pauses for a beat, all eyes turning toward her as she snaps the photo, her camera clicking as she captures the moment. With a quiet smile, she sits back down.

"Can you grab one later, by the tree?" I ask, my voice casual, knowing she's always happy to help.

"Yes, ma'am," she replies, already nodding.

I reach for my glass, then glance at her, my tone light. "Saylor, call me Iris. It's your day off. Have some eggnog. Relax."

She laughs softly, the sound like a breath of fresh air. Pouring herself a generous serving of my homemade eggnog, she raises her glass toward me.

I lift mine in return, the rich warmth of the drink settling into my chest. "Merry Christmas," I say with a smile, my voice filled with love.

"Merry Christmas," she echoes, and we both clink our glasses, a quiet cheer that holds the weight of years, memories, and the bond between us all.

We settle back into our meal, the clinking of silverware filling the room again, when suddenly, Oliver's voice breaks the rhythm.

"I heard Bobby's out of jail."

The words hit like a shock wave, and the sound of silverware clattering against my fine China echoes loudly through the room. I gasp, my breath catching in my throat, and suddenly, silence falls over the table like a heavy curtain.

"Oliver!" Evan barks, his voice sharp and angry.

"What? I didn't know it was a big deal," Oliver defends, his tone steady, but the tension in the room is palpable.

Bobby is Chelsea's ex-boyfriend, a man who had once filled their lives with pain. He went to jail for various offenses, including harassment and stalking Chelsea. The thought of him still lingers like a shadow over us all.

"My dad's in jail," Chad announces matter-of-factly, his voice cutting through the quiet. There's a string of curses muttered around the table, and I pretend not to hear them, focusing instead on how my heart tightens at the mention of Bobby's name.

The air feels thick with discomfort, but then Eliza stands up, breaking the tension.

"I think I'll have some egg nogg," she says casually, as if nothing unusual has happened, and the simple statement is a welcome distraction.

I grab my eggnog and take a long sip, finishing the small glass. "I'll have some more too," I add, trying to steer the room back to normalcy.

Without a word, Saylor pours more into my glass.

After the dinner plates are cleared, I rise from my chair and head toward the kitchen. The soft padding of footsteps follows close behind. Chad's lighter, quicker steps mix with the steady thud of Harvey's.

I reach for the apple pie, its golden crust glistening under the soft glow of the kitchen lights. A buttery, spiced aroma wafts through the air.

"Do you want me to grab the ice cream?" Harvey's asks, already halfway to the freezer.

"Yes, please," I reply, glancing over my shoulder. "And thecream."

Chad sticks close to Harvey's side, his gaze fixed upward with quiet admiration as Harvey opens the freezer door. The sight of them melts me. Chad's eyes wide with curiosity, Harvey's calm, steady presence makes something tender in my chest, a warmth so sudden my knees feel unsteady. They're not just moving together. They're in sync.

By the time they return, Chad's arms are stretched wide, gripping the ice cream tub with both hands, as if it's a treasure, his face beaming with pride. "Can I help scoop it out?" he asks eagerly, eyes darting between me and Harvey.

"Sure," I say with a nod, already moving to grab the bowls from the cabinet.

Harvey finds the scooper in the drawer, the metallic clang of it hitting the white countertop with a sharp bang. I watch as he takes the cream to the table, pausing long enough to glance back at us, his eyes crinkling with amusement. Chad's already digging into the ice cream, his small hands working hard. The first scoop doesn't make it to a bowl. Instead, he pops it straight into his mouth, glancing at us with a big grin like he's been caught doing something sneaky. He's too quick for us to stop him, the taste already his. I hold back a laugh, but Harvey's on it right away.

"Hey," he says, his fake stern tone that's more playful. I'm already giggling, knowing exactly what's coming next. Harvey's grin grows as he steps closer, eyes locked on Chad. "Make sure you share that," he adds, tilting his head and opening his mouth expectantly, his hands resting on his hips like he's about to be fed.

Chad's laugh bursts out, light and happy. He lifts the next scoop straight into Harvey's open mouth. Harvey's gasp is loud and dramatic, his eyebrows shooting up like he's just witnessed the most shocking thing ever.

"Two peas in a pod," I mutter, shaking my head as I turn my attention back to the pie. The crust cracks under the weight of the knife, revealing soft, spiced apples baked inside. I'm careful with each slice, placing them into bowls like small works of art.

"Chad, you take the pie and serve as much ice cream as you want," Harvey says, his tone gentle but clear. "Then sit down and eat it, okay?"

"Okay, Dad," Chad says, his voice sweet but so casual it takes mea moment to process it.

My hand pauses on the spoon, fingers gripping the cold handle as I glance at Harvey. He's looking right at me, a small grin tugging at the corner of his mouth. My chest tightens, a wave of happiness hitting me out of nowhere. I drop my gaze to the pie, focusing on cutting the next slice carefully. The steady motion keeps me grounded, each slice clean and precise. I'm aware of Chad nearby, carrying his bowl to the table.

"When did he start calling you Dad?" I ask, eyes still on the pieas if the answer is written in the crust.

"It's been a while now," Harvey replies. He's scooping ice cream into bowls, his focus split but steady.

"And how does it make you feel?" The words come quieter than I mean them to, my fingers tracing the edge of the pie dish.

"I love it," he says, grinning.

"Will the dynamic change when the baby comes?" The question's out before I've had a chance to rethink it; the words hanging in the space between us.

Harvey's quiet for a beat, just long enough for me to glance up. He's shaking his head, eyes locked on me like he's making sure I hear every word. "Jemima and I have talked about it. We're going to make sure to spend quality one-on-one time with Chad and all together as a family." He doesn't waver. It's not a hope. It's a promise.

I'm still holding the spoon, but my grip's looser now. Family. It's not just in the words we say, it's in the glances across kitchens, the warmth of shared meals, and the conversations that fill the spaces in between.

Saylor enters the kitchen to carry the bowls to each family member.

I finish serving and move to the table to retake my seat. Saylor lowers my bowl with a soft clink of ceramic against wood. The room is filled with the rich aroma of spiced pie and sweet vanilla ice cream. I'm just about to begin eating when a sharp voice cuts through the quiet hum of conversation.

"Shit!"

My head snaps toward Oliver's voice. He's on his feet, brushing at his jeans, a smear of pie filling and melted ice cream on his denim. His eyes dart up, catching mine, and he stills under my gaze.

"Oliver," I say firmly, my tone carrying the weight of a thousand lessons on respect and self-control. I'm not bothered by the mess, that's easily cleaned. But swearing? I've always been clear about that.

Saylor's eyes flick toward us, and without a word, she's already moving. She's quick but calm, a sponge in her hand like she's grabbed it from thin air. She offers it to Oliver with a small smile. Her quiet competence is something I've always admired about her. "Thank you," Oliver says, his voice filled with genuine gratitude. The look in his eyes stirs something deep in my chest. Moments like these remind me why I'm proud of my grandsons. They're not perfect, but kindness is something they've never lacked.

Oliver's hands work the sponge over his jeans, dabbing at thedarkened fabric with care. Once he's satisfied, he drops back into his chair,rolling his shoulders as if to shrug off the minor accident. Dessert resumes,the clatter of forks against plates a steady rhythm that fills the quiet spacesin our conversation. We eat, we talk, and slowly, the mess is forgotten.

Once the meal is over, I push back from the table with a soft grunt and make my way to the living room. The plush cushions of the sofa welcome me like an old friend, and I sink into them with a sigh. I wave Chelsea over, patting the empty spot beside me.

She's quick to respond, her smile warm as she crosses the room. Her hair bounces with each step, loose waves catching the light. She settles in beside me, her body angled toward mine, as if ready for whatever's coming next.

"How are you, dear?" I ask.

Her eyes drop to her lap, fingers fidgeting with the edge of her sleeve. She lets out a long, controlled breath. "Yes, it's still sinking in that he's out," she admits, her voice low but steady.

My eyebrows knit together, concern slipping into my features like an old habit. "Do you need Evan to hire security?"

As her eyes lift to mine, I see the resolve there, stronger than I'd expected. "No, thank you," she says. "He spoke to a friend, Jonathan Black, whose girlfriend went through something similar. It's been helpful for figuring out a plan."

"What do you mean?" I'm leaning forward now, eyes locked on her, ready for every detail.

"I have security wherever I go. They're on rotation, so there's always someone fresh and alert," she explains.

I nod, but a new worry finds its way into my mind. "Evan has one too, I hope?" I ask with sudden urgency. My chest tightens at the thought of my grandson being vulnerable.

"Yes," Chelsea says quickly, her hand reaching out to lightly pat my arm. "Sometimes two, depending on where we're going."

Relief seeps into my muscles, the tension melting away. "Good," I murmur, leaning back into the cushions. My eyes shift to hers, searching her face for any sign of strain she's trying to hide. "And how's the new house?"

Her whole face brightens at that. "It's great. We can't wait to have you all over."

"Evan's been trying to work out a date for Sebastian to drive me," I tell her, already picturing the house from the photos she's sent. It's modern but warm, with large windows that let in a lot of natural light. "It's beautiful. I can't wait to see it in person."

Chelsea's grin widens. "My parents are equally excited to see you again."

"Well, I'll have to make sure I'm at my best, then," I reply with a small laugh, my heart lighter now than it's been all evening. Moments like these, where family gathers, talks, and makes plans for the future, are what I live for. No amount of spilled pie or heavy conversations can dull the glow of that.

"Can I join?" Nova asks.

I glance up from where I'm seated, my gaze settling on her. Her dark curls frame her face. Nodding, I pat the spot next to me on the sofa. "Please."

She sinks into the cushion with a sigh. "How are you going?" she asks, tucking a curl behind her ear.

"I'm alright," I reply as I shift to face her. "What's going on, dear?" I notice the subtle change in her expression, the slight downward tilt of her lips.

"I need to look for another job," she says, her voice quieter now. "And it's been a little harder than I thought."

"Jeremy offered her a job," Chelsea chimes in from across the room, her voice kind but edged with a knowing look.

"And you don't want to take it?" I ask, curiosity laced with concern. It's a good opportunity, and I can't help but wonder what's holding her back.

Nova shrugs. "I might. I just... I don't know if it'll be too much. Working together and then coming home together."

"Could you trial it out?" I suggest, leaning forward slightly.

Her eyes flicker with thought. "Yeah, maybe. Save up some vacation time and, instead of taking a trip, I could try working with Jeremy."

"Then you'd miss out on a vacation," Chelsea mutters, scrunching her nose.

Nova nods.

"I know, but if you work for Jeremy, I'm sure he'd look after you," I add with a small wink.

Her face flushes a pretty shade of pink. "I don't want to take advantage."

"I'm sure he wouldn't mind," I reply with a grin. Her eyes soften, and she pulls lipstick from her bag. As she applies the bold red shade, it's like watching her armor click into place. The red stain against her skin gives her a lively, youthful glow. I'm a lipstick lover too, though I prefer pink tones, an old favorite that's seen better days but still does the job.

"Is it present time?" Chad's eager question pulls our attention. He's practically bouncing on his heels, eyes darting toward the Christmas tree.

"Yes, if everyone else is ready?" I glance around, checking for nods of agreement. Jeremy settles beside Nova, while Evan sits next to Chelsea. Harvey and Jemima claim the seats next to me, and Oliver and Karley take their spots on the floor near the tree, ready to assist with the gift distribution.

"Alright, Chad, start passing them around," I encourage.

Chad's grin stretches wide as he rocks forward to grab the firstpresent, reading the tag carefully. "This one's for Nova," he announces,beaming as he hands it over. As he collects his own pile, his excitement growswith every present he finds. "Another one for me." Grinning, he stacks them ina pile.

I'm given five gifts, one from each grandchild, and one from my son and daughter-in-law. I open them slowly, savoring the moment. There's a mix of candles, picture frames, cardigans, Debbie's Cakes, and a beautiful photo of each family, the one I'd been hoping for. My heart swells as I think about adding it to my mantel. I open the final gift, and it's from Karley: a painting of my garden. My eyes look up to her, and she's grinning. I mouth *thank you* before I look at the beautiful watercolor of the roses, gardenias, sunflowers, and hedges. It's stunning. I'm lost in it until Chad approaches, and I lower the painting to the side.

His eyes meet mine, a shyness I don't often see in him. "Thanks, Nan, for my gift."

The word "Nan" catches me off guard, warming my heart so deeply that it brings tears to my eyes. I glance at Harvey, whose blue eyes meet mine with a knowing smirk, as if to say, *See how sweet he is.*

"No problem," I reply, my voice thick with affection. "I hope youlike it."

"I love them." Chad's face lights up as he glances at his stack, the board games, reading books, Lego, toys, video games, and new clothes.

Nearby, Jemima's conversation with Karley catches my ear. "Would you have kids?" Jemima asks, her tone soft but curious.

Karley's answer is firm. "No. I told Oliver I don't want to."

"How did he take it?" Jemima's eyebrows lift.

"He's been amazing," Karley says, glancing at Oliver. "But I'll always worry he's settling for me."

Her words tug at me. She's talented, kind, and I'm proud of her for standing firm. We didn't have that choice in my time. My gaze shifts back to Chad, but my ears stay tuned to them.

"Sorry, Grams, but we need to head off." Evan's voice breaks the moment as he rises from his chair. I check my watch. "Of course," I say, getting up to hug and kiss them goodbye. One by one, Jeremy, Nova, Oliver, and Karley head for the door. The house slowly empties including Saylor.

"I'll go, Sebastian. Let you and your mom relax," Eliza says.

"I'll drive you home first," Sebastian says, already reaching for his keys.

"Good idea," I say with a tired smile. "I'll probably head to bed and watch a classic Christmas movie while finishing this." I hold up my half-full glass of eggnog.

"Merry Christmas," Eliza says as we walk to the door.

"Merry Christmas." I close the door behind them and walk to my room.

With a full heart, I change into my tartan pajamas and settle into bed. The soft glow of the TV lights up the room as the movie plays. I sip the rest of my eggnog and close my eyes, thinking about my family, their laughter, and the love that filled the house today.

It's easy to get caught up in hard times, but days like this remind me to be grateful. And tonight, I am.

I nod off to sleep, and I wake to the soft hum of the television, its glow flickering against the walls like candlelight. The Christmas movie, *The Polar Express*, plays on in the background. My eyes blink open slowly, and for a moment, I'm disoriented, unsure if it's morning or still night. But the clock on the dresser tells me it's just past midnight. Christmas is over, at least by the calendar's count, but not in my heart. Not yet.

I'm still wrapped in the comfort of my flannel pajamas, the scent of peppermint clinging to the fabric. My fingers brush over the sleeve, tracing the familiar softness that's been with me for years.

I shift in bed, propping myself up against the pillows, and take another sip of the eggnog I'd saved. It's sweet, spiced, and a little strong, just how I like it. My gaze moves to the window, where I keep the curtains open. Snow isn't common every year, but there's a dusting covering the glass. It's beautiful.

My thoughts drift to Chad and the way he'd hugged me, the way he'd marveled at the "real" Christmas tree. His wide-eyed wonder reminded me of his father at that age. Sometimes, it's like looking back in time. Harvey's calm, steady presence hasn't changed a bit. And when Chad called him "Dad"... well, that's the kind of thing that stays with you. I'll hold that moment close for as long as I'm here.

The floorboards creak just beyond my door. It's a light sound, cautious but familiar. I know who it is before I hear the knock. "Come in, Sebastian," I call out.

The door opens slowly, revealing my son's silhouette. He's in his jeans and a sweater, his hair slightly tousled like he'd run his fingers through it one too many times. "Hey, Mom," he says, stepping inside with that careful quiet he's always had. He's not a loud man, never has been, but his presence fills a room just the same.

"Couldn't sleep?" I ask, tilting my head as he moves to the armchair by the window. He sits heavily, elbows on his knees, hands clasped together like he's got something on his mind.

"No," he admits, eyes flicking toward me before settling on the window. "Just... thinking."

"About?" I'm careful. I've learned over the years that asking what's wrong makes people shut down. But "about"... well, that's an open door.

He's quiet for a moment, his jaw working as if he's chewing on the words before he says them. "Dad." The single word lands heavily in the space between us. He doesn't have to say more. I know exactly where his mind has gone. Mine's been there, too.

"I miss him," I say, filling the quiet with honesty. "Especially on nights like Christmas."

Sebastian's lips press into a line, and he nods, gaze still locked on the frost-lined window. "He'd..." He stops, rubs a hand down his face, then tries again. "He'd love all of this, you know? The big table, the grandkids everywhere, the..." He gestures toward the ceiling, where faint music still plays from the living room's stereo. "All of it. He'd love it."

I'm nodding before he's even done speaking. "Yes, he would." My chest tightens, not with grief, but with love so strong it's almost unbearable. "He's here, though. You know that, right?" I tap my heart gently. "Here. Every year, every Christmas, he's right here."

The End.

ALSO BY SHARON WOODS

www.ingramcontent.com/pod-product-compliance
Lightning Source LLC
Chambersburg PA
CBHW072018020726
47501CB00006B/1861